MEMORIES OF THEN

STEPHANIE MAY

INSPIRED BY TRUE EVENTS

IMPRESSUM

Memories of Then

Published by Impressum, Newcastle NSW
November 2021
www.impressum.com.au

www.stephaniemayofficial.com

Cover design by Nada Backovic
Internal design by Impressum

National Library of Australia Cataloguing-in-Publication entry

Author: May, Stephanie

Title: Memories of Then/ Stephanie May

ISBN: 978-1-922588-16-6 (print)
978-1-922588-15-9 (ebook)

A catalogue record for this book is available from the National Library of Australia

DEDICATION

In loving memory of Corey.
You will always be my sunshine.

'To live is to suffer, to survive is to find some meaning in the suffering.'
Friedrich Nietzsche

Chapter 1

THE GRANDFATHER CLOCK chimed away another hour of his life, pervading the silence of the freezing-cold house. Sheba was out the back burying a chicken neck, while in the kitchen a pot of Irish stew bubbled on the stove.

Irish stew, he thought without a stitch of enthusiasm. It wouldn't have been a terrible choice if he hadn't consumed the same thing for the previous four nights in a row. But Coles had a two-for-one special, so he'd licked up the opportunity to save some coin and stock the bare cupboards. Now he regretted his decision as his stomach grumbled for something more substantial.

While searching for a magnifying glass to aid his task of completing the daily crossword puzzle, the *damned telephone* rang. The only people who ever called were telemarketers or sales reps from funeral companies trying to get him 'on board'.

Exhaling, he picked up the receiver. 'Who the hell is it and whaddaya want?' His eyes rested on his teeth soaking in a glass of watery solution on the coffee table.

'*Jesus*, Eli, could you try having a bit more tact the next time you answer the phone?'

Grace's voice was haggard from years of chain-smoking, but it still held a glimmer of humour, even if she sounded like a rock star at a concert after-party.

After he secured his teeth and manoeuvred his jaw, Elijah Samuels settled into the man-made groove on his favourite rocking chair and smiled.

'I knew it was you, old girl.'

'Ah, you put your teeth in,' Grace said, like a mother praising her child for taking their first steps. 'Good boy!'

His stomach grumbled as he glanced at the blank crossword puzzle that lay open on his thigh. 'What can I do for you?'

Grace sighed in an unsettling manner, which he was quick to pick up on. 'I wanted to check up on my favourite sibling.'

'I'm your *only* sibling.'

'Well, you win by default.' After offering a weak laugh she paused, and he heard the click of a lighter before she inhaled. 'I haven't heard from you in a while. Perhaps a phone call now and then would keep you in the loop on family situations?'

'I hate phones. Always have,' he said, eyeing the images that flashed across the TV screen, the sound on mute. *Apocalypse Now.*

She suckled again on the cigarette and exhaled. 'Yes, I know all too well how you won't conform to the twenty-first century and our methods of communication.'

Elijah scowled as his fingers strummed the fabric of his chair. Her going round and round the mulberry bush did little to help his growing unease that something regrettable had happened. 'You'd hardly call just to ask me how I am.' He waited for an interruption, a protest. None came. 'What's up? Are you okay or are you out to irritate me worse than my bowels today?'

Grace clicked her tongue curtly. 'You got me; I'll cut straight to the chase.' She took another drag. 'I, ah, wanted to let you know Audrey is in a coma.'

Chapter 2

WALKING THROUGH DUNMORE Nursing Home's private facility, Chloe Tawny's feet dragged across the floor. Each step felt like lead weights were attached to her feet, with an anchor chained around her neck for good measure. She hadn't seen her grandmother in a while, so the guilt atop her other emotions was piled like an accountant's desk at end of financial year.

When Chloe's mother, Angela, received the upsetting call from Dunmore Nursing Home, the two of them had left for Woolwich as soon as they could manage. Angela appeared strong, but Chloe supposed she was keeping calm to seem brave for the sake of others. Classic first-born child syndrome that had carried on through the years; something others (including Chloe) sometimes mistook for Angela being taciturn. At this tender age, Chloe had only dealt with the loss of her grandfather, Buck. Chloe had few memories of Buck, but she still felt sad whenever she thought about her poppy and all the good times they *could* have shared had he lived longer.

In the spacious recreational room that Chloe and Angela walked through, elderly residents were playing board games, watching TV, or doing arts and crafts such as knitting and crochet.

Winifred Mildred, a middle-aged southern American, approached Angela with drooping jowls. Nurse Mildred was Chloe's favourite; she was warm, compassionate, and had a wicked sense of humour that included poop and fart jokes, even if they were ill-timed.

'Thank ya fo' comin'; I'm sorry ta have been the bearer of bad news,' Nurse Mildred said, deep frown lines accentuating her weathered face.

'Sorry I couldn't get here sooner,' Angela said. 'I was in the middle of a meeting, then I had to collect this one from school.' She gazed at Chloe, who was staring at Nurse Mildred as if to telepathically say *Please save my nanna*.

Nurse Mildred was clad in a typical blue nurse uniform, with a fob watch attached to her breast pocket and a stethoscope around her plump neck. Her downturned mouth and slumped shoulders conveyed her fondness for Audrey Arlington – and her sadness at the elderly lady's sudden deterioration.

The double doors behind them swung open and Chloe's Aunt Jamie walked in, puffy-eyed and with a wad of crumpled tissues in hand. When Angela and Jamie spotted each other, they embraced in a tearful hug. Jamie whispered incoherent words until Angela broke away with a slight sniffle.

'Hi, g-g-guys,' Jamie said, acknowledging Nurse Mildred and Chloe. After Jamie wiped her red nose with broken bits of tissue, Nurse Mildred shook Jamie's other hand, decorated with a sterling silver ring and charm bracelets dangling from her wrist.

'Mayhap we should walk 'n' talk?' Nurse Mildred said, turning on her white sneaker heels.

They strolled along the sterile corridors; an endless enclosure of white-washed walls that seemed cut off from the outside world. Chloe couldn't understand half of what Nurse Mildred was prattling on about, but she didn't like the sound of words like 'morphine' or 'palliative'. Deep down, she knew the situation wasn't good. Chloe kept a crucifix around her neck, even though her family was not religious in the slightest. The only time Chloe had heard her father speak of Jesus Christ was when he stubbed his toe on the coffee table a few months back. But there was something comforting in having a ubiquitous symbol close to her heart, so she clasped onto it like it was some sort of personal saviour. After passing a room where an elderly woman (who reminded Chloe of the Old Hag in *Snow White*) was talking to a stuffed doll resembling Raggedy Ann, Chloe began praying to a greater power, asking Him for more time.

They entered the luxurious room 217, draped in the finest materials from curtains to cupboards (even the bathroom befitted royalty). Jamie was on her smartphone, leaving a voice message to her partner, informing him of the situation as she walked across the polished linoleum flooring towards her motionless mother. Angela approached the bed hesitantly, as though her carefully stoic facade might tumble like a house of cards at any second. She held onto Audrey's limp hand as Chloe glanced at the patient monitor beside the bed, which emitted a troubling beeping sound every ten seconds that jangled her nerves as though someone were plucking piano wires.

Audrey Arlington had an endotracheal tube protruding from her agape mouth, an IV drip stood beside the bed – hanging from it, a spiked bag of saline with a plastic tube snaked into the back of Audrey's wrinkled hand. Leads running from an ECG machine were secured to her chest, covered by her gown. Sinus rhythms twitched across the cardiac monitor.

Chloe noted that the room smelled of disinfectant and soap. While she observed the monitors, a man walked in with shoulders perched back and a fat head held high like he was walking on stage to explain how to get rich quick.

'Good evening, everyone,' he began, smoothing over his navy-blue silk tie. 'My name is Doctor Nathaniel Grant, and I am Audrey's primary attending physician. I'm sorry to meet under these circumstances.'

Chloe gazed up as Nathaniel shook hands with her mother before turning to her aunt.

'What's the diagnosis, doc?' Jamie asked, taking his outstretched hand into her own.

He cupped his muffin top hips while Nurse Mildred looked on from the doorway. 'Well, Audrey – sorry, your mother – had a fall earlier today. We administered barbiturates through an infusion pump, ensuing in a medically induced coma. She struck her head on the toilet bowl and, as a result, a scan showed swelling in the frontal lobe. It controls significant cognitive skills such as emotional expression, language, and also memory. It's the control panel of our personality and our ability to communicate …'

Chloe's heart plummeted. She surmised this doctor had the compassion and empathy of a debt collector.

'We hooked Audrey up to a ventilator as a precaution,' he said, pointing. There was micropore tape on the left side of Audrey's face covering part of a tube protruding from her mouth to a machine that replicated a pair of lungs. 'Given she's had trouble breathing these past few weeks.'

Doctor Grant walked to the bed and lifted the sheets where Audrey's feet lay, then reached for his breast pocket. 'As you can see with this Babinski test' – he produced a ballpoint pen and then grazed it against Audrey's foot, to which it jerked upwards – 'the natural response would be downward. An upward reaction indicates brain trauma.' Jamie cupped her mouth, muffling an anguished cry. 'We commenced Audrey on IV therapy and administered NSAIDs – nonsteroidal anti-inflammatory drugs – which will help with any pain and prevent further swelling. We're monitoring the electrical activity of her brain through an EEG. As I'm sure she discussed with you all, it was her wish not to be moved to a hospital if she went downhill. We're going to make her comfortable here.'

Staring at the floor, Chloe listened to Nathaniel Grant quoting statistics and odds of those who have been in the same predicament as her grandmother. After fifteen minutes of listening to Jamie and her mother asking questions and receiving answers about the side effects and ramifications of a medically induced coma, Doctor Grant and Nurse Mildred stepped out of the room with solemn goodbyes.

The three of them stood in silence until the beeping became unbearable.

'Do you want to stay with Nanna while we step outside?' Angela asked Chloe.

Chloe nodded, eyeing the half-filled bag of dark urine dangling beside the bed.

Angela grabbed a pack of Marlboro Reds from her Gucci bag and turned to Jamie, who rummaged through her suede fringed handbag for her own cigarettes.

Chloe watched them leave the room before turning back to her immobile grandmother. She inhaled and tears stung her eyes. Once more she grasped her necklace with a silent plea.

After ten minutes of Chloe talking to her about school and new books she was reading, in the hope her grandmother would miraculously awake, Chloe decided that sketching might take her mind off the fact she could soon be saying goodbye to her beloved nanna.

Chloe wiped her eyes, stood up and went to the mahogany tallboy next to the bed. Opening the top drawer, she searched for blank paper and pens. No luck.

Next she looked through the blackwood buffet, the bedside table and the bookcase, but could find no stationery, not even a Dunmore Nursing Home notepad with its logo imprinted at the top.

On a hunch, Chloe checked a red cedar chest of drawers near the floor-to-ceiling window. Nothing but clothes and accessories, along with a time-worn Arnott's Biscuits tin containing earrings and bracelets. As she was about to close the drawer, something caught her eye: a maroon-coloured book partially hidden under a pair of folded beige slacks, and because it looked so out of place, Chloe had to feed her curiosity.

After inspecting its faded leather cover and running a hand over the cracks, Chloe concluded it was an old diary. And as it was concealed, it had to be a *secret* diary.

The curious youngster looked over her shoulder to ensure no-one was entering the room; she knew there was a hint of danger at being so intrusive. Seeing and hearing nothing to cause immediate alarm, she turned around and opened the cover. The smell of dusty pages and mothballs flooded her nostrils, making her wince. Chloe lowered the book and marvelled upon seeing a dog-eared page with a date – 27th November 1964 – written at the top in faded black ink.

Wow, that's over half a century ago!

Chloe looked at the words written on the pages in her grandmother's cursive writing: *Chevy Impala, freedom riders* and *jazzed* jumped off the page ... then she heard Jamie's smooth-as-silk voice and the unmistakable clacking of her mother's high heels echo through the hollow corridor. Chloe shut the diary and slammed the chest of drawers closed before running back to her uncomfortable chair.

When the two women entered the room, Chloe looked at them in silence, clutching the diary to her stomach. Her heart pounded like a mouse's beneath a cat's paw as she noticed out of the corner of her eye that a pair of pantyhose had fallen out of the drawer onto the floor.

'Everything okay?' Angela said as she walked over, emitting the faint odour of tobacco smoke that permeated her clothing.

Chloe nodded. 'Yes, but I might go for a walk.' She already formulated a lie that if they noticed the diary, she'd say it was just a blank notepad she'd found on her grandmother's table.

Angela consulted her Guess wristwatch. 'Don't be long, and be mindful of those trying to sleep.'

Stepping out into the garden, enlivened by a light breeze, Chloe walked past a sizeable water fountain with cherubs lit up by LED lights, surrounded by terracotta tiles and a semi-circular, manicured box hedge. Sandstone pillars formed a gateway to a black Victorian cast-iron spiral staircase, which led down to a fenced-off area with picnic benches placed near a pond. Beyond the confines of the encircling black wrought-iron fence, the Sydney Harbour lights were luminescent. Chloe looked towards the slumbering silver moon haloed by a scattering of stars, but a fresh wave of tears blurred her vision.

She wiped her eyes with the palm of her free hand, and found a sandstone bench next to a hedge of coniferous shrubs and a row of knee-high solar lamps – perfect to aid her sight. Chloe knew that reading the diary was a major breach of privacy, but she felt that her grandmother's words might conjure up her wonderful, sweet voice and make it seem like she was there beside her. Chloe was also dying to get a firsthand account of what the sixties were like – surely it couldn't hurt to read a little …

'Have you told Tim yet?' Jamie said, glancing out the window to observe the stars flickering amid the black velvet sky. She wondered if their father, Buck, was looking down on them. God, she missed him. His infectious laugh. His sense of humour. She even missed the smell of Imperial Leather talcum powder (something he used to douse himself in after every bath). Jamie turned to her sister.

Angela raised her manicured eyebrows, which suggested their brother hadn't crossed her mind. 'No, I haven't had a chance; I was busy at work when I received the call.'

They stood in silence before Jamie focused on the stars once more.

'I always get side-tracked these days; too much is going on,' Angela said.

'What's the time in London now?' Jamie plucked a piece of thread from her black poncho.

'I'm not sure; I haven't spoken to Tim in a while.'

Jamie consulted the world clock on her phone for the time difference between Sydney and London – noting that her partner, Boyd, had yet to acknowledge her voice message.

While Jamie peered at her phone, an elderly gentleman holding a bunch of lilacs poked his head around the open door.

Jamie and Angela both stared at him, then at each other, with the same curious expression: *Who's this stranger?*

'Can we help you?' Angela asked.

'Oh, um …' The man peered at the door number with a furrowed brow. 'Sorry to … ah, I must have the wrong room.'

'Who are you looking for?' Jamie took a step towards him, noting the scents of Old Spice and talcum powder – a marriage of smells that only silent generation folks would think of pairing.

'Um, I was looking for Audrey.'

'Yes, but who are you?' Angela said.

The old man fidgeted with the lilacs – he appeared nervous, but his rumpled forehead suggested he thought these innocuous questions irritating.

Everyone then directed their attention to Chloe, who came to an abrupt halt behind the man standing in the doorway.

Chloe's eyes widened and her mouth curled into a grin. 'You're *him*, aren't you?!'

Chapter 3

ELIJAH SAT IN the room with Audrey and, it appeared, her family, still not quite believing how this had unfolded. While he stared at Audrey lying on the bed only a few feet away, hooked up to various machines, reduced to senseless flesh, he could feel the eyes of the young girl and two women appraising him.

One woman was a fresh-faced bohemian-type, probably in her early thirties, wearing a red beret and a black poncho that partially covered a pair of jeans. The other was more businesslike in a grey pencil suit and hair tightly pulled back into a bun, which to him looked like an economical attempt at an instant facelift. *No doubt she thinks her shit doesn't stink,* he thought.

'Here, let me take these for you,' the bohemian offered, taking the flowers from him with a nervous smile.

'Thanks,' he muttered. He handed over the lilacs and turned to the grinning young girl, who now sat in a chair beside him. He wanted to flick her like he would a persistent fly.

'So, how do you know my mother?' Miss Prim-and-Proper asked, folding her arms across her chest as he turned to answer her.

'My name is Elijah. I knew your mother a long time ago.'

'Yeah you did!' the little girl said, grinning from ear-to-ear.

Elijah shifted in his chair. What the hell was she doing, grinning like that? He had no time for childish games. He could be at home doing the *Take 5* crossword for a chance to win fifty bucks!

'Do you know something we don't, young lady?' Miss Prim-and-Proper asked with a raised eyebrow.

Yeah … do you? Elijah thought, looking at the girl he assumed was Audrey's granddaughter.

'Maybe,' she said, smirking close-mouthed.

'Well, spit it out,' the bohemian said in a light, amused tone.

The girl shook her head in defiance. 'No, he's got a mouth. He can use it.' She looked at Elijah with a quick nod, as if giving him an opening.

Jeez, how fuckin' thoughtful, twit.

All three now stared at Elijah. This was too emotional, too overwhelming. He cleared his throat. 'Ahh, what's the update on Audrey's condition?' he asked the older woman, whose attitude and upturned nose exuded a sense of superiority. She reminded him of his late mother – and it didn't sit well.

'I'm sorry – Elijah, is it?'

He dipped his head.

'I've never heard of you. Are you sure you have the right room or even the right person? This is Audrey Arlington.' She pointed to the bed. 'My name's Angela, and this is Jamie.' She motioned to the one in the red beret, who then gave a short wave and grin, as though she was a contestant on a game show. 'And next to you is my daughter, Chloe.'

Chloe held out her hand and gave Elijah a wide smile, showcasing every tooth. 'Nice to meet ya!'

Angela scoffed like she was clearing phlegm. 'Chloe, there is no such word as "ya"; it's "you". We've spoken about this before, young lady. Remember?'

Oh yeah, definitely like my mother, Elijah thought; it only added to his indigestion.

He enclosed Chloe's hand within his calloused paw, saving his temper for the one with the pugnacious scowl. 'I know where I am, lady. I ain't senile!'

Jamie glanced at Angela, who looked back at her in astonishment as if to say *How dare he speak to me like that.*

'Well, pardon me … Elijah … but I've never heard of you!'

'Of course not,' Elijah mumbled.

'What's *that* supposed to mean?'

'It means, lady, that I'm not surprised by anything *this* woman has or hasn't done,' he said, pointing to Audrey. 'I haven't seen Audrey in a *very* long time. I heard from a relative that she was in here, so I wanted to come and … pay my respects.'

Hearing himself say *those words* for the first time made it more real. His throat tightened as he struggled to keep emotionally balanced. *I knew this was a bad friggin' idea*, he thought, chastising his foolishness.

'But we don't know who you are,' Angela said. 'We've never heard of you!'

Elijah grumbled and threw his hands in the air as though he were fighting a losing battle.

'It's all right, Mother,' Chloe said. 'Nanna would want him here.'

Angela turned to her daughter. 'Really, young lady, and how could *you* possibly know that?'

Chloe held out the maroon diary she'd concealed from the group – the ace up her sleeve.

Elijah stared at it without blinking; without saying a word. As if in a trance, he reached into his grey woollen jacket and pulled out an identical book, which also had a faded leather maroon cover. Everyone in the room remained silent until Chloe turned to Angela.

'I know this, Mother, because Elijah was … is … her soulmate.'

No-one dared move. The only sounds came from the ventilator beside the bed.

Elijah stared at the diary the girl held, while everyone else looked at *his* diary, clasped in his frail and shaky hands.

Seconds passed before Angela clasped either side of her head as though trying to stop her brain from hurting. 'I'm sorry, but you're going to have to be more damn specific about what's going on. Are you a resident here too, or what?'

Elijah glared at her, clamping his jaw shut until it throbbed.

Angela lowered her register. 'Look, I've had a tumultuous day, and I think Mum's final moments should be with the ones she loves. Mum has *never* once mentioned you, so until more explaining, I'm afraid I'm going to have to ask you to leave us in peace – out of respect and privacy.' Angela ran her hands over her skirt while looking directly at Elijah, whose eyes were blazing with hostility. Blind Freddy could have seen his look said *Fuck you, lady.*

Angela took a hesitant step back towards Jamie, who hadn't uttered a word.

Elijah's heart hammered. After all this damned time – even now, in a coma – *she* still affected him like no other.

'Okay, lady, sure. You want specific details?' Elijah said, nostrils flaring as he opened his diary and adjusted his glasses. 'Fine, then you got it. So sit down, shut up, and *listen*!'

Chapter 4

'THE YEAR WAS 1964. I remember well: it was a Friday afternoon and the blazing sun was nestled above the horizon as I travelled along the Wollongong coast in my EH Holden. I swore it was the most mesmeric sunset I had ever seen. It was like I had just been born; like I was seeing the world through fresh eyes. Little did I know it was a perfect opening scene.

'The Swinging Sixties was a fabulous time to come of age in Australia, and as a twenty-four-year-old ex-army cadet, I thought I had it all. I had the money, the friends, and the girl. She was a hot piece of ... well, I won't be crude in front of the youngster, but people used to say my girl was the spittin' image of Jean 'The Shrimp' Shrimpton. Her hair was always fashionable, she always wore either baby pink or white lipstick, and her love for those bloody Mary Quant miniskirts had men wishing they were me. Her bodacious bosoms were something to write home about, let me tell you! Sure, she had a bit of a reputation, but that's what made the mystery of her come alive.'

Jamie lowered her head, but Elijah caught the beginnings of a snicker, while Angela's jaw dropped open like a clown's head at a carnival game.

'I needed to see what the fuss was all about, and that I did! On the streets she was a lady, but in the sack ... holy hell, mama—'

Angela held up a hand. 'Um, I don't think we need to hear this. How disrespectful! Chloe's only twelve.'

Elijah scowled then shot back: 'Have I finished talking?'

Jamie's chin was now touching her chest, and Chloe's eyes appeared to be propped open with toothpicks.

Angela mustered a murderous look that would have scared a hardened criminal.

Hmm, so the apple doesn't fall far from the tree, Elijah thought, remembering all too well Audrey's fiery temper that would rival Ares, the Greek god of war.

Elijah grinned, tongue lubricating his bottom lip. 'My girl's name was Georgie Brown.'

Angela's lips shrivelled, her face resembling a furnace. 'I don't appreciate that! You did that deliberately; you *knew* we would have assumed you were talking about Mum, that we—'

'You did all the assuming of your own accord,' he corrected, remaining composed. 'I was merely telling a story, which you prematurely interrupted.'

'Bastard!'

'The gutter becomes you,' Elijah said, still poised. Angela diverted her attention to her flashing phone. Elijah cleared his throat. 'As I was saying, the controversial Swinging Sixties couldn't have been better. The music, the culture, living avant-garde on the beach – it was the greatest *damn* time to be alive.' He paused and smiled with a sense of fondness. 'I feel sorry you all missed it and live in an age where everyone is glued to their phone instead of looking at the beauty of this country.' Angela shot him a scowl. Her mobile phone had pinged again. 'At about five-thirty on the 27th of November, I screeched into the parking lot of Betty-Sue's ice cream parlour. Upon walking to the entrance, which faced the street, away from the ocean, Georgie stood near a barber's pole, wearing a light pink dress and white thigh-high boots. It was quite the Nancy Sinatra-look, with her dark hair all fluffed up and a yellow band through it – she even wore white lipstick. Mind you' – he glanced around the room – 'I was rockin' it in my brown bell-bottoms and black dress shirt. Back in those days, see, even if you were going to the shops for bread and milk, you put effort into your appearance. Not like today: girls wear skirts the size of eye masks and boys wear jeans halfway down their backside and think they're a modern-day Sammy Davis Jr.'

Chloe giggled, even though he knew she wouldn't have a stinking clue who the Rat Pack were. Elijah visualised that Angela's family sing-a-longs in the car were to Beethoven, Chopin and Bach.

'Anyway, my girl ran over with a squeal and kissed me like I was a returned soldier, much to the disapproval of passers-by, I'm sure. Not that we cared. I've never been fond of getting other's approval; it's an unnecessary waste of energy,' he added for good measure, before smiling towards Angela. Her nostrils flared like a bull about to charge.

'Georgie ran her fingers through my hair while my hands travelled down to her backside, having a good old snog until someone yelled: "Hey, get a room!"

'We broke free and saw Alison, Lawrence and Jonathan – he was the one who'd shouted out.

'Lawrence's red eyes conveyed he'd been puffing the magic dragon, while Alison drifted over like the orange-haired flower child she was. The five of us high school delinquents were inseparable. We did everything together, and no-one felt left out, even though we were an odd number. A favourite pastime of ours was going sailing at the beach to catch some rays, or heading to the passion pit to—'

'Passion pit?' Chloe said, head tilted.

'He means the drive-in,' Angela said, shaking her head. 'He's deliberately provoking us all with his filth, degradation and—'

'Actually, come to think of it, Angela, I think I *know* you,' Elijah said, straight-faced.

Angela's eyes narrowed to slits as she cocked her head.

Elijah removed his index finger from his withered chin and nodded. 'Yeah ... yeah, weren't you the author of *Mein Kampf*?'

Jamie let out a small squeal, but soon clamped her lips tighter than a clam, whilst Angela's face flushed scarlet.

'Moving on,' Elijah muttered. 'That afternoon, we had planned on going to the parlour before surfing the waves. Simply put, life was picture-perfect. When we entered Betty-Sue's ice cream parlour, they blasted us with the latest song from the British Invasion: "House of the Rising Sun". The UK bands were producing hit, after hit, after hit, and us Aussies felt like they left us for dead in the music scene. I happened to play the guitar and used to jam to get my kicks. I dreamed of being in a band, playing my latest song about heartbreak, or being an advocate for a countercultural movement.' Elijah paused and remembered his old lady's face when he'd told her he wanted to quit private school and become a musician. He had to give her a paper bag to stop hyperventilating, and in the days that followed, Margaret Samuels treated her son like he was an escaped prisoner begging for food and a place to stay. He had become a nobody; the scum of society on which people could lay blame for the world being such a cesspool of corruption and poverty.

Shaking his head from the hurtful memory, Elijah continued. 'Anyway, we took our usual seats in the green booth at the back corner, along the wall opposite to the counter and ice cream selection. It was right next to a window with venetian blinds, which gave us a partial view of the beach behind the building. A framed picture of Patsy Cline overlooked our table, and her knowing gaze seemed to say *I know all your secrets, you hip-cats!*

'The ceiling fans did a mediocre job of keeping us cool, so we were looking forward to our shakes and sundaes. After all, it was the summer of '64 and it felt like we were in hell's mouth.

'"Give us our usual, doll," Jonathan yelled out to pretty Sylvia Flores, who was rocking her new Vidal Sassoon bob cut.

'After Jonathan's outburst, the elderly couple in the adjoining booth left. I can't say I blame them, and they had probably witnessed the unlawful act of public affection outside between Georgie and me.' Elijah chortled through his nostrils at the memory. 'Over in the car park beside the building on my left, surfies with blonde mop-tops attempted to unload their boogie boards, while widgies pointed and giggled at them, acting like they'd never seen a shirtless man before.'

'Widgies?' Chloe said, a smile creeping up.

Elijah realised much of the jargon of that turbulent decade had changed; he may as well be speaking gibberish. 'Sorry, it was a term given to the youth subculture that existed in Australia back in the day. A "bodgie" was a male, the "widgie" was his female counterpart—'

'In other words, useless degenerates of our society; a complete waste of space,' Angela said, her raised eyebrow challenging Elijah to say something to the contrary.

'You know, I am trying to see things from your perspective,' Elijah said, 'but, honey, I'll be damned if I can get my head that far up my rectum.'

Angela bared her teeth as Jamie concealed another smirk while soothing Angela's arm to calm her down. Chloe's face was now paper-pale.

'Getting back to my story,' he said with a deliberate eye roll, consciously deciding to turn the notch down from boiling to a gentle simmer. 'Jonathan said, "Hey, buddy, here's to good fortune."

'I looked at the table where Jonathan tossed me a penny for the Ask Swami chrome napkin dispenser.'

Chloe's crinkled brow told him she was confused as all get-out.

'See, back in the day, some diners had napkin dispensers where they also told your future for a small fee. It was great fun; I believe they did a story about it for an episode of *The Twilight Zone*. Anyway, I laughed as I inserted the penny and pushed the black lever down. Out popped a white paper strip, which read: YOU WILL FIND A NEW LOVE.

'I looked up, shielding the piece of paper from everyone – especially my girl, Georgie, who was sitting opposite me, playing footsies. Georgie had a wicked smile going as she slurped on her strawberry milkshake through a straw.

'Lawrence was next to me, craning his neck. "What's it say?"

'I chuckled. "It says: you will win one million pounds!"

'They all cracked up – they knew how much scratch I had. Georgie turned to Alison sitting next to her and they giggled like no tomorrow, but I think partly because Alison had had an oh-zee's worth of grass.'

Angela's heel slammed to the ground. 'I'm warning you!'

Elijah glanced towards Chloe, accepting the fact if he wanted to continue the story he was going to have to omit references to sex, drugs and alcohol. *Shit, this is going to be tough*, he conceded. As they say: if you can remember the sixties, you obviously weren't there. However, he dipped his head in acknowledgement and continued. '"Gimme a kiss, baby," I said, leaning over the table to smooch Georgie.

'As everyone "woo-hooed" and clapped, I used that time to discreetly put the obviously phoney fortune strip into my pants pocket before settling back. At that moment, the front door of the shop swung open … in walked a girl – and it hit me like a battering ram.'

Elijah glanced at Audrey, picturing in his mind as clear as day, her swaying hips as she strolled past the booths all those decades ago.

'That's the best way I can explain it,' he whispered, frowning. 'I looked over my right shoulder towards the entrance and saw rays of golden sun shining through the door behind her, and *that*, along with the way she walked, stole my breath. I've never forgotten it to this day. She was the closest thing I'd ever seen to an angel on earth and, as if serendipitously, the jukebox spun its needle around to Roy Orbison's "Oh, Pretty Woman".'

He observed Jamie clutching her heart and Angela gulping.

'I like the next part,' Chloe said, which revealed she'd read a few pages of Audrey's diary.

'So do I.' Elijah looked at Audrey's open diary that lay in Chloe's lap. 'Her ethereal beauty had me stunned; I even recall Alison making a comment on her good looks, something like "What a fox!"

'Jonathan shrugged as if indifferent, but his eyes were fixated on Audrey, too. I forced myself to turn away from the mirage and focus my attention back to Georgie.

'"They forgot my cherry," Georgie said with a pout and a few rapid blinks with her fake Almay lashes that she'd become glued to – pardon the pun. As soon as women from across the globe caught Sue Murray on the front cover of *Vogue* that year, every girl, woman and transvestite decided they needed, wanted, and couldn't live without fake bloody eyelashes. For some, it was like the defining event of our generation.

'Georgie pushed her milkshake towards me so I said, "I'll get you a cherry, baby." My heart had sped up like I'd taken too much LSD. I wanted to shake it off, so I gladly volunteered to get out of the confinement. I excused myself from the booth, climbing over Lawrence, and made my way over to the counter. The angelic apparition was now putting her scarf and handbag on a rack. With every step I took, it felt like a lifetime before I reached her, as though I were walking on the spot. I didn't know what was happening, but I remember wondering why she wore a scarf during summer.

'She placed a white boat-shaped hat over her rich, beautiful blonde hair. Her yellow-and-red uniform did wonders for her hourglass figure, which she knew how to move. As I approached the counter, I realised she was tall – taller than the average chick, anyway. I stared at her slender back, not wanting to speak, not wanting to interrupt her, as though it would be rude of me to do so. It seemed oxygen was no longer available to me. At that moment, she looked up at the mirror in front of her, as if sensing my presence. Everything around me ceased to exist as our eyes connected through the reflection, and I swore I heard her gasp – or maybe it'd been me.

'"What the hell do *you* want?" a voice to my left said.

'I broke away from the magnetic pull to face Betty Wallis, the old sweat hog who owned the parlour, and man did Ol' Bet know how to throw a party to end all parties. She used to have 'em on her acreage and we sang and drank the night away while bonfires outshone the night sky. She was like the mother I always dreamed of having – a bit of a redneck with a heart of gold – instead of the proverbial high-class rollers I was born to. Betty was onto husband number three, who unfortunately was as sick as a dog by this point. She never had any kids of her own. Except us foster kids, I guess you could say.'

Elijah grinned before continuing. '"Sweet cheeks, you forgot to give Georgie a cherry with her milkshake."

'"Dammit, Eli," Betty said, "they're only given with sundaes and you know it!" She placed her hands on her meaty hips, her sleeves rolled up to reveal part of the heart-shaped ***My Heart Belongs to Elvis*** tattoo on her upper right arm.

'There was tension in the air before she cracked first and started laughing – the kind of laugh that comes straight from the pit of your gut. She went back through the swinging doors into the kitchen to retrieve the maraschino cherries while I stood there and slowly swung my head back to the right. Pretty Woman was now facing me, wiping the front counter with a dishrag. I swallowed hard; it was as though I'd never seen a chick before. She must have known I was watching, so she raised her baby blues and her arm stopped circling. She offered a timid smile, but I had nothing to contribute. No smile, no words; in fact, I frowned. The girl then gave her attention to Betty, who had now come out of the kitchen, effectively putting a stop to any more interaction between the two of us.

'"Now get the hell outta me sight!" Betty cackled, her croaky laugh reflecting the many years of smoking a pack of Rothmans per day.

'I grabbed the ramekin of cherries and kissed Betty's cheek, ravaged with deep ravines carved by nicotine. She swotted me away and I darted back to the booth, where Georgie eyed the goodness I held. I jumped over the back rather than squeeze past Lawrence, and handed my girl the cherries.

'"Neato – you're my hero!" she said, inspecting her lipstick in the chrome napkin dispenser. She then grabbed the dish of cherries off me and stuck one in her mouth seductively, playfully hinting at what she planned to do to me later that night—'

'Disgusting. You're truly *disgusting*,' Angela said, lowering her phone that she'd been typing on as Chloe frowned and looked from one person to the next.

Elijah fixed his steady gaze on Angela's. 'Lady, you can point the finger all you want, it ain't nothing you haven't done before. Her right there is living proof,' he said, pointing at Chloe, causing Angela to wheeze. 'So don't act all bloody high and mighty, or are you the Blessed Virgin Mary's incarnate, claiming Immaculate Conception?'

Angela made to slap him, but Jamie intervened and held her raging sister back by the upper arms.

'Calm down, Ange.'

Slicing through the chaos, Chloe said, 'Mother, I don't know what you guys are talking about, but Nanna wrote about that day in her diary. I think it'd be fun to read it and compare notes, don't you?'

'No! You're only twelve, Chloe. I will *not* let you listen to this filth.'

Elijah felt a pang deep in his stomach, but concealed his emotions – an act that had become second nature after the torture he'd gone through. 'Why not? I have the time, and everyone else seems to be all ears.' He grinned whilst looking at the two sisters. One of them smirked, whilst the other conveyed through blazing eyes that she was plotting his demise in a way not even Vlad the Impaler could conceive.

Chapter 5

'27th November 1964. *Dear Diary, last night I dreamt of my parents. The images of blistering skin peeling from their faces and eyes full of fear will forever linger, it seems. My recurring nightmare. The pain continued flowing through me as I woke to hear Uncle Lloyd below, yelling at someone on the telephone. Misty was sleeping at the foot of my bed and I wanted to stay like that forever – curled up in a ball like my cat – and disappear from the world. I hate the person I've become and I haven't made any friends since arriving in Wollongong. Although, Sylvia Flores from the ice cream parlour seems pleasant, and she doesn't treat me as different. I hate when people do that. This afternoon I arrived at the parlour for my shift, but something felt gnarly as soon as I walked in. I didn't realise what it was until I looked in the mirror and saw the most attractive man I've ever laid eyes on, standing behind me. Stupidly, I gasped – not just because he was attractive – but because it startled me. I honestly didn't hear him approach. I stared at him until my boss, Betty, interrupted us. When she left for the kitchen, the gorgeous man turned to me and we locked eyes. Green pinning blue. Golly, it was a queer feeling. I tried to smile, but he looked angry about it. Why? He rejoined his friends, who seemed jazzed – as they appeared to behave and carry on like riff-raff. The man started kissing a glamorous girl – in public! The handsome couple looked happy together, but I felt bummed out because I know deep down a cat like that would never go for a dud like me. He'd like good things, expensive things. More importantly: things that actually function! He wouldn't want anyone dragging him down. He seems like the textbook bad boy who floats from girl to girl, and it wouldn't surprise me if he came from money. I don't know what happened today with that strange feeling I experienced, but I hope I never see him around again. Something way-out occurred, but I for one do not want an encore. Love, Audrey.'*

Chloe lowered the diary to her lap and faced Elijah.

Elijah smirked, running a hand over his chin. '*Riff-raff,* really, she wrote that?'

Chloe nodded with a short laugh.

'That's not a stretch of the imagination,' Angela mumbled, thumbs tapping away on her phone at lightning speed.

Silence hijacked the room once more, apart from the steady beeping of the ECG, and the *whoosh-click* sounds of the respirator.

'I still don't think you should read Nanna's personal diary, Chloe,' Angela added, still typing.

Elijah regarded the uptight woman and rationalised he should probably go easy on her – as stuck-up and bitchy as she was. They clearly had no idea who he was; they only knew what he'd presented himself as: a grumpy old man. 'I might get going now.' He reached for the arms of his chair.

'I think that's a wise idea; the brightest thing you've said all night,' Angela said before chucking her phone into her Gucci bag.

Elijah fought the urge to give her one of his famous quick-witted comebacks. This was not the time or the place for a donnybrook. After struggling for a few seconds, Elijah was upright and bade everyone a good night. He looked at Audrey and tears surfaced, brought on by an internal storm that had been raging for decades. His stomach mimicked a dinghy tossed around on a rip-roaring ocean – the kind he used to surf in his youth. It enraged him that *she* still had such power over his emotions. *Damn you, Audrey.* He left the room without another word, feeling their gazes bore into his back.

'Wait, please!'

Elijah turned as Chloe stood alone in the corridor, clutching her grandmother's diary to her chest as though she had sole guardianship of some sacred artefact – it was *her* Holy Grail.

'Please don't go,' Chloe whispered, inching closer. He felt her radiating warmth and saw the desperation in her soulful eyes. He'd always been a sucker for the allure of innocent eyes.

'I have to,' he said, choosing to focus on a sign on the wall behind her: **Cleanliness is in Your Own Hands!** with step-by-step, diagram-by-diagram instructions on how to wash your hands. What any basic, dim-witted individual should have learned in pre-school, he thought. 'Besides, I don't want the Wicked Witch of the West sending her monkeys after me.'

Chloe frowned and looked at him blankly.

He scoffed, slapping his thigh. 'What kid these days hasn't seen *The Wizard of Oz*?'

Through tears, she said, 'I love my nanna more than anyone. Reading this diary, and yours, might help me. I know she's still here, but I'm not silly. The doctors say she doesn't have long. Please stay with me and tell me more about her. I want to know *everything* about her, and how she came to be the greatest lady I've ever met.'

Elijah looked deep into the girl's sapphire-blue eyes as he felt the ice inside his heart dislodge, just like the first time Audrey had flashed her baby blues at him – he'd melted like butter on warm toast.

The greatest woman she's ever met, huh? So great minds do *think alike.*

'Well, I don't think we should go back in *there* with Nurse Ratched hanging around.'

Chloe frowned. 'You mean Nurse *Mildred*? No, she won't mind—'

'No, Nurse Ratched is from *One Flew Over the C*— never mind, I don't think we should go back, do you?'

Chloe shook her head. 'No, sir. But I know the perfect place.'

Chapter 6

CRICKETS, NOCTURNAL BIRDS, and a variety of insects attracted to the solar lamps kept them company, as an orchestra of maritime sounds floating from the harbour acted like background music.

'Okay,' Elijah said, suppressing a dry cough, 'have I bored you so far?'

Chloe shook her head, smiling. 'Not for a single second, sir.'

Elijah observed her. She was understandably desperate to find out more about her grandmother's clandestine past, so who was he to deny her request?

'Pay attention now; I don't want you missing a single beat.'

Chloe sat straighter, smiling while nodding.

'Ah, let's see,' he said, holding his diary. 'Two days later on the Sunday, I was at home, dining on salmon. Around the dinner table sat my mother, Margaret; my father, Howard; and my older sister, Grace. Arthur Moore, our butler, stood in the corner of the large dining—'

'Butler?'

Elijah swotted a bogong moth flying around his face. 'Yes. Servant, valet, butler, shit-kicker, whatever you want to call it, we had one. I came from a wealthy background, see.'

Chloe rolled her eyes. 'I *know* what a butler is. What I mean is, were you *really* that rich?'

'My father was a top barrister who wore the funny, long, horse-haired wigs and red robes, and my mother worked for the premier of New South Wales as a secretary. So, we were loaded, to be frank.'

Her eyes darted to the left. 'Who's Frank?'

'No, it means honest.'

'Oh.'

He looked on as Chloe ran a hand over his diary's leather surface, but despite the years that had passed, he was certain he knew the story word-for-word. Such memories never disappeared; they were merely covered by the sands of time.

'As my parents were discussing the pros and cons of the Civil Rights Act, Grace and I chucked peas at each other, using the tips of our silver spoons. We were well and truly past that stage of our lives, but we wanted to prove we could do anything at the dinner table and it would go unnoticed by our parents. Over time, my presence at the dinner table diminished, and Grace had been living with some guy, Roger, until she broke it off a week prior, and then moved back home. Due to my circumstances, I also moved back in with the understanding it would be temporary. It wasn't too bad being back home, because I was usually at a girl's house, anyway. Not anyone in particular, just whomever I fancied.'

Chloe frowned. 'But you were with Georgie?'

Elijah covered his mouth with a fist and coughed. 'Sorry, excuse me.' He patted his chest. 'At this point in the story, yes, but before that I had, err, I had had a few skirts that were, um, friends.'

Chloe's eyes narrowed. 'You had sex with them, didn't you?'

Elijah almost fell backwards off the sandstone bench. There wasn't any point in lying to this precocious child, so he said, 'Maybe,' and cleared his throat once more, avoiding her sceptical gaze. 'Now, getting back to my story. I was growing restless at the dinner table, so I excused myself; not that my mother or father heard – or even cared. They had transitioned into a full-blown argument about the *National Service Act*, which was introduced that month. Things were getting pretty heavy at the dinner table, but my old man was a proud hawk and a blue-blooded patriot, acting as though bumping off the commies was no more effort than brushing off pesky ants at a picnic. The Vietnam War had been going on for years, but it didn't fully reach the height of opposition from the public until the sixties. Still, news coverage was round the friggin' clock, as it was the first war to be televised. It frequently made the headlines – from political radicals to protestors, from jingoistic leaders to war fanatics—'

'Jig …?'

'Jingoistic, yes – extreme love for your country.'

'And commies?'

'Sorry, I'm not good with talking to people. Communists. Communism is a bad ideology; there are only five communist countries in the world, and although you might not understand it, thank your lucky stars we ain't one of 'em.' Chloe frowned. 'Sorry, I'll try and speak—'

Chloe's spine straightened like a wooden ruler. 'No, don't. Then you'll dumb it down and talk to me like I'm stupid. I'm not, you know?'

Elijah offered an honest smile. 'I know that. I can tell you're right up there with Einstein.'

She rewarded his flattery with a smile that could only be interpreted as *cute*, and then bobbed her head to indicate he should proceed.

'I walked outside my house, loathing the fact I couldn't stop thinking about the blonde girl. There was something about her; something unique. My feelings bothered me. I had to put a stop to this nonsense. She was just another sheila, right?' Elijah leaned down with a raised eyebrow, and Chloe flashed a big smile. 'I jumped into my EH and drove down the mountainside to see this girl, but when I got to the parking lot, I sort of … froze.'

'Why?' Chloe whispered, wide-eyed.

'Well, I realised I didn't want any bloody part of it. I was content with Georgie; I didn't want to go on the make with some stranger, ya know?' Chloe nodded, her eyes and mouth wide. 'Georgie gave to me without me even asking. She was somewhat wealthy, my parents loved her – as did Grace – so why meddle where there shouldn't be any meddling?

'As I sat in my idling car, my stomach grumbled. I'd only had two bites of the pretentious salmon, and dessert always follows dinner, right?' Chloe nodded once more. 'Right, so why not indulge in a little ice cream? To hell with *her*; this was *my* local hangout!'

Chapter 7

THEN – 1964

ELIJAH FLICKED HIS Camel cigarette butt into the nearest bush, and with shaky hands he opened the door to Betty-Sue's. No-one was behind the counter on the right, adjacent to the seafoam-green booths lined against the wall. *So far, so good*, he thought as he made his way over to the ice cream selection, intent on getting in and getting out. 'You Really Got Me' by the Kinks blasted from the dome-shaped AMI Continental 2 jukebox in the corner beside a provocative full-length poster of Gina Lollobrigida. Elijah stopped and shook his head. *Very funny*, he thought with slight irritation at the felicitous song lyrics. Elijah then positioned his hands on either side of the glass and searched the ice cream selection, acting like he didn't have a care in the world. He tapped his fingers on the frosty glass to the beat of the song, when the swinging doors to the kitchen opened. He looked to his left, and it was *her*. She appeared as radiant as when he first saw her – probably even more so. Her lips parted when she saw him, and for a moment Elijah thought she had ceased breathing too.

'Hey,' Elijah said, breaking the palpable tension before pinning his eyes on a sign above the counter: **PETER'S ICE CREAM – THE HEALTH FOOD OF A NATION**. He watched her out of the corner of his eye, noting her chic, pinned-up hair. He'd never stared harder at ice cream in all his life, but he was following her movements through his peripheral.

She cleared her throat as she went behind the counter and in a sweet manner said, 'What would you like, sir?'

Elijah continued looking at the daily selection as she stood opposite now, fidgeting with her apron. 'Mmm ... whaddaya recommend?'

Audrey took a second before speaking. 'The butter pecan is pleasant.'

Elijah fish-hooked his upper lip. 'Nah, had that the other day. What else?' He still hadn't looked at her. He must have seemed like a total wanker, but he honest to God *couldn't*. He felt ill-equipped, like an unarmed soldier going into battle. He was unprepared to handle the same strange heart palpitations as before, and cursed himself for being in this situation.

'Um ... well, we have cherry surprise, which is topped with lime, orange, strawberry, and pineapple candy chips. I know you like cherries ...'

Elijah looked up – and wished he hadn't. The connection was instant; it was like something he'd only read about or seen in a Columbia picture. Then he noticed it, the reason she was reserved and acted like everything frightened her. She had a hearing aid with a wire travelling to a transistor pouch. *How did I miss this the first time?*

Elijah realised he'd stared too long at the device when his eyes returned to her flushed face. She'd caught him gawking. From then on, she didn't look at him. In fact, as she turned away, he caught her welling up. Elijah needed to change the subject quick-fast; this wasn't how he wanted their first encounter to play out.

'How about I try maple walnut? You can't go wrong with walnuts, can you?' Elijah chuckled.

Her jaw tightened as she focused her attention beyond him, looking anywhere at all but at *him*. 'Would you like a cup or cone?'

Elijah swallowed hard upon hearing her deflated tone. He'd hurt her. *What do I care, anyway? She's nobody to me*, he told himself.

'A cone is fine, thank you, miss.'

After Elijah gave her the money, she handed him the cone, then turned and left for the kitchen. He had no idea what to say or do; he was left staring at the doors swinging on their hinges. When his chest constricted, he had to remind himself to breathe.

As he exited the parlour, he tossed the cone into the nearest bin and ventured off for some alone time with Georgie.

Chapter 8

CHLOE GLANCED AT the open diary across her knees. 'Would you like me to read what she wrote about that night?'

'I can only imagine,' Elijah mumbled, cringing as he relived the awkward encounter.

'*29th November 1964. Dear Diary, he's just like the rest! I hate him. He entered the shop tonight, all suave in his black jeans and black leather jacket, looking dangerous and forbidden. His gorgeous, thick, jet-black hair shimmered, and his emerald-green eyes were just as piercing as when I first saw them. But good looks aside … as I was serving the cool cat, he stared at my aid. He stared for so long that I almost threw chocolate fudge at him to snap him out of it. I knew he'd be like the others. When will people wake up? I'm an actual person with feelings; they didn't discover me at the Roswell crash in 1947! I'm a good person, but people judge what's on the outside. I only hope they wipe civilisation clean out so we can start with friendlier folk, who are more understanding of people who are "different". If I ever see him again, dear Diary, I'll let him have it! Yours angrily, Audrey.*'

At that moment, Nurse Mildred emerged from the shrubbery, appearing from the darkness like a creature in a B-grade horror flick, prompting a high-pitched squeal from Chloe.

Elijah patted his chest over his beating heart with a sigh of relief and Nurse Mildred said, 'Chloe, yer mama is lookin' fo' ya, darlin'; it's past visitin' hours. Yer'll both have ta skedaddle on home now.'

She's crazier than when I met her in the foyer, Elijah thought, smirking. *I like her though, even if she is a Charlestonian.*

'No problemo,' Elijah said, but Chloe moaned like a child told to sit in the time-out corner.

'T'was fetchin' ta meet ya, Mr Samuels,' Nurse Mildred said.

'And you. Perhaps we shall see each other again?'

'Darlin', only if the creek don't rise.'

Both Chloe and Elijah swapped frowns as the crickets chirped away in the darkness.

'Well … night, y'all.' Nurse Mildred walked away, chuckling to herself.

Chloe closed the diary and turned to Elijah. 'Sir, are you going to come back tomorrow?'

'I don't think so,' he whispered, picturing having to go through hell and back with Angela. He would rather have someone use his eyeballs as voodoo dolls than have another encounter with the she-devil – much less excruciating. Chloe placed a hand over Elijah's. He looked down, noting the softness and warmth of her skin – a stark contrast to his own. Despite himself, he glanced into her eyes.

'Please come back. I need to hear this story, sir.'

Short of torture (even then, probably not) he'd never admit that his undoing had been her gentle touch alone – not her pleading words or the sorrow in her innocent eyes.

'Chloe, what do you think you're doing?' Angela yelled from the lower-floor balcony as though the nearby residents sleeping was of no significance, even though she had previously warned Chloe about being conscious of this. Do as I say, not as I do. They both looked at Angela, and Chloe removed her hand from Elijah's.

As Angela trotted down the wheelchair-access ramp, Chloe turned to search Elijah's eyes. 'We haven't much time. Please don't let me down.'

Elijah closed his eyes and gritted his teeth in silent anguish. *Please don't let me down.* She had no idea how much that tugged on the few remaining heartstrings that hadn't yet been severed.

Angela clasped Chloe's arm and shot Elijah a brief look of dismissive contempt as she towed her daughter away. 'I assume I won't see you here again? Thank you for taking the time to say goodbye to an old friend. Take care!'

Elijah glared at Angela, anger lighting up his rheumy eyes. *I'll be seeing you real soon.*

Chapter 9

LATER THAT NIGHT, Elijah plonked himself on his rocking chair and grunted. He thought about Angela's vindictive expression when she'd made it clear he wasn't welcome back. *What a bitch.*

His right leg throbbed like a strobe light, so he breathed through parted lips, in and out, closing his eyes. After the pain eased, he swivelled left to the side table and switched on the radio (always tuned into 2CH), drowning out the loud hum of a helicopter overhead with a catchy tune by Gene Vincent. Elijah pricked fork holes into his charity-delivered dinner tray and marvelled at the sorry sight as condensation rose. Even through his fogged-up glasses, it looked like the meatloaf with mashed potatoes and peas had been whizzed in a blender, then poured onto a Styrofoam plate. *Bugger the fork; I need a soup spoon!*

He removed his glasses to clean the lenses before replacing them. As the steam escaped in snaking tendrils, he glanced at his diary lying beside him on the two-seater lounge. Audrey had bought him an identical one from the same discount store where she had bought hers when she moved to Wollongong. He'd never thought he'd be the type of guy to keep a journal, but some things were worth remembering.

It was a privilege to go back in time and recapture the essence and beauty of one's life, whether through a diary, photo collection or video footage. Some days he stared at his reflection in the mirror, wondering who was staring back. His withered, leathery face and bumpy scalp was almost laughable compared to his once-youthful good looks and luscious locks.

But this wasn't a joke. His life was almost over – that was the harsh reality. He'd reached the end of the line. So wasn't it normal to reflect on one's life as the end of it, just months away – a year at best – was closing in? He'd had a lot of time to reflect on where he went wrong in his younger years and, of course, Audrey was always at the top of his list. He glanced up from his shit-for-dinner tray as 'Be-Bop-a-Lula' ended, and pictured Audrey walking into the living room with two bowls of her lip-smackingly-good spaghetti bolognaise, settling in beside him before eating in companionable silence. He pictured holding her until they both passed out while watching some crap on TV that qualified as entertainment these days. It was a cruel reverie that he'd allowed himself to slip into on numerous occasions. But that's just what it was at the end of the long, lonely day: cruel. When he looked at the space beside him, he saw nothing. Nobody at all, not even an arse impression, which proved he'd endured this tiresome marathon called 'life' on his lonesome. *What the hell was it all for, then?*

He eyed his surrounding belongings: tattered books piled on a chair, the grandfather clock ticking away the passing moments with mechanical precision, dust-covered knick-knacks that adorned the shelves, framed pictures on the wall. All pieces that had personal memories attached. After his death, every item he owned would either be in the hands of someone else, or thrown in the trash. Everything that he'd bought or collected or received as presents – none of it mattered at the end of one's journey, did it? You couldn't take a single fucking thing with you into the afterlife. Except maybe for memories.

He picked up the diary and, in that moment, 'She Loves You' by the Beatles emanated from the crackling radio. A single, traitorous tear trickled down his wrinkled cheek, dripping onto his TV dinner as vapour still rose in a thin spiral. Trembling fingertips hijacked by the early stages of

Parkinson's traced over a tiny piece of yellowed paper that was sticky-taped to the inside cover. The ink was faded, but he didn't need to visit memory lane again to know what it said:

YOU WILL FIND A NEW LOVE.

Chapter 10

'WHAT AN INSUFFERABLE man!' Angela said into the mouthpiece. 'I have no clue what Mum saw in him.'

When the clock had struck nine that night, Angela decided it was time to brave it and call her younger brother in London to deliver the news. However, her verbal tirade about the strange old man dominated their tête-à-tête.

'Wow! Mum sure as hell never mentioned him to me,' Timothy said. 'I don't know what to say.' Angela heard him typing away on his computer keyboard.

'Do you think his story is true? I mean, do you think maybe he's mixed up?' Angela said, googling the name 'Elijah Samuels' to see if any headlines akin to *ESCAPED MENTAL PATIENT* came up.

Timothy inhaled and took his time before responding. 'Well, to be honest, I don't know much about Mum's life as a teenager or even her early twenties – do you?'

Angela stared at her client's documents on the desk in front of her as she sat in her study, desperately longing for a glass of red. It had been an emotional day and her blood was still bubbling, thanks to the crazed stranger who'd interrupted their private family time a short while ago.

She ran a finger over her bottom lip as she pondered her brother's question. 'You're right. She seldom spoke of the past, and we never got to meet Grandma or Grandpa on her side because of ... well, you remember. God, I can barely remember her uncle – he died from an aneurysm while

I was young.' She paused again to reflect. 'I don't even remember seeing any old photos, really, but it was always the case so I never questioned or thought anything of it.' Angela grabbed a steel ruler and tried to multitask – something she had been forced to learn well.

Angela's boss, CEO Bruce Maxwell, was not a man to be tested. If he said he needed a soy decaf mocha at 7:13 am, there was no other option – it had to be 7:13, not a minute later. Since Bruce Maxwell had demanded sketches from Angela at 8:30 am tomorrow for their pitch meeting with Kensington Inc., there was no fighting it. Even if her mother were to pass during the night, Bruce would still expect Angela there bright and early, along with his soy decaf mocha.

The joys of advertising, she thought, grabbing a red ballpoint pen.

The proposed drawing was halfway complete, but a considerable amount of detail still needed to be incorporated to meet the *Maxwell Standard,* so this conversation would have to be cut short, even at a time like this.

'I suppose there's no harm in him being there, is there, Ange?'

Angela scoffed. 'He's crude and full of sexual innuendo! It's *weird*, and I don't want to subject Chloe to his wicked stories. She's too young.'

'I don't know what you want me to say or do. I mean, I can't hop on a plane and leave Tida here by herself.'

'I know you have obligations, but newsflash, we all do! So face up to your responsibilities.' His mocking laughter in reply was like a lighted matchstick dropped in a haystack. Angela battled to control herself. 'I get it, you have baggage here, but once again ... we all do. You only have one mother. You need to come home, no ifs or buts.'

'I'll make it to the funeral; you just have to understand—'

Chloe popped her head around the study door, hair dripping from her recent shower, the smell of strawberries wafting into the room. 'I'm going to watch *Beethoven* and make popcorn. Do you want to join?'

Angela shook her head and placed her hand over the receiver while Timothy prattled on, shoving food into his gob between his 'I'm so busy' and 'Tida needs me' bulldust.

'It's a school night, young lady.'

The corners of Chloe's mouth tilted upwards. 'Half-day tomorrow, remember?'

No, Angela hadn't remembered. She couldn't remember what she'd eaten for breakfast this morning, let alone conversations pertaining to school that may or may not have been uttered some time ago.

'Oh. Right. Sorry, but I have to work on this presentation. Where's your father?'

'He's on some important phone call.'

'Right. Well, I'm sorry, Chloe, but I'm going to be up for hours as it is.'

Chloe nodded without protest and closed the door just as Timothy finished justifying why he couldn't come a moment sooner than required.

'That's not good enough, Timothy. You need to say your goodbyes.'

'"Timothy"? Wow, now I *know* you're being serious.' He chortled before slurping his noodle soup, telling her he'd just improved it with a packet of soy sauce. Angela couldn't have cared less about goddamn condiments. 'Look, by the sounds of it' – *slurp* – 'she won't be around by the time the plane lands.'

Angela moved the phone away from her mouth, a hand clamped over her quivering lips and her eyelids pressed tightly together.

Timothy once confided in Angela that he'd gone batshit crazy after their father passed away. He told her he'd have welcomed the Grim Reaper himself with open arms. But after a stint in rehab, her younger brother left Australia for his own peace of mind and went to London. It ended up being the best decision of his life, as he'd substituted drugs for work, and alcohol for a woman. Timothy had never been much of a warm person, but six months after arriving he'd fallen in love with a Malaysian woman, Tida. They were now expecting their first child.

Being the eldest, Angela wanted everyone to get along, so she played mediator whenever possible. But in the years since Buck's passing, when Audrey was placed into a home and as the pressure of work accumulated, Angela felt like her smile had been replaced with a permanent lour, and monthly calls to Timothy and other family members had petered out.

Timothy cleared his throat, interrupting Angela's thoughts. 'This is part of life. Kids outgrow their parents; our kids will outlive us; it's all part of the master plan.'

Angela felt like plonking her head down on the desk and blocking everything out. It wasn't in her nature to let things beat her down; she was used to being in charge, and this situation was no different. She bit her tongue, stifled a yawn, and listened to Timothy's excuses.

'Am I upset? Of course I am. She's my *mother*; I love her. But nothing I do will save her. I can only be there to say goodbye and pay my respects—'

Angela hung up as she usually did when this sort of dead-end, brick-wall scenario played out. If she had to convince her brother to fly home to say goodbye to the woman who had borne and raised them, then something was wrong, and she didn't have the time or the patience to handle his delicacies. The events of this evening rattled her. She hated to admit that she was irritated her mother once had a life before she was born.

A secret life.

Had their father known?

Angela deduced that none of it mattered, as Elijah Samuels would never enter room 217 again – she would speak to Nurse Mildred to guarantee it!

Angela glanced at the clock on the wall, each tick of the second hand sounding louder than the last. It built to a crescendo until she shook her head and loosened her shoulders. She'd need to invest at least another three hours into this project to even consider adding it to the *Maxwell Standard* stockpile. She hopped up, walked to the stereo and turned on Mozart to calm her mood and put her in the right frame of mind. Rolling her head down and around, she pushed the thought of Elijah aside and poured herself a generous glass of Malbec.

Chapter 11

THE NEXT MORNING, Elijah lay in bed and stared at the ceiling with its peeling paint, cobwebs and cracks. Part of him had been hoping that God would have heeded his prayers and ended his torture in the night, but *c'est la vie*, here he still was. Ironically, he *felt* non-existent.

It seemed the only way he was going to cast his eyes on a set of pearly gates would be in a Dunn & Farrugia Fencing and Gates catalogue. No doubt he'd lived a life of too much sin. But had it been worth it?

What is the use of lingering when I don't need to? he thought, as a dull throbbing erupted through his right kneecap. *Goddammit, this isn't living, it's existing!*

'Quantity versus quality,' he whispered, clenching his eyes and waiting for the pain to subside.

His mind travelled to Sheba. He'd have to give her breakfast, so he got up slowly and made his way to the bathroom to relieve himself.

As he wiped his wet hands on a cotton towel, the *damned phone* rang. Grumbling and cussing, Elijah limped as quickly as he could to see who was selling what now. Maybe he had the start of dementia, because he had a momentary hope of it being Audrey. *Wouldn't that be something?*

'Yes?' he barked into the mouthpiece, huffing.

'Are you coming to the nursing home today?'

It took Elijah a second to register. When it did, his mouth dropped open. 'Is that you, little girl?'

'Chloe!'

Elijah raked a hand over his bumpy scalp that reminded him of the surface of the moon. 'How the hell did you get my private number?'

'From Facebook.'

This impressed Elijah; not even he would have thought of that. But, of course, Grace had set up a profile for him a few years ago, even though not *once* had he ever looked at it or so much as thought about the dumb idea. He thought the notion was as ridiculous as standing under a tall tree with a sheet of metal during a thunderstorm. Grace said it was so he could keep in contact with the family, but his firm response was 'if they need me, they can write me'. So, Grace had listed his *private* number under his contact information, eh? It was a minor annoyance that Grace would soon rectify, of that he would make sure.

'I can't. I'm too busy.' He mentally listed the things he needed to accomplish: complete the *Take 5* crossword; take blood-thinner tablets; buy Oz Lotto tickets from the corner store ... the jackpot's now three million dollars—

'You said last night you would.'

Elijah was careful not to pluck the few remaining wisps of silver hair he had left, so he brought his hand down and glanced at the clock: 7:41 am.

'You're right, I did. It's because of your whingey mother, but anyway, I have to set a good example, don't I? If you make a promise, you must keep it.' Chloe was more than likely the type of kid to show up at his doorstep and camp there until she got her way, he mused. 'I shall be there soon. Just don't bug me or irritate me; I've had a terrible morning!'

'I won't do anything except listen to a story that I'm desperate to find out the ending to.'

Elijah opened his mouth, but nothing came out. It wasn't often that a young child could bewilder him – although some had tried in earnest.

'Are you *sure* you're only twelve?'

'Yes; why? I *am* turning thirteen in January, you know ...'

'Is that so?' he said, trying to avoid beaming from ear-to-ear. 'Well, you don't sound like a normal twelve-year-old.'

'How else am I supposed to converse with you?'

Elijah sputtered. 'You see! That right *there*, you talking like *that* and using sophisticated words.'

'Is that a bad thing?' She sounded confused, even a little hurt.

Elijah realised that whilst her vocabulary seemed beyond her years, her feelings and emotional understanding were not so well-formed. *More than likely kept under wraps, like a good little girl.* He pictured his own deplorable childhood.

'No, not at all. You remind me of my sister and how she was raised. It's not a bad thing.' He waited for a response. 'I'm not having a go at you; you're just well ahead of your years. In some ways it's a damn shame.'

Chloe remained quiet, unsure, on the other end of the line.

Elijah exhaled, thinking he would do well to tread lightly with his next choice of words. 'Well, is your mother going to be there?'

'Probably later, but I want to see you as soon as possible. When can you be down there?'

Elijah's spine stiffened. *I want to see you as soon as possible.* The last person he'd heard those words from was his proctologist. Elijah chastised himself for getting emotional over simple words uttered by a stranger, so he turned his attention to Sheba, who had now wedged her way between his legs.

'Sir?'

Elijah lifted his glasses, pinched the bridge of his nose and screwed his eyes shut. 'Ah, I suppose I can push things around. Can you be there in a few hours?'

'Yes, sir!'

Elijah could picture her giving a fine salute and meaning everything by it. It was a damn shame about her childhood – or lack thereof. Had she ever played with a Barbie, or was that considered lacking intellect and 'gender equality'?

'Well, ah, you do what you need to, and I'll see you soon.' Elijah slammed the receiver before Chloe could reply.

Try as he might to stop it, a thin smile spread across his face.

Chapter 12

THEN – 1964

DAYS HAD PASSED since Elijah's disastrous encounter with the chick he couldn't stop thinking about. He hated the way she looked at him – like he was a fucking jerk. He wanted to make up for it, but at the same time, he didn't. He'd argued back and forth with himself about going down and seeing her at the parlour, but the sensible part of him said *No, don't mess with her. Just forget about the mysterious girl.*

But Elijah was like a hard-luck diabetic faced with a piece of gooey chocolate cake. He already had a reputation around the Gong for being a badass; he sure as hell didn't want one for being offensive to people with a disability. He needed to set the record straight. All he'd wanted was ice cream and yet he'd left with a guilty conscience. It was, to date, the most expensive ice cream he'd never had.

Elijah marched inside the shop and waited in line for Audrey to serve him. Elvis was crooning 'King Creole' over the jukebox as those seated were either flipping soda bottle caps using the edge of their table to see who could flip the highest, or stuffing their faces with greasy burgers between slurping on milkshakes. Elijah did everything he could to make sure he didn't look at *her*, especially at her aid, even though he swore it honest to God didn't bother him. She was so pretty it made no difference. She could have had a purple birthmark the size of a tennis ball on her forehead, and Elijah still would have thought she was the most beautiful girl in the world.

The waiting line shuffled forward and Elijah's heart *thwack-thwack-thwacked* with each step. To pass the time, he glanced around the crowded parlour at posters of Marilyn Monroe, Betty Boop and James Dean adorning the walls. As he checked to see if anyone was in his gang's favourite seafoam-green booth, some jocks in his usual spot seemed to be pointing at Audrey and laughing. Elijah couldn't tell for sure, though, so he kept his mouth shut as he took another blind step forward. But his temperature gauge rose.

'Can I help you?'

Elijah turned around to come face-to-face with the beauty, who spoke like a lady with class and that, to him, was a major turn-on. Her voice was as silky-smooth as nylon stockings. Elijah noticed the vertical crease between her eyes as she recognised him, but despite that, he tried to smile and make the most of it.

'Hello, again. How are you?'

Audrey glanced about the room, head tilted. 'What can I get you?' She couldn't have looked more bored if she sat through an eight-hour sermon.

Elijah's head reeled back. 'Oh, okay. Straight to the point, huh? No sweat, um ... I think I'll try the pink pineapple today.'

'Cup or cone?'

Once again, she chose not to look into his eyes. Elijah swallowed with an open mouth as his thoughts struggled to find a foothold.

'Cone,' he said, staring. She carried on like he was an insignificant bug, one not even worth squashing – that's how low he was to her. She scooped the creamy goodness and handed Elijah the cone before holding out her hand. He was just about to pop the money into her palm when he pulled back and placed a forefinger to his earlobe. 'I'm sorry, what was that?'

She looked at him then. 'That will be threepence,' she said through gritted teeth. Oh, she was a feisty tigress all right, one he wanted to hunt badly.

'I didn't hear the magic word,' he said with a slight smirk. A vein in her neck throbbed, her cheeks redder than Santa's. He could practically see the mushroom clouds burst from her ears.

She squinted as she pressed her plump lips together, which Elijah figured was to keep from screaming before she said, 'Please.'

Elijah had discovered a newfound passion in life: making Audrey squirm. No matter how irritating he was, she couldn't say a thing back to him; not if she wanted to keep her job.

'No, say the whole thing, this time with feeling.'

She stared at him through narrowed eyes as her lips parted. 'That will be threepence, *please*.'

Elijah grinned and popped the coin in her hand. 'Good girl.'

After that, Elijah walked outside into the searing heat. He felt like a wanker, but seeing her face change colour faster than a chameleon had been amazing. He obviously affected her, and admittedly she affected him. However, he understood he was being too harsh and wanted to speak to her one-on-one about their situation. Sitting on the scorching bonnet of his sky-blue EH, he finished his ice cream and lit a Camel. As he took a deep drag, he swivelled around as Pretty Woman walked out of the shop in a huff. He loved the way she walked, her backside wiggling all feminine-like, and he believed she didn't bung it on to attract a guy's attention. It was all natural – just like her sweet voice.

Elijah studied her as she walked away from him. His Adam's apple bobbed up and down as he dry-swallowed, a faint trickle of sweat slid down his left temple, as slow as molasses. For a moment, he contemplated following her to see where she lived, but he conceded that was stalker behaviour. However, he was going to have to sort out her attitude; he didn't dig it one bit. As he was trucking along a fair distance behind, a couple of shirtless, muscled jocks who were on a front lawn, soaping up their souped-up Ford Mustangs, approached her.

Elijah scowled when the tanned guys stopped her. A pinprick of jealousy hit him. God he hated that feeling; jealousy was a weakness. Then, a queer swirling in the pit of his stomach told him something wasn't right. While Audrey was talking to one guy who blocked her path, the other one walked around the back of her and, before Elijah knew what was happening, the scuzz sprayed her hearing aid with water. As water dripped from Audrey's uniform onto the pavement, they cracked up laughing. At their laughter, Elijah lost all sense of control.

He sprinted to their driveway and swung at the guy holding the hose. *Crack*! He fell faster than a dropped anvil. The second guy held his hands out in surrender, but Elijah socked him in the stomach, regardless. Emitting an *ooff,* he too fell hard, hitting his head on the pavement with a *boink*, like someone knocking down pins in a bowling alley. Elijah grabbed the first guy around the throat, who now signalled a deuces and said, 'Hey, m-man, don't flip your wig; it was only a joke.'

Elijah clenched his teeth and brought the guy's face closer to his. 'If you dare mess with her again, my face will be the last thing you *ever* see.'

Chapter 13

'WOW, MISTER, DID you really say that?' Chloe said, taking a sip of her apple and blackcurrant juice. She'd only arrived a while earlier after running from the bus stop to the nursing home. There was much to get through and so little time, but at least it was just the two of them – no outsiders interfering every second. Nurse Mildred had greeted Elijah in the recreational room, and he was pleased to have had a few moments alone with Audrey before sneakers skidded across the linoleum floor of the corridors. Chloe had parked her butt on the closest chair to the bed and then told Elijah to start.

'Well, I had to clean it up a bit for your sake but, yes, I did.' Elijah wasn't sure how to read her expressionless look, so he added: 'But, ah, I don't agree with resorting to violent tendencies to get a point across.'

Chloe's incredulous stare said *Come on; give me more credit than that!*

'Ah hell, your mother ain't here. In life, kid, some people deserve a dose of their own medicine. If I could go back in time, I would have done the same thing over again.'

Chloe grinned, satisfied that he'd cut the baloney. Taking another sip of her juice she said, 'By the way, what is a doose?'

'Oh, *deuces* – peace sign. Like this.' He held up two fingers in a V. 'You never saw this before?'

She marvelled and nodded. 'Yes, but from Winston Churchill.'

'Correct. It also means victory. You're an astute little girl, aren't you?'

She pinched her brow together and shook her head. 'No.'

His eyebrows rose. 'No?'

'No, I am not "little".'

Elijah Samuels once again felt his heart thawing – like frost from flower petals as the morning sun reaches them – and he stifled a laugh as Chloe appeared as serious as the Queen's Guard.

Chloe then produced her grandmother's diary from her schoolbag. 'It was difficult not reading anything else last night, but I managed. Would you like to hear how Nanna felt that day?'

Elijah smiled, remembering too well what happened next, but he reminded himself that Chloe was hearing this for the first time. He nodded, steepling his fingertips into a pyramid and placing them at his lips.

'2ⁿᵈ December 1964. Dear Diary, the most amazing thing happened today! I'm still in shock as I write this. It started off bad – HE came into the shop dressed in a pair of dark Wranglers and a black Ban-Lon shirt. His jet-black, tousled hair looked like silk, and he even smelled alluring. But Mr Hunk was so smug and arrogant, he enjoyed taunting me. Today was a hot one and the parlour was busy, so I was rushing through the customers. But he wouldn't let me rush him. He took his time, provoking and playing – he even had the nerve to stand in front of me and lick the ice cream as people in the queue waited. I was still sore at him, yet he acted like he was angry with me! I wasn't the one who had been rude enough to stare at an impediment!

'I finished my shift when Denise relieved me soon after, and I headed home with this man who irritates me beyond buggery on my mind. As I walked along, some guys hosing their cars stopped me and asked questions. They said they knew me; they'd heard I was new in town and that we should all hang out. I thought one guy was kind of cute, but it was a set-up all along. He distracted me while his friend moved to the back of me and sprayed my hearing aid! I stood there, frozen in shock, as they laughed and pointed. The next thing I knew, I heard a primal scream followed by a crack, then a crash. I turned to see Mr Hulk storm over to the guy who had distracted me, and he hit him in the stomach! The guy who'd sprayed me was already sprawled on the ground, crying for help as Mr Hulk walked back over to him and held his fist over the

guy's face while explicitly telling him to stay away from me. The ordeal shocked and embarrassed me, so I turned and fled. Mr Hulk shouted after me, and as soon as I rounded Church St, he grabbed my shoulders and swung me around ...'

Chapter 14

THEN – 1964

'HEY, ARE YOU all right?' he asked, spinning Audrey around.

She sobbed like a newborn into her hands, shielding her face. He wrapped his muscular arms around her as she continued to cry. He rubbed his hands over her back, soothing her jangled nerves. Then he grabbed her hands and pried them away from her face.

'Are you okay?' he repeated, looking deep into her eyes.

She managed a feeble nod.

Elijah pointed to his own ear. 'How's your, um ...?'

'It's called a hearing aid, get over it. I don't have cooties!'

Audrey knew she'd surprised him because he shouted back: 'I know that! I just helped you out!'

That afternoon, her knight in black armour walked her home. It was pleasant, but she was still embarrassed, and her mind fixated on how cruel some people could be.

Her fingers intertwined, twisting with anxiety, but she caught him glancing at her, although he tried to hide it by gazing at a shopfront behind her head. They strolled past J. Dean's Tailor, Elaine's Haberdashery, Jenny's Flower Boutique and California Milk Bar.

Morris Minors and Volkswagen Beetles whizzed past in a kaleidoscope of blurred colours, yet they still hadn't uttered two words.

When their silence became unbearable, much to Audrey's relief he said, 'So, um, did you just move here?'

'I moved here a while ago, but only started working at Betty-Sue's just recently.'

'What do you think of Wollongong so far?'

She scowled and eyed him.

'Oh, yeah, stupid question.' He smacked his forehead. 'But we're not *all* like that, you know.'

'Maybe, but I saw you staring at it, too!'

He stopped Audrey by coming to a halt in front of her. 'Look, about that. It wasn't my intention to offend you, and not everyone thinks you're different, okay? I am sorry I looked; I didn't mean to come off rude. I'm just not used to seeing people with one; I never meant no ill intentions.'

I don't know whether he's telling the truth, or maybe he's setting me up. She continued along the pavement, her bumblebee-yellow skirt swaying in the afternoon breeze.

Elijah began walking backwards in front of her as he spoke. 'Hey, what are you doing this Friday night?'

'Why?' She eyed him as they walked through a crowd of theatregoers on the corner of Church Street and Globe Lane. The eager assemblage at the Savoy Theatre was waiting to see the matinee screening of *My Fair Lady.* The young couple soon found themselves tangled amongst the jostling bodies. Elijah reached for Audrey's hand through the sea of people to help pull her out, but he could only latch onto her wrist.

As soon as she was free, she released herself from his grip and offered a curt nod of appreciation, adjusting her ruffled hair. As they continued walking she kept looking over, begging to hear the rest of his idea for Friday night.

'Do you wanna come to the drive-in with me?'

She eyed him. 'Why don't you take your *girlfriend*?'

Elijah stopped and stood inches away from her. 'Because I want to take *you.*'

Audrey's heart rate accelerated as she looked into his drop-dead gorgeous eyes. 'Look, Mister …'

'My name is Elijah Samuels, but my friends call me EJ, or Eli.'

She stared at him until a red-over-white Plymouth Fury tooted its horn at some young kid in denim overalls on his KTM bicycle and made her jump. She turned back to Elijah's green jewels, which hadn't moved from her face.

'And … this is the part where you share the same information with me.'

She tucked some hair behind her ear and smiled. 'My name is Audrey Hughes.'

He held out his hand, which she hesitated to accept. That was when she had to acknowledge the electricity between them. Elijah's lips parted as his chest expanded but held her gaze. 'It's lovely to make your acquaintance, Audrey Hughes.'

Her name practically rolled off his tongue, which sent shivers down her spine. *This man has pure magnetism, like Steve McQueen,* she thought, diverting her gaze to a torn *Playboy* featuring Kai Brendlinger on the cover, discarded on the pavement near a bottlebrush.

She pulled her hand from his firm grasp. 'Mr Samuels, I don't want any trouble. I attract enough as it is. Thank you for the kind offer, but I don't need pity.'

She turned and strolled off, but Elijah put his arms on her shoulders. 'Whoa, hold up. That's what you think this is?'

She felt very aware of the heat in his touch; it bore into her skin like someone directing a blowtorch over her shoulders. She wanted more, but believed she deserved nothing all the same. 'Most likely. You already have a girlfriend who you can do these things with. Why would a man like you want to go out with someone like me? I don't need pity; I've had enough of that to last me a lifetime.' She walked off again as vivid memories surfaced of her parents' funeral, and at school where teachers would overprotect her like she was a handicapped child – making things worse when she was alone and vulnerable.

Elijah strolled right alongside her, as she glimpsed an anti-Vietnam sign stapled to a tree: *Bombing for peace is like fucking for virginity!*

'What do you mean "a man like me"?' His eyes bore into hers. 'And you're right, I have a girlfriend to take out and do other things with, but I am asking *you*.'

He stopped her by blocking her path once more. This time, she stayed put. His eyes challenged hers. Audrey wanted to say yes, but she had no desire to fall for a man like him. She reasoned by his touch (residual heat lingered on her shoulders) that there was a real danger of falling – and falling fast.

'It's not a bright idea, but thanks for helping me out back there, Mr Samuels.'

The wind curling around them carried away his exasperated sigh. 'Why are you so stubborn? I'm offering you a groovy time out, all expenses paid, to see a movie simply for the pleasure of your company and to get to know you better. Is that too much to ask?'

She shrugged her heavy shoulders and they continued on, walking past a shirtless middle-aged man mowing his front lawn. He tipped his Stetson as he pushed the mower forward one-handed, a lit Viceroy protruding from his teeth. They nodded back before wading through silence once more, the smell of cut grass lingering in the hot air.

'Think of me as the neighbourhood welcome wagon, welcoming you to the neighbourhood. I will not try to get fresh with you. I'll act like the gentleman that I am, and have you home by eleven on the dot. How's that?'

A tingling sensation expanded in her stomach. The blazing sun had begun its descent, as beams of light stretched out with sepia tones, casting a gorgeous streaky effect in the sky behind him. To her, he looked radiant, his face aglow from the tangerine rays. His green eyes were to die for – she wondered if he knew the effect he had on her, just by looking into her own eyes.

'What are you afraid of?' he whispered, his lips bearing the semblance of a smile, hinting that he was enjoying this, searching for the truth behind her eyes. After much deliberation, she agreed. After all, he had come to her rescue, so it was only fair she reciprocate.

Chapter 15

ELIJAH JOLTED FROM the sound of a trilling mobile phone. He glanced around the room until his eyes focused on Chloe. She gazed at him from the opposite side of Audrey's bed, with her head perched on her hands, propped up by her elbows. The way she stared at him in awe made him feel like he was some world-famous philosopher whose ideals she truly believed in.

Realisation set in and Chloe rummaged through her schoolbag to retrieve her ringing mobile phone. To Elijah, this was about as annoying as receiving a call from a telemarketer right at dinnertime, as if they *knew* he was about to take his first bite of slop-on-a-plate.

Elijah could hear Angela shouting at Chloe, even from all the way over his side. It was almost comical, as he couldn't hear her exact words; all he heard was muffled sounds – like someone shouting underwater.

'Don't be mad; I'm at the nursing home with Nanna.'

More shouting. *Don't laugh. Christ, whatever you do, do not laugh!*

'I didn't want to go to school, so I caught the bus here. Besides, it was only a half-day, remember? I missed nothing of importance.'

Elijah picked at his teeth with the nail of his pinkie as he heard: 'Um, he's not here yet, but he might be soon.'

Elijah smiled broadly as he gazed at Chloe, whose cheeks were glowing.

Chloe chewed her bottom lip before saying, 'Oh, that's funny – he's just walked through the door. I have to go, see you soon.'

Chloe hung up on her mother, which caused Elijah to beam from ear-to-ear. They continued to stare at each other until Nurse Mildred popped her head around the doorway, and the smell of vegetable stew followed thereafter.

Nurse Mildred was doing the routine noon lunch drop-off (Narelle, the cook, had fallen down the stairs while chasing a rat, thus leaving Mildred to lend a hand for the lunch service) and had decided to check in on the most talked-about room in the place. No event inside a singular room had ever reached the height of taboo since the time sultry Nurse Francinfold embezzled money from a bedridden Jimmy Falkaki when he was about to pass.

'Ya two 'kay in here?' Nurse Mildred peered over her horn-rimmed glasses with a wry expression, as if she knew what was going on and how Angela would react to being lied to about a complete stranger. That in itself made Elijah feel as though he'd won a minor victory.

One small step for man …

They both nodded with matching mischievous grins.

'Anyone wantin' some lunch? We have leftovers due ta the fact two residents croaked it this mornin'. So if ya want some pipin' hot grub, it's all yers.'

Both Chloe and Elijah stared open-mouthed.

'I'm *kiddin'*! I grabbed extra. Supposed youse would be hungry by now; but ya shoulda seen the looks on yer faces!' She slapped her knees and bellowed out a deep, guttural laugh.

'That's very thoughtful; thank you,' Elijah said, as Nurse Mildred wheeled in a silver trolley with meal trays stacked amongst shelves.

Nurse Mildred placed a tray on the overbed table near Elijah, just as a resident in the adjacent room banged something hard against a metal object.

'Nurse … nurse … I'm *hungry!*' a sickly voice yelled as the banging continued.

'I'mma comin', Montgomery, hold yer horses!' Nurse Mildred shouted, causing Elijah to jump from her foghorn voice blasting in his ear.

'Appreciate it,' Elijah mumbled as his stomach gurgled like a sink being drained of dishwater.

'Not ta worry, it's a pleasure!' She sighed and glanced at Audrey. 'I best be goin'; I'm busier than a one-legged cat in his crappin' box.'

Elijah guffawed as another metallic bang billowed from room 215, just as Nurse Mildred placed a tray on Chloe's lap.

'I *said* I'mma comin'!' With a slight roll of her eyes, Nurse Mildred shuffled back to the trolley and wheeled it out of the room.

Elijah uncovered the lid of his tray and discovered creamy vegetable stew on a bed of mashed potatoes next to a dinner roll. The tray also contained a Berri apple juice cup, a small fruit salad, and a vanilla bean yoghurt tub.

'Shall we?' Elijah grabbed his silver spoon. *This outshines Irish 'spew' by a mile.* His tastebuds were now finally reacting to something; it was a goddamn miracle!

As they ate in comfortable silence, commotion emanated from room 215.

'Dang it, Montgomery, eat yer lunch!' Nurse Mildred yelled in the distance, her voice quivering with undertones of fatigue, as though this type of dramatic performance was one she'd been experiencing every single day since the day he had arrived.

Chloe smiled at Elijah and nibbled on a piece of watermelon. All the while Elijah observed Chloe's behaviour. This kid doesn't come from the slums, he noted. When she wiped her mouth with a folded napkin, it was more of a delicate blot on either side. The expensive gilded clips in her silky brown hair were a dead giveaway, too.

Chloe placed her tray on the floor and sat upright. 'Now, where were we, sir?'

Elijah wiped his greasy mouth with the back of his hand and pushed the overbed tray away before clearing his throat. After taking a sip of cool apple juice, he opened his diary.

'That Friday night, I arrived at Audrey's house ten minutes early, which I can say was a first for me – being early, I mean. I think I'll be late for my own funeral; I have never been good with timeframes and following rules.' Chloe laughed as she reached for her yoghurt tub. 'I was as nervous as friggin' hell walking up to the gate of her home. I first saw the house she lived in when I walked her home after the hose attack. Looking at the house and the overrun garden, I knew she hadn't come from money. It was as obvious as dentures, and some labelled the area as "the eyesore of the Gong". That didn't bother me, though, and I never mentioned that degrading description to her, either. Anyway, I opened the rusty gate and walked along the broken, uneven path before knocking on the fly screen with a sweaty hand. A man carrying a few pounds more than necessary appeared and introduced himself as Lloyd, her uncle. I wondered where her parents were. I shook his firm hand and introduced myself. We stood in awkward silence until Audrey appeared at the door wearing a yellow full skirt dress and white gloves – the ensemble suited her well. She'd put effort into this, which made me giddy, as it told me she was excited and wanted to make a good impression.

'After she said goodbye to her uncle with a kiss on his plump, rosy cheek, we walked down the crooked pathway and I told her she looked boss. While we exited the front gate, she said I did as well. I glanced at my ironed dark-blue shirt and charcoal-grey slacks, thinking we made a handsome couple indeed.

'"I have something for you," I said, facing her and catching the glimmer of excitement in her eyes. She looked at me, frowning, as I opened the boot of my car.

'I handed her a wicker basket. "Welcome to the neighbourhood!"' Elijah paused to look at Chloe. 'Remember how I made a joke about being the neighbourhood welcome wagon?' Chloe nodded. 'Well, I got a basket full of stuff: comic books like *Creepy* and *Daredevil*; board games including Buccaneer and Concentration; Cadbury's Golden Crisp chocolates, and a copy of the book *Charlie and the Chocolate Factory*, plus a bottle of red wine. Audrey thought it was a riot, which delighted me because I wanted her to feel at ease. As we sat in my car, I noticed her clasped hands resting in her lap and her eyes focused towards the road ahead. She had me hooked, and her hair smelled like a coconut–passionfruit blend. Audrey was downright feminine, and I was fast slipping under her spell. I was nervous, too, but I hid it well.'

Chloe sniggered. 'Um, it says here you didn't.'

Elijah's forehead crinkled. 'Huh?'

'Nan wrote here: "He looked nervous, like a little boy standing in front of the classroom about to give a speech on algebra".'

Elijah scrunched his nose. 'It doesn't say that.'

Chloe tittered. 'It does.' She held the diary up – not that he could see at that distance. 'You weren't as good an actor as you thought.'

Elijah grumbled as Chloe lowered the diary. 'It also says *you* chose the movie!'

Elijah shifted in his chair. 'Hey now, from memory we tossed a coin. We sat in my car deciding what to see, as there were two options. One was for some movie directed by Hitchcock, if I remember right, and the other one we heard people talking about with anticipation. I said fair and square, "How about we toss a shilling?" and she said, "Yes." I did so without cheating, and the ram's head won. So, what was the movie I took her to see on our first date?'

'*Goldfinger!*' Chloe and Elijah chorused.

Chapter 16

'5ᵀᴴ December 1964. Dear Diary, yesterday EJ and I had our first outing. It was … interesting. First, he took me to see the latest yawn-fest instalment of James Bond. Those movies are rubbish and full of nonsense, but I kept looking at EJ and he was munching away on popcorn, slurping Coca-Cola through his straw like a little boy. And I will admit, Sean Connery is easy on the eyes.

'EJ is fascinating; he seems like a two-sided coin. One side is dangerous, dark and foreboding. The other is more light-hearted and fun-loving; a promise of good things to come. I know where we stand though, because he is courting Georgie. Then again, this was just one night out and nothing even happened. He didn't touch me, he didn't kiss me, he didn't place his hand on my knee or anything. I'm worried because yesterday morning I heard from Cynthia Green at work that he has a reputation with the ladies, and I don't want to be another notch on his belt. Apparently he took out Cynthia's cousin and slept with her on the first date, but didn't even have the decency to call her again – can you imagine? That aside – I had a groovy time and I am appreciative that he paid for everything, but I can't get Georgie out of my head and neither can he – obviously – because he never made a move. I'm not disappointed, honest. I'm glad he didn't touch me. I don't want that sort of reputation; can you imagine that label on top of my disability? I'd be the laughing stock of the town. But what made the night interesting, dear Diary, was that he drove to a lookout, and we talked. That was the part I enjoyed the most. We talked about everything while music from his radio played in the background.

'We put our car seats back as far as they would go, and faced each other as I asked him questions about his family and he asked me questions about mine. Naturally, he was shocked when he discovered that my parents had passed. I saw sympathy in his eyes. Then, to change the subject, I told him about my passion for ten-pin bowling and my love of movies. He told me he liked to play the guitar and when the song "Do Wah Diddy" by Manfred Mann came on, we both got excited and started singing along to the radio. What fascinated me the most was I found out there's a lot more to this man than I thought.

'He is wealthy (as expected), but he is also intellectual. He is learned and well-read, plus he seems generous, as he paid for everything and bought me a gift hamper. When EJ gets excited, his eyes light up, and he has a cheeky, boyish smile – making his 'tough' half seem like a brave front. Even when he met Uncle Lloyd, he looked nervous. He is breathtaking to look at, with his tall stature, his not-too-short black hair, and his bright green eyes. God help me. We chatted about subjects ranging from ancient history to philosophy; he even quoted from Aristotle! His broad knowledge astounds me and it is a very attractive quality ... he left me and my presumptions speechless.

'I know he took me out because of the bullying incident and he felt sorry for me, but that's as far as it goes and I have to remind myself that – not surprisingly – he's a taken man. Upon arriving home it was well after midnight, but we sat in the car – neither one of us wanted to call it a night. He asked when he could see me again, as he lit up a cigarette (red flag). I told him it was not a bright idea to continue seeing each other because of Georgie (the biggest red flag). He took a drag before turning to me with blazing eyes and told me he'd pick me up tomorrow (today)! Then, he actually thanked me for the evening, and something about the way he said it made me fumble for the door handle. I don't think I have ever seen a more attractive man in my entire life – and that includes Gary Cooper (green flag). However, after I walked inside my house, I got into a terrible row with Uncle Lloyd (who had been waiting up for me) and he banned me from seeing Elijah.

'Apparently, after we left, Lloyd checked up on EJ in local joints and found that he has a tarnished name. According to town gossip, he has been in fights, *he gambles and he has even been arrested – something I did not know. Of course, none of this looked good to Uncle Lloyd, who admittedly tries hard to protect me after all that's happened. And let me remind you, EJ has a ladies' man reputation that he can't shake off. Uncle Lloyd is all I have left in this world now; I cannot disobey him, even though I am far from the little girl he once knew. This is his house, which means his rules—'*

'You have some nerve, don't you?' Angela said, striding into the room. Chloe and Elijah swapped wide-eyed expressions as neither heard her travelling up the corridor. She came aptly dressed in a fiery red business suit that Elijah thought matched her satanic eyes, which glared at the empty lunch trays.

'Hello to you, too,' Elijah said, smiling as Chloe slammed Audrey's diary shut after placing a ribbon on the page she was up to. Chloe wouldn't be able to read another extract while this idiotic nuisance was flying about, acting like he was being 'inappropriate with a minor'.

'I want you to stay away from Chloe, do you hear?'

Elijah shrugged and, with immense effort, crossed one leg over the other. 'No problemo, I'll just sit right here and you guys can take off.'

'How dare you!' Angela marched over to him as he interlaced his fingers like a pretzel.

'No, how dare *you*. Look, I know, Miss Hoity-Toity, that you are used to wagging your skinny finger in people's faces, demanding whatever you please, but I am not your servant and this is not your castle. I understand you don't know me from a bar of soap – or even shit from clay – but I am not leaving. You're not the only one who cares about *her*.'

Angela looked from Chloe to Audrey before settling on Elijah. 'I'm going to talk to Mildred about this!'

He cupped a hand to his mouth as she turned on her black Prada heels. 'Don't let the door hit ya where the good Lord split ya, Cruella!' Elijah chuckled and turned to Chloe, only to discover tears in her eyes. He soon lost his victory smile. 'I'm sorry; I know she's your mother. You can't help that.'

Chloe sniffled and sat straighter in her chair. 'I believe, sir, that people even within the deepest of comas can hear what's happening around them. I would hate for Nanna to be hearing this while she's trying to get better.'

Elijah, for the first time in his life, had nothing smart to retort. Even if he did, he would have capitulated if it meant stopping Chloe's tears.

'Perhaps I should go. I never wanted to cause this much drama, for Christ's sake.'

'No!' Chloe stood and walked over to him. 'No, I want to hear more, but please, no more fighting. I *know* Nanna can hear everything.'

Elijah regarded her for a moment before turning to Audrey. The sound of the respirator subtly reminding them she was still alive. 'You're right. And for the record, I believe she can hear us, too.' He removed his eyes from Audrey and had to refrain from touching Chloe's hand, which now rested on the edge of the bed right next to him. Others might not appreciate such an act, and it was high time things changed for the better. Although he had laughed off Angela's childish antics, his ulcer had borne the brunt of each nerve-wracking moment she'd scolded him like he was scum akin to a paedophile. 'If your mother can play fair, then so will I.'

'Thank you, sir.'

He watched Chloe swipe at her salty tears that had run down her youthful face, causing her button nose to turn puce. 'Hey, um, kid …'

Chloe peered up, wiping away a tear that clung to her lower lip.

'My, err, my friends call me EJ.'

Chapter 17

THEN – 1964

ELIJAH BELTED ALONG to the latest song to reach the shores, 'Baby I Need Your Loving' by the Four Tops as he cruised down the meandering mountainside in his sky-blue EH Holden. Upon reaching Audrey's front door, he rapped on the chipped wooden panel, waited two seconds, then knocked again. Lloyd appeared, lips pursed around a protruding Chesterfield. Elijah's beaming smile was not returned.

'What are you doing here, boy?' Lloyd said, his breath reeking of beer and tobacco.

Elijah double-blinked, but retained his grin. 'I'm here to weed the garden, sir. Should I start here or out back?'

Lloyd's head tilted as he squinted, the cigarette smoke wafting in front of his face. 'Oh you think you're funny, do ya?' He removed the butt from his lips.

Elijah stifled a smirk. 'No, sir, just thought it was obvious I'm here for Audrey, that's all.'

'Ah, so she hasn't told you,' Lloyd said with a click of his tongue and a sadistic smirk, as though he took great pleasure in what he was about to say. 'You're banned from this house and you're banned from seeing Audrey.'

Elijah waited for the bubbling anger to subside, because he admitted sometimes he let his emotions get the better of him. He glared, non-blinking. 'Don't sweat it, what do you think this is, 1955? You cannot control Audrey like a puppet. You have no right to tell me who I can and cannot see, and that goes the same for her! She's not a child and we haven't done anything wrong. Now, if you'll excuse me …' He attempted to push past Lloyd's burly figure. It was like the wolf trying to huff and puff his way into the brick house. It was brazen, but Elijah couldn't stand strangers telling him what to do, or how to act; it pushed him to the precipice between staying sane or going berserk. Lloyd took it a step further by pushing Elijah backwards onto the weed-choked lawn. Elijah bounded to his feet, fist clenched and ready to go, but he heard Audrey gasp as she looked on from the foot of the wooden staircase. She would never forgive him if he socked her uncle out cold. It took an abundance of self-control, but Elijah unclenched his fists and stared at Lloyd, chest heaving.

Lloyd jerked his thumb sideways. 'Get the hell outta here, punk, before I call law enforcement.'

Elijah couldn't remember a time when he'd seen a hotter shade of red; not even when three guys attacked him for his wallet. It took all his willpower not to bop Lloyd on the nose. Instead, he slammed his heel into the rusty gate, jumped in his car, and drove to Percy's Grill Room to get blitzed with Lawrence, Alison, Jonathan and Georgie.

Chapter 18

'SUGAH?' NURSE MILDRED said, popping through the door with Angela in tow. 'I think it's best ya go. I don't want Aud's family gittin' upset durin' this stressful 'n' sad time. Ya dig?'

'No.' Elijah stared straight ahead at the whitewashed wall with its charts and mounted television set.

Nurse Mildred sighed, and he believed deep down that if it had been her choice, she would have let him stay. But defying a witch like Angela would likely see Nurse Mildred staked to a pole, ready for execution without trial. Still, he was rebelling more for Angela's sake than for Nurse Mildred's; he wanted everyone to know he meant business, and a woman with an upturned nose who thought the sun shone out of her arse couldn't convince anyone otherwise.

'Fo' the sake of the family, ya don't want this ta git nasty. Think of how Aud would feel; Angela is Aud's proxy – ya dig?' Nurse Mildred said, and Elijah almost believed she was regretful. He *wanted* to believe that.

Elijah slapped his thighs. 'You know, throughout my entire life I have had people misunderstand me. People telling me what to do, what not to do, who to see, who not to see; it's been one person after the next trying to pry me away from Audrey.'

Elijah thought Angela mumbled: 'Here we go,' but he couldn't be certain.

'After all this time, I'm still here by her side because I've always found my way back to her. So you can all get stuffed, because as far as I'm concerned, I have more of a right to be here than you lot!'

'How do you figure that out?' Angela said, pushing past Nurse Mildred at the door.

For Elijah, it was like looking the beast square in the eyes. 'Because if it weren't for me, you wouldn't even be here!'

The room went quiet enough to hear Chloe's tears dripping onto her hands and thighs.

'This isn't helping the situation, guys,' Jamie said, pushing past Nurse Mildred. 'I could hear you lot out in the rec room.' Nurse Mildred looked from one person to the next as Jamie held up both hands. 'I think we need some time to focus on what's important here.'

'Now you're siding with this geriatric?' Angela said with a jerk of her thumb in Elijah's direction.

'You're just a nasty person, right down to the bone,' Elijah said, shaking his head. 'Even your snarl could rival a pit bull's.'

Angela gave a watery snort. 'You're nothing but a dotard!'

'Ange, come on, don't be like that. Mum wouldn't have wanted this.' Jamie placed a hand over her own chest. 'The most important thing is that we're all here for each other. If we can't support one another, then we need to adjust our priorities.'

Angela's jaw clenched as she inhaled through engorged nostrils. 'Jamie, I will not have this stranger warping Chloe's mind about Mum – if that means anything to you at all.' Elijah caught Jamie shaking her head as Angela gave weight to her argument. 'She idolises her nanna, so I'm not sure hearing these stories about sex and drugs will do anyone any good. No, we never knew that side of Mum, but does it matter? I know *I* got up to mischief that my child doesn't need to find out about, so why do we need to have a tell-all right before Mum passes? Can we not remember Mum for how she is?'

Jamie held up both hands in a placatory manner. 'Calm down, I just think there's no actual harm in him telling stories about Mum; things that we never knew and, moreover, is there anything he can tell us that will change how we feel about her?'

Good point, love, Elijah thought. He glanced around the room to see if someone else agreed.

Jamie licked her lips, lowering her hands. 'For me, the answer is no. No matter what's in that diary of his or hers, it won't change the time we've spent with her, the times we've laughed and cried and argued; nothing can change that nor can anything take it away.'

Angela gave a desperate last glance towards Nurse Mildred, but Nurse Mildred's eyes fluttered to the window, as if she saw something of interest there. Angela shook her head and pressed her tongue to the side of her cheek, eyes flickering aloft.

'What happened, happened,' Jamie continued. 'And I don't want to tell you how to raise Chloe, but she's eager to hear about Mum's youth.' Her shoulders rose like an elevator. 'I am, too.'

Angela inhaled and threw her head back. She remained silent for a heartbeat before opening her eyes. 'Think about the fact that this guy could have stalked and harassed Mum.' Jamie's lips parted. 'He could have attacked her or been obsessed by her. God, for all we know, Mum's blood is boiling at him being next to her.'

Elijah somehow relaxed his crumpled forehead to say, 'Angela, you're about as cold as a widow's—'

'Be my guest to sit around for storytelling time – by a complete stranger – and let him manipulate the way we see Mum. I'm going for a coffee.'

'I'll have a flat white with two sugars and cold soy milk on the side, ta,' Elijah said, straight-faced.

Angela's eyes turned as cold as a sleety day in July. Nurse Mildred's lips pressed together as she stepped out of the way to let Angela storm off, heels clacking thereafter.

'Well, that went over like a fart in church!' Nurse Mildred said, stepping back into the room. Elijah smiled, but his drooping lids overshadowed it.

Chloe looked to Jamie, then to Nurse Mildred. 'What do we do now?'

Everyone turned to Elijah; it was an act that said he was now in control and could do as he pleased. 'If you want to know why I am so intent on being here, then gather around for some insight.'

Chapter 19

THEN – 1964

LATER THAT NIGHT at Percy's Grill Room, Elijah drank his weight in booze to forget about Lloyd, and he smoked a full pack of Camels. He'd lost around eighty pounds on the pokies, and got into a fistfight with a bloke who started giving his buddy Lawrence a hard time over money he was supposedly due to hand over. When they got kicked out, Elijah drove home as pissed as a poet, despite Georgie offering her pad for him to stay.

The next day, with a raging hangover, Elijah went to the ice cream parlour to confront Audrey and ask her what they should do about their situation, because he couldn't stop thinking about her.

True, Lloyd had banned Elijah from the house, but there was no way Lloyd would interfere with his local hangout; over his dead body. So for all intents and purposes, the ice cream parlour became Elijah's sanctuary.

It was another scorching day in paradise. The queue of people snaked outside the parlour door, and parking spaces were as scarce as honest politicians. It was so dry the trees practically begged the dogs. Elijah stood in the ice cream queue waiting to talk to Audrey, although there were only two people serving: her and Cynthia. Betty and Sylvia were clearing tables and taking out fatty food to red-eyed, greasy-haired teenagers, so Elijah passed the time trying to mask his anxiety by tapping his foot along to Elvis's 'Viva Las Vegas', which blasted from the jukebox. When Audrey spotted him, he was between breaths; his chest wouldn't expand to take another one. Would she be able to tell he had gone on a bender the night before? One glance at his bruised knuckles would have revealed part of the story, and he didn't want Audrey to think he solved his problems with violence.

As he moved closer to the counter, Audrey glowered, but she fumbled with an ice-cream cone and her cheeks reddened. As he ogled Audrey, he took note that her rich hair was well-groomed. She had an endearing smile and a pin-up figure, but what he adored most about her was the way she could be both innocent and sweet, but within the next second she could be a little spitfire, jumping to conclusions, such as him being like the jocks who'd teased her about her aid.

Upon reaching the counter, Elijah got stuck with Cynthia Green.

'What would you like today, EJ?' Cynthia asked in a no-bullshit tone.

'I want *her*.' He pointed at Audrey, who was looking at him, looking at her.

Cynthia scowled. 'You cannot have her; what else?'

'Um, gimme cherry-vanilla.'

'In a c—'

'Cone!'

Cynthia prepared his order while he looked across at Audrey, whose hands were shaking while she squirted Reddi-Wip whipped cream onto a hot caramel fudge sundae.

'I need to see you,' he whispered, as Cynthia eyed them while wrapping a napkin around the base of a cone.

'No,' Audrey whispered, focusing on her task at the register. The grey-haired man she was serving, dressed in Hawaiian swimming trunks and a matching shirt open at the chest, remained silent, his eyes darting between Elijah to Audrey as beads of sweat glistened on his forehead.

'I'm not taking *no* for an answer. Didn't you have a gas at the drive-in?'

'Yes – that will be one shilling, sir,' she said to Mr Blue Hawaii. He passed her the coin, exchanging glances with Cynthia before collecting his order.

'Dammit, then what's the problem?'

'I'm too busy.' Audrey fiddled with the ancient cash register and its old typewriter buttons.

'Bullshit!'

Her wide eyes connected with his. Customers stopped their conversations and stared, so Elijah lowered his register. 'Who's got to you, Audrey?'

Audrey's cheeks appeared as red as a Moulin Rouge showgirl, and she diverted her eyes to the next customer. Her chest rose and fell, and the chatter from patrons behind him intensified once more. By now he had a sweat moustache, and Audrey's hair clung to her damp temples as 'Hit the Road Jack' played over the jukebox.

Elijah raked a jittery hand through his sticky hair. 'I'm sorry, but I don't understand why you let people walk over you; why you allow people to tell you what to think and how to feel. Can't you be yourself?'

She snapped a wide-eyed glance at him. 'I don't know what you're talking about – why is there a bruise under your eye?'

Elijah raised an eyebrow and matched it with a crooked smile. 'Oh – have a touch of compassion in that heart of yours for little old me, do you?'

Audrey's next customer gave a deliberate cough.

'Don't be absurd – hello, madam, how may I be of service?'

Elijah's eye twitched. He was frustrated, hungover and hacked, so when Cynthia handed him his cone, he slammed the coin on the counter and walked over to Audrey as she scooped black raspberry ice cream. The lady in a brown jumper dress gasped as Elijah held his palm to her face, so he slipped her a one-pound note to shut her up and turned to Audrey.

'At least talk to me about this, Audrey; don't just shut me out!'

'No!'

A man yelled from the back of the queue: 'Yeah, hit the road, Jack!'

Elijah's lips thinned at the outburst, his cheeks heated, and his pounding heart could have knocked that fucker out. 'I thought you were stronger than this.'

'I'm not an idiot.' She turned to face him. 'You have a girlfriend; her name is Georgie Brown, remember?' Audrey pointed towards the glass door as Georgie, Alison, Lawrence and Jonathan loitered outside near a red-and-white barber's pole. Admittedly, to Elijah, Georgie looked cherry in a yellow-and-white shift dress and white Mary Jane heels. Upon opening the door, which had a bell attached, they spotted Elijah. Standing at six-foot-two, he usually stood out amongst crowds.

Georgie ran over, squealing. 'I thought you said you had plans today, baby?' She wrapped her arms around his waist, transferring her baby pink lipstick over to his tight-lipped mouth. 'Oh, bangin'! You got me my favourite flavour!' She took the ice-cream cone off him and licked it, keeping the eye contact. 'Wait … make that my second – *you're* my favourite flavour!' She winked.

Elijah pushed her away, ignoring her gasp, and glared into Audrey's fiery eyes before storming out.

***

That evening was Grace's twenty-ninth birthday dinner. Along the way to the restaurant, Elijah collected Georgie, but it was Audrey who swamped his mind. She'd shot him down faster than Annie Oakley lining up tin cans. This was a first, and he didn't care for it – it was a crushing blow to his ego and it had happened in front of everyone, too. He was determined, however, to make the most of the night and tried to forget about the elusive Audrey; he didn't want to fall for a chick like her, anyway. Too bad she'd already left her mark. He'd have a better chance of forgetting his own name than Audrey Hughes. If Elijah tasted a sample of what she had to offer, he was afraid he'd become addicted, and the only thing he wanted to be addicted to was rock 'n' roll.

The Samuels and Georgie sat inside Bessy and Pete's Grill Room, with Elijah's arm resting over a wooden ledge behind Georgie's back, chewing the thumbnail of his other hand. The swank restaurant had leather-studded chairs, snow-white napkins folded into intricate frills, and the smoke from meat fat dripping into the fire wafted through from the kitchen. Bessy and Pete's was a place Grace and Elijah liked to frequent, but their parents detested it, which was part of the appeal. Grace played with the circular mahogany cruet-stand presenting a merry-go-round of sauces and other pungencies, while Howard Samuels popped the cork from a bottle of Moët & Chandon, and Georgie fanned her face with the menu.

'You look distracted, Elijah,' Margaret said while studying the fold-out menu, cringing at everything she saw.

'I'm ... thinking,' he said with a quick smile, glancing at Georgie, who was sipping from a bottle of creaming soda through a striped straw, still fanning her face.

Elijah was thinking that what he liked most about Audrey was she was the only one who seemed interested in his life's plans. Their conversations had been intimate. Elijah supposed that when you've never had that, it doesn't register. His past relationships had been based around balling, so Audrey had got him thinking. Deep. She was thought-provoking and that was perhaps what equally intrigued, yet scared him the most.

'Thinking about *what?*' Georgie said, eyeing him. By now he guessed she'd worked out that something was suspect, as he was distant and had stopped touching her. A rarity considering their hangout dates typically consisted of Georgie scratching his back.

Elijah tugged on his shirt collar, grimacing. Every damned thing agitated him, even the ceiling fans, which did nothing but blow hot air around.

'You've been acting funny all day,' Georgie added, not leaving the damn ice cream parlour incident alone. Elijah had told her his stomach contents were about to erupt, which was why he fled. But Georgie wasn't stupid. Silly, perhaps, but not stupid.

'What are you going to order, son?' Howard asked, adjusting his kipper tie.

I wonder how soft Audrey's lips are, was all Elijah could think, while the smell of a char-grilled steak wafted by their table as a young waitress rushed past to deliver it to a scowling customer, who tapped an invisible wristwatch.

Georgie gave Elijah's ribs a hard elbow. His head snapped up and looked around. 'Huh? Sorry, um, I think the broiled mutton and mash will do me fine, Dad—'

Elijah sensed something like a telekinetic buzz, so he glanced towards the front doors and there *she* was. Audrey, dolled up in a purple drop-waist long-sleeved dress with a white collar and white cuffs. A teal band pushed her hair back from her forehead. The rest was brushed straight but with a flick at the ends. And although it was plain to see her threads weren't from Dior, Elijah thought she rocked it like no-one's business. As Audrey stepped aside for Lloyd, she turned to Elijah, as if she knew he was there – as though she *felt* it.

Their eyes connected like a conduit transferring electricity, and it proved Elijah's theory: there *was* something special – not only about her – but about *them*.

Audrey narrowed in on his arm around Georgie, and turned away as she followed Lloyd (who hadn't seen Elijah) and a waiter over to the smoking area behind a partition, ensuring the Samuels party wouldn't see her throughout the night.

Turning back around, Elijah's heart acted like it was trying to break free through his throat. He tried to ignore it, but it pissed him off that even his bodily functions spoke the truth. He gave Georgie a reaffirming smile before reaching for his bottle of Carlton Draught.

Elijah's food lay untouched, forming a hardened outer layer. He'd focused on how ticked off at Audrey he was for taking control of his emotions. To him, it was foreign. He wasn't putting on his best acting skills, as Georgie kept looking over as if to analyse his strange behaviour. Apart from his lack of appetite, he wasn't involving himself in the conversation circulating the table. As they waited for Grace's Pavlova birthday cake to be brought in by the owner, Pete, Elijah excused himself from the table and headed for the men's room, where he looked over and saw Audrey cocooned by a cloud of plume Lloyd was manufacturing. Her mouth was downturned as she pushed a fork around her plate, moving her food from one side to the other, while Lloyd chuffed on a cigar in between mouthfuls of lamb's fry and gravy.

Audrey glanced up. For Elijah, their sizzling eye contact was like staring into the blazing sun and feeling twice as hot. As he walked towards her, the tension thickened, like wading through a dense swamp, and his heart beat faster as they stared at each other with apprehension. Still sore from being rejected, Elijah diverted his stormy eyes – walking past her table as Lloyd coughed and spluttered.

Yeah, choke on it, you bastard.

As Elijah entered the gents, he placed his clenched knuckles on the porcelain sink and looked at himself in the mirror, panting.

'Keep it together!' he said to his reflection, grinding his teeth against the rising emotions. His inner strength seemed to have vanished like dust in the wind. 'Keep your shit together!'

Chapter 20

THEN – 1964

ELIJAH CONCEDED HE couldn't ride two horses with one arse, and he didn't want to hurt Georgie or prolong something that had died – for him, anyway. The night after Grace's birthday dinner, he told Georgie they needed to talk. She met him at seven o'clock at a posh restaurant called Josephine's on the east-end side of town. Every table was occupied. The air was redolent of fried onion and garlic. Georgie glared at him across the round table as he downed a bottle of Carlton Draught as soon as it was served.

He used a knuckle to wipe foam from the corner of his mouth. 'Georgie, I've, ah, had some time to think, and I believe it's best we remain … friends.'

Her glossy lips parted. 'What?'

Elijah fidgeted in his seat and wiped his sweaty hands over his thighs. 'I know this is sudden, but I just don't think I feel that way about you anymore.' He paused for breath, then quickly added: 'It's not a reflection on you; it's just something that happens, I guess, over a long period.'

She stared at him, incredulous. 'EJ, we've been going out for eight months.'

Elijah glanced at the middle-aged waiter walking past with plates in either hand, wondering how many times he'd witnessed couples break-up in this swank joint.

'I know; I am sorry. You're a great chick ... but, I don't think it's going to last. I hope you understand.' Georgie scowled, her lips twisting. 'I hope we can still be friends, though?'

She folded her arms over her chest. 'Why the sudden change? A few weeks ago everything was cherry. Who are you sleeping with now?'

Elijah wet his lips and shook his head. 'I swear to God you are the last person I slept with; I haven't been playing up on y—'

She scoffed. 'Isn't that what you told Karen Sanders when you left her for—'

Elijah tsked, leaning forward. 'Please lower your voice; I am speaking hand on heart. I haven't slept with anyone else, and boy we have had some crazy nights that I'll never forget, but in the long run how do you think we'll go, ya know? What do we actually know about each other? What of our dreams, and plans for the future? Do you honestly think we're built for the long haul?'

Georgie flicked her hair and shrugged before glancing at her polished nails. 'Hey, it's no skin off my nose. Brad's already asked me out ... so, like, whatever. Your loss.' She grabbed her Babycham while Elijah tried to recall who the hell Brad was ... *Oh, Bradley Edwin Jr.* – heavily tattooed guy who loved cricket, beer, and car racing. A high school dropout and the epitome of white trash. Elijah wasn't covetous, but he thought she deserved better. Although if he verbalised his concern she might take it as a sign of weakness and jealousy. All he could do was wish her luck because he knew they weren't destined to be.

Elijah paid the bill, led Georgie by her elbow to her canary-yellow Ford Zephyr, and offered a peck on the cheek. She retracted from his kiss, turned around, hopped in the car and drove off without so much as a goodbye.

Two days rolled by without Elijah seeing Audrey, and he felt no closer to inner peace. He needed to sort this shit out; at the very least, he needed her not to hate him every time he showed his face around her. He didn't understand what had happened between their flawless night at the lookout, to now where she loathed him.

Wollongong became a small place once you'd lived there for a while; everyone seemed to know one another, hence the execrable reputation associated with Elijah's name.

He didn't need another enemy in town, so he decided to be an adult and go to the parlour and try to sort it. He shaved and decked himself out in a schmick ensemble, prepared to extend the olive branch. He sped down the mountain, smoking at least three cigarettes before pulling into the parking lot of Betty-Sue's in his usual spot, next to a gargantuan weather-worn ice-cream cone. Running a shaky hand over his mouth and chin, he pushed open the front door. Audrey cleaned a table with a bottle of Ajax and Bounty paper towels. Her downcast eyes narrowed when she saw him. She stood straighter and jutted her chin as he approached. No customers were inside; they were all alone.

'Hey,' he said, swallowing a lump that felt like a cotton ball.

She turned away.

'I bought you some chocolates.' He handed her the wrapped box of Pascall Clinkers he'd hidden inside his breast pocket. She glanced at it until he placed it on the shiny, custom-made Formica table featuring abstract art. 'Listen, I, um, really want to talk to you.'

She shrugged. 'I don't see what good that will do; why are you bothering me?'

'Because you bother *me*!'

'Well, flake off then!' She stormed away, heading for the kitchen. 'Go back to your girl!'

'Wait!' He dashed after her, grabbing her wrist to spin her around. Their faces were only inches apart and for a second neither one spoke, but she flinched like he had scorched her. He put his hands up and stepped back after she shot him a surprised look at the manhandling. 'Sorry,' he whispered, as she turned back around and sauntered off. God, she was draining all his energy. '*Please* hear me *out*!'

She spun around and looked him square in the eyes. 'Maybe you've had too much Chateau Tanunda to understand my request, but it is simple: leave me in peace and go back to Georgie. I know all about you, Mr Samuels, you're only here because I don't want you. You want the challenge and the chase. If I gave in, you would leave me as soon as the thrill ends, so bugger off.'

Elijah wanted to correct her assumptions, but she gave him no chance. Looking into her eyes was like looking into an inferno.

'I've done nothing to you or anybody else, yet people keep hurting me,' she said, teary-eyed.

'Audrey, *please*,' he whispered.

When she closed her weary eyes, he believed she was going to break down. 'I have experienced a gnarly couple of months, so please go. I wish to live a drama-free life, if that's all right with you?'

Elijah creased his brow and refrained from screaming at the top of his lungs. 'You think I see you as just a catch?' Her watery eyes opened. 'Yes, I enjoy chasing you, but that's because you have something I want more than my next breath. I, too, have no desire for drama and I apologise, okay? I am sorry if I upset you; that's why I am here – to straighten things out so it won't be weird between us anymore.'

'There is no *us*!'

When three people walked into the shop, Audrey put her cleaning products aside and walked to the register. Elijah glanced at his untouched box of chocolates on the table. He walked to the ice cream selection and propped his elbow on the chilled glass to rest his head on his hand. By the way she wiped her hands over her apron, he felt smug glee over her nervousness. If he affected her in any way, it was a good sign. Anything was better than being ignored, right? Something he'd learned from his childhood.

'What would you like, sir?' she asked a handsome young chap with mutton chop sideburns. His staring at Audrey made Elijah's jaw clench.

'Chocolate marshmallow, please, missus,' Mutton-Chops said, grinning. Elijah told himself to hang loose and unclench his fists; that he was overreacting to Mutton-Chops undressing her with his eyes.

A young couple peered at the ice cream selection, talking about *Hush … Hush, Sweet Charlotte,* which had finished its session at the Savoy Theatre. It was a flick starring Bette Davis and Olivia de Havilland, and had opened to rave reviews. Elijah thought if the young couple stayed around long enough, they might see *another* epic scene of murder if that joker kept ogling his girl. Two for the price of one, folks! Get your tickets here for half price!

'You're new here in town, aren't you?' Mutton-Chops said to her.

She flashed Mutton-Chops a flirtatious smile – one that Elijah wanted her to reserve only for himself. She was taunting him; he fucking knew it. If she wanted a reaction, Mutton-Chops' face would pay the price – and maybe result in him visiting his dentist afterwards.

'Yes, I moved here a while ago to live with my uncle.'

Elijah's eye twitched as Mutton-Chops' gaze lowered south of Audrey's chin.

'Welcome to the Gong; I hope you'll have a good time.' Mutton-Chops flicked his long brown hair away from his face. 'My name is Les; if you ever need a tour guide, I'd—'

'I've never seen you before,' Elijah said.

Mutton-Chops turned to him, frowning. 'Excuse me?'

'I was born and raised here; never seen ya.'

Mutton-Chops looked at Audrey with a half-hearted smirk as if to say *Is this guy for real?* 'Ah, well, *may*be it's possible you don't know everyone. Ever think of that, friend?'

Elijah stared at this guy as Audrey looked back and forth between them like she was watching a tennis match. Elijah removed his elbow off the cabinet and stood upright.

Mutton-Chops pointed at him. 'Wait, are you that guy who hit Robbie and Ken the other day?'

'Who the hell are they?' Elijah creased his brow, mentally recalling the names of all the guys he'd been in a fight with.

'They're friends of mine, and you're that rich, spoiled ex-army brat who lives up the mountain, aren't you?' He wagged his index finger. 'Yeah, yeah you attacked my friends.'

'It's possible,' Elijah said, shrugging. A fresh wave of customers came in, and Audrey appeared to be looking at the strangers for help by communicating with her eyes.

'Yeah, I know you. You've got a mean junkyard dog-thing happening, but I'm damn sure you cowardly hit Robbie and Ken.'

Elijah held both throbbing fists beside his body. He didn't want Audrey to think the only two things he knew how to do were frig and fight. 'Do they own Ford Mustangs?'

'Yeah ...'

'Now I remember. They were the bastards who disrespected *her*,' he said, pointing to Audrey, her face as pale as cream. 'And who the hell do you think you're calling a coward? It was two-on-one and they had the upper hand, *friend*.' Elijah inched closer before poking Mutton-Chops' solid chest with his index finger. 'Not to mention they messed with the wrong girl by damaging her property – so tell me again up close: Who's the coward?'

'Elijah, don't,' Audrey said as Mutton-Chops inched backwards. The young couple from the Savoy left abruptly, bell clanging in their wake.

'Why don't you bug out now while you still can; she's with me, anyway. Better luck next time, pal.'

Mutton-Chops held up his hands in defence. 'Man, why don't you cool your jets; you don't want this to get hairy.'

Elijah raised a mocking eyebrow and laughed before pushing Mutton-Chops' chest. 'Don't I?'

'No, you *don't!*' Mutton-Chops shoved Elijah back further than he had him.

Elijah stepped forward with a raised fist, but the sound of Audrey's timid voice filled the room as onlookers gasped.

'Elijah, please – for me?'

He looked at her as if spellbound, then back to the prick, who was now grinning, running the tip of his tongue along his lower lip. Elijah clamped his jaw to stifle the rage.

Mutton-Chops chuckled and then patronisingly patted Elijah's cheek twice. 'Silenced by a skirt, hey? Your reputation is just a flake, man. I'm outta here.' He looked at Audrey, almost with disdain, and back to Elijah before he scoffed and walked away.

Elijah looked at Audrey, who looked at him with a stony expression as she held the ice-cream cone in her trembling hand. A lady clutching a purse adjusted her pink pillbox hat and approached the counter as Elijah's emotions bubbled away. He couldn't believe Mutton-Chops had touched his face and got away with it.

'God, do you see what you're doing to me?' Elijah said, feeling disgusted with himself. He didn't know Audrey from the next broad, yet he was letting his reputation slide for her? What the *fuck* was going on here? Had his testicles slipped off without him knowing about it?

Audrey glanced at the ice-cream cone as if contemplating what to do with it.

Elijah sighed before taking it off her. 'Here.' He reached into his pocket before slamming a threepence coin on the counter.

As Audrey prepared the lady's banana split, Elijah leaned against the counter and said, 'So, getting back to where I was, when can I see you alone?'

Audrey flashed him a scowl, then looked away as her face went as red as any rose in June.

'Would you like caramel or chocolate fudge, ma'am?' The lady Audrey conferred with reminded Elijah of Twiggy, with her expressive eyes and short haircut, which was fast becoming a trend.

'God, you are *so* beautiful,' he whispered to Audrey, trying to change his approach.

'Fine! Come around tomorrow after six – would you like anything else tonight, ma'am?'

'I'd like to leave as soon as possible.' Twiggy eyed Elijah behind fake Almay lashes, which to him looked like cockroach antennae. She handed Audrey the money.

'Keep the change,' Twiggy said before strutting away, but making a point of giving Elijah the once-over one last time. He puckered his lips, which sent her moving out the door like a cat with its tail on fire.

'Hold up, sir,' Elijah said, blocking her next customer – a frail, scowling old man. Facing Audrey, he said, 'Are we going to tell Lloyd about *us*; is that why you want me to come to your house?'

'Don't be silly. Lloyd's playing euchre at a friend's place, so I will have the house to myself. We can talk then. Besides, I just said there is no *us*; you have a lady-friend already.'

The front door opened in the background, the bell clanging, but neither one of them looked. He leaned in closer. 'Not anymore I don't, because I want *you*. And I always get what I want.'

Her nostrils flared. 'Not this time, you don't! I'm not interested in you *that* way.'

Elijah glared at her until the old chrome-dome cleared his throat from behind, so Audrey focused her attention on him. Elijah blocked her view with his body.

She exhaled, glaring into his eyes. 'Do you want me to lose more customers and get fired? I said we can talk tomorrow!'

Elijah would not argue the point, but her statement about not wanting him had stung. He looked forward to proving her a liar. Upon walking towards the front door, he spotted Georgie at the back of the snaking queue, glaring at him.

Chapter 21

SOMEWHERE BETWEEN ELIJAH pausing for a coffee break and to relieve his bladder, Angela rejoined them, Styrofoam cup in hand. Her back and shoulders appeared less tense. Perhaps she was just too damn tired to continue battling. When Angela had stepped into the room, Jamie held out her hand, which Angela clasped. They stood side by side until Elijah returned, giving Angela a side-glance.

'Welcome back,' he mumbled. He positioned himself in front of his chair and plonked down, panting and reaching for his hanky, not at all giving a damn that Angela had to play catch-up.

Once composed, Elijah opened his diary and adjusted his glasses. 'Continuing on, I couldn't handle this love triangle situation any longer, and I knew that even if Audrey and I weren't to get together, that if I had these feelings for another chick, then it meant I wasn't in love with my current girl. One thing I also came to realise about Georgie was that she was all show and no go ... a real mirror warmer.' He paused, coughing into a fist.

'Shall I read something Nan wrote?' Chloe said as the sound of voices passing through the corridor outside became louder, then faded.

Elijah nodded, his right leg pulsing like a second heartbeat. 'Sure thing; why not?'

Chloe licked her lips. *'9th December 1964. Dear Diary, tonight EJ is coming over because Uncle Lloyd is playing euchre at Jack's; he'll be gone for hours. He refuses to lift the ban off EJ after the scuffle between them, but I don't want to miss out on having friends, either. I am nervous about EJ coming over, but I know nothing is going to happen between him and me. I'm only letting him come over because frankly, he embarrassed me yesterday at work – I didn't want Betty hearing about the altercation EJ had with Les, and then firing me, as I need money to buy a new aid. Betty is already under enough stress with her sick husband. Right now I'm trying to calm my nerves because who am I kidding? I am smitten with this man, and it's just my luck he's off-limits. Believe me, I don't even* want *to feel this way about a criminal playboy. When he arrives, I will say to his smug face that we can be friends and that's all! Because it will be 6 o'clock, I may as well make him dinner, too, whilst I am at it. It's the least I can do, really. In the freezer we have pork chops, so I will whip them out and serve them with roast veggies, broiled cabbage, and Bospur's gravy. I hope he doesn't laugh when he sees what I have planned. Anyway, I'm confident that after dinner I will tell him I am* not *interested in being a playboy's mistress. Audrey.'*

Chloe lowered the diary with a smirk, and looked at her mother, then Aunt Jamie, and then Nurse Mildred – who had got caught up in the story when she came to change the IV drip, administer more morphine, and check Audrey for bedsores.

'This doesn't sound like the woman we know,' Angela said, stirring her steaming coffee with a plastic stick.

'I know, it doesn't,' Elijah said, creasing his brow.

Angela used her free hand to massage her neck, easing out the kinks. 'Listen, Mr Samuels, I think we should call it a day, if you don't mind? I'm hungry, and I'm sure these guys are, too.'

Elijah observed Audrey breathing from a tube, fighting to stay alive. 'I understand. I will leave soon.'

Nurse Mildred's pager beeped, so she took off like a bullet exiting a gun, right as Angela received a call from her husband. Seth Tawny wanted to shout the ladies dinner, presumably as an apology for his absence when his presence as a stable figure was much-needed.

As Elijah listened to the two sisters determine where they should eat, he caught Chloe staring at him. He turned away.

After the brief phone call, the ladies got all their personals packed and ready to go, then each said goodbye to their mother, kissing Audrey on the cheek. They then said goodbye to Elijah, who simply dipped his head and hoped it would suffice. Chloe, however, went over to Elijah and hugged him around the neck, catching him off guard, especially when she slipped a note into his quivering hand. 'Night-night, Eli.'

After they left and the room was once again silent save for the respirator, Elijah sat alone, observing Audrey before he glanced at the piece of paper Chloe had left: *Please come back tomorrow!*

Elijah smiled because deep down, despite his best efforts, Chloe was growing on him. He rose and tottered over to stand beside Audrey. His eyes trailed over her thinning hair and her purplish eyelids; her skin as crumpled as old parchment. The last time he'd laid eyes on her all those years ago, she'd shone brighter than the sun. Her smile was as wide as he'd ever seen. Raw emotions raked across his chest like a pickaxe. He blinked away the blinding agony and leaned over. As his lips brushed against her pallid skin, a thousand memories came flooding back, from the first day he'd said hello, to the day he had to say goodbye. It was too surreal; he'd believed he'd never see her again. Over the years he'd begged God for a reunion with his beloved, and this is what He served: Audrey in a coma, nearing her final days. In a morbid way it was humorous, because this type of thing was just his rotten luck. *Yeah, fuck You, too, pal. You better believe I've got a thing or two I'd like to say to You when my time is done.*

'Sugah, if ya didn't feel like trottin' on home jist yet, ya can catch the tail-end of tonight's movie out in the rec room,' Nurse Mildred said, interrupting Elijah's kiss as she popped her head around the door.

Elijah straightened, but he didn't take his eyes off Audrey. He never had been able to do that. 'What movie is it?'

'*Face Lift.*'

He faced Nurse Mildred then. 'Never heard of it. What the heck is it even about?'

'Ya know ... *Face Lift*! The one with Nick Cage 'n' the handsome fella from *Grease* who has the nice butt.'

'You mean *Face Off*.'

'Nah, *Face Lift*.'

'I'm pretty damn sure it's *Face Off*—'

Nurse Mildred folded her arms. 'I *said* it's *Face Lift* 'n' there'll be no more arguin' 'bout that. If ya aren't keen on watchin' the movie, would ya like ta order some grub? I'm sure the kitchen can arrange somethin' fo' ya.'

'I would like that, thank you.'

She handed him a two-fold, off-white menu. 'Here's what we can offer; ya jist choose 'n' I'll fix up the payment later. I can even bring it in here, so ya can eat with Aud.'

Elijah swallowed hard. It had been such a damn long time since their last meal together. As he skittered through words he'd never heard before, like 'quinoa' and 'açai', Nurse Mildred whispered: 'She's gittin' weaker, Eli.'

His eyes drifted up to nothing in particular, nostrils flaring.

'Nathaniel Grant is gunna have a yarn ta Ange 'bout future options.'

Elijah's bottom lip quivered. 'S-Sometimes I see her eyelids flutter, like she's trying to open them.' He gulped to suppress the bubble of emotion floating like a balloon to the surface. 'Her hands will flicker and I believe I hear sounds. I think she'll come back to us.'

Nurse Mildred's lips folded inwards and she closed her eyes. 'It's normal fo' that ta happen, sugah. It's jist what's left of the system.'

Elijah shook his head, his jaw set.

'I ... I don't want ya ta suffer, Eli.'

He looked into her moist eyes and choked out, 'I already have.'

She caressed his cheek and offered a smile. 'Oh, bless yer pea-pickin' heart!' She removed her hand, but continued to stare.

He struggled to find the courage to ask, 'Do you think she knows I'm here?'

A tear rolled down his cheek when Nurse Mildred nodded. 'I surely do.'

'Has she ever ... ever mentioned *me*?'

The look on her face matched the kindness in her tone. 'No, sugah, but then ah-gain, folk won't like ta drudge up the past if it hurts too much. The big regret in these halls is those that never took the chance ta fulfil a destiny, but the biggest one is love. Everybody in here has a love they cain't git over; there's always been "the one".'

Elijah believed something flickered in the nurse's eyes, like a flash of lightning across a dark and gloomy sky, but he refrained from being too inquisitive. 'Do—' He paused, clearing his throat and glancing away. 'Do you think it might give her the strength to come back to me? I've heard about this thing: terminal lucidity. A final moment of lucidity before a person kicks the bucket. It's a last surge of brainpower where even the catatonic can stir from a coma and speak one last time. This lucidity thing doesn't last long; it's one final moment of awareness before they cross over. Well, that's what I'm waiting for.'

Nurse Mildred placed a hand on his shoulder. 'Ya'd be surprised what miracles I have witnessed durin' my time, darlin'. The power of prayer an' thought fo' the ill is damned miraculous. Never stop believin'; never stop the optimistic thinkin' an' prayers, 'cause ya never know. Mayhap she will return ta us after all.'

Chapter 22

THE FOLLOWING DAY marked the third occasion when Chloe and Elijah were in each other's company.

For Elijah, her company was becoming a pleasure rather than a hindrance. Chloe, who had arrived ten minutes earlier, wore a lemon-yellow floral knee-length dress and white buckle shoes. Once again she was alone, choosing to take the bus to Dunmore instead of going to her North Shore private school.

A springtime breeze swirled around the building, causing leaf litter to be swept into a whispering conglomeration. After giving Audrey a bed bath and changing the bedsheets, Nurse Mildred had opened a window to let fresh air into room 217 before anyone arrived. Chloe said she was thankful the room had ceased smelling sterile like a hospital and was now more akin to a flower shop. She and Elijah took a moment to appreciate the view of the surrounding trees and flower beds, which were filled with blossoming roses, sunflowers and jasmine. Sydney Harbour glittered vividly in the background, its beauty beyond measure.

'Yoo-hoo,' Nurse Mildred sung, poking her head through the doorway. 'How are we this mornin'?'

'Very well; yourself?' Elijah said, looking at the tray she carried.

'Darlin', I'm happier than ol' Blue layin' on the porch chewin' on a big ol' catfish head!'

Elijah cupped his forehead with a shaky hand. 'Jesus H. Christ, give me strength.'

'Hush now 'n' never use the Lord's name in vain.' Elijah peered up. 'I thought ya might like mornin' tea, kiddies.' Nurse Mildred handed them a plate each of strawberry gateau with whipped cream and flaked almonds. The tray also included two cups of white tea with white sugar satchels and stirring sticks, and packets of assorted biscuits.

So very thoughtful, Elijah thought, smiling with gratitude, noting the faint fragrance of vanilla from Nurse Mildred's black hair, which showed streaks of silver and grey.

As if right on cue, banging from room 215 erupted, just as it had the day before, and the day before that. 'Nurse ... nurse ... help!'

'What'd I tell ya?' Nurse Mildred yelled over her shoulder. 'Hush yer whistle; I'll be there in a doggone jiffy!'

No wonder she has grey hairs, Elijah thought.

Nurse Mildred sighed and closed her eyes for a split second. 'Arguin' with that fella is 'bout as practical as puttin' a steerin' wheel on a mule.' Her whole body jiggled with laughter.

Elijah considered how hard people like Nurse Mildred worked to ensure that elderly people were properly taken care of, but he knew a job like this must have its limits, and patience was a prerequisite. Some poor folk in here didn't even know what day it was, let alone how demanding and sometimes discourteous they were to those caring for them. Elijah was about to suggest she take the load off and shoot the shit, but he guessed she'd decline and he couldn't take her precious time away from folks who needed her help.

After Nurse Mildred left, Chloe dunked an Arnott's Scotch Finger into her steaming English breakfast tea, while Elijah began to recount the day he arrived at Audrey's.

Chapter 23

THEN – 1964

CARRYING A BUNCH OF LILACS and dressed in a smart new slack suit, Elijah knocked on the door at six o'clock. The price tag dug into his neck, so he reached up, tore it off, and stashed it in his pocket before wiping his sweaty hand over his pants.

Audrey opened the door, and he was stunned not just by her pink pastel dress, but also by the appealing, homely smell wafting from the kitchen. Elijah knew right then what he wanted most.

This. To come home to this type of situation every day would make him the happiest man alive. Within that split second of her opening the door, she held the answer to every question he'd ever had; the key to all the doors that needed unlocking, and the solution to the problems he needed help solving. With just one look, he saw the rest of his life in front of his eyes, and no-one painted a better picture of his future than she did.

'Come in.' Her eyes darted to the lilacs. Knowing he was in dire straits, Elijah wanted to run on the double. Accepting her offer was like a double-edged sword – it could be the best thing, or it could be the worst. With a pounding heart, Elijah surmised that if she chose to exercise her power over him, she could be the type to bring him to his knees and make him beg for more.

With his pulse beating fast, he stepped over the threshold, offering her the flowers. There'd be no turning back now.

'They're beautiful,' she said, taking the flowers, her cheeks flushing as red as her seductive lipstick.

Elijah couldn't stop gawking at her as she buried her nose into the fragrant posy. One minute she'd been a stranger, next minute he wanted her to become his *everything* in a world full of nothing.

Something fierce swept over him; he wanted to possess her the way she possessed him, so he pushed her against the wall, captured her face with both hands, and caved in to his consuming desires.

From the moment their lips collided, he wanted everything she had; everything she was going to have. He wanted them to share their hopes and dreams, and he wanted it all *now*.

Audrey's body froze as his lips crashed down onto hers. It was as if they were fused together by natural causes, like waves crashing over the sand. When Audrey's body slackened and she threw her arms around his neck, they made out against the wall before moving to the lounge room on the right, tumbling onto a sofa that'd seen better days, kissing and grabbing wherever they could. They *needed* to merge: it was the only logical thing to do.

Elijah pulled back, looking deep into her wide-set eyes as she panted. 'I thought you said you didn't want me?'

He didn't want to let on that her words at the parlour had hurt, so he masked it with an arrogant snarl. 'Tell me you lied,' he whispered, searching for the truth in her eyes.

She turned away, her bottom lip trembling. 'No!'

Elijah grabbed her chin between his thumb and forefinger and turned her face towards his. 'Admit it.'

A tear slipped out and trickled down the side of her face as she closed her eyes. 'I lied.'

Upon hearing her confession, Elijah kissed her hard as they sank deeper into the sofa – deeper into a world of their own.

Elijah leaned back to remove her white heels before starting on her nylon stockings. She was trembling like a dog in a thunderstorm. Hell, so was he, but he went slow for her sake, offering words of comfort as he removed her clothing like he was unwrapping a long-awaited present on Christmas Day, while his hungry eyes roamed over her uninhibited, flawless body.

'Wait, I-I can't do this.' She pushed at his bare chest just as he unclasped his belt buckle.

Elijah's fingers stilled as she sat upright, covering her exposed breasts. 'Why?' He feared she didn't want him nearly as much as he wanted her, but they both panted like wild beasts.

Someone knocked on the front door, stealing their focus. They both froze, thinking the same thing: Lloyd had come home early.

'Shit,' Elijah whispered as he held her head against his heaving chest, but then he realised if it was Lloyd, why would he knock if he had his own set of keys?

Audrey dressed faster than someone sneezing, and Elijah zipped up his fly – with difficulty.

Audrey yelled out: 'Coming!' which caused Elijah to moan in anguish as he ran to hide behind the wall of the lounge room. It was right beside the front door so he could hear an Avon representative talking to Audrey about cosmetics.

Audrey politely told the lady she needed nothing before sending her away. Elijah glanced at the trampled flowers on the floor, conceding it was probably a good thing – at least Audrey could bin them and wouldn't have to lie to Lloyd, who would no doubt ask who gave them to her.

After closing the door, Audrey peered around the corner. Her blue eyes spoke of guilt or shame – he couldn't tell which – but it made him smile because there was nothing wrong with the way they had been carrying on, in his humble opinion.

'Oh golly, look at the flowers.' She bent to retrieve the dishevelled posy.

'Don't sweat it,' he murmured with a slight smile, hauling her into his embrace as she wrapped her arms around his waist, nestling her head under his chin. He closed his eyes. 'Has it been as hard for you as it has for me, these past few days?'

Her response was a meagre nod before she choked out, 'Yes.'

Elijah held her as they spoke to each other with their body language. He never knew how fulfilling a hug could be, but it seemed Audrey was going to keep teaching him new things. It felt exquisite holding her feminine frame to his body.

Audrey broke free from his arms, her eyes wide. 'Oh no, the dinner!'

She sprinted to the kitchen as he stood there, smiling, while Audrey cleared the smoke wafting from the oven.

He wanted to feel like this forever.

Chapter 24

'IT'S HARD TO imagine Nanna as sexy, because she has white hair, wrinkles, false teeth, and whiskers,' Chloe said, straight-faced.

Elijah chuckled, almost choking on his soggy Monte Carlo. 'Trust me, she didn't always. She was *the* most beautiful woman in the world. Even better than Sophia Loren!'

'It sounds like you really loved her.' She opened Audrey's diary with her free hand.

He glanced into his cup of tea where floating crumbs swirled amongst clouds of milk. 'Kid, you have *no* idea.'

'Let's read more, okay?' Chloe smiled, then looked at the diary. *'9th December 1964. Dear Diary, tonight was heaven. After dinner, which I thought was a success despite the chops being a little crisp, we went upstairs to my bedroom and watched some telly. I uncovered our mutual love for* The Twilight Zone, The Flintstones, *and* Gilligan's Island. *It was bliss, and he swore he is no longer with Georgie. I wasn't watching what was on the boob tube, although I think I put on* The Munsters, *I was more aware of the fact I was cuddling up to his chest. It was so romantic and as he stroked my arm, I looked up and caught him smiling. I asked him straight if the rumours of his arrest were true. He said they were. One night he'd been walking down the street around midnight, admitting he was completely blown, when three guys attacked him for his wallet. EJ lost his marbles and fought back – 3-on-1. By the time the fuzz came, one guy was out cold on the pavement and the other two had scrammed. EJ was intoxicated and had been in fights before, so they hauled him down to the station where he was locked up, but all charges got dropped when his parents intervened. Over the years he said he'd heard the story getting bigger and more fanciful. I may be off my rocker, but I believe him. EJ kissed me all throughout the evening. It held so much promise for the future, and like some hussy, I couldn't get enough. If I am being honest, we almost made love as soon as he walked through the door! He makes me feel alive. He makes me feel like I am protected in a world full of people who are out to hurt me because I'm "different". We heard Lloyd come through the front door at around midnight, where he stumbled over to the staircase and passed out. EJ kissed me passionately at the top of the stairs before climbing down, stepping over Lloyd's body, and tiptoed to the front door. I felt so special when he blew me a kiss before leaving. Golly, I think I am falling in love. Audrey.'*

Chloe tore away from the diary with a wide, closed-lipped smile.

'Thank you for that, kid.' Elijah gave an appreciative nod, wiping a crumb from the corner of his mouth as he eyed Audrey.

Chloe licked her lips and popped the last of the gateau into her mouth, washing it down with the hot tea.

'Pardon?' he said, looking over.

She frowned and shook her head. 'I didn't say anything ...?'

'Oh, sorry, mind's playing tricks on me again.' He laughed it off and then cleared his rusty pipes. 'Is there an entry the next day? I would like to know from her point of view what happened, because the next day after our special night, I drove over to the ice cream parlour to surprise her with a visit.' Chloe put down her teacup and flicked through the pages. 'I was walking towards the shop when, through the window, I saw Georgie and a woman called Shelley Adams talking to Audrey at the front counter. I watched them like an eagle, but to this day I still don't know for certain what they said.'

'Here it is,' Chloe said. *'10ᵗʰ December 1964. Dear Diary, what a day! It started off well, but as I was in the parlour, Georgie and her friend Shelley came in, looking fab in identical knee-length plum-and-chocolate suede platforms, and checkerboard mini-shift dresses! As they approached the counter, they started talking to me, but I couldn't hear what they were saying and I felt embarrassed as I thought my batteries had conked out. I turned away from them and turned the volume up as high as it could go. But when I turned around, they yelled in my transistor, nearly blowing my drums out. It had been a set-up all along! They'd convinced the few people in the shop to keep quiet, and they turned the jukebox off. They compounded the hurt by laughing at me, and so did EJ's friends, Jonathan and Lawrence, who were sitting in a booth. Before I knew it, EJ bounded through the door with a scowl that had indignation written all over it ...'*

Chapter 25

THEN – 1964

'WHAT THE HELL do you think you're doing?' Elijah yelled, rushing towards the counter.

'EJ, w-what are you doing here?' Georgie said.

He stood close enough their breaths mingled. 'Answer my damn question!'

'Don't have a cow, we were just getting some grub,' Shelley Adams said, flicking brown hair behind her shoulder.

By this point, the few patrons gathered closer.

'Hey, man, what's going on?' Jonathan said from the booth.

'You're a bunch of fucking losers,' Elijah spat out, his chest heaving. 'I can't believe you treat people like this, it's disgusting.'

'Whoa, what's your beef?' Lawrence said with a shoulder shrug.

Elijah turned and pointed a forefinger in Lawrence's face. 'I swear to God, you guys say one more word and I'll knock you flat. We're no longer friends; you can all get stuffed.'

Audrey grabbed her bag and ran out the door. As she hurried up the street, he bounded out the front door of the parlour; the door slamming with a resounding *BANG!* behind him.

'Wait, please!' he screamed, running after her. Elijah soon reached her, grabbed her around the waist and held on tight from behind as she struggled against him. His cheek pressed against the back of her head as he panted, saying, 'Shh, it's all right.'

'Just let me g-go,' she pleaded, sobbing.

'I *can't* let you go! Haven't you worked that out by now?'

She clawed his forearm. 'I just want to be alone.'

He spun her around, rougher than intended. 'Why? Why are you trying to push me away?'

She sniffled and clenched her eyes shut. 'Because you deserve better than hanging out with this freak of nature.'

He sucked in a huge gulp of air. '*What* did you just say? You take that back right now!' She whimpered, trying to shield her face. 'Listen to me well.' He grabbed her shoulders with both hands. 'You're better than any person I have ever come across. You're kind-hearted, you're caring, you're hard-working; you're better than those scum back there in the parlour.' He paused, breathing hard as she continued to cry. 'You're better than that.' His eyes softened and he lowered his register. 'Why are you letting them get to you? Why are you so concerned about the opinions of people who are lower than you? Don't let them get in here.' He tapped her temple. 'You're stronger than this; you're the strongest person I know. Don't let them win.' He kissed her forehead and she clutched his forearms as he grabbed her face between his hands. 'I don't want to see you like this again, do you hear me?' He brushed tears away from her flushed face with the pads of his thumbs before planting a kiss on her red, salty nose. 'Seeing you like this hurts me, too, Audrey.'

She looked up, snuffling, staring deep into his eyes.

'I ... kinda like ya,' he said. 'I am not afraid to say it out loud. No matter what life throws at you, that's okay, because I will protect you. I will *always* have your back, no matter what.' Fresh tears cascaded down Audrey's face. 'I need you, like you need me. Believe me, I don't want anyone else – just you – if you'll have me?'

And just like that, as the sun shone brightly upon them and kids played marbles in a nearby yard just like any ordinary day, extraordinarily, Elijah Samuels – the 'bad boy of the Gong' – had asked Audrey to be his girl.

'Yes,' she whispered through trembling lips, 'and good luck.'

Elijah laughed and kissed her, wrapping his arms around her body, pulling her close.

After they finished kissing, Elijah lit a cigarette and draped his arm around Audrey's shoulders. Now they were official. As they walked back past the parlour, he instructed her to wrap an arm around his waist. At first she hesitated, worried that it would stir the pot. A chill ran through his body at the exhilaration of holding her, plus *they* were all inside watching. Elijah knew Audrey wouldn't glance inside Betty-Sue's, but he looked with his head held high – a protective arm around his girl as he led her to his car, where they discussed their next date.

'How about the drive-in again?' he said, taking a drag as they leaned against the warm bonnet.

When Audrey sniffled again, he retrieved a box of Scotties from his glove compartment.

'Thank you.' She took one and blew her nose. 'Why do you have a box of tissues in the car?'

Fuck! 'Ahh, just out of habit. Never know when you'll need 'em.' Technically that'd been true on many, *many* occasions.

'I thought you were going to a party tonight?' She glanced over her right shoulder as if fearing his now ex-friends might burst out of Betty-Sue's brandishing weapons.

Elijah blew a plume of smoke away from Audrey. 'Don't sweat it. I'd prefer to see a flick with you, anyway.'

Audrey sniffled again, peering out beyond the sandy shores of the beach as a seagull squawked.

'I will let you pick the movie,' he coaxed, knowing full well she thought *Goldfinger* was a bummer for some strange reason.

Her face lit up as she stood in front of him, gazing into his eyes. 'You'll let me pick?'

Elijah took one last drag, flicked the butt into the nearest bush, and got off the bonnet. 'You bet, because you're my girl now and I promise you, you'll want for nothing.' He grabbed her hands. 'Whatever you want shall be yours, I swear it.'

Elijah pulled her in for an embrace as more tears ran down her face. When her tears subsided, he leaned back. 'Do we have a deal? I'll pick you up at seven and you choose the movie?'

She bit her bottom lip and stared at the asphalt. 'Uncle Lloyd won't let me go with you.'

He kicked the grille of his EH with the heel of his boot. 'Goddammit to hell, Audrey, you're not a child, he doesn't have dibs on you!'

She double-blinked before standing taller. 'I know that; I'm not stupid!'

They glared at each other for a split second before melting into a passionate kiss.

Chapter 26

CHLOE LOOKED UP from the diary, shaking her head with an open mouth. 'Wow, you had mean friends.'

Elijah's jaw hardened. 'I didn't know it at the time, or maybe I did; maybe it took an incident like that for me to realise how we looked in other people's eyes. I've done a lot of bad things in my time, but I never belittled someone with a disability.'

Chloe glanced at her grandmother. 'You can't tell she has a hearing aid, though.'

'How far technology has advanced since the sixties, eh?'

Chloe returned her gaze to his. 'I am glad you told off your friends!'

'They deserved it; they were lucky I didn't strike out because I was pretty angry.'

Chloe's lips retreated and she tilted her head. 'Forgive me, but it seems like you were an angry person with an attitude problem.'

Elijah let his head fall back as he chortled. 'Truer words were never spoken, kid; it was part of the reason I joined the army. I suppose it stemmed from my upbringing. I hated being privileged because folks around me were always facile.' Chloe gazed into the distance as if pondering her own fortunate childhood. 'I was rebellious at a young age because I didn't have a stable upbringing – does that make sense?' Chloe's nod wasn't convincing. 'See, I had a nuclear family, but we weren't a true *family*, if that's clear?' Chloe's lips twisted as she *ummed*. 'I was never disciplined because my parents weren't ever there to give me a clip around the ear or a stern talking to if I did something wrong.' Chloe lowered her eyes and nodded. She now understood. 'That's why I think I acted out: partly because of my want for their attention, and partly because I damn well could. My parents weren't around for most of my upbringing. They didn't come and see me perform in school plays, they didn't cheer me on at sports carnivals, they just didn't care. When I didn't get anywhere with them, I lashed out my anger on people who sometimes didn't deserve it, so then others would chalk it up to me being *the spoiled rich kid.*'

'Are you still rich?'

Elijah was quick to grin. 'Why, do you want to club me over the noggin?'

Chloe shook her head as though she thought he believed she was capable. 'No! I don't like violence. I was just wondering if you were.'

Elijah grabbed his hanky just in time to capture the black muck he hacked up from his congested lungs. He thought it resembled something you'd fill potholes with. She raised an inquisitive eyebrow as he cleared his throat. 'Sorry. Well, look, not by today's standards. I suppose the money I have could buy me a second-hand car and a loaf of bread, but that's about it.'

Chloe grinned. 'You are an odd person; you're the only person I've met who can yell and get angry while blushing.'

Elijah leaned over and lowered his voice to a conspiratorial whisper. 'Don't tell anyone; it'll ruin my reputation.'

They both shared a laugh before Elijah stopped to cough into his hanky once more. He wiped the spittle off his lips and faced Chloe, who'd opened her mouth to say something, but as she looked towards the doorway, her face broke out into a wide grin.

'Who the hell are you, friend?!'

Elijah pivoted towards the man's baritone voice, as Chloe shouted: 'Uncle Tim, Uncle Tim!'

'Hey, Chloe!'

Elijah eyed the tall man, who swept Chloe into his arms. His light-brown hair and dark, stormy eyes were not attributes from Audrey.

His name's Timothy? Interesting, Elijah thought as he observed the joyous family reunion in front of him.

Just like Angela, he, too, had an air of superiority about him, with his designer suit, expensive-smelling cologne, and gold-plated wristwatch. Elijah knew this would not end well – for Timothy, that was. Elijah used to eat pieces of crumpet like him for breakfast when he was younger, but age was nothing but a number and he was in no mood to be bowled over.

'My God, you're so big now!' Timothy said, inspecting Chloe from head-to-toe.

Seconds later, in shuffled a woman with silky black hair and Oriental features – she smiled upon seeing Chloe. Elijah's nostrils flared at the sight of her, his heartbeat accelerating at an alarming rate.

After completing his assessment of Chloe, Timothy turned to glare at Elijah. 'Well?'

Elijah focused his attention back to the forty-something bloke, regathering his strength, breathing deep into his diaphragm as his toes uncurled. 'Well, who the hell are *you*?'

Timothy exhaled and released Chloe from his arms. She looked back and forth between the two men as Timothy said, 'I'm Audrey's son, and I repeat my question. Who the hell are you?'

Elijah glanced out the window to admire the silver oaks swaying in the wind like sultry flamenco dancers, as varicoloured leaves whipped up in a cyclical frenzy near the garden. 'I must say, I'd never forget a face but Christ, in your case I'll make an exception.'

Timothy inhaled sharply. 'Here I thought you were a brain-dead idiot, in which case I could have forgiven you. But the fact you're as sharp as a tack means I'll have no qualms in telling you to piss off before I remove you myself.'

Elijah remained staring out the window. 'I've come across some shitty people in my lifetime, but you and your goddamned sister win the gold trophy, you know that?' He turned to face Timothy. 'And I'm speaking with over eighty years' worth of experience.'

Timothy's teeth clenched. 'I ought to—'

Elijah sat forward. 'What? What, bucko, come on! You just try it and I'll knock you so hard you'll see tomorrow, today!'

Timothy pawed the air and chuckled. 'I could kill you in a heartbeat, old man.'

Elijah's eyelids narrowed. 'I've killed thirteen people in this lifetime and there are two things I hate: arseholes and odd numbers.'

'What's goin' on here?' Nurse Mildred said, rushing in.

Elijah slapped his knee. 'Can't I have a minute's peace here, please, Winifred? Bring Apollo Creed over there a bucket of ice cubes and tell him to cool the hell down.'

Timothy expelled pent-up air. 'Excuse me—'

'You're excused,' Elijah said.

Timothy tsked. 'I'm Audrey's son, Tim. I've just arrived from London with my wife, Tida' – he pointed to his partner, who frowned – 'and I find this jerk in here alone with my niece.'

Elijah cocked his head to the side. 'What exactly makes me a jerk? That I'm sitting here having an adult conversation with Chloe about her grandmother?' Timothy glanced at Nurse Mildred before Elijah continued. 'No, I think you and your shit-for-brains sister believe I'm the sort of man inclined to take down her panties when no-one is around!'

Nurse Mildred bowed her head and turned towards Timothy. 'Could ya step over yonder fo' a jiffy?'

'Yeah, get outta here,' Elijah mumbled, but Nurse Mildred ushered Timothy outside before he could retort, with Tida in tow.

Once Timothy and Tida were out of sight, Nurse Mildred stepped back inside the room and folded her hands together. Her sunken eyes portrayed regret, yet her straightened spine said she was a professional who hadn't spent years training only to be fired for not following protocol. 'I think mayhap ya should leave, Eli, jist so Tim can have some quiet time with Aud.'

'You're kicking me out?' Elijah asked with a bitter smile. 'You siding with him, is that it?'

Nurse Mildred held up her hands, palms outward. 'Sugah, right now he's hotter than a jalapeño's coochie! I jist think it's too nice a day ta waste on bein' inside.' She smiled with a scrunched nose and gave a petite shoulder shrug. 'Mayhap ya two should run off 'n' enjoy the sun fo' a change?' Elijah looked at Chloe, who had a downturned mouth. 'Let Tim 'n' his wife enjoy private family time with Aud. After all, they have flown all this way 'n' he is next of kin.'

Nurse Mildred was right. To them, he was a nobody. His name wouldn't appear on anything Audrey owned or possessed – heck they hadn't even heard of him until now. If roles were reversed, he might have acted the same way.

'Ya'll should go play outside 'n' I'll fix up some sandwiches 'n' iced tea fo' ya. How does that dill ya pickle?'

Elijah Samuels conceded Nurse Mildred was right about one thing. Outside, the sun radiated in a cloudless sky, so it would be a shame to let the day go to waste cooped up inside a room where you could skim the tension off the air with a ladle, and every few seconds were filled with a monotonous beeping sound that could, at any moment, become a continuous bcccccccp.

Chapter 27

'ELI?' CHLOE INTERRUPTED his train of thought. They sat on cast-iron, ivory-coloured chairs at a round mosaic table sheltered by a white umbrella. 'I believe Nanna really loved you.'

Elijah's lips formed what he hoped would suffice as a smile while gazing at the glistening harbour, hearing boat horns toot and magpies' warbles above the whistling wind.

'I know I am only halfway through the story, but I really mean it. The fact that she kept this diary with her after all this time means something. I find things stuck on the pages – like this.' Chloe showed him a drive-in movie stub and business cards from restaurants she and Elijah had visited. 'I know it must hurt that none of us know who you are, but I don't think she hid you from us because she wanted to forget. I think she did it because she really did love you.'

Elijah turned away from the swaying willows to see his withered face reflected in her youthful eyes. 'Again, I must ask to be sure, are you really only twelve years old?'

Chloe smiled and lifted her shoulders to her ears. 'Yes, but as I said, I am turning thirteen in a few months. You're welcome to come to my party if you want.'

'Thanks, kid,' he said with a tender smile, scratching his stubble. She was such a sweet child; it seemed kindness and compassion had skipped a generation in her family.

Elijah wanted to humour her gesture, so he said, 'Where are you having it, McDonalds?'

Chloe frowned. 'I hope you're joking.' His mouth dropped open. 'But in case you aren't, no, I am having it at the Art Gallery of New South Wales.'

What ever happened to kids being kids? he thought, gazing out at the iconic view once more. What he wanted to know was, how many more sunsets did Audrey have left?

As Elijah pondered how on earth he would survive the pain of knowing he and she no longer existed on the same plane, Nurse Mildred appeared, carrying a tray with a silver platter of exquisite-looking sandwiches, and cheese and crackers. Elijah salivated over the sandwiches: cheese and tomato; salmon and cream cheese; egg, lettuce and mayonnaise; and (his personal favourite) beef and mustard. She'd also brought a jug of peach iced tea, stating that it would go down well on a hot day like today.

'Lordy, I jist saw a young woman inside wearin' pants so tight I swear ya could see her religion!' Elijah bent forward to laugh as Chloe frowned. 'Boy, I'll tell ya, Eli … ya got that fella inside sweatin' like a Mexican racehorse! Yer actin' like a right gizzard!'

Elijah's shrug was more of a jolt. 'How the hell do you want me to act? Like some friggin' pushover?'

Nurse Mildred pursed her lips and gave him a playfully stern look. 'Sugah, if yer lookin' fo' sympathy, it's in the dictionary between shit 'n' syphilis – excuse the potty mouth, pumpkin!'

Chloe waved this away; her attention was on the platter as her tummy rumbled.

'Hey, I'm not looking for anything. I just want to be by Audrey's side; am I asking too bloody much here? Am I asking for mountains to be moved? All I goddamn want is to be around her again, why is this so *fucking* hard to comprehend – I, too, am sorry for the potty mouth, kid, please excuse my French.'

Chloe shook her head, her lips holding back a grin.

Nurse Mildred regarded him; her double chin more pronounced as she tilted her head. 'Ya know somethin'?' Elijah shrugged *What?* 'Yer startin' ta grow on me like fungi.'

Elijah couldn't help but grin. 'Christ, if that's not Hallmark-worthy, I don't know what is.'

She placed her hands on her hips and chuckled. 'Now stay outta trouble, ya hear?'

After Nurse Mildred winked and left, Elijah shook his head and smiled. 'Winifred's a lovely lady – wouldn't you agree, kid?'

Chloe nodded but was focused on the cheese and peppered crackers.

As she picked up the silver knife, Elijah said, 'You, ah, need any help with that?'

She gave him a sassy, offended look, and he tried in vain to conceal a grin as she sliced off two pieces of creamy camembert.

Chapter 28

'AUDREY CHOSE *MARY Poppins*. As soon as I connected the wire to my car window, she squealed and bounced, her head almost hitting the roof of the car. That's all I could have wanted. I often wondered from what point it was that I started changing for the better; perhaps it was that night.

'The truth was, Jordan Tattle *had* invited me to his party, but the last one I attended turned into something the adults called a sweat party. I didn't want a bar of it. That wasn't my gig, but what Jordan did best was burn rubber. We used to race near an abandoned factory out past Fairfield – me in my Ford XB Falcon, and Jordan in his Corvette Stingray. On a few occasions, the coppers almost busted us for drag racing, sending all the partygoers scrambling like roaches under torchlight. They never could catch us.

'Whenever punks tried to walk in on our turf and stir the pot, it was always Jordan by my side during the brawl, which sometimes included pickets from wooden fences. There was a time where I chose Jordan and his wild ways over anyone, including Georgie.'

Elijah smiled broadly when he remembered comparing his evening – which would have included drinking, smoking, and drag racing in front of pretty girls in miniskirts – to being with Audrey watching a bloody Disney flick.

'When "Supercalifragilisticexpialidocious" came on, I wanted to drive off, but Audrey's face lit up and I knew I could never intentionally disappoint her. So, I stayed, ate the popcorn, and watched her sway away to "Chim Chim Cher-ee". I would have done it over again if it meant making her smile.'

When Elijah turned the page, he caught Chloe suckling a dollop of creamy cheese stuck to her thumb. Realising Elijah was watching her, her eyes widened, and she removed her thumb, offering a sheepish, apologetic smile.

Elijah frowned, patting his congested chest. 'Why did you stop?'

Chloe's cheeks flushed scarlet. 'I'm sorry—'

'Hell, I don't need an apology! All you did was lick your finger, who gives a damn?'

Her eyes fluttered. 'It's not considered polite.'

'I don't give a flying rat's arse about that, do you understand?'

She nodded, but her rumpled brow indicated a mental tug-of-war between right and wrong. Good and bad.

'Jesus, I think there are bigger things to worry about than licking your finger, or knife, or dinner plate. Christ, does your mother reprimand you when you're "insubordinate"?' he said with air quotations. He thought he detected tears in her eyes, but his failing eyesight was unreliable – with or without glasses.

'I don't understand.'

Elijah coughed into a fist, causing his eyes to water. 'You can break wind, burp, stick your whole friggin' fist into your mouth, but never apologise for such trivial things – not to me, not to anyone – do we have a deal?'

She stared at him, breathing hard before she bit her lip and finally made the deuces sign.

Elijah gave an honest laugh, which brought on a fit of coughing.

'Are you okay?' she said as he spat into his hanky, which was becoming ever-present in his hand these days.

Elijah nodded, swallowed, and gulped for air. 'Now you're catching on.'

She sniggered. 'Shall I read now or are you just going to babble on?'

Elijah waited for her to begin while he struggled to lift the heavy jug that was filled to the brim with ice cubes, mint leaves, and assorted seasonal fruit slices.

'11ᵗʰ December 1964. Dear Diary, yesterday I had the pleasure of going to the drive-in and watching Mary Poppins, *starring Julie Andrews and Dick Van Dyke. I LOVED IT! It was clever and innovative for a film of this calibre. I know EJ hated it, but he didn't complain once, nor make any sounds of disgust or boredom. In fact, after we left the drive-in, he asked me about the film and we spoke about the intelligence of the director. I think this movie will be a hit – it is just so far out. After the movie ended, I should have gone home as I was already pushing the envelope with Uncle Lloyd.*

'But, I wanted to show EJ I care about him and that I am serious about our future. So I stayed out until one in the morning to continue on from the buzz. EJ took me to a lookout at the highest peak in Wollongong, which overlooks the beach and surrounding lights. It was breathtaking, for lack of a better word, and we were near a lighthouse. After he opened my car door and led me outside, we laid on the grass, gazing at the twinkling stars with his transistor radio beside us. He tuned into 2CM and our night started off with "House of the Rising Sun". Honestly, I have never heard a song quite like it.

'Critics say we're going through a British Invasion and now I know why. England is producing some of the greatest songs in radio history. It is that groovy, I feel blessed to witness firsthand the frenzy their music is causing. I had never believed in the power of music until Elvis, the Beatles and now, the Animals. EJ and I have many things in common, but our biggest one is music. We might not agree on movie choices, but when the songs kept on playing over the radio, we found we knew most of them, and word-for-word, too. Evidently, I feel like this is where I am meant to be.

'Yes, I have Uncle Lloyd, but I feel distant from him – like there's a generational gap. That's where EJ comes into the picture. I am positive those above sent him to protect me and save my future – I wouldn't be surprised if my parents were behind this. Lord knows how painful it is for me to wake each day without them; struggling for reasons to get out of bed. I miss them so much. Maybe EJ is my saviour? But, as he and I were getting to know each other more, I asked him straight about the number of women he's bedded. The look he gave me said it all—'

'Ahh, I'll take over from here,' Elijah said, shifting in his chair as Chloe tittered while reaching for a twig of green grapes. This was a conversation Elijah remembered as though it had happened yesterday …

Chapter 29

THEN – 1964

ELIJAH'S EYES DRIFTED to Audrey's, and in the moonlight her face appeared more youthful – no longer nineteen years old – more like a child. His chest expanded on a deep breath. 'I'm not going to lie; there's been a couple of women in the past.'

'A couple as in two?'

He sat up to view the royal-blue ocean. The water seemed to merge with the grey clouds on the vast horizon, above which the night sky was clothed in twinkling stars. A gust of wind disturbed the ocean's surface, giving it the appearance of shattered glass, mirroring how this conversation was headed, he thought.

'Um, a little higher than two, but it's just a number, really.'

'How old were you when you first gave it away?'

It was blatant Audrey needed to know if she was destined to the same fate as the others. Would Elijah ditch her like he had Georgie when someone new, shiny, and different came along?

'Sixteen.' His fingers fumbled with his chrome lighter to ignite the Camel dangling between his lips.

Her spine extended. 'I see.'

Elijah jetted smoke from his nostrils, his eyes focused on her as she averted her gaze. 'It isn't what this is.' He reached out to touch her, but she stiffened. 'I'm not here just to get into your skirt. I mean, I have thought about it, of course, but … it's not like that.' He stole a deep breath. 'I mean to say, I am attracted to you, but it's not *all* I want.'

Audrey's furrowed eyebrows and downturned mouth made Elijah want to disappear into the vast ocean in front – the anxiety and nerves were getting to them both.

'Audrey, please. I am no saint – I'll be the first to admit it. Hell, we almost kicked it back at your place the other day.' Audrey's body tensed at the memory of what had almost happened on the sofa. 'But you're different and I'm happy to wait because I know it'll be worth it, and for the first time in my life I am not talking about scoring.' He raised her chin with a forefinger, but she focused on the lighthouse.

'Is this a line you tell all the chicks?'

'No,' he whispered, attempting to caress her face as she smoothed over her green swing skirt.

Audrey surveyed the ocean, watching the waves do the bidding of the moon's gravitational pull, crashing against the rocks and lapping the sand with lacy foam before retreating. The onshore breeze carried with it the smell of salt and seaweed. 'A Hard Day's Night' came over Elijah's Zenith Royal 40-G transistor radio, as a cherry-red Hillman IMP rolled into the car park, gravel crunching like cereal upon its arrival.

'Can I be honest?' Elijah said, fingering her ribboned curly ponytail tied high upon her head.

'Oh, why stop now?!'

Would she ever get over his tarnished past? He drew on the cigarette as though gasping for air. 'The truth is, I think most guys go through a stage of meaningless free love and maybe even drugs, but at the end of the day all a man wants more than anything is to be loved. We are no different to chicks when it all gets stripped back. To have that one special person to come home to is something we do eventually think about. We might be foolhardy and it may take a while for us to realise that, but if you think I introduce all these girls to my folks, then you're wrong.'

Audrey faced him, waiting for the shrieks of baked laughter coming from the Hillman's occupants to cease. 'Did you take Georgie?'

His lips pressed together as his flying thoughts struggled for balance. 'That's different – my parents play bridge with hers. Plus, Georgie and I went to school together, so we were friends first.'

'It's okay, you don't need to explain.'

Audrey rose to her knees, so Elijah grabbed her forearms and brought her down. 'Yes, I do. I am not a model citizen but I *know* I can improve, and you ... you make me want to be a better man.'

Audrey's body and hands relaxed.

'I don't know what it is about you, but you're so different from anyone I have ever met. We actually *talk*, ya know? Just being around you makes me want to straighten up and fly right. I don't know what you've done, but thank you. As for the sex part, for the first time in my life, I don't need it and I find myself craving other things from you; things that are more significant. Don't get me wrong, I can't wait to experience *that* with you, but if you suddenly took away what we have now and only gave me sex, I wouldn't want to be around you.'

They pulled up out the front of Lloyd's house a short while later. As Audrey reached for the door handle, Elijah grabbed onto her waist and pulled her to his chest, whispering into her ear from behind. 'Come here.'

She twisted in his hold, grunting.

'Audrey, I'm not going anywhere. I know you're scared. In the big scheme of things, words mean shit. If you want proof of how I feel then that's no problem, it's the you-believing-in-what-I-say part that'll be tough. I have never once told a girl I love her, not once. I didn't have to lie to get into girls' pantyhose – they willingly gave it, so I took it. It's never meant more to me than giving and receiving pleasure.' When she struggled and made sounds of protest, he held on tighter. 'I don't lie, so when the time comes be ready for it, because I am going to shower you with more than you've ever dreamed of. I know you've had a rough year but rest assured, sweetheart, I'm your family now.'

Chapter 30

ELIJAH KNEW A lingering problem wouldn't go away just by avoiding it. It hadn't worked with his testicular swelling, and it sure as hell wasn't going to work now. 'Listen, kid, perhaps you'd better spend some time with your aunt and uncle; after all, they have flown a long way. I'll be fine sitting here in the sun for a bit.' He gazed out towards the harbour. 'I could even work on my tan.'

'I don't really know my aunt – we don't talk much – and Uncle Tim will be around for a while. What we have is a time constraint, don't you agree?'

Twelve years old my wrinkly arse.

'Never assume that a person is going to be around, because before you know it, you're pining for them and wondering how the hell they escaped your grasp. For all we know, I could get hit by a bus and squashed like a pancake on my way home from here.'

Chloe loured. 'Let's just read some more stories. Uncle Tim can spend time with Nanna and then we'll go in soon.' Elijah raised a sceptical brow, so she held up both hands. 'I promise!'

He raked a shaky hand over his chin to remove the crumbs clinging to his skin like fluff on nylon fabric. 'Your mother is going to be here any minute and she wouldn't like this.'

'But Nanna would.' Her chin jutted forward. 'I'm sure she's smiling right now, knowing that you and I are sitting here together talking.'

Elijah swallowed a mouthful of refreshing iced tea while entertaining that thought, and noticed a book protruding from her pink schoolbag. 'I've seen you with that book for the past few days. What is that; your diary?'

She followed his eyeline to her bag. 'It's a visual diary. I don't write words; I draw what I see.'

'You're an artist?'

Chloe shrugged and tucked strands of silky brown hair behind her unpierced ears. *Probably not allowed such bodily harm until her thirtieth birthday.*

'It's only a hobby. Do you want to see some pictures?'

'Sure.' He flashed her a warm smile as she handed him the A4-sized pad.

Flicking through the pages, he marvelled at how well she drew and how she excelled in pretty much all areas of life. The man who was lucky enough to snatch her up one day would be one lucky son of a bitch. Well, it would come with a heavy compromise. A beautiful, talented wife with a fire-breathing dragon as a mother-in-law.

Elijah stopped at a black-and-white picture of her family sitting around a dinner table. Angela was focused on papers that lay next to her dinner plate. Elijah assumed it was Chloe's father, Seth, in the picture, sitting at the head of the table in a suit, mobile phone pressed to his ear. The picture was outstanding, yet paradoxically it was intrinsically sad. The image showed the most intricate details, including a crack in the centre fruit bowl and a crooked painting on the wall. Elijah swallowed his pain because when he looked deeper into Chloe's picture, he saw a reflective piece of his own childhood, and she had no idea how raw and vulnerable that nerve was. Most people would look on the surface and think *Wow, this is great for a twelve-year-old,* but only a select few would see it for what it really portrayed. *Most people look but never actually take the time to see,* he mused. Prime example: Angela.

'Did you really draw this, kid?'

Her narrowed eyes said she didn't know which way the conversation was heading. 'Yes.'

Elijah glanced down, refraining from running his oily fingers across the work of art. 'How long did it take you?'

Out of the corner of his eye, he saw her shoulders relax. 'I drew a little each night, sitting in the same place across three-and-a-half weeks.'

'And this is just a hobby of yours?'

She murmured in the back of her throat. 'It's a passion, but my parents don't think it's suitable.'

His head snapped back. 'What, as a vocation?'

'If that means job, then yes.'

Ah, finally a word this whizz-kid doesn't comprehend.

'They're unsure about it; they would prefer me to have a reliable job.'

He raised a mocking eyebrow and enunciated, 'Oh, really?'

She nodded while slurping the rest of her drink. Elijah noted that if Angela were here, that slurping would warrant a reprimand.

'Yes, being an artist doesn't bring in the best money in the beginning.'

Elijah slapped his knee and choked back a cough of rage. 'Who cares about money? Damn you people, there's more to life!'

Chloe jumped, but she held her own. 'I know that, but how will I live if I don't earn money?'

Elijah handed the book back to Chloe. 'How often do you think about being an artist?'

Without hesitation she said, 'Every day.'

'Then you mustn't quit, especially if it's a passion and if it's something you can't stop thinking about.' He clenched his brittle fists together and held them in front of his heaving chest to emphasise his advice. 'You must not give up, do you hear?'

She blinked and nodded as if she appreciated his words, but it would take more than a few words to undo her parents' mantra of making it clear this was only a pipedream. 'Yes.'

After Chloe showed Elijah more pictures with added narration (including a stunning portrait of a blue-black satin bowerbird) they resumed storytelling whilst enjoying the last of the sandwiches.

Chloe licked her lips and rubbed her arm. 'Can I ask a question?'

'I reckon you can ask me anything you like.' Elijah paused, wiping a crumb off his lip. 'Doesn't mean I'm going to answer.'

She frowned.

He laughed, a hand to his stomach. 'I'm joking, kid! I'm as open as a prostitute.' She gasped. 'What do you want to know?'

She stared at her hands, disregarding his lurid comment. 'How did her parents die?'

Elijah straightened his back, his eyes trailing from hers. 'Sweetheart, it's not gonna make for proper lunch banter. Perhaps we'll leave that for another time.'

Chapter 31

'*14*TH *December 1964. Dear Diary, last night opened my eyes, and it begs the question: Can a leopard change his spots? EJ called me, and luckily Uncle Lloyd was downtown doing business, as he would have hung up the phone straight away. I told EJ I had the flu and couldn't come out, even though I was dying to see him – it has been two drawn-out days since I last saw his gorgeous face. After he hung up, I thought that'd be it – but no. While I was cuddling Misty and watching Johnny Chester's* Teen Scene, *I heard banging on the front door. As I opened it, EJ held out a container of fresh chicken soup that he told me he'd cooked. I was so overwhelmed and embarrassed, as I didn't look too flash, but he picked me up like a baby and took me to the kitchen to get a spoon, and then carried me up to my bedroom. It was there that he pulled up a chair beside the bed and spoon-fed me in silence. After* Teen Scene, *he introduced me to a new fad called* Homicide *– he said it was "prime watching". However, I couldn't keep my eyes off him. He wore a red-and-black polo shirt with faded Levis. His dark hair glistened – he'd obviously showered before coming, and his piercing green eyes danced whenever he looked at me. He spoon-fed me until I finished, then he kissed me on the forehead and whispered, "Good girl". Then EJ jumped on the bed beside me and held me until I fell asleep. When I awoke hours later I was alone, but Uncle Lloyd had returned, his snoring rattling the walls. Beside my pillow, EJ left a box of tissues, Medic's vapour spray, and Halls cough drops with a note saying "Get better soon, I miss being with you!" He is such a cool head! I want my future-self reading this to know that as of*

14ᵗʰ December 1964, I am swooning in love with ELIJAH SAMUELS and nothing will EVER change that. A thrilled and smitten, Audrey.'

Chloe gave Elijah the thumb of approval. 'Good job, Mr Smooth.' She gave a curt head nod, which caused him to cackle. 'Who was Misty?'

'Her cat.'

'I love cats! We don't have any pets, though. Do you?'

'Sure do. A German shepherd – best type of dog out there. Her name's Sheba, and I would be lost without her.'

Chloe beamed. 'I think you're both lucky to have each other. We don't even have a goldfish.'

'That is a shame. Every household needs something.'

'Maybe one day.' She ran a finger back and forth under her nose. 'Anyway, back to the story.'

'Yes, I'm pleased to say from that moment on, when Audrey knew I wasn't dickin' – sorry, muckin'—'

'It's too late for that,' Chloe said, shaking her head.

He tsked. 'Dammit. Look, the point is we were inseparable. Even the wrath of Uncle Lloyd couldn't stop us from sneaking around. Every single day, after that night, we made time for each other – even if it was only for half an hour. It was getting to the point where neither of us could breathe without the other. I would take her to the movies, to theatre shows, even roller-skating around town. We would go for picnics, or scenic drives where I attempted to teach her how to drive a manual transmission – which was a balls-up, by the way – and for romantic moonlit walks along the beach … during one of those was when I confessed something to her.'

'Oh?' Chloe leaned forward.

'It came about one Saturday night in mid-December. I picked my beloved up from Lloyd's, whistled at her outfit choice, and kissed her like I'd missed her …'

Chapter 32

THEN – 1964

ELIJAH PULLED AWAY from Audrey's lips. 'Honey, I have a surprise for you.'

Audrey's face lit up as she gave him a breathtaking smile. Her eyes danced as she showcased every single tooth. 'What is it?'

Elijah raised his eyebrows before he drove down the road, pulling into their local ten-pin bowling alley: Elroy's Bowl-O-Rama.

'Oh, *groovy*, bowling!'

Elijah clamped a hand around one of hers and walked her inside. 'Baby, I confess,' he began, facing her profile as her eyes roamed the mammoth crowd. By the way her pupils expanded the size of a vinyl record, anyone would think she'd landed on Mars. She stared, mouth agape as she tried to take everything in. The noise. The palpable excitement. The people rushing about.

'We are here tonight because I have entered you into a competition.'

'P-Pardon?' She stared bug-eyed at the banners placed around the room announcing Wollongong's annual ten-pin bowling tournament.

'I want you to show the locals what you have to offer,' Elijah shouted above the noise.

She turned and grabbed onto Elijah's shirt, almost ripping it. 'EJ, I've only played with friends and family back in Penrith; never a competition in front of hundreds of people. I can't do this!' Her erratic breathing blew the hair away from his forehead.

'Baby, let's look at the facts, shall we?' He pried her shaky hands off his shirt, walking her over to a nearby vacant table. 'Let's say you come dead last,' he began, while she glanced at the people who darted around them. 'What is the worst that can happen?' She moaned and placed her head in her hands, so he reached out and pulled them away from her bright red face. 'Don't let fear win, otherwise then it's a life half-lived. I want you to put on a pair of bowling shoes and play not to win, but for fun. You said it's been a while since you've played.' He shrugged. 'So, just get up and play.'

She looked towards the front door.

Elijah brushed his lips over her knuckles. 'Come on, honey. I thought you said you loved to play?'

'Yes, but as I said, only recreationally – not at a professional or competitive level.'

'If you don't push yourself, how will you know what you're capable of?'

She snatched her hand away. 'I'm not looking to find out in front of all these people!'

Elijah glanced at the competitors wearing professional blazers, some spit-shining their red-and-white shoes. He turned back to her and held her gaze dead-on. 'I believe in you.'

Audrey's eyes softened as though she'd never heard those words directed at her before, so he pulled her in across the table for a quick kiss. When they stood, he took her over to the marshals taking care of the competitors and paid her fee. The night started off with all twenty lanes being occupied by groups of up to three to four people. The best player from each lane then played the winner of all twenty lanes until they narrowed down the top ten, then the top five, then those five players would compete on one lane against one another until the winner prevailed. Third, second, and first place would win a prize, but Elijah wanted to prove to Audrey that prizes and money weren't everything – merely a bonus.

Elijah didn't know how good his girl was at bowling, but when she'd spoken about it previously her eyes had danced, so passion lurked somewhere. He kissed her sweaty forehead, wished her good luck, and then sat at the spectators' stand after he'd grabbed an American hot dog and Coca-Cola from the indoor café.

Elijah couldn't keep his eyes off Audrey, or the smile from his face. He was proud of her; only Jesus knew he would never have done such a thing. He wanted her to hold her head up whenever she walked around town. She didn't seem keen to interact with people. She was like a dog that had been whipped and mistreated its entire life, so it didn't expect or understand any better. People either looked down on her or made her feel stupid, especially now she was being spotted out with Elijah Samuels – *the lady pleaser of the town* – she wanted to disassociate herself with the image.

The MC of the night, Yvette Holliday, dressed in a black-and-white geometric dress, raised the microphone and did her usual spiel about the history of the annual tournament. She introduced last year's winner, Eric Burdon, who stood and bowed. Eric had taken home the crown three years in a row, knocking out the town favourite, Maria Nesbit, every time. Eric was an English fellow who made a living out of doing small-time competitions, loving the fact that he was a foreign cat amongst local pigeons. Eric didn't come to make friends. His scare tactics worked, as most players watched him in awe when he grabbed his personalised purple-blue Ebonite bowling ball out of a black duffel bag and polished it with a yellow shimmer cloth. His red-and-white shoes sparkled like mica under the fluorescent lighting. Elijah imagined he'd be the type of guy to blow a kiss to himself each night before bed.

He was a stereotypical Pommy with crooked teeth, a thick accent, and a pompous attitude to boot. Most players trembled when he walked past in his fancy Ivy League get-up, and some even shuffled out of his way. But in reality, all Elijah saw was a plump, balding, middle-aged gadger who stood no taller than five-foot-six on a good day, played amateur ten-pin bowling for a living, had no real stability in his life and no wedding ring around his sausage finger. However, Elijah would never forget Eric because he proved that image and deception are powerful tools to carry in a kit of personal weapons. Maria Nesbit was sitting this one out – probably due to fear of losing to Eric – again. Elijah didn't know for sure, but the only other amateur players representing Wollongong looked like their understanding of a 'split' was something you did with bananas.

Audrey began on Lane 19 and she kept glancing at Elijah, wide-eyed and pale-faced. When Audrey bowled the first time, she only knocked down four pins. It was the lowest score on the board across the twenty lanes. She turned back and breathed in and out as she collected another ball, stopping to look at Elijah with a tight-lipped mouth.

'Play for fun,' he mouthed. As she stepped up and bowled her second turn, she got a spare. Elijah clapped and whistled, but she didn't smile or look at him again as she took her seat. She was scared and nervous; probably even ticked off at him, but his faith never wavered. Elijah looked at Eric Burdon on Lane 2; he had bowled a strike on the first go, walking back with an arrogant grin on his smug face, dismissing outstretched hands to give him a high-five.

While watching some orange-haired man in a preppy sweater line up for a 7-10 split, an old flame of Elijah's strutted past in a black miniskirt and a light-brown top that showed off her ample assets. Deborah Malloy winked and approached as Elijah's mind's eye went to their wild encounters, of which at the time he'd had no complaints. But she was like a dime a dozen, and as Paul Newman once said: 'Why go out for hamburger when I can have steak at home?'

Her white boots came to a halt just in front of him, so he glanced up to offer a smile.

'Hi, *Daddy*; I've missed you.'

'Excuse me, you're in my way, darlin'.' He leaned to the left, looking past her frame.

She clicked her tongue as a cluster of women waving signs in the air, shrieked over a middle-aged man who'd bowled a turkey. 'So the rumours are true. The wild cat of Wollongong has been captured.' She turned to watch Audrey retrieve a fuchsia-coloured bowling ball.

'For once, the rumours about me are spot on.'

She turned back and curved her baby pink lips around a straw that dangled out of a 7-UP glass bottle. 'Don't you miss it?' She sucked on the straw.

'Nope.' His knees bounced up and down, not because he was getting his kicks, but the thought of Audrey turning around and seeing this attractive chick with him could throw her off. It would throw *him* off. He would have raced over and bopped the guy on the head with his fingers still attached to the bowling ball if this scene was reversed.

'I can tell you do just by looking at her. Why have that, when you can have *this?*' She ran a tongue over her pink lips, causing them to shine. Elijah recalled Lawrence's summation of lipstick colours: 'Red is for women, pink is for children', and almost laughed out loud over her abysmal attempts at seduction.

Elijah leaned forward as cheers erupted around them. 'Let's get this straight, sweet thing. The only thing I miss about ballin' you is the fact you kept your trap shut for once.' Her eyes widened as her jaw dropped. 'Close your mouth, it's never gonna happen again.' Rosebuds stained her cheeks, her eyes darted left and right. 'Now once more, I'm sorry it didn't work between us, but hopefully you'll find someone honest, smart, and ambitious … because I hear opposites attract.' Elijah left her gaping at him as he walked off to find another seat.

As time rolled on, and after smoking half a pack of cigarettes while watching his girl knock out player after player, it got down to the wire. The final five battling it out were Eric Burdon, Marjorie Waintek, Patti Boyd, Derek Carver and, Elijah's personal favourite, Audrey Hughes.

The first four players had bowled and now the pressure was on for Audrey and her last throw, as she needed to knock down ten pins – a strike – to win by one point. It became so quiet Elijah swore he could hear his own hair fall out. Within a minute, Audrey stepped up to the lane, eyes as fierce as a shark zoning in on its prey, lifted her hand backwards while taking a few steps, and swung it down to release the ball. It went flying across the shiny surface before knocking down nine pins. She'd equalled Eric's score of 243, a personal best for Audrey, and as she knocked them down, everyone in the room clapped like raving lunatics at their new champion – even if Eric Burdon shared the title. By the time Elijah jumped over the handrail and raced over, the townsfolk of Wollongong had picked up their new ten-pin bowling champion, thrusting her in the air. Streamers and balloons held by a net suspended from the ceiling came tumbling down. Tears glistened on Audrey's cheeks as everyone chanted *Aud-rey … Aud-rey … Aud-rey!*

Tears stung Elijah's eyes.

When she looked over with the biggest smile as Elijah fist-pumped the air, she stretched out her arms to him. As he reached up to grab her from some guy's shoulders – who Elijah thought was enjoying it a little bit too much – she slipped into his waiting arms and he kissed her like crazy, the sound of wolf whistles erupting around them.

Yvette Holliday ran to them, a hand keeping her white cap in place, before presenting Audrey a trophy. Unfortunately they had to split the prize pool in half, but Audrey still got a whopping two hundred pounds. Eric Burdon never even shook her hand, but it went to show what happens to people who walk in, acting like they own the damn place. Audrey held the trophy in her hands as she skipped out the front doors whilst everyone carried on the celebrations.

At Wollongong Beach later that night, a blue moon shone upon the two lovers, illuminating the ocean's ripples as they tiptoed barefoot along the coarse sand. Audrey was the most *fascinating* person Elijah had ever laid eyes on. She smiled from ear-to-ear whilst looking across the ocean, a light breeze blowing the hair away from her face. Elijah Samuels felt free.

'EJ, I was thinking tomorrow night after work—'

He grabbed her shoulders and turned her to him, placing his forehead on hers. 'I love you.'

She gasped, the trophy falling to the sand. He cupped her face and stared into her eyes. 'On my life, I do. If I were to die tonight, I'd *need* you to know how I feel. I am crazy in love with you, Audrey Hughes.'

Tears rimmed her eyes as she grabbed him around the waist. It took a moment for her to say, 'I love you, too, EJ.'

He breathed a sigh of relief and laughed nervously, before their lips sought union. Afterwards, Elijah drew their initials in the sand with a stick and encased them in a heart shape. He could almost see the love hearts beaming from her eyes. They hardly spoke that night. The feeling of finally admitting they loved each other was too intense, so they revelled in the adrenaline and walked along the beach, intoxicated with raw emotion.

The next night, they consummated their love for the first time. Lloyd had gone on one of his usual gambling extravaganzas. Elijah didn't miss the irony of Lloyd's irritation that he gambled with cards, too. After they'd eaten Audrey's delicious homemade spaghetti bolognaise by candlelight, Elijah gave her a piggyback ride up the stairs to her room, where he lay her on the bed. They were laughing hard as the Lindeman's Sparkling Porphyry Pearl that Elijah brought over had gone straight to their heads, but there was also a sense of giddiness and liberation. Elijah knew Audrey was a virgin (he'd had a few of those before), but in some ways it felt like it was the first time for him, also.

'I love you,' he whispered, staring into her beaming eyes. For Elijah these words sounded foreign, but it was like some sweet drug being released into his system each time he told her the truth.

'I love you more.' She kissed his nose and eyelids. And for the first time, Elijah Samuels believed that someone really *did* love him.

'Not possible,' he said, marking the segue into the most unforgettable night. His only regret was that after making sweet, intense love to this girl he worshipped like a deity, he couldn't wake up with her in his arms the next morning.

Chapter 33

THEN – 1964

SEARING HEAT COILED around Elijah's limbs like a hot-blooded serpent the next day. Even the blades of grass stood still as if it were too hot to move, so he'd taken his girl to the beach. They found a shaded spot away from those who dared to play volleyball in the disorienting haze, so they could fool around without being noticed. Elijah only wore swimming trunks and black shades, while Audrey wore a modest yellow-and-white flowered bikini dress, although she was self-conscious for reasons he didn't understand.

Even the clouds had succumbed to indolence as Elijah placed a blanket on the scorched sand and grabbed his transistor radio out of a wicker picnic basket before removing his thongs. Audrey salivated over the food Elijah had prepared as he started laying out the good stuff in front of her: Hillier chocolates (now liquefied), Mastercraft scored peanut bars, fresh strawberries, assorted sandwiches with their crusts cut off, and UDL Rum and Cola cans to wash it all down.

After a liquid lunch, as the arid heat burned their lungs, Audrey grabbed a bottle of Coppertone QT lotion from the basket and applied the oil to his sizzling skin. He leaned back onto her supple body and emitted low, rumbling moans at her heavenly touch as she rubbed his chest from behind. She massaged his upper chest in a circular motion and he gazed up at her, thinking he couldn't get enough of her taking care of him. Elijah puckered his lips, so she giggled and bent over to kiss him. As she did, he hooked an arm around her neck and, with the other hand, wiped lotion over her forehead. She squealed and jumped – wriggling to get away – but he released his hold on her neck, only to spin around and grab her ankle as she scrambled away, pulling her back. Elijah pinned her beneath him and tickled her. She squirmed and screamed so hard tears escaped her clenched eyes. In that moment, Elijah felt like he was a little kid again, without a care in the world.

Amid them laughing and carrying on, a song came on the radio: 'Under the Boardwalk'. As serendipity would have it, that's exactly where they were: under a boardwalk.

Elijah stopped tormenting her and looked down at her before exploring her lips with his. Her giggling soon faded away as she met him with the same passion and enthusiasm. Their sun-kissed skin felt blistering to touch, the unrestrained heat stealing the breath from their lungs while sweat-slicked hair clung to their scalps.

'I love you,' she said, kissing his damp forehead. 'I love you.' She kissed his cheek. 'I love you' – his eyelids – 'I love you' – his neck. '*God* I love you, EJ.'

***

'Marry me,' he breathed into her ear the next night, while they made love at their usual spot underneath the boardwalk.

She froze, panting. 'P-Pardon?'

He leaned back, frowning, as if shocked by his own words. He'd never thought of saying it, let alone uttering it aloud to a girl. His heart pounded as he stared into her wide eyes as she lay beneath him. He didn't know why he'd chosen *that* exact moment, but he had. He'd asked her to be his wife in an unorthodox way.

The moon's light infiltrated the cracks of the boardwalk as foam-tipped waves pounded the sand behind them.

Elijah admitted to himself just the night before that making love to Audrey was so indescribable that he wondered whether he'd been doing it wrong all this time. It wasn't the act of sex itself; it was how she affected him. So perhaps that's why he had felt the urge at that moment in time – a moment of pure rapture – to propose.

'Listen to me,' he said, as 'Louie Louie' blasted from his transistor resting in the sand beside them. 'You've made it clear in the past you think I'm better than you. But let me tell you: I've never cared about money or status. If I only ever had you in my life, I'd be richer than anyone ever could be.' He paused as she dug her nails into the bare flesh of his shoulder. 'I never imagined falling in love with you like I have, but now that it's happened, I can't turn away. I want us to walk together as husband and wife. I want us to grow old together, and I want to sleep by your side every night, protecting you in my arms. Audrey ... I would sell my soul for you.' Audrey made little gasping sounds as tears trickled down her face, which he brushed away with a thumb. Hell, he was close to crying, too. 'Wait, before you say anything, tell me straight: D-Do I make you happy?'

She let out a squeal and wrapped her arms tighter around his neck, pulling him down to kiss her. When they broke, she placed a loving hand on his cheek – the sea behind them kindling its own symphony.

'Because,' Elijah continued, 'you make me happier than I ever thought I could be, and if you let me, I promise I will try to make you feel the same for the rest of your life.' He cupped her cheek while his other hand palmed the coarse sand beside her head. 'Please, for the love of God, make me the happiest man alive and marry me.'

'Do you even have a ring?' She snuffled and then smirked, hooking her index finger through the chain of his dog tags that swung around his neck.

Elijah gave a nervous laugh, which sounded more like a cough. 'No, honestly I don't. I wasn't planning on doing it like *this*.' He looked between their bodies at his embedded situation. 'I wasn't planning on even asking you today, but why wait? I need to know if you feel the same as me.'

Audrey's bottom lip trembled as her eyes squeezed shut. '*Believe* me, I do.' She inhaled. 'You make me feel like a different person; the fact you overlook my disability means everything because when people look at me, that's *all* they see.' Tears spilled down the sides of her cheeks and onto the sand. Her hand resting on his shoulder moved behind his head so she could hold him still and look into his eyes. 'I love you, Elijah Samuels, and I would be more than happy to accept your proposal – when you have a ring – and also one more thing ...'

Was she thinking of her loving parents? He understood Audrey no longer had her mother to help with the wedding plans and finding a bridal dress. She no longer had her father to walk her down the aisle and wipe away a solitary tear as he told her she looked beautiful. Did Elijah's proposal (even in a sticky situation like this) conjure up those emotional thoughts for Audrey?

'Anything you want ...' he said.

'I have to meet your parents first.'

Chapter 34

'OH, NO!' CHLOE said, flipping through the pages of Audrey's diary.

'Oh, yes,' Elijah said, watching a nearby duck with remarkable plumage, whose quacking interrupted their colloquy.

'I can only imagine how your parents would have treated her.'

'It was a night that even dementia couldn't make me forget.'

At that point, two nurses walked past the windows, pushing two wheelchair-bound 'inmates' as he referred to them. There was a lot Elijah could be bitter about, but he thanked his lucky stars he could still function without the aid of strangers, or soiling his trousers without knowing it. Elijah loathed this place – not just because of Audrey's situation – but because it was like a holding cell for people waiting to die. It was like where his father ended up, and watching Howard's deterioration into skeletal remains still gave Elijah nightmares. His mother had dropped dead of a heart attack back in the early eighties during a bridge tournament (cigarette holder still protruding from her mouth). At least Margaret Samuels avoided the disgrace of ending up in a place like this, where strangers wiped your arse, inmates marinated in their own urine, and money meant fuck all to folks who didn't even know what their name was.

The inmates here were waiting to die, wondering when they'd be next in line to meet their Maker. Elijah observed those walking the grounds or doing outdoor group activities – picturing them in their prime, wondering what they would have looked like, what their jobs would have been. They were once active, able-bodied people – flash-forward fifty or so years and here was where many ended up. Alone, and praying to God to end their life – no – their *existence*.

Let those anti-euthanasia arseholes live here for a week, Elijah thought, remembering an article in the *Daily Telegraph*, Thursday before last: *'Suffering is a grace-filled opportunity to participate in the passion of Jesus Christ. Euthanasia selfishly steals that.'*

An emaciated man wearing blue flannelette pyjamas strolled past their table, leaving a mephitic waft of urine in his wake. He had severe Parkinson's. *Is this a prelude for what's to come?* Elijah glanced at his own quivering hands.

The elderly man acknowledged the two of them with a curt nod as he waddled along, holding out his leftover sandwich crumbs to a magpie, which began its descent from a nearby grey gum.

'Hello, Maggie,' the man croaked, his thin, cracked lips forming a smile across his withered face, each wrinkle like a badge of honour for making it this far in life. The magpie's clawed feet clamped onto the man's shaky hand, feverishly pecking the crumbs from his open palm.

'They say if you make friends with a magpie, you'll have a friend for life,' Elijah whispered to Chloe.

I hope you're okay with that, pal, Elijah thought. *'Cause by the looks of it, she'll be the only one missing you when you're gone.*

Once the bird had eaten the last remnants of the man's sandwich, she flew back to her squabbling chicks waiting in their nest.

'Bye, Maggie,' the old man croaked, drool slipping from his pallid lips as he raised a feeble arm that looked no stronger than Maggie's wing, to wave goodbye.

'That was probably the highlight of his day, feeding that bird,' Elijah said, watching the old man toddle back inside the prison. Elijah thought of Sheba at home and was thankful God had at least granted him one small pleasure amongst the turmoil – a dog. Man's best friend, indeed. If it weren't for Sheba, he might not have made it this far. She kept him on his toes and kept him active, at least for the portions of the day when she wasn't sleeping or slobbering on his slippers.

'You know something, kid? Very few old folks are happy; I'm not the only grumpy bastard out there. Most of them are poor, their health has gone down the crapper, and they've said goodbye too many times to people they've loved. It's the most difficult and fragile time of a person's life, more so than childhood because all that's left in the future is death, and rarely is it dignified.'

Chloe's eyebrows shot up. 'Where did *that* come from?'

The corner of Elijah's mouth curled. 'Just voicing my thoughts. Promise me one thing …' Chloe remained silent as she looked at him. 'Enjoy your youth while you have it, for it is an ace up your sleeve. Enjoy life to the fullest, even if it means doing things your parents don't approve of. The only things you'll regret in the end are the opportunities you've missed. Trust me.'

'I promise.'

He nodded and gave a mirthless smile.

'Um, shall I read another story?'

Elijah inhaled through his nostrils and closed his eyes. 'Sure. Please take me back to a time I would give anything to travel to again.'

Chloe turned the page and cleared her throat. *'19th December 1964. Dear Diary, this evening, after EJ carved our initials inside a love heart into the timber under the boardwalk at Wollongong Beach, he took me to meet his parents. It was a spur-of-the-moment thing, as he's proposed to me! Yes, Elijah proposed to me on the beach. It was clearly impromptu; he didn't have a thing planned, but I still said yes – on the condition that I meet his parents first. I thought it was a good idea to meet them, seeing as Christmas is coming up and maybe we could do a family thing together.*

'How silly was I? As soon as EJ pulled up to the electric gates, they opened to reveal a mansion on top of the hill. My breath caught in my throat. I thought it was a joke. EJ lives nestled in the lap of luxury and I am really embarrassed

now that he has even seen my home. But, he grasped my hand and held on tight as if to protect me against the looming three-storeys high homestead. Lantern sconces illuminated the sandstone walls. A lion head fountain and large palm trees were in the courtyard; their house even has a four-car garage. When we entered the mansion, the decor blew me away, but above all, I felt foolish standing in my Salvation Army dress and faded Mary Jane's.

'When his mother, Margaret, appeared, she startled me; she reminded me of a Hollywood star like Joan Crawford or Ava Gardner. I still thought it had to be a joke – she even had a cigarette holder sticking out of her mouth. Her wavy brown hair had not a stray hair out of place, and her make-up was flawless – like a Madame Alexander doll. Her purple silk gown reached the floor, and her emerald necklace looked like it weighed more than me. But most of all, I noticed her pursed, honey-coloured lips and judging eyes ...'

Chapter 35

THEN – 1964

ELIJAH BRAVED A smile. 'Mother, this is Audrey … the girl I've told you about.'

'Charmed.' Margaret held out a dainty hand encased in a silver lamé glove. Audrey put a quivering hand into hers, but Margaret pulled away as if Audrey's hand was on fire.

'Oh, honestly, Elijah … you have sand in your hair.' Margaret then looked at Audrey's ruffled hair with the subtleness of a despot.

She must know what we've been up to, Audrey thought, evading eye contact, her cheeks flushing hotter than hell under the blatant scrutiny.

'Howard, you must come at once,' Margaret called out, her inquisitive brown eyes never wavering from Audrey.

Elijah, Margaret and Audrey stared at one another in awkward silence until Elijah's father, dressed in a brown cotton suit, walked around the corner, a copy of *The Australian* shoved under his left armpit. He stopped, stared, then planted his best team-player smile as he overemphasised: 'HELLO, LOVELY TO MAKE YOUR ACQUAINTANCE. I'M HOWARD.'

Audrey's heart shattered like a crystal goblet. Elijah must have told them she was deaf. Audrey looked to Elijah, who was holding her hand, as he shot his father a warning glance.

They invited Audrey to dine with them; it would have been impolite for her to refuse. Angel-hair pasta with mussels, oysters and king prawns in a creamy, rose-coloured sauce was the main course.

Audrey appraised the furnishings of the dining room whilst Arthur Moore cleared their plates, and conceded (with dread) that she did not fit into this world of champagne and limousines. She'd lived on a farm in Penrith in Western Sydney until she lost her parents. That was a far cry from this place. Throughout the night, Margaret and Howard asked intrusive questions: 'What are your plans for the future?' and 'How does Elijah fit into that?' and 'How did your parents die?'

Audrey felt as though they were dissecting her under a powerful microscope, and what's worse was Elijah knew it, too. The entire time he gripped her quivering hand under the teak dining table that had a golden candelabrum in the centre. Elijah interjected where possible, but apart from that, there wasn't much he could do to save her.

By the time dessert arrived, Audrey was on the verge of tears. It was spiced-apple pie with custard and strawberries. She thought it was exquisite, as was the champagne and the cheese and grape platter Arthur served afterwards.

At one point, when Elijah had gone to the bathroom and his parents were chatting about a tennis tournament with Rod Laver, Grace turned to Audrey, leaned in and said, 'You know, you're officially the first chick he's brought home as a girlfriend?'

So, he *had* been telling the truth! Audrey clutched the silverware that glimmered like the hope in her heart.

'Yeah, dig it, sister. Georgie and he were friends first, so that means you're officially the first girlfriend. Don't let my parents put you off. EJ is a bit unconventional with his thinking and his actions, but I know my little brother, and he really digs you. Sure, he can be a tad aggressive sometimes, but he's had a bit of a hard life.'

Audrey swallowed a mouthful of Piper-Heidsieck – a luxurious champagne her parents would never have had the means to purchase. 'What do you mean "hard life"?' She licked her lips, which tasted of green apples and white peaches.

'They picked on him at school because he always hung around the unpopular kids. He didn't want to be associated with the stuck-up ones, so people who were more popular than him showed him who was boss. Eventually, EJ fought back, but then he'd be the one getting in trouble and having our parents come down to the private school to talk about his behavioural problems.' Grace glanced at her parents, who were now bickering at the end of the table. 'Despite being aware of his antics, I don't believe they ever went to see what they could do to help their "troublesome son". Anyway, trust me when I say I know EJ can be a bit much, but he's always been protective of people.' She leaned closer across the table as Margaret and Howard segued into a full-blown argument, and it was at that precise moment Audrey realised what was wrong with the picture: there *were* no pictures. No framed photographs on the walls of dead relatives looming over the dining room table – no childhood photos of Grace or Elijah, or family pets or family vacations. The place was as bare as a birch in winter, devoid of all sentimental objects, heirlooms and nostalgia.

Grace continued. 'When Nanna on Dad's side – who was more like a mother to him than our mother – passed away, EJ felt responsible because he wasn't by her side when it happened, and personally, I don't think he's been the same since, 'cause that's when he ramped up the rebellion.'

Audrey cocked her head to the side. 'Rebellion?'

Grace smirked and rolled her eyes. 'You know: drinking, gambling, street fighting … then he discovered girls – or should I say – they discovered *him*.'

Audrey felt what little colour she had left in her face drain away as a car pulled into the courtyard, headlights permeating through the red velvet drapes. Grace explained one of Margaret's friends and her husband wanted to show off their baby daughter, who had been born days prior. That would be the last Audrey saw of Margaret and Howard that evening.

'In saying all of that,' Grace continued, 'I've never seen EJ act the way he has been since he met you and that's the truth. Not even the army could straighten him out.' She smiled, thoughtful. 'I don't think he ever loved any of those girls; I think they were more of a distraction than anything.' Grace plopped the last of her strawberries into her mouth. 'Anyway, I've said too much, but I want my brother to be happy and I can clearly see it when he looks at you.'

Audrey's smile resurfaced. Something about the look in Grace's green eyes gave her statement weight.

'Stick with him because I think he'll surprise you.'

Audrey's round cheeks burned.

Grace shrugged. 'I just call 'em as I see 'em, and man does he have it bad!'

Audrey smiled tenderly at Grace and nibbled on a purple grape, not because she was hungry, but because it gave her something to do as she slipped into a reverie about their potential future.

Then she had a thought. 'How old was he when your grandmother passed away?'

Grace's eyes flew skyward while thinking. 'Sixteen.'

Chapter 36

THEN – 1964

'PLEASE LET ME go,' Audrey said. Elijah clamped his hand on her forearm. They had pulled up outside Lloyd's house, and Audrey couldn't have scrammed faster if she'd had a rocket strapped to her.

'No.' He gripped her forearm tighter. When she slackened, he let go long enough to light a cigarette. 'Not until we talk.'

She looked at him as the spark of his lighter illuminated his face. Holding the cigarette to his lips, he drew deep on the butt.

'I don't feel like it.'

Elijah shrugged before exhaling the smoke. 'Well, I don't feel like letting you go, so how about that? Stalemate.'

She glared at him. 'Why are you such a bastard?' Even through the darkness, she saw the hurt flash across his eyes when he glared at her.

'You've been quiet the entire way here. There's something on your mind and I would love to hear it.'

She focused on her entwined fingers resting in her lap. 'I don't feel like I … fit in.'

'No, you don't.' He drew on the cigarette. 'And I'm glad.'

She shot him a wide-eyed look. 'It doesn't bother you?'

Elijah let out a short laugh. 'Bother me ... are you foolin'? Baby girl, don't insult me, I'm *glad* you're nothing like them; that's what I love about you.

I adore you. Hell, I never want you to become like them.' He shifted in his seat, facing her front on. 'In fact, *promise me* you will never become like my parents.'

Audrey laughed and rolled her eyes. 'Trust me; I promise.'

Curling tendrils of smoke jetted from his nostrils as he grazed the back of her neck with his fingertips. 'I'm sorry you didn't enjoy your night with them, but please don't think about going anywhere because I am telling you, I don't care what anyone thinks, do you hear?'

Audrey used her index finger to rub the base of her nose. 'But, don't you think you deserve someone better; someone who is normal?'

'Baby girl, you are *not* abnormal. Jesus, sometimes I think you're your own worst enemy.' He leaned forward, their cheeks grazing as he whispered into her ear. 'I am in love with you. I don't know what else to say; maybe I have to show you more?'

Audrey shrugged and sat rigid as a Holden station wagon approached, blaring 'Ring of Fire' by Johnny Cash. Elijah leaned back, positioning his face so they were cheek-to-cheek, witnessing the beefy male driver of the station wagon chugging on a bottle of Jack as the car swerved across the road from side to side.

'Do you see?' Elijah turned to her. 'Do you see what women do to men?!'

Audrey chuckled as the music dissipated and the driver's taillights vanished.

'All I know is how I feel inside and I don't even think about your aid; it doesn't change how I feel about you. Whether or not you had it, I would love you the same; in fact, maybe I love you *more* because you have it. I feel like I have to protect you from the world.' He placed his free hand on her thigh. 'You're my baby girl; you were meant *only* for me, do you hear? No-one else is going to marry you, but me – promise?'

Audrey gave a cute smirk as if to say *Don't be silly, of course that's not going to happen.*

He wiped her tears away, then after taking another drag, he disposed of the cigarette into the nearest front yard, landing beside a Hasbro G.I. Joe jungle fighter.

Their heads turned to the right at the sound of the rusty fly screen at Lloyd's house being flown open, and Lloyd stepped out under a dimly lit bulb to stare at them with his burly arms folded.

Audrey sighed, looking straight ahead. 'I have to go now.'

Elijah grabbed her face between his hands and kissed her deep as her hands gripped either side of his waist. When he broke away his dreamy eyes roamed over her face. 'I love you so *fucking* much, Audrey.' His brow furrowed as though in deep concentration. Her forehead rested against his rosy lips as she closed her eyes. 'Never forget that.'

***

Upon Elijah's return home, his parents ambushed him, telling him they were disappointed with the girl he'd chosen. Audrey was the only girl he'd ever cared about; the only one with self-respect, and here were his parents, telling him to go with someone like Georgie Brown, who was a dope smoker and far from virginal.

'Oh, honestly, Elijah, you cannot see that girl ever again, do you hear me?'

'Do you hear *yourself?*' He stormed up the spiral staircase. 'You're off your rocker!'

'Howard, tell your son she cannot step foot inside this house again!'

'Son, you get back here,' Howard yelled.

'Get stuffed!'

Margaret gasped. 'You *cannot* talk to us like that!'

Elijah turned around to see them standing on the black-and-white tiles, dressed like movie stars from the Roaring '20s. 'Nor can you tell me who to love. I'm going to marry Audrey, whether your precious North Shore golf club comrades like it or not!'

That night, Elijah tossed and turned like his mattress was made of cobblestones. He didn't *want* to sleep, anyway, so he drove back to Audrey's place and did the old throw-the-pebbles-at-the-window routine. Light shining through the chink in the curtains meant she was still awake.

A minute later, her head appeared and Elijah stepped back upon seeing her eyes at half-mast.

Audrey braved a smile, genuinely surprised to see him standing below her window. She lifted the screen and whisper-shouted: 'What are you doing here?'

'I came to see if Lloyd maybe wanted to play gin rummy with me?'

She poked out her tongue. 'He's just gone to bed. I'll meet you downstairs!'

As she opened the rickety front door, he took her into his arms and sighed. He kissed the top of her head and she led him by the hand up the wooden stairs, past Lloyd's bedroom from where deep snores echoed, and into hers.

After she closed the bedroom door, she made a point of slamming her open diary shut before offering him a place to sit on her bed.

Her eyes were as puffy as pastry; her button nose red. 'They hate me, don't they?'

He reached for her hands. 'I can't predict the future, Audrey. All we have is now. I promise you I will not take you for granted, because I recognise how rare *this* is.' She lowered her head as tears fell. He squeezed her hands with a quick pump. 'Hey, I promise you that I will never stray, and that I will one day tattoo your name across my heart as it already metaphorically is.' She whimpered, then inhaled through her nose. 'I promise, baby, that if you stand by my side each day, then nothing can tear us apart. We will have a nice house, we will be husband and wife, we will have children, we will grow old and grey together, and I promise that even when we die, I will be right by your side – as I believe it is my purpose here on earth. Don't let what we have go because of what you *think* will happen. Live in the *now*. Just promise me, day-by-day is all I am asking – *say* it!'

By this point tears poured down Audrey's face and she moved closer to clasp her hands around his face. 'I promise you, EJ, that we will be with each other until the end.' He leaned over and kissed her as her fingers raked through his hair. Audrey whimpered while they kissed. When he pushed her shoulders, she lay back and Elijah followed as though their bodies were conjoined.

That night they made love in a way that was more spiritual than it was sexual. It was unadulterated love, mixed with a tinge of desperation and uncertainty.

Chapter 37

'WAS IT REALLY that bad?' Chloe said, refilling both their glasses with iced tea.

'Does a bear crap in the woods?'

Chloe frowned. 'Pardon?'

Elijah grinned, noting the sun shifting higher in the sky. He believed Angela would soon arrive, as the wind had picked up, and much like dogs, he could sense evil afoot. 'It was; her diary entry wasn't exaggerating at all. When Audrey went to the bathroom, I pulled my folks aside and told them they were being a pair of ars— um … I said they weren't being nice.'

'They *were* arseholes.'

Elijah stared at Chloe. 'For God's sake, don't tell your mother I let you say that word. I don't want another fight with her; I'm too old, kid.'

She twisted an imaginary key next to her lips and 'threw it' into the nearby hedges. 'Don't worry, Mum's the word.'

They shared a smile before Chloe flipped through the diary, skimming the pages.

Elijah covered his mouth to cough, noticing what looked like a drop of blood on his shaky hand as he lowered it. He dismissed it, chalking it up to bad eyesight.

'Whoa, back up, mister …'

Elijah glanced up to see Chloe scowling. 'What just happened?'

Chloe stabbed her finger at the page open on her lap. 'Why does it say in here you guys had a huge fight months later in April 1965?'

Elijah held up his hands. 'Just hear me out.'

'You ditched my grandmother for that hooker, Georgie?!'

Elijah glanced around. 'For goodness' sake, first things first.' He paused. 'She wasn't a hooker, and that's a word you shouldn't say—'

'You can't get out of this on a technicality!'

Elijah sighed, raised his glasses and pinched the bridge of his nose. 'Please lower your voice. I don't want the walking dead to think I pay for hookers.' He chuckled at his own joke and peered up, but Chloe wasn't laughing. 'Christ, will you let me explain before I'm led to the guillotine?'

Chloe picked up her iced tea and sipped through the straw without taking her eyes off his. When she'd sucked it dry, causing an irritating slurping sound for Elijah, she slammed it back on the table and continued to stare.

Elijah exhaled through his nostrils and turned the pages of his diary, flipping through the months of 1965. 'Just be patient on this one, kid.' He licked his cracked lips, jiggled his shoulders, and breathed deep. 'After months of courtship, on Thursday, 29th April 1965, I woke up snuggling her in bed. Because I woke first, it gave me the opportunity to look at her while she slept in my arms. Her lips were parted as she breathed. She looked peaceful, so I brushed a golden strand of hair back from her face and kissed her forehead, careful not to wake her. Judging by the sun's position, I guessed the time to be around six o'clock, which meant I had to duck out before Lloyd woke up and found us stark naked in bed together, although the thought gave me smug satisfaction, I must admit. I wanted to remain like that all day, but Audrey had to work at the ice cream parlour and I had tutoring to attend to – a secret I was keeping from my girl. I climbed out of bed and threw my clothes on before writing a note: I LOVE YOU! HAVE A GOOD DAY, and placed it on the pillow next to her head, before kissing her nose. I left without Lloyd noticing and walked around the block to my car – where I'd been parking it so Lloyd wouldn't realise when I was around. On the way home, I drove past a group of anti-Vietnam protestors lined up along Edward Street. A foreboding feeling settled in my stomach, and as I rocked up to my house I found the answer for the newfound rise of anger from the public. There on my front doorstep was a copy of *The Sun* with the headline in bold, black writing: **MENZIES TO TELL PARLIAMENT TODAY: TROOPS TO VIETNAM.**

'That night, Audrey and I had a tremendous blue. A new discotheque had opened on the shores of Wollongong called Calypso. It was the latest craze in town; all the hit songs of the fifties and sixties were being played, and it was the hottest thing this town had seen since Audrey arrived. Calypso had a vibe about it that no other nightclub could match. It brought people together as a community, and because it was in the "lower class" part of Wollongong added quaint humour, because the fancy snobs had to come down to everyone else's level for the night if they wanted to enjoy what Calypso offered.

'The menu comprised Australian and modern French cuisine, and had a reasonable-sized dance floor for the people who had an itch for the Madison, bush dancing or the jitterbug. They also had a competition, which I was dying to enter with my baby girl as it seemed like a gas. It was a *bop till you drop* competition where couples had to do the twist – the couple who danced the longest, won. It might sound silly now, but it was all the rage and sometimes went for days as there was a generous cash prize on offer. Heck, they didn't call it the Swinging Sixties for nothing.

'Anyway, Audrey and I fought because when I told her I'd pick her up at eight, she heard seven.'

'Mm-hmm. And why so late?' Chloe said, giving him the old stink eye. 'What were you doing, or should I say *who* were you doing?!'

Elijah went slack-jawed as Chloe folded her arms over her chest. When she cocked an eyebrow, he said, 'Jesus H. Christ, maybe I am a bad influence after all.'

He heard rather than saw her foot tapping. 'Well?'

'Do you honestly think I was out fooling around?'

Chloe shrugged. 'Well, I just don't know. Did you ditch my nan for Georgie?'

Elijah stumbled. 'Look, technically—'

'I've heard enough for one day.' She closed the diary, standing to leave.

Elijah palm-slapped the table. 'Have patience and listen! You don't want to end up like your mother, do you?'

Without hesitation, Chloe took a seat.

'Just as I thought. Getting back to my story,' he said, inhaling, 'I was *about* to leave the house in my brand-new tuxedo when I opened the door and came face-to-face with Georgie.'

Chapter 38

'EXCUSE ME, COULD I have a word, please?'

Elijah peered up, just as a sharp pain shot through his ribcage like a spearhead. He raised his hand to block out the sun as Timothy loomed above him, hands on hips.

If this is some sort of intimidation method, it isn't working, dickhead. 'Sure, what word would you like? I know a few of 'em.'

Timothy exhaled and then turned his attention to Chloe, who was smirking. 'Sweetness, could you please give Mr, um ...'

'Samuels.' *Something tells me you already knew that.*

'Mr Samuels and I – er – a moment alone, please? Why don't you keep Tida company; I know she'd enjoy that.'

Chloe conferred with Elijah with a glance, which he responded to by giving a reaffirming wink. She moseyed up the wheelchair-access ramp and disappeared inside the building, which was now buzzing with a fresh wave of visitors. Performing their obligatory annual visit, Elijah thought, probably to find out whether they were any closer to gaining their inheritance. He turned his attention back to Timothy.

Timothy pursed his lips. 'Mr Samuels, I'm going to be honest; nothing more, nothing less. The flight from London was arduous, and I've come all this way to say goodbye to my mother. Instead, I have some old guy being a pain in my arse. My sister told me you're here for story time or something like that, with Chloe?' Elijah chuckled and shook his head, gazing out to the horizon. 'Well, I think you've had your fun. Now, out of respect to my mother, I am asking you to please leave. Take your crummy old book and leave, now, without a fuss. Even a bum like you can respect we want Mum's final moments with us to be memorable, not filled with feelings of anger towards you.' Elijah kept quiet and still, despite all his fibres screaming *Knock him out cold.* 'If you were that influential to my mother, then don't you think she would have brought you up in conversation at least once in the past; that she would have … attempted to contact you?'

Elijah glanced up, shielding the sun blazing into his dowdy eyes as he caught sight of a murder of crows careening above. 'You said your name was Timothy, didn't you?'

Timothy broadened his shoulders. 'Yes.'

'Well, here's the thing, arsehole … I am not going anywhere. I don't intend to make this any more difficult for you than it already is. But once upon a time, believe it or not, your mother and I were inseparable.' He crossed two fingers together to help Timothy visualise that he meant as close as close could be. 'I made a promise to her many years ago that I would be by her side, even in death.'

Timothy smirked and stepped closer, giving Elijah the shade from the sun he desired. 'That's very heroic, but as I said, *none* of us know who you are, or even who you were to my mother.'

Elijah swallowed a glob of metallic-tasting mucus. *Shit, it's getting worse,* he thought as another sharp pain struck his ribs. 'What exactly bothers you?' He paused for breath – maintaining a straight face despite the discomfort. 'Would you prefer it if I kept my mouth shut? Would you allow me to sit in that depressing room with you all and to not say a word about the past or your mother?'

Timothy's eyes travelled north, pondering. 'Truthfully? No, because I don't know who you are and this is a private matter.'

Elijah shrugged. 'But your wife is here.'

'She's family!'

'Why, because she married you, so that automatically makes her family, huh? How many times has she even met Audrey – if ever? And because she's attached to you – with no other reason apart from a ring – you're telling me she deserves to be in that room over me?'

Timothy's eye twitched. 'It doesn't matter if she's met my mother or not, she's family!'

'Son, you don't even know the definition, so do me a favour and stop using gargantuan words you don't comprehend. By the way, can your wife even speak English?'

Timothy's nostrils flared. 'You racist son of a—'

'Calm down, Clancy, it's just a simple question with a yes or no answer.' Elijah thought he witnessed a blood vessel burst like a gel ball being squashed in Timothy's left eye. 'If you had the slightest idea …' He held his index finger and thumb a centimetre apart. 'If only you knew, Timothy. I knew your mother inside and out – better than anyone. Probably even better than you, which is why you're scared.'

'Scared?!'

'Correct, *scared*, because there's a chance that this old geezer – who's a complete stranger to you – knows more about her than you ever allowed yourself to. No doubt you're feeling ashamed right now.' Elijah shrugged and clamped his fingers together, resting them in his lap. 'I don't blame you.'

'I doubt that scenario very much.'

'There's no actual way to measure that theory, is there?' Elijah paused, hearing the droning of a helicopter in the distance and the piercing squawk of a bird. He stared Timothy straight in the eyes with a look of sheer determination. 'I am more than willing to make this easier for you, but I don't take to authority well. I don't take to pencil-pushing, suit-wearing dipshits who think they can tell me what to do. I've been around you for all but thirty seconds, and I infer that any similarity between you and an intelligent, fully functional man is purely coincidental.' Timothy's right eye blood vessel burst. 'I am not leaving Audrey's side. You can try to keep me away from her just like all the rest, but you won't succeed … just like all the rest.'

Timothy spoke through gritted teeth. 'You do not want to make an enemy out of me.'

'I understand you perfectly. Lashing out at everyone around you is a way to assuage the guilt you feel for throwing your own mother into a hellhole and flying off to London to leave everyone else to deal with the "big stuff". Boy, it's a wonder how you sleep at night.'

'Hello, gentlemen,' Jamie said from behind Elijah.

As Elijah swivelled to her direction, Timothy walked over to envelop his younger sister in a bear hug, then leading her by the elbow towards a hedge of flowering pink azaleas.

Timothy jerked his head towards Elijah. 'What's his plan? Swoop in and hope Mum will change her will to include him because he came to say goodbye at the last minute? Where the hell was he all her life?'

Jamie's head reeled back. 'First, great to see you after all this time and, second, I'm well … thanks for asking!'

Timothy screwed his eyes shut, shaking his head. 'I'm not callous; I'm trying to sort out this situation and protect my family.'

Jamie's face softened; her shoulders relaxed. She'd never heard those words uttered by him before. 'Am I the only one not bothered by him?'

'You and Nurse He-can't-do-no-wrong, who stuck up for him as I was telling her I wanted him gone.'

Jamie pursed her lips, searching the best way to approach the situation. 'Maybe you can't imagine Mum being happier – or at least happy – with this stranger, but it's clear from what I've heard that Mum and this bloke were in love.' Timothy threw his hands up in exasperation, as though he were losing *this* fight as well. 'I don't know why he's here, maybe it's nothing more than him wanting to say goodbye to an old flame and if so, then what's the harm?'

'That's what the funeral and wake will be for, for him to say his good-byes. *Here* is where immediate family should be, not some stranger who looks like the Crypt Keeper provoking us.'

'He hasn't bothered me or Chloe. Maybe if you and Ange spoke to him civilly, things would improve?'

'Why are you siding with Walter Matthau?' He jerked a thumb in Elijah's direction. 'Plus, has it even crossed your mind about how disrespectful it is to Dad? Yeah, remember that guy?'

Jamie grabbed her brother by his upper arms as if to shake sense into his thick skull. 'You're going too far! It's not like they had an affair behind Dad's back and here we all are, laughing about how funny it was. Dad wasn't even around then, and I have to say, this new melodramatic trait of yours is a big surprise. Is it something you picked up in London?'

'Wake up! It is disrespectful and if you don't see that then there's something wrong with you.'

Jamie's chest expanded as her eyes closed. 'I'm trying to strike a happy medium where we all benefit. I would hate to push him out of here before he came to do what he had to. Look into his eyes, there's nothing there.'

'Yes there is, it's called glaucoma.'

Jamie shook her head. 'Elijah came here to do something; he has a purpose. It doesn't really bother me who's here, because if he wasn't around, you, me and Ange would probably be arguing, anyway, and we really are only here watching her pass—' Timothy interrupted his sister with a prolonged scoff. 'Well, I'm sorry,' she continued, holding out her hands, 'but that's how I see it. We are standing around waiting for her final breath. There's nothing else they can do, and now it looks like she's got pneumonia. To me, this guy gives her life again, even if it was in a time that we never knew. I think he actually makes the mood lighter. Only you and Ange have a problem with him, and that's why he's acting out.'

Timothy turned around and they both observed Elijah throwing breadcrumbs into the lake, feeding an array of ducks that quacked and flapped with excitement.

It was clear Angela had whispered into Timothy's ear before he could make up his own mind; she'd influenced him before he'd met Elijah. It would take some time and a lot of convincing, but Jamie vowed to dismantle the preconceptions Angela had constructed in his mind, plank by plank, nail by nail.

Jamie believed the way Angela was carrying on was as if Elijah wasn't to be trusted around children. She knew better. Underneath his tough (*very* tough) exterior, there was nothing but tender feelings. Just like a tortoise shell, it protected the vulnerable parts inside.

'I know this is bizarre, but I'm sure if Mum were awake, she would love to have him by her side. Some of what I have heard so far is touching – for lack of a better word.' Jamie didn't miss the look of fake amusement in Timothy's eyes. 'Hey, I'm not asking you guys to join hands and sing "Kumbaya", but just take it easy on him and maybe let him finish his story. You might even get into it a bit if you keep an open mind – and I know you're a fan of modern history. Plus, it is also helping Chloe through this process of transition, too.'

To distract himself whilst Mr Fucking Big Shot spoke to Jamie, Elijah grabbed a handful of crumbs off the sandwich platter and chucked them into the clear-as-crystal lake, with weeping willows draped over the surface of the water. Among the hungry shovelers and whistling ducks, Elijah saw his image in the water below, but when a duck swam close, the rippling effect made his reflection vanish, as though his existence was being wiped out before his eyes.

Even so, Elijah welcomed the distraction and found pleasure in feeding the beautiful ducks that swam before him, but the tranquillity faded when someone behind him deliberately cleared their throat.

'Listen, Mr Samuels,' Timothy began, which made Elijah shudder. 'My family and I are going to grab a bite to eat from a nearby restaurant and, uh ...' He inhaled. 'We'd like it if you would come along, too. My shout, of course.'

'Thank you, but I will be all right here by myself.' Elijah threw the remaining chunk of bread and watched it sink until a blue-and-green

Cayuga dove head-first, grabbed it in its beak and swam away to eat in peace.

'No really, I insist.' Timothy paused. 'I think it would make us all feel more comfortable if you came along and told us a bit about yourself.'

'Please come,' Chloe said. 'I really want you to.'

Elijah turned around upon hearing her fragile voice, to see Angela in all her pompous glory, holding Chloe's hand. Upon seeing Angela's crinkled brow, he dusted his hands off on his trousers, outstretched his arms and gave a dashing smile. 'Beelzebub! I was wondering where you were.'

Jamie grabbed Angela by the waist, as she was in full stride. Jamie pulled her red-faced sister to the side, stating both she and Timothy had agreed that maybe things would be better if Elijah told them more about himself and his agenda for being here. Eventually Angela relented (still grinding her teeth), partly because they outnumbered her, and partly because she hadn't had a bite to eat since Bruce Maxwell had blown her up at midday.

Elijah grimaced at the glare Angela projected to him. 'Do yourself a favour, Angela, and ignore anyone who tells you to be yourself. Bad idea in your case.'

'Come on, guys,' Jamie began, walking over to him. 'Let's all calm down and grab a bite to eat—'

'He's *not* welcome!' Angela dragged Chloe by the hand up the ramp.

'Fine by me, ya prissy *twit*!'

'Nanna would have wanted you to come,' Chloe said, her heels digging into the concrete as Angela grappled with her.

Elijah's nostrils flared as he averted his face.

'I said *no*, Chloe!'

'Come on, what else do you have to do that's better than eating dinner with us?' Jamie said, placing her arm around his taut shoulders.

Elijah thought of the *Take 5* crossword puzzle resting on his cushion at home. 'A lot, actually!'

Jamie whispered into his ear, which caused him to flinch. 'Don't be scared of us. We're not going to hurt you, too.'

Chapter 39

JAMIE OFFERED ELIJAH a lift and he accepted, because if it had been Angela or Timothy, he might have done interior damage to their car.

'I don't, um, know why you've come back into Mum's life, especially now, but I for one am glad.' Jamie placed her hand on top of his, giving it a quick squeeze as she concentrated on the road in front.

'Thank you,' he murmured.

When Jamie's phone rang, she answered by pressing a button on her steering wheel.

'Yo, babe!'

The sound of a man's voice blaring through the car speakers made Elijah jolt. Jamie looked at him with a bemused grin, then looked back at Timothy's hire car in front, brake lights flashing arbitrarily as he rounded a bend and then took a narrow side street.

'Christ, can this guy drive, or what?' Elijah mumbled, looking at Timothy's car in front as the brake lights flashed red again. Jamie hit the brakes, while in front Timothy swerved, avoiding a parked silver Prius by mere millimetres.

'Babe?' the man said.

'Sorry, honey. So, are you coming down to eat with us? Tim and Tida are here now.'

Elijah stared at her dashboard in amazement, thinking how things were so different back in the '60s. The cars he used to drive didn't even have seatbelts until it became mandatory in the '70s.

'Nah, I can't. I'm going to be late, so you guys go ahead and eat. I'll get takeout or something. I've got a shitload of work to do tonight.'

'So … are you staying and eating at the office?'

'Yeah, babe. I'll do that and I can catch up with you guys tomorrow or something?'

Elijah didn't need to see her face to know it was masked with disappointment.

'Oh, okay, no worries. Well, good luck with work. I'll, um, I'll see you when I get home tonight.'

'Hey, look, don't wait up for me, yeah? I've got a long, hard night ahead of me. I'm sorry. Love you.' Boyd followed this with kissy sounds.

'Love you.'

Clunk.

'Dump him,' Elijah said to Jamie once she'd pressed the DISCONNECT button on the steering wheel.

Her lips pressed into a pale slash as she slowed down at a set of traffic lights. 'Excuse me?'

'Dump him,' Elijah repeated in the same tone and delivery.

The car came to a complete stop.

'Why would I dump my partner of over ten years because you say so?'

'You deserve better. Your mother is about to pass and he's your partner, which means you come first, work comes second. That's how it should go, no excuses.'

Jamie opened her mouth but fell short of speaking. The traffic lights turned green, and she crept forward.

'I don't remember asking for your opinion, Dr Phil.'

Elijah focused his attention on the procession of blurry objects they passed, including someone being lifted by a stretcher into an ambulance. 'No, but you asked me along for the ride and you did zilch to keep that conversation just between the two of you. My advice is to dump him before you catch him fooling around in your penthouse with his busty secretary.'

He turned to gauge her reaction.

Jamie's mouth was agape as though a pair of hands had encircled her throat. 'I think you're being quite rude,' she finally managed to say.

'I think I'm being quite honest. The tone in his voice, the delivery; the way he made out like you should have a good time while he slaves away in the office … oh yeah, he's cheating on you all right, and he's using this opportunity of your mother's welfare to his advantage – the smug prick.'

They continued the journey in awkward silence.

When he saw tears in her eyes, he had to remind himself of the aphorism: *You have to be cruel to be kind.* 'Jamie, I'm an old fart, I have no need to keep things to myself anymore; to chew things over, if you will. My life is too short now; I need to say what I see, while I'm able.'

Her hands tightened around the leather steering wheel. 'Chloe and I are the only ones on your side right now, yet you're treating me like dirt.'

He lowered his register. 'Hey, I'm just a stranger to you lot, remember? My thoughts and feelings shouldn't affect you at all.'

When they pulled up to another set of traffic lights, he glanced over and caught her knuckle a tear away. 'I know what will help, love. How about we join hands and sing "Kumbaya"?'

Chapter 40

ANGELA'S MERCEDES LED the convoy to a red-bricked Italian restaurant called L'Ultima Cena: The last supper.

Elijah licked his lips as he was partial to Italian cuisine, and he remembered how Audrey used to make the most delicious pasta sauce that would shit all over any native from Bologna.

Everyone hopped out of their cars and walked over to the restaurant, which appeared crowded – a testament to the good food and wine, or so Elijah hoped. Tida glared at Elijah as they walked through the chock-a-block car park, while Chloe gazed at him like he was a deity. It touched Elijah's heart that this little girl loved and cared for her grandmother the way she did, but it wasn't hard to understand why.

A waiter with a moustache and gapped front teeth motioned towards a six-seater table covered with a red-and-white checked tablecloth. As they took their seats, Elijah couldn't miss the lugubrious expression on Jamie's face. The waiter, who introduced himself as 'Juan', passed them each a threefold menu and filled their glass tumblers with Santa Vittoria water. Angela ordered two lots each of garlic bread and bruschetta for the table, while Dean Martin serenaded overhead through the speakers as they studied the menu.

Elijah held the menu up close and regarded the pizzas; it'd been a damn long time since he'd had a decent one.

It didn't take long for Angela to quiz Timothy about his life in London. As Elijah suspected, Tida hardly spoke English. When she did, it was broken and full of non sequiturs. A smile crept onto his face. He'd already pushed Timothy too far, but it was good to know he still had back-up ammo.

'What are you going to order?'

Elijah looked up at Chloe, who sat opposite him. 'If the pizzas taste as good as they smell then hallelujah! I'll be as happy as a pig in crap. What about you?'

She snickered and shook her head, side-glancing Angela, who was talking to Timothy. 'Hmm, I think I will have the vegetarian lasagna.'

Elijah frowned. 'Are you in fact a vegetarian, or do you just like boring food?'

'Eating animals is wrong! They shouldn't have to feel pain just so we can eat!'

Well, shit! Elijah would need to change his mind about the meat-lover pizza in order to keep her happy, and save himself from the lecture she would undoubtedly deliver. Back to the drawing board.

After Elijah placed his order for a simple Margherita pizza, he excused himself from the table – not that anyone was listening. Jamie left two minutes prior, leaving Timothy to voice his concerns to Angela about his apprehension of becoming a first-time father.

Outside the front of the restaurant, Elijah spotted Jamie leaning against a guardrail with a cigarette in one hand and her mobile phone in the other. The wind had abated, but a breeze was still present as he strolled towards her, watching her hair ripple about her drooping jowls.

'Got a spare?'

When she turned to him, pain gnawed at his tight throat over the tear tracks in her powdered face.

She cleared her throat, sniffling. 'Sure.' She held out a JPS packet, wiping her nose with the back of her other hand.

After igniting the tip with his Zippo, he turned to her. 'I didn't mean to upset you. I don't know what I am on about; I'm a silly old codger—'

'Boyd didn't answer.' She waved her mobile phone.

Elijah almost choked on the smoke he'd inhaled before he blew it out and stared at her in reticence.

She shrugged, turning away. 'I tried his work office, our home phone and his mobile, but they all rang through.' Strangely, Elijah felt livid – as though some punk had cheated on his own daughter – a daughter he'd never had.

'I had noticed this has been happening more often but I, um, didn't know how obvious it was till you mentioned it before.' She chuckled slightly.

'I'm sorry; I didn't want to be right. I just wanted to save you the pain.'

'It's not your fault; you speak your mind.'

Elijah twisted his face as he inhaled the cigarette's toxins. 'I could exercise more decorum.'

'That's true,' she said, sniffling through an attempted smile.

There was a moment of silence between them as they listened to cars zooming past, a train running on its tracks, and the sound of endless, incoherent chatter from inside the busy restaurant.

Jamie took a deep drag before looking at the sizzling, red-tipped cigarette almost in disgust. 'I am going to quit. I know it doesn't look too good, me smoking while trying to conceive, but some days it's just so *hard*.' She chucked the cigarette into the nearest bush as she exhaled smoke, turning to him. 'When did you become a philosopher?'

'I suppose as you get older and reflect on the years wasted on worry and anxiety, you realise how redundant it was. I have no need to hold anything back, but I suppose it's different for me, because I don't have the fear that you do. I say it how it is, because I have nothing left to lose. I understand you can't put an old head on a young person's shoulders. But I mean, Christ, over ten years and he hasn't even put a ring on your finger? *C'mon* … something's not right, love.'

Jamie glanced at her phone once more. 'I suppose I've been putting a lot of pressure on Boyd lately, as we're trying for a baby. It's my fault we can't get pregnant; I can *feel* that it is. There have just been so many appointments and tests and scans – perhaps he's over having sex on a time schedule these days. There's no romance in it; sex has become a chore to him. I've been so wrapped up in the thought of having a baby that I've let our relationship slide.'

'So, you're telling me that gives him the green light to fuck around behind your back – 'cause he's having too much sex at home?'

Her head lowered as tears glistened on her cheeks.

'You're still a spring chicken and you have the heart of your mother. But because of that, people will trample all over you and not even look back – just like some people did to Audrey.' He swallowed for much-needed lubrication. 'You don't need shitbags like that in your life. Kick him to the kerb to make way for Mister Right.'

She scratched her throat while looking at him. 'Oh, like it's that easy.'

'It's never easy. But things don't always turn out like you want them to, no matter how hard you try. And let me tell you something else. People think that love and compatibility are the foundation to any great relationship, but I can tell you from experience, it darn well isn't.' That piqued her interest, Elijah noted. 'The most quintessential thing a relationship *must* be built on is timing. Timing is of the essence in every part of life. I believe that two fantastic people who are compatible, can meet at the wrong time. It doesn't matter if the love they share is pure; bad timing will pull them apart like, like Velcro.' They both stepped aside on the footpath for an elderly couple leaving the restaurant, smelling of garlic, red wine and oregano. A minute later, their gold Hyundai i40 backfired as it took off. Elijah jolted as a result and placed a hand over his erratic heartbeat.

Jamie stepped towards him; her hand outstretched. 'Oh my God, are you okay?'

He exhaled, wincing. 'Yeah, just scared the bloody crap out of me, that's all.'

Jamie laughed and rubbed his arm.

Elijah shook his head, chuckling while straightening his spine. 'Do yourself a favour and never get old.'

'Duly noted. Now, where were we before you lost it?'

He smiled, glancing at the asphalt. 'Love, how can you meet the right person when you're holding on to the wrong one? It's time to let go, and whatever is meant for you *will* happen, but only when—'

'The timing is right.'

Chapter 41

AFTER DESSERT, CHLOE told Angela she'd left her artist's pad in Audrey's room, so they *had* to go back to get it.

Elijah admitted to himself that he'd had a good time, although it had more or less been him listening to stories the siblings shared between themselves.

Jamie drove Elijah, with Alanis Morissette's singing softening the awkward silence. Elijah couldn't apologise. Not if it would save Jamie from the heartache she'd endure at seeing her boyfriend entwined between another woman's thighs on their kitchen bench. Elijah was so certain Boyd Patterson was cheating on Jamie that he would have bet his left testicle.

'Nice meal tonight, wasn't it?' Elijah whispered, looking out at the blurry patches of streetlamps and traffic lights as they passed by.

Jamie nodded, trance-like while 'You Oughta Know' played in the background, like a befitting musical score. She grabbed a cigarette and then offered him the pack.

'Ta.' He took a protruding stick, then retrieved his Zippo. They both lit up and inhaled synchronously.

'Are you going to come back inside to say goodbye to Mum?' Jamie said, exhaling smoke through the wound-down window.

'If it was up to me, I'd never leave her side.'

***

'Do we have time for one more diary entry, Mother?' Chloe said, already settling back into her self-proclaimed chair.

'No.' Angela shut the curtains before tidying up tissues, Styrofoam cups and Arnott's biscuit wrappers that had accumulated around the room. 'Did you grab your art book?'

'I'd like to hear another one,' Jamie said, looking straight into Elijah's eyes. He caught on pretty quick, but knew his vote to stay a little longer would hold up like plastic in fire.

Angela turned to Jamie. 'What about visiting hours? People are trying to sleep.'

Jamie shrugged. 'No-one's said anything yet, have they? I think we have a bit of leniency given the fact this is a palliative situation. C'mon, just a bit longer.'

'Yeah, to tell you the truth, we're still wired from the trip. We probably won't be going to bed for a while – will we, honey?' Timothy asked Tida, putting his arm around her shoulders.

Tida nodded and smiled.

'Can you make it quick?' Angela said to Elijah, who was studying Audrey.

'I'll try to.' He realised he was at the part where Georgie came to his house the night he planned to dance with Audrey at Calypso.

Chapter 42

THEN – 1965

WHEN GEORGIE TURNED up out of the blue, Elijah presumed his parents were trying to set them up again. She was all dolled up in a YSL Mondrian dress and buckled winklepickers. His nostrils closed when her usual choice of Chanel perfume knocked him about. Her lips pulled back taut into a manufactured smile as her hands fidgeted in front of her.

'I'm sorry to come unannounced,' Georgie began, 'but I want to apologise.' Elijah stared at her, trying to figure out her angle. 'Honest to God, I am *so* sorry for how Shelley and I treated Audrey that day. It's been on my mind ever since and I have felt sick in the stomach because of it.' She wiped her hands over the sides of her dress. 'The truth is, I was spewing that you'd dumped me for her, but it was no excuse. It was totally no excuse, and if I ever raised a daughter who acted like that, I would feel like a failure.'

Tears streamed down her face and that's when he believed she was being genuine; not even Katharine Hepburn could act this well.

'It was a shitty thing to do.' He gritted his teeth at the memory.

'I know, I know, I know, I've been so unglued since, and the group isn't the same without you. All I want is to make peace with you both. And I don't want you back 'cause Brad and I are kinda getting serious, but I don't want this on my conscience, either.' She stopped twirling the ends of her hair and looked up as if making a solemn oath to God. 'I need to work on being a better person. There's a nasty streak in me and, like, I don't know where it comes from, but I want it gone. So please, tell Audrey I want to make it up to her, that I meant no harm. She can scream and cuss at me if she wants. I just want to stop feeling like I'm a total scuzz.'

Elijah held the eye contact before nodding once. 'I will tell her you popped over.'

'Right on! Y-You believe me though, right?'

Elijah shrugged, conscious of time slipping away. 'I want to know why it took you so long; if you felt guilty, then why didn't you come sooner?'

She fidgeted with her fingers, twisting them this way and that. 'I was a coward. I still am. But this is better than having that awful feeling inside of me. Plus, I wanted the guys to come, too, so we can all be a gang again.'

Elijah chuckled at the thought. 'That's not going to happen. I appreciate you coming here alone, it took guts, but I refuse to hang with those who think that people with a disability are a source of entertainment.' He brushed past her. 'If you'll excuse me …'

Georgie grabbed onto his tux, splitting a seam. 'Please don't say that! I only did it because that was the most obvious thing to hurt her with. The truth is, she's cherry! And I couldn't think of anything else to tease her about, so I went straight for that. It was crass, but I was hurting and high on dope at the time – we all were. The boys miss you. Alison misses you. Please come back to us, it ain't the same.'

He brushed her hands off his tux. 'Nah, but thanks for dropping by.' He began walking past the lion head water fountain over to his car.

Her ear-splitting shriek caused him to stop in his tracks, but he refused to turn around. 'Let me prove it to you!'

Elijah dropped his head, car keys dangling in his hand. 'Prove *what*?'

She stepped out in front of him so the house lights behind his frame now illuminated her briny eyes. 'That I am being sincere and want to help you guys out.' Her eyes roamed his stony face, breathing in and out. 'Are you planning on marrying her?'

Elijah nodded, not sure where she was going with this or whether that information would hurt her.

She smiled and dipped her knees. 'Groovy! Roberta owns a jewellery store down near Milson's Point – I think I told you about it?'

Elijah didn't remember much apart from the fact that Georgie's sister, who was busty yet svelte, had once tried to hit him up by grazing his crotch at one of Betty's shindigs when Georgie had gone for a toke. He'd spurned her advances and kept that little secret to himself.

'She'll give you a discount on an engagement ring, and I can tag along to help you choose the perfect one. It'll be rad! EJ, on my mother's life, I want to show you I mean I am sorry. Things with me and Brad are, like, totally grouse, so this isn't some lame attempt at making a play for you. You and I weren't meant to be; I realise that now that I have Brad.'

Elijah couldn't imagine that her being with an alcoholic womaniser like Bradley Edwin Jr. would have gone down great with her well-to-do parents, but he refrained from being too inquisitive. 'I'm glad you're in a better place and I'm glad you realise I never meant to hurt you. I think you need to lay off the drugs, though, and concentrate on getting your shit sorted.'

She shook her head from side to side, causing her go-go disc earrings to flop about. 'Right on! I agree – one hundred per cent. So, will you let me help you?'

He regarded her for a moment. 'I suppose, since I don't know what to look for with rings, yes.' He wondered how Audrey would take the news. *About as well as adding gasoline to a bonfire*, he guessed, but he needed Georgie to leave pronto. 'If it's not weird for you, then I suppose you can help me out this one time. But I'm not coming back to the gang. Audrey is my family now.'

Chapter 43

'WOW, YOU'RE IN the doghouse!' Chloe said as she flipped through the pages of Audrey's diary.

'Where did you learn "doghouse" from?' Angela said, one eyebrow raised.

Chloe looked up with a serious expression. 'From Dad.'

Everyone in the room erupted in hysterics.

'Sounds about right,' Elijah mumbled to himself with a know-all smile, before an unexpected cough ejected from his lungs.

'Just read the next chapter so we can get on with it,' Angela said, and Elijah noted the faint beginnings of a blush.

Mmm, well, what do you know? he thought, before gazing down and detecting a drop of either blood or Napoli sauce on his pants. He chose to believe it was the latter.

'29ᵗʰ April 1965. Dear Diary, I hate him! We had a massive blue because he's cheating on me with Georgie! EJ told me to wait outside my house because we were going to a new nightclub called Calypso. Well, I was waiting in my best dancing outfit that Mum had bought me (the nice blue one), and he stood me up! I waited for ages before I went back inside. While I was in my room, he started throwing stones at the window. Instead of opening it up to converse that way, I ran downstairs and confronted him. He was talking nonsense, so I asked him this, dear Diary: Were you with Georgie? His reluctant response: Yes. I turned around after he admitted the affair, and he tried to talk to me, but I didn't want to listen. I made it to the front door and locked it behind me,

with him pleading for me to listen; he even pounded on the panel, claiming it wasn't what it sounded like. Yeah, right! Is he fair dinkum? I feel at an all-time low and it makes me wish I had my mother to talk to. I hate my life. I always knew he would break my heart, but I didn't think it'd be so soon. Audrey.'

As Chloe lowered the diary, everyone stared at Elijah as if to badger him with questions.

'Read the next entry, Chloe. Please ... be my guest.'

Chloe flipped the page of her grandmother's diary and smiled upon seeing the date at the top of the page. 'This is the same night.'

Elijah intertwined his fingers.

'Wait!' Everyone turned to Chloe, who looked into Elijah's eyes. 'How did my great-grandparents die? Don't avoid telling me any longer, please.'

Elijah looked at Angela, who looked at Timothy, who looked at Tida, who was looking at the wall clock. 'Well, kid, they, ah, they died on the HMAS *Voyager* in February 1964.'

Chloe cocked her head. 'What do you mean; how?'

Elijah shifted in his seat. 'The ship was involved in a fatal collision with an aircraft carrier, HMAS *Melbourne* – I believe it was. It sliced the ship clean in half, killing everyone on board as it ... went up in flames.' He cleared his throat. 'Joyce and Henry Hughes were among those who perished on the ship.'

Chloe's eyes filled with tears as she shook her head. 'You mean – they burned to death?'

Elijah glanced towards Angela for back-up. There was nothing to be said except the truth – if not from him, then from the Internet. 'Yeah, kid. Unfortunately, they did.'

Chloe closed her eyes as tears splashed the pages of the diary. She covered her face with one hand and whimpered, bending over. Elijah looked at Angela as if to ask if she should put her arms around her daughter, when at last Chloe removed her hand and inhaled with a quivering lip.

'Thank you for telling me.' She swallowed, opening her eyes. 'I th-think we should move on.'

'You don't have to; we can go home and—'

She wiped her face, sniffling hard. 'No, Mother. I wish to continue, please.'

Elijah lowered his eyes on remembering the countless times he'd wiped away Audrey's tears of pain. The countless times he held her in his arms as she wept uncontrollably, especially after waking from night terrors, and especially leading up to, and on, the one-year anniversary of her parents' passing.

Chloe clutched the diary tighter before she cleared her throat and began: *'Dear Diary, I am completely in love with him! I just experienced the most amazing, romantic night of my life. I am writing to you from the day after, but it all started last night. When I was crying, thinking it was all over between us, out of nowhere, I heard some rock 'n' roll-type tune blasting from outside. I jumped out of my skin, but what did I see below my window? I saw MY MAN with a guitar and amp. He waited for me to open my window before he strummed the guitar and began singing 'Keep on Running'. Uncle Lloyd, who had returned home from poker night, went ballistic and threatened to call the fuzz. A neighbour turned on her porch light and came out into the front yard, wearing a pink robe with curlers in her hair. It seemed the performance annoyed most people considering the time, but not me. Even if it wasn't his original song, it is a song that I adore by the Spencer Davis Group, and EJ did a remarkable job singing it, despite my neighbours yelling at him. I ran down during mid-song, with tears streaming. What else is new, right? I hugged him around the neck and kissed him senseless ...'*

Chapter 44

THEN – 1965

'BABY GIRL, IT'S *not* how it looks with Georgie, I swear on my nan's grave. You gotta let me explain,' Elijah said before Lloyd shouted out again, informing them the police were on the way.

Elijah grabbed her shoulders. 'Let's move in together. I don't want to be apart from you; it's killing me!'

Audrey grabbed his face and grinned as more tears developed. 'Yes.'

Elijah placed his cherry-red Maton guitar on top of his Goldentone Bassmaster amplifier, and grabbed her hands. 'Y-You want to move in with me; to get our own place far away from here to start a new family of our own?'

When Audrey nodded vigorously, his hands held hers tighter and he grinned, then put his head down so she couldn't see the emotion on his face. They turned towards the sound of approaching police sirens.

'I'm coming with you!' Audrey shouted over the wailing.

His head shot up.

'Take me with you!'

He took her arm and led her to his car, despite Lloyd's protesting as he bounded down the rickety steps. 'Shit, I left my guitar—'

'Drive!'

Elijah screeched off just as Lloyd reached the footpath. 'You make me feel so alive!' His smile reached his earlobes as he pushed against the steering wheel with outstretched arms.

'You're telling me. Now the fuzz are after us!' Audrey burst into laughter – the kind of laugh brought on by sheer liberation.

'God, what have I done to you?' Elijah glanced at his girl.

Audrey leaned over and kissed the side of his face. He twisted his neck to kiss her lips, keeping his eyes on the road all the while.

'I love you too much,' she whispered into his ear.

'I crave it, baby. It's never going to be *too* much, so keep it comin'.'

The sirens continued yowling, and through the side mirrors the young lovers could now see the red-and-blue flashing lights materialise from the darkness.

'What's going to happen?' Audrey looked out the back window as Elijah lit a cigarette while driving one-handed.

'Not much. What can they do? But I don't want you getting mixed up; I should let you go somewhe—'

'No, you won't! We're in this together!'

'I don't know what I was thinking.' He scowled and punched the steering wheel. 'I'm so sorry; it was selfish of me—'

'EJ, you're part of me. Wherever you go, I go! Now shut up and drive!'

Elijah glanced into her eyes for a split second before looking back to the road and raising the cigarette to his lips. He'd seen the love, felt the happiness, and she, too, looked like she wanted to scream with joy.

Elijah changed back a gear on an S-shaped bend and sped down the mountainside, losing the police before eventually parking his car in a concealed spot on the sandy beach and flipping the lights. Darkness entombed them, apart from a faint blue glow in the sky. The roar of the thundering ocean in front of them was their orchestra, conducted by the moon.

They sat still and let what had just happened sink in, before looking at each other and cracking up laughing. Audrey climbed onto Elijah's lap as he reclined his chair and they kissed, tearing off each other's clothes. Once naked, Elijah pulled her into the back seat, positioning her underneath him, where heavy breathing soon replaced laughter.

'Let's never grow old; let's stay young and reckless for the rest of our lives,' he whispered afterwards, looking down at her in the shadows as his thumb grazed her cheek.

'But we have so much to look forward to when we get older.' She nipped his prickly chin with her teeth.

'Hmm, that's true. Fine, let's grow old together, but let's remain happy and in love like this forever – deal?'

'Deal.' She pulled on his dog tags so he could kiss her senseless.

***

Audrey awoke the next morning as an orange sun rose over the azure-blue ocean. Far out to sea, streams of pulsating light saturated the undulating surface of the water with a golden haze – the promise of a new day. The blanket Elijah had wrapped around their naked bodies still covered them, and the moment made Audrey shiver in delight. In the comfort of his arms, with his warm body behind her, she slowly turned to inspect his face, which looked peaceful and angelic. She brushed his lips with hers. Elijah's lips spread into a smile, then he opened his eyes to focus on hers before shutting them and pulling her closer. Nestled under his prickly chin, Audrey listened to the waves hitting the coarse sand, and the call of gulls and terns circling high above; their raucous cries reverberating off the towering cliffs. A tear trickled down her cheek when she placed a hand over his beating heart and discovered it was in sync with hers.

Chapter 45

THEN – 1965

A FEW WEEKS after the police chase, Audrey and Elijah began the search for their dream home. Because Lloyd grounded her again after Elijah's guitar stunt, she had to tell him a fib about going to work just so she could see her paramour. Elijah picked her up from the parlour and they split to the Black-and-White Milk Bar on the corner of Keira Street, where a gathering of angry anti-Vietnam peaceniks were handing out propaganda pamphlets.

Inside the milk bar, they sat in one of the walnut veneer booths along the wall near a wall-to-wall mirror, and ordered spider soda drinks (lime for Elijah and raspberry for Audrey) with a plate of lamingtons and scorched almonds, while 'Sherry' by the Four Seasons played overhead. Pert uniformed waitresses delivered steak and eggs or sundaes to other patrons, or worked on the soda fountain pumps, keeping up with demands from ravenous customers who'd become addicted to the American influences. Audrey and Elijah loved visiting this milk bar, which was a marriage between food and fantasy with its round windows, curvilinear art deco style, and an endless list of soda flavours for just sixpence, but Elijah would never have dared say this to Betty Wallis. No fucking way in hell.

With their bellies full and hearts expanding, the two young lovers set off on an adventure: looking for a house to call theirs.

While Audrey inspected things in the houses they viewed, Elijah kept his eyes focused on her. As he stared at her with hungry eyes, he silently thanked Cupid that Audrey fancied him the way he fancied her. Months before it may have appeared that he was saving her, but actually, she had saved him. He had cut down on smoking, he'd stopped gambling and punting, he'd ditched his low-life friends, his hands hadn't seen blood for a while and he felt much calmer, all thanks to her. He had no doubt the senders of this angel from above were his father's parents, Joseph and Elaine.

The third house they ended up at was a single-storey fibro house up on the hills at Carmel – a tranquil country town that was on the verge of major expansion, including a new variety store called Coles and a new department store called Big W.

They inspected the house with Dick Carpenter from Martin Morris and Jones Realty. Enthusiasm was printed on Audrey's face like a tattoo. Elijah felt enthusiastic, too – not just about the house, but what the house would represent. A home; something that was the epitome of the word 'family'.

As Elijah ran a finger over a waxed cabinet top, he pictured Audrey pregnant, running around, chasing their little son who'd be dressed in cute overalls. He pictured them with a magnificent garden, a beautiful dog in the backyard; he could even smell Audrey's homely cooking wafting from the kitchen. In his reverie, he pictured coming home from work to see his loving wife standing there in the hallway with open arms, encircling his body, shielding him from the outside world that too often dealt harsh and unfair circumstances.

It struck him like a blow to the face as he watched Audrey appraising the kitchen: she was not only his drug, but the supplier as well.

After viewing several houses, they both agreed on one. It was a modest house – nothing too flash – situated upon a high cliff overlooking the ocean. The elderly owners wanted to retire to the countryside near Orange, having looked at the ocean their entire life. The asking price was well within Elijah's budget, plus (unbeknownst to Audrey) he added another few thousand pounds on the asking price for good measure. It wasn't a mansion – but that's what he loved about it. It was the type of place that could be called *home*, not just a 'house'. He didn't care how many rooms it had; he cared about the memories they would create there together.

As they stood in the backyard, Audrey said she would take on two jobs to help pay the bills. Over his dead body, he told her. She said she didn't want it to seem like she was sponging off him.

This made him twitch, because the fact she knew he was loaded and yet she still offered to work two jobs showed the type of person she was. They left the house after Elijah made an offer, and took a stroll in the neighbourhood, stopping in front of Rickard's Tackle and Bait.

Audrey turned to Elijah with unshed tears and he knew why – he felt it, too. They were high above sea level as the wind danced around them seductively. The sky looked like streaky chalk on a blackboard, stony grey clouds moving overhead with unnatural slowness. Elijah pretended to study them as an excuse to cling to his lover, his best friend, his absolute everything.

'I can't believe this is happening,' she said, hugging Elijah tight as though at any moment the wind would pick up and carry him away.

'I know. This is outta sight! Thank you for not giving up on me.' Elijah rubbed his nose against hers at the precise moment thunder clapped in the leaden sky.

'Oh, look!' Audrey squealed, so he turned as she pointed to a German shepherd pup in the window of Bryce's Pet Store. The adorable two-tone fluffball was curled up on sheets of *The Illawarra Mercury*, mouth open with his tongue hanging out as he slept – probably dreaming of a T-bone.

'Do you want him?' Elijah whispered as she gazed at the doggy in the window.

Audrey leaned back to face him. 'Is it an option?'

The corner of his mouth lifted as he searched her eyes. 'Of course; you won't go without while you're with me, do you hear?'

Audrey shrieked and hugged him tight as a gust of wind delivered a carnival of smells, including fish and chips and salt water.

Elijah's chin rested on top of her head as he closed his eyes in contentment. 'Is that a yes, baby – do you want the dog even though you already have a cat?'

Audrey nodded, her face pressed against his chest, so he kissed the top of her head and said, 'Then he shall be ours.'

She screamed and jumped up and down. He laughed at her infectious enthusiasm, adoring how her eyes lit up whenever she was excited. After her parents passed away, her happy days had been like sunny days in Greenland: brief and rare. Now she was the cheeriest girl in the world and it filled Elijah with emotion so overwhelming he almost toppled over.

They held hands, swinging them like a pendulum from side to side. 'This is it, baby. Just you and me, and well ... now the dog – and Misty – but no-one else around to tell us what to do. No-one around to hear you *scream* at night,' he teased, facing her with a wicked smile. Her cheeks coloured and she turned away to focus on the dog, so he kissed her cheek and laughed at her blushing. 'What are you going to call him?' He adjusted his black beanie as the icy wind accelerated.

She looked from the dog, then to Elijah. 'Mmm ... Corey. Like the male lead in the book I'm reading. He's strong and loyal. Yes, Corey suits him, I think. You?'

Elijah squeezed her around the waist as they stared at little Corey. 'Sounds good to me.'

'Misty and Corey will be the best of friends – I can feel it!'

Thunder clapped like cannon fire around them again, but no precipitation appeared. All the same, Elijah held her tighter.

She turned to face him, teary-eyed. 'EJ, I want you to know I love you as deeply as I possibly can. I am grateful I found you. But I must warn you: now you're stuck with me!'

Elijah laughed. 'I hope that's a promise?' He rolled up a sleeve. 'The time, according to Mister Rolex, is 6:29 pm on the dot. I hereby declare

to you that from this day forward we will remain side by side, tackling'
– he pointed to the tackle and bait shop for a laugh – 'life's obstacles
together. We are going to give our kids a better life than what we had,
and I *swear* to love you for as long as I breathe. So, the next time you
look at a clock and see 6:29, think of me here and now, making a solemn
oath with my grandparents as witnesses, that I will be your protector,
your shelter, and your guardian for as long as you'll have me. I love you,
Mrs Samuels.'

***

Elijah whistled a merry tune when he waltzed up the carpeted stairs
towards his bedroom later that night. The next thing to do was to make
it official by claiming her his own with a wedding ring. God, he was one
lucky son of a gun; he must have been a saint in his previous life because
things didn't add up.

'Son, we're glad you're home,' Howard said.

Elijah turned around at the top of the stairs to see his father, dressed
in red silk pyjamas, sipping brandy from a snifter.

'We need to talk.'

Elijah grinned. 'Why, yes we do, Daddy-O. I have an announcement
to make.' He cupped a hand to the side of his face. 'Mother dearest, where
are you?'

Grace and Margaret appeared around the corner to join Howard at the
bottom of the stairs.

Margaret leered at her son. 'Oh, honestly, Elijah! What's got into you;
are you drunk again?'

Elijah placed a hand to his chest. 'Very kind for asking. I am announcing
that Audrey and I are going to be moving in together. I put an offer on a
house today. I am also going to propose to her – properly this time.' He
held up the palm of his right hand. 'Now-now … I know I don't need your
approval; I can tell how eager you are to have her as your daughter-in-law.
I can see it every time you mention her name.'

Elijah stared at his parents with a smart-arse grin, but they didn't waver. However, Grace folded an arm across her stomach, her shoulders slumped, and her downcast eyes gave Elijah the impression something sinister was at hand; her face was bereft of colour.

His face dropped as his spine straightened. 'What's wrong; what's happened?'

Howard ascended the stairs one at a time, a hand concealed behind his back. 'I'm afraid that won't be possible.'

Elijah raised a mocking eyebrow. 'Got better plans mapped out for me again, do you?'

Howard shook his head as Grace cupped her face with both hands, chest heaving. The last time Elijah saw his sister cry was at their grandmother's funeral years before.

'No, son, but the government does.'

Elijah's mocking sneer straightened and he looked at Howard, dumb-founded, before his father shoved a service letter in his face.

'You've been called up for Vietnam.'

Chapter 46

'NO!' NURSE MILDRED screamed from the doorway, which started a domino effect. Elijah snapped his diary shut in a fright, Tida shrieked, and Angela shot Nurse Mildred a displeased glance, because she had also jumped.

The room went quiet enough to have heard a mouse fart. Everyone directed their attention to Nurse Mildred.

'I'll be back in a jiffy,' Nurse Mildred said before rushing off with a stifled sob.

'I didn't even know she was standing there,' Timothy said in a low tone, placing a hand over his chest.

Jamie's eyes were misty. So were Chloe's, and so were Angela's.

'I think that's enough for tonight, Mr Samuels,' Angela said, clearing her throat and diverting her attention to her wristwatch. Elijah didn't have to be an expert on human behaviour to know Angela was angry she'd let her guard down by getting wrapped up in the story. He found it touching.

'So that's how you two ended,' Jamie said, more to herself, as if realising it was the answer to a puzzle she'd been trying to solve. 'The whole time I've been listening to this beautiful and touching love story, I've been wondering what separated you two lovebirds. And now I know: it was 'Nam.'

Nurse Mildred returned, blowing her nose into a tissue, just as Elijah coughed into his hanky. The acidic tomato sauce from the pizza was causing havoc with his reflux. As he pulled his hand away, he was certain this time he saw clumps of dark red blood. He crumpled the hanky and shoved it back in his jacket pocket before clearing his throat. 'Yes, it is very late and I've already taken up too much of your time. Besides, if I don't get up now, I'll more than likely get piles.'

Chloe's head tilted. 'What's piles?'

'That's when ya git cherries on yer clacker, pumpkin,' Nurse Mildred said, straight-faced.

'Pardon?'

'God, why me?' Angela whispered, looking towards the ceiling as Jamie laughed.

Chloe turned to her mum with pleading eyes. 'He's only halfway through his story; there's so much more that needs to be told. Please let him come back tomorrow.'

Angela's chest expanded.

Elijah had risen from the chair and shuffled over to kiss Audrey's forehead before he turned around to catch everyone staring at him as though he were still some stranger kissing their mother. 'Goodnight, everyone.'

They all mumbled words of farewell as he limped out the door without another word.

Elijah had travelled halfway down the sterile corridor and stopped to inspect the bloodied hanky under the monochromatic lighting above, when he heard: 'Mr Samuels.'

Shoving the hanky back in his pocket, he turned around in a heartbeat as Angela faced him at the entrance to Audrey's room.

She inhaled, folded her arms and held his gaze. 'My family and I would like to see you back here tomorrow, if you're not too busy?'

Elijah dipped his head. 'Thank you. However, I never planned on staying away.'

Chapter 47

JAMIE DROVE HOME that night, barely blinking. It was as though someone had yanked the plug and all her emotions and thoughts had drained away.

Subconsciously she'd known Boyd was cheating on her – didn't every victim of infidelity on *some* level know?

She pulled into the driveway, high beams illuminating the cobalt garage shutters, and sighed. The only sign of Boyd Patterson's car was an oil stain on the concrete, which she'd discovered this morning after he left for work. The absence of his car at night was becoming the ordinary. She didn't know if she should cry or laugh that a complete stranger had the guts to say what was going on, when she herself didn't even want to think it.

Jamie dragged herself inside her loft and thought about the love affair between her mother and Elijah as a welcome distraction. Anything was better than visualising Boyd pumping into another woman from behind.

Jamie switched on the lights and shook her head as if to dislodge the repugnant images, and focused on the stories Elijah spoke of that day. It certainly seemed to have affected Elijah, and deep down she knew it would have shaken her mother to the core. Sometimes love can do that to a person, but realisation dawned – it hadn't happened to *her*. When Jamie met Boyd, he didn't sweep her off her feet; in fact, from memory, she'd despised him. But the hunky football player with the red Corvette had persisted, and eventually she'd relented due to the premature fear of ending up a spinster.

Now, Boyd had a steady job as a systems analyst (his football days long gone thanks to beer and deep-fried food) and he took care of her, but their relationship had become weighed down by monotony and recurring patterns of ovulation charts and (for Boyd) ejaculating into a cup beside a porno mag in a private room to identify whose fault at failing to get pregnant it was. Their relationship was steady; dependable. The type that people married for forty years find themselves in. A stage (or rut) where everything becomes predictable and expected, and based on tolerating each other because putting effort into finding someone new is too damn hard. Better the devil you know, right?

They seldom had fights, but all in all, their relationship was stagnant. Their life together hadn't plummeted into the pits of the earth, but then again, it hadn't catapulted to the peaks of ecstasy, either. Jamie couldn't remember the last time they had gone out on a random date, or even for a scenic drive while listening to classic rock (belting out 'Bohemian Rhapsody' in a duet) like they used to in the early days.

Scooby (their golden retriever) ran to her, tail wagging and tongue protruding like a pink slippery dip. Jamie knelt to scratch behind his ears before planting a kiss on his wet nose. But his nose was wet from her own tears; tears produced by the realisation Scooby loved her more than her high school sweetheart.

While Jamie filled Scooby's bowl with kibble, she compared her own relationship to the one between Elijah and her mother, and laughed. First, there was no way Boyd would have gone for a person with a hearing aid.

Jamie knew her mother hated what God had cursed her with, but Audrey had never played on it, or used it as an excuse for anything.

No, Audrey had wanted a normal life – and *that* she had received in abundance.

Chapter 48

ELIJAH SAT IN his rocking chair, glass of milk in hand to combat the reflux, watching a movie about soldiers battling it out in the jungle; men screaming in agony while they waited for air support.

He eyed his blank *Take 5* crossword puzzle and contemplated for a long time whether he wanted to complete it. His mind was too wayward, so instead he opted to go to the cupboards near the foot of the staircase and unlock the small vault – something he hadn't done in years, yet he still had the key to the lock on his master keychain. The door gave an eerie squeal as if the gates of doom were opening, and he found the photo album he desired beneath soot and cockroach faeces. It was damn near sacrilege, he thought. His maroon diary didn't fit inside here with the other meaningful items; he'd packed it away in a cardboard box with other books and it had remained in a spare bedroom until the night he'd received a call from Grace.

Elijah blew dust off the album cover with what little air came out of his congested lungs, and waddled back to his chair before plonking down with a grunt, ignoring the dull ache in his belly.

He turned the TV volume down when the soldiers' screams became unbearable.

Opening the inscribed cover, Elijah looked at the picture inside the first sleeve. It was a black-and-white photo of Audrey and him, taken on Christmas Day, 1964 – roughly five weeks after they'd met. Audrey gave him this album months later, on one of the worst days of his life. Through tears, he stared at the photo he hadn't seen in decades, but same as before, the first thing he zeroed in on was their infectious smiles.

With bated breath, he steeled himself to once again read the sweet message Audrey had written on the inside cover:

Dearest EJ,

I love you more than words can describe. We may be apart for a while, but it will only strengthen what we have.

When you get back, we will fulfil our dreams of having our own family, and together we shall battle whatever life throws at us.

You need to believe that nothing will EVER change my love for you.

I know you will find a way back to me. I know because we were meant to be together, forever.

Thank you for loving me unconditionally for who I am and for putting up with my insecurities. There may only be one photo in here, but think of it as a promise of good things to come; of the things to look forward to when you come back to Australia.

Please return home in one piece so we can stock up this album with pictures of our dreams that we fulfil over the years. As you can see, I've left the second page free for our furry son, Corey.

My heart will always beat for you, my darling, so I will be right here waiting for you with open arms, no matter how long it takes.

All my love,
Audrey xoxo

27th May 1965

Chapter 49

THEN – 1964

FOR CHRISTMAS, ELIJAH surprised Audrey by booking a cabin at Jenolan Caves. Audrey was too embarrassed to have Elijah go to her house for Christmas (not that Lloyd would have allowed it), and he was damn certain he didn't want to associate with his side of the family, either.

Jenolan Caves was to be an unforgettable experience for both of them, and it revealed Elijah's romantic side as he had booked a remote cabin, complete with a fireplace and kitchenette. Although Audrey felt bad that she'd left Lloyd alone over the Christmas period, she soaked up every second she spent with Elijah.

They made love night after night on a rug by the blazing fire as Christmas carols played over the ham radio. On the first night, they snuggled in bed, sipping hot cocoa as special re-runs of *The Twilight Zone* aired, and later on they played card games, drank brandy custard and ate gingerbread cookies.

The next day – Christmas Eve – they explored the dazzling Imperial Cave with a tour guide, and later on endured a nature hike before the frigid chill of the afternoon set in, when they retired to their cabin.

When Christmas morning came around, Elijah wore only a Santa's hat and checked blue-and-white pyjama pants as he knelt beside the bed, looking at Audrey's angelic face. He wished he could give her the gift of bringing her parents back, but showing her how much he loved and needed her would have to suffice.

'Wakey-wakey,' he whispered, but she moaned and turned over.

Elijah laughed and caressed her bare back with his fingertips. 'Merry Christmas, sweetheart.'

Audrey shot up and blinked rapidly. Her eyes danced when she discovered Elijah had decorated the entire cabin with tinsel, and set up a small tree in the corner by the burnt-out fireplace.

'Merry Christmas!' she said, high-pitched and wide-eyed. 'When did you do all this?'

'While you snored your head off, young lady.' He grinned, stood and stretched as she wiped her tears away. After he booked the cabin, he'd chucked whatever dusty decorations he could find into the boot of his EH and, considering he'd never been allowed to decorate his parents' house, or even the Christmas tree (even as a child), he thought he did a pretty all right job. Elijah admitted he'd enjoyed himself, and he pictured the two of them and their children decorating their own tree in a few years to come.

As he stood next to the bed, Audrey wrapped her arms around his naked waist while he gazed down at her – a pretty impressive sight, considering she had just woken up. He tried to absorb her pain as best he could, swallowing deeply when her hot tears soaked his naked torso.

Later they sat on the bed and exchanged gifts before Audrey made breakfast from the supplies they'd bought along the way – fried Spam and eggs on toast – and Elijah put on a pot of fresh Bushells coffee while he serenaded Audrey. They ate on the back veranda, gazing out into the vast wilderness of flora and fauna, seeing wallabies and kangaroos going about their day as the bright orange sun peeked over the tops of the native trees, allowing light to streak through the boughs in both brilliant and shadowy beams. The rich fragrance of leaves and loam tantalised the lovers' nostrils.

After they ate, Elijah motioned for Audrey to sit on his lap. He rested his head against her shoulder and hugged her body, wrapped in a white robe. Audrey placed her chin on his head and encircled her arms around his neck and shoulders.

Elijah sighed in contentment and closed his eyes as the morning sun warmed their faces, while birdsong and cicadas chorused throughout the dense forest. A lyrebird appeared near a collection of pine trees before darting off and for a moment, the young lovers felt ensconced in a magical world of their own.

They remained cuddling until Audrey lifted her head and brushed aside a strand of Elijah's hair that covered his black lashes. She looked deep into his eyes before dipping her head to kiss him as his hands roamed over her back. After Elijah had kissed her thoroughly, he swiftly patted her backside and suggested they explore the Devil's Coach House, a vast cave near the Jenolan Caves House, free to all guests. He also told her he'd booked them on another cave tour, this time in the Temple of Baal.

That night they ate in the Chisholm Restaurant of the main building – a short drive from their secluded cabin – as dinner was part of the Christmas package.

Elijah wore a pink-and-black pinstripe suit, while Audrey chose a red V-neck swing dress and black Mary Jane heels (he had told her to pack clothes for any occasion).

A Christmas bon bon and tealight candle was on each table, and they both donned the conical striped party hats provided. Christmas dinner was turkey with cranberry sauce and apricot stuffing, assorted veggies and a damper roll, plus a complimentary glass of warm spiced-apple cider. Dessert was Christmas pudding with custard and berries, which they both heartily delved into. A waiter clad in a suit and braces went around to each table and took a picture of the guests, promising to mail it out to them once printed, with a watermark logo and the date. Elijah had pulled Audrey onto his lap, ignoring shocked onlookers, and clamped his arms around her waist as she laughed and leaned her head on his, while the charismatic photographer snapped the moment that would last a lifetime, with a mere quick flash of his camera.

After waiters cleared the empty dessert plates, Elijah held out his hands flat on the table and Audrey took them in hers with a smile. He glanced at their entwined fingers and moved his thumbs over her soft skin, focusing on one finger in particular. When Elijah looked up, he zeroed in on her downturned mouth and asked what was wrong.

Audrey wiped a solitary tear away and shook her head. 'Gosh, I feel guilty for saying this when my parents are no longer around, but I never thought I'd be happy again. I didn't think it was an option for me. And then you came into my life. But I am *so* scared of losing what we have because I don't think I'll be the same again. Ever.'

Elijah focused his attention back to their entwined hands, his forehead crinkled. 'Wild horses couldn't tear me away from you.' He gripped her hands tighter, his nostrils flaring. 'Thank you for loving me the way you do. You've completely changed my life.' Elijah's stormy eyes pinned Audrey's as he leaned over the table to seal the moment with a kiss.

The staff had games organised, including trivia. Elijah was impressed how knowledgeable Audrey was on subjects he wouldn't have expected. Overall, out of twenty teams, Elijah and Audrey came second, and only to a group of eight. Their prize was a box of Hoadley's chocolates and a bottle of Barossa Pearl. After various groups had played Etch-A-Sketch and bingo, the guests took to the waxed dance floor. Elijah took Audrey into his arms and spun her around, watching her red dress twirl like a whirlwind as guests side-stepped out of their way. They both smiled as she draped her arms around his neck and they stared into each other's eyes. He dipped his head to kiss her before jazz music replaced 'The Twist', and all the guests attempted the Lindy Hop.

Later that night, Elijah suggested they do the 'spooky ghost tour' of the Lucas Cave, which he loved because Audrey snuggled to his chest when she got scared. After that experience, they settled by the crackling fireplace in their cabin and began making sweet love to the sound of Frankie Valli.

'Can I tell you a secret?' he whispered through laboured breathing, leaning back and watching the shadows of the blazing fire dance over her glorious skin, which shone like the embers.

She nodded, interlacing her fingers around his damp neck while unwrapping her ankles from around his bottom.

'I knew I loved you from the moment I saw you walk through the door of Betty-Sue's.'

She stared at him through half-dazed eyes, panting softly. 'I thought you hated me; why did you act all pompous?'

Elijah paused and swallowed, looking deep into her baby blues. 'Because I was scared.'

Chapter 50

ELIJAH FLIPPED THE pages over in the photo album; blank page after blank page that were supposed to be filled with photos to match the captions Audrey had written at the bottom. Page two was captioned *Corey*; page three, *First House*; page four, *Wedding Day*; page five, *First Child*; page six, *Second Child*; page seven, *First Family Vacation …*

It was soul-crushing for Elijah to flip through an empty album that had once held so much promise of things to come.

When the pain became unbearable, he slammed the album shut with a loud *thud,* as abruptly as life had shut down his hopes and dreams.

Through blurry eyes, Elijah glanced at the TV to the image of a soldier bleeding out as his buddies tried to cauterise a wound.

A small whimper of pain emerged from Elijah's trembling lips and his nostrils flared as he grappled with swirling emotions. He struggled to suck in air as a sharp pain jabbed his ribs. *Shit!*

The grandfather clock ticked incessantly and he knew his days, just like Audrey's, were drawing to an end; it was only a matter of time. He'd never imagined in a million years saying goodbye to Audrey. He'd always assumed due to his habitual smoking, he'd be the first to go.

Audrey's condition hadn't improved since she first went under. Her organs were shutting down and he understood now: she was just *tired*.

Nathaniel Grant had been discussing with Angela, who then informed everyone else, that he was considering upping her morphine dosage. There was nothing they could do to save her. There were only so many times you can fix an old, beat-up car before you had to accept it was a lost cause. That was the state of the nation, folks. Medicine did not equal miracle.

Sheba wandered in from the backyard and plonked down next to her master, placing her head on his slipper as she gazed up. Elijah stared at her for a moment. The album slipped from his trembling hands, landing only inches from Sheba's head, as the dam wall collapsed. Hot tears squeezed out of his clenched eyes and his chest heaved as if an invisible pair of hands were performing compressions. Elijah breathed heavily, gasping handfuls of air, while stabbing pains assailed his heart and stomach, before *PING!* the sound of the microwave made him jump and clench his brittle fists. He had lost control, yet again. With shaky hands, he leaned over to scratch his loyal dog on the head and reasoned she deserved a treat; it was the least he could do, as she had given so much already.

After Elijah regained his composure, he fetched Sheba a chicken neck from the near-empty refrigerator, and while listening to her crunching away he decided to call his lawyer to see what last-minute changes he could make to his will. After shuffling back into the living room with a warm lavender wheat bag, he grabbed the remote control, intending to switch off the telly. Then he realised – it had never been turned on to begin with.

Chapter 51

THE NEXT MORNING, Elijah made a cup of tea, then stared into the mirror to comb his wispy hair. He visualised having the silky, jet-black hair that women used to love raking their fingers through. Time did not treat people well, but that was part of life. He'd had a fairly long shot at it; too bad he regretted most of it … *Better luck next time, pal,* he imagined God saying.

After he fed Sheba, buckled his cufflinks and locked up the lonesome house, he moseyed down the street and bought a bunch of lilacs for Audrey – the same flowers he'd bought her that first time back in 1964.

He made his way to the bus stop, which was a short walk from his house, ignoring the lingering pain in his right leg until he arrived at the nursing home where Audrey would draw her final breath.

Upon entering room 217, the family sat in silence. The atmosphere felt off, like the moments leading up to an electrical storm. It was as if they'd been quarrelling – *About me, no doubt,* he thought, looking from one solemn face to the next. *Tough titties.*

For a heart-stopping moment, he thought maybe Audrey had passed because they regarded him stoically, but then the respirator *whoosh-clicked*.

'Good morning,' Jamie said, her bloodshot eyes focusing on the flowers in his shaky hand.

'Morning.' He shuffled over to Audrey's bed and placed the fresh lilacs beside a Ming vase containing wilted roses that looked like they'd come from Morticia Addams' garden.

As he turned around, all eyes were on him.

He frowned. 'What? Did I forget to put my trousers on again?'

'No,' Angela said with a short laugh. 'We, ah, would appreciate if you could tell us the rest of your story.'

'I don't think I want to.' Elijah shuffled over to where Tida sat. 'Get out.'

Timothy rose, his chair legs scraping against the floor. 'This is *exactly* why we have a problem with you! You don't need to be rude.'

'Forgive me, but back in my day healthy people were supposed to give up their seats for the elderly, sick or pregnant.'

'She *is* pregnant, pops!'

Timothy's stance didn't faze Elijah – in fact, he thought it comical, like a chihuahua facing off with a lion. 'Well, I can't see anything.' He pointed to Tida's stomach. 'How am I supposed to know? She has the body of a ten-year-old boy.'

Timothy's top lip curled inward. 'We only spoke of it *all* last night, you senile bastard!'

'I never pleaded to the contrary – why is the fan on?'

Everyone looked towards the ceiling fan, which was spinning on a medium setting, as Elijah tried in vain to rehash last night. For the life of him, he swore he didn't know Tida was up the duff. They hadn't mentioned it. Or had they? *Jesus, I'm friggin' falling apart at the seams.*

Jamie stepped forward. 'Tida's flushed, so we thought we'd—'

'Christ, it's not that bloody hot,' Elijah muttered. 'Can we turn it off now?'

Jamie looked at Angela, whose right eye twitched. Nobody moved.

Elijah tsked. 'Is anyone going to give up their seat for me?' He caught Timothy looking towards Jamie with upturned eyebrows. *So they have been arguing then,* Elijah concluded. No doubt Chloe and Jamie stuck up for him, whilst the others battled it out, highlighting his faults to prove to the others that he shouldn't be here. What else was new when it came to democracy whenever he was concerned?

Chloe walked over to him. 'You can have my chair.'

Elijah's glasses emphasised the sadness in her eyes and knew he was being a royal knob. He was a professional at morphing his pain into anger. Looking at the message from Audrey last night, which he hadn't read in decades, had opened Pandora's box. He'd had a terrible night's sleep; the pain and bitterness hadn't gone away even after all these years – in fact, it was getting worse now that Audrey was on the verge of crossing over.

There was always a part of him that held onto the hope – like that of the parent of a missing child – that Audrey would find her way back to him. But hope in general is dangerous. Hope can be the loose thread that pulls apart one's sanity.

The corner of his mouth tilted. 'No, kid, you sit in the chair. I might get some fresh air for a while.'

Everyone remained silent as he limped out of the room. He didn't want to be remembered for being an arsehole, but the weight of the world seemed to rest upon his shoulders and he could only keep up a brave face for so long.

As he reached the immaculate garden near the pond, a forlorn tear trickled down his face. A salty breeze carried the sounds of beating wings and squawks from above. There were so many things he wanted to tell Audrey. He wouldn't even know where to begin if she suddenly changed for the better and they were blessed with being able to speak to each other again. He was waiting for her moment of terminal lucidity.

'Why do you have to be such a jerk? We'd only just arrived ourselves; we were going to get you a chair once you came!'

Elijah uttered an expletive and wiped his face. He turned to face Angela, who stood at the foot of the steps with hands on hips.

Shit; anyone but her. He regained masculine composure with a quick inhale through the nostrils and shoulders lifted.

'You're making it *very* difficult for us to want to be in the same room as you.'

'I never came here looking to make friends.'

Angela threw her hands in the air. 'What is your goddamn problem?'

'I don't want to get close, okay? I'm an old man now, let me be. I'm too set in my ways.'

'Why do you have to push us away at all?'

'Because I'm afraid!'

Angela's head reeled back. Silence.

He stared at her as his chest heaved. 'Age doesn't make someone invincible from feelings.' He swallowed in an attempt to put the kibosh on his tears. 'No matter how old I get, I still *feel*!' He pounded his chest – which prompted a small cough. 'I still feel pain, I still feel betrayal. I still feel guilt, sadness, love, anger. It doesn't pass with age; in fact, I think it gets worse. So there, are you satisfied? I'm afraid.'

'Afraid of what?' Angela said, the grass whispering as she inched closer.

Elijah's bottom lip tremored, so he turned to watch the ducks as they swam in circles. Water shone off their backs in glistening blues and greens, and a caw from a certain magpie squawked high above. It was almost feeding time for Maggie and her chicks.

'You're the only remaining link to the woman I lost my heart and soul to many years ago.'

'You don't have to be afraid of us. We won't hurt you.'

Elijah scoffed. 'Like mother, like daughter.'

'That is so unfair; you don't know me and I don't even know the woman you're talking about.'

He spun around, pointing a finger. 'You're damn right! The truth of the matter is the woman I love seems to have disappeared. I have no idea who that person in room 217 is. The woman seems to be a fragment of who she once was, and I mean that with no disrespect.'

Angela turned her focus elsewhere, hands dropping from her hips.

'The Audrey I fell for barely had two pennies to rub together, and now here she is, surrounded by her family in one of the wealthiest suburbs in Sydney.' He shrugged. 'I suppose it's like Norma Jeane morphing into Marilyn Monroe – she was two different people. You all address her so formally – '*Aud*' – it's plain to see I'm just an old fool because of course, people change.'

'Why did you come – honestly? Please tell me the truth. Were you hoping to rekindle the flame; did you secretly father one of us?'

Elijah looked out over the glistening harbour as yachts and catamarans bobbed on the turquoise surface. He had nothing left to lose by being honest. Maybe he'd even be welcomed into the room if he relaxed a bit more. 'Honestly? Because I've lived a life of regret and I want answers. That's all there is to it. Not one day has passed where I didn't think of Audrey and wonder *why*.' He inhaled, looking down at his wrinkled, liver-spotted hands. 'I suppose I want to know what it was all for. What did my existence in this life contribute to? Because right now, I-I cannot think of a single thing.' He turned to face Angela, who came closer still. The drumming of a helicopter passing above them drowned the awkward silence.

Angela mashed her lips together and focused her eyes on the sky.

With the helicopter gone, Elijah continued. 'So, Angela, apart from wanting to say goodbye to Audrey and the life I once knew, I suppose I simply want to know *why*. I think it's safe to say a song I can relate to more than any other is "Yesterday" by the Beatles.'

She inhaled, licked her lips and cleared her throat. 'I, um, don't know what to say.'

He threw her a lopsided grin. 'Gee, that'd be a first for you, wouldn't it?'

They stared at each other momentarily, before sharing a laugh as Angela walked over to Elijah and hugged him. It took a moment, but eventually he placed his arms around her, his eyes stinging. Her body went from concrete to cotton in his embrace.

'I haven't always been like this,' Elijah mumbled. 'This is one for Ripley's, but … I was happy at one point.'

Angela leaned back. 'And I haven't always been like this.' She used the knuckles of both index fingers to wipe streaked mascara from under her eyes. 'I wish Mum was awake so she could answer all the questions we have. I wish parents lived forever, but it's the circle of life.' She thumbed a tear away from Elijah's cheek, her own lip trembling. 'One day, Chloe will be beside my bed with her children saying goodbye, and the cycle will repeat for her, and for her children, until one day we are all forgotten. There isn't anything we can do about it, but we can make the most of it while we're here.'

Elijah patted her hand that rested upon his shoulder. They stood in comfortable silence, gazing out towards the busy harbour as life carried on regardless.

Thirty minutes later, Angela and Elijah walked back into room 217, arms linked. Timothy's mouth formed a perfect O, but Chloe and Jamie sported huge grins as they exchanged knowing glances.

'EJ will read more of his diary today,' Angela said.

As Angela helped Elijah into her chair, he looked at her and whispered: 'Did you just call me EJ?'

'No, I did not,' she stage-whispered, leaning down while helping him ease back.

'Yes you did. I like it.'

'Shut up; I didn't.' She stood and turned, clearing her throat. 'I will be back in a tick. I'm just getting another chair from the rec room.'

After Angela returned with a chair, she placed it next to Timothy and Tida, giving them both a reassuring wink.

'I believe you were at the point of telling us how you told Mum you were heading to Vietnam,' Jamie said, leaning forward in her chair, elbows on knees.

His index finger rose to his chin and he looked up to address them all.

Chapter 52

'I GOT INTO a severe argument with my parents, who told me they wanted Audrey out of the picture. My cunning parents had opened my letter from the government, forged my signatures where necessary, and then kept my departure – my little first-class ticket to hell – a secret until the day before I was due to leave.'

Shocked sounds erupted from everyone in the room.

'How is that even possible?' Timothy said. 'Weren't you enlisted in the army?'

'I *was* in the army. They'd kicked me out – well, technically an indefinite suspension – for insubordination.'

Angela let out a curt: 'Ha!'

Elijah ignored her and continued. 'I hadn't seen my superiors at the Holsworthy Barracks in months, so I couldn't have heard about *who* was going, but the entire nation read about Menzies' Ministerial Statement delivered to the House of Representatives on the evening of 29th April 1965. Sir Robert Menzies ordered an infantry battalion of 778 men to be deployed on operations to cooperate with the United States' military advisers, to support the Government of South Vietnam. My parents forged my signature on a few documents, sent in phoney reports and medical checks, and because the Australian Government was pretty much desperate, the army stamped its approval on my medical report.' Elijah coughed into his fist, prompting a short spasm in his left side, which he struggled through, ignoring the concerned looks. 'The lack of communication was to ensure that Audrey and I wouldn't have time to plan anything in case I went AWOL. My dad reminded me what the punishment was for skipping out and I knew deep down I had to go; it was better for us both if I went and served my time.' He paused, remembering the abhorrence wash over him. 'I swear I could have killed my deceitful parents, but rather than waste any more time, I drove straight to Betty-Sue's, smoking at least three cigarettes along the way. I did a brody into the car park and stormed inside to see Audrey chatting and laughing with Cynthia, whom she'd become close with.'

'Brody?' said Chloe, and Elijah registered they all looked curious.

With hand actions, Elijah said, 'It's when a car skids in a semicircle with the brakes locked.'

'Oh,' Chloe mouthed.

Elijah peered over the rim of his spectacles. 'I didn't have time for indicators or green lights; I'd declared it a state of emergency.' He pulled his hanky out of his trouser pocket just in time to catch parts of his lungs and a spot of blood as he coughed into it. 'Excuse me.' The others exchanged worried glances as they watched Elijah regain his composure. 'Audrey's open-mouthed smile was welcoming because it held a hint of excitement, but it was not a conversation she anticipated ...'

Chapter 53

THEN – 1965

'BABY, WE NEED to go,' Elijah said, breathing hard, perspiration running down his face.

'What do you mean; what's wrong?' Audrey said, a hand rising to the base of her throat.

Elijah ran behind the counter and reached Audrey within a heartbeat. 'We need to split on the double; it's urgent. I'm sure Cynthia can handle the night shift by herself – can't you, Cynthia?'

Cynthia twirled a strand of hair. 'Excuse *me*—'

'Goddammit! Audrey, we don't have time, you're coming with me!' Elijah grabbed her by the elbow and forced her out of the shop, the bell above the door ringing loudly as they left.

'You're scaring me!' she said as he bundled her like a child into his car. Elijah stood there for a second, panting, observing her fearful eyes. He closed her door before jumping in the car himself and drove in silence to the nearest lookout. Elijah screeched to a halt, killed the engine, and faced her before grabbing her trembling hands.

'EJ, you're scaring me; what's happened since I saw you a little while ago?'

'Baby,' he began, choking on his pain, 'I don't know how to tell you this but, um; look … I'm just going to lay it on you.' He gulped before sucking in oxygen. 'I've been called up for Vietnam.'

Audrey stared at Elijah, as if suspended in time, her lips slightly parted as tears trickled down her motionless face. Elijah lowered his head to where he grasped her hands, and tried damn hard to hold the emotions back before he kissed her knuckles and glanced up into her unblinking eyes. She remained immobile, mouth agape.

'When do ...' she croaked at last. As she mouthed the words, her tears increased.

'Tomorrow.'

She frowned and clutched her stomach. 'What do you *mean*; how can it be so soon? What about the house ... and Corey? What about *me?*'

Elijah clenched his stinging eyes, forcing the tears back. 'It's a long story – you have my parents to thank for this.' He caressed her wet cheeks. 'I needed to see you and tell you that tonight will be our last night ... our last night until God knows when. Christ, I hate my parents. Damn them to hell!' He punched the steering wheel three times, wincing as he wrung his hand out. Audrey's face had drained of all colour as quick as a snap of fingers, yet Elijah believed the information still hadn't fully sunk in.

'I don't understand,' she said in a thin voice. 'Please don't leave me.' She shielded her face in both hands to muffle a bray of pain, and that's when Elijah's tears burst free. Yes, he was scared about dying, but most of all he hated the possibility of never seeing Audrey again, which to him was a fate worse than death.

'Aren't you on suspension? You haven't even done training or a physic—'

'But I have, my love. I did my mandatory six weeks' training in Wagga Wagga back in '61 and passed with flying colours. I'm a registered 1-A classification, which means I am eligible for military service.'

'Six *weeks?* Is that all they prepare you with?'

These questions were infinitesimal compared to the bigger picture. Elijah leaned over and hugged her tight, because deep down he knew something beautiful was dying and they were powerless to stop it.

She clutched his shirt like a drowning person reaching for a lifebuoy. 'What happens if you don't go? What happens if we run away together, tonight?'

Elijah leaned back, looked at her wet face and made some sort of anguished sound he'd never heard before. 'I love you so much.' He placed his forehead onto hers and she started heaving. 'But you know what happens to men who go AWOL and abandon their country. I could end up in jail and cop a hefty fine; my family will think I'm a yellow-belly – not that I give a damn about my parents right now, but the rest of my family would live in shame because of it. I thought of it, too, for a split second, but eventually my luck would run out.' Audrey gulped and clung to him tighter, a breath away from hyperventilating. 'Baby, as hard as it is to admit, the best thing for me to do is serve my time and have you waiting here for me when I get back. Can you do that for me?'

'Please don't leave me all alone; you're all I have.' She wheezed, shaking her head. '*Please* don't do this.' She climbed onto his lap and into his arms as if to stop him from hopping out of the car – and out of her life. There was nothing Elijah could do to help her; there was nothing he could say that would make their fears diminish. The statistics of fallen soldiers in 'Nam was way too high; the suicide rate of young men forced to defend their countries, staggering. The odds were not good, at least not as good as they *should* have been for a fairly advanced country with America as its ally.

They were young lovers having to face something beautiful having to end, at least for a little while. Or so they hoped. Elijah couldn't calm Audrey down, not with soothing caresses, nor with tender kisses. It seemed the more she thought about it, the worse it felt. She went on and on, to the point of storming out of the EH, cursing God, letting her voice trail with the wind, down the mountainside and over the valley of Wollongong. Elijah eventually got out of the car, drying his eyes with the backs of his hands before leaning against the bonnet and lighting a cigarette. After she finished cursing, she collapsed onto the ground, weeping. He went to her.

'We only have tonight. Let's go away – I don't care where – let's hire a room for the night.' He discarded his cigarette, bending down to hold her. 'I would rather die than go back home to spend my last night here with my parents.'

Audrey's response was a feeble nod, so he helped her to stand and she hobbled to the car as if physically crippled by the pain. Elijah opened the door and helped her inside before kissing the top of her head. He then hopped in behind the wheel and took a scenic drive far away from the Gong, to spend his last night in Australia with the only girl he'd ever truly love.

Over forty minutes later, they reached a bed-and-breakfast near Picton. The trip was arduous because Elijah concentrated on Audrey, imagining what life would be like without her during his term. Audrey mumbled and whispered to herself. 'Please, God, please don't take him away, too.' Her eyes were closed, her hands clenched together in her lap. She was obviously thinking of her parents and it squeezed Elijah's heart, as she had already been through hell and back.

As Elijah pulled up to the quaint lodge, Audrey's eyes were open, but she was a million miles away. She looked utterly defeated, as if she had no more fight left in her. Elijah paid for a room, and the preppy man who served them turned his nose up about the fact they were sharing a bed, because they were clearly not husband and wife. Getting knocked up before marriage could be enough to drag an entire family name through the mud – appearances and social status were everything in the sixties.

Elijah opened the door to their room with an old-fashioned key, flicked on the lights, took his girl by the hand and led her over to the queen-sized bed positioned in the middle of the room, opposite the en suite.

'This can't be happening,' she whispered, plonking down on the floral quilt cover.

Elijah's knees cracked as he bent down to edge his way between her legs and wrap his arms around her waist.

She glanced down with lifeless eyes. 'Please don't go.' She inhaled sharply. 'I will die without you, you son of a *bitch*, you cannot leave me!' She struck his chest as her tears splashed his face.

'Hit me again,' Elijah said. She slapped his face as he gritted his teeth. 'Harder!' Before long, Audrey was striking him with closed and open fists, screaming in pure agony. He forced her backwards, his weight pushing her into the soft mattress while he clasped her. She wailed straight from the heart as she clung onto him like a scared monkey clutching its mother after hearing a predator's roar. Elijah cried into her neck for a moment until he regained composure. They kissed with desperation and agony, despite the looming darkness and knowing their prospects looked bleaker than a winter's night. They kissed knowing their plans of buying a home, of raising a family and spending the rest of their lives together were now on hold. And in this strange room, they made frenzied, passionate love.

Afterwards, Elijah held Audrey in his arms until her tears subsided. He stroked her naked skin as she stared at the ceiling, motionless. He eventually hopped up and ran a bath, as sleep was the last thing on his frazzled mind.

They were fortunate enough to have bubble bath supplied, so Elijah poured the miniature Soaky bottle into the porcelain tub before grabbing cotton towels and a packet of Lux soap. Once the bathtub was half-full, he stood in the doorway and regarded Audrey, who was lying naked on the bed, appearing catatonic. She didn't even seem to blink. He walked over to the bed and kissed her from her feet to her head before grabbing her hands to help her stand.

'I can't,' she whispered.

Elijah popped a steady arm around her waist to support her. 'You can't have a bath with me … why not?'

'Because I can't get my aid wet.'

'That's fine; you can take it out.'

She shook her head. 'But we won't be able to talk; I won't be able to hear what you're saying.'

'Yes, you will. Come on, baby, please do it for me.'

When they had stayed at Jenolan Caves a few months prior, the bathtub in the cabin wasn't big enough for a Pomeranian, let alone two adults, so they hadn't yet experienced bathing together. Audrey removed her earpiece with much trepidation and bit her bottom lip before placing the transistor pouch on a bunch of folded towels. She glanced up at him with childlike eyes, and his heart splintered with a deep yearning. He believed his only purpose on earth was to protect her; she was the reason he breathed at all. He planted a kiss on her perfect nose. She'd told him before that she had been deaf since birth and that without her hearing aid, she heard nothing; it was like being alone in a sealed room. He often wondered what it must be like.

Elijah helped her into the steaming, fragrant bath and collected her in his arms so she lay back on his chest. Her body convulsed as she emitted stifled sobs. He lay his chin on top of her head, listening to the little popping sounds from the surrounding bubbles. Audrey couldn't even hear them. He held onto her for dear life with his eyes closed, cursing the fact he had been born into a ridiculous family. If he never saw his parents again, it'd be too soon.

After a while, she sat up and slid to the other side of the tub, staring into space. Elijah's pulse quickened, but there wasn't a more suitable time to do what he had planned. This was months in the making and he still felt like a novice. *Fuck it, here we go.*

He raised a hand from the water and keeping his ring finger and middle finger down, palm facing outwards, he signed: *I love you.*

Her eyes widened and her lips parted.

Elijah put his hands out flat and wiggled his fingers, then touched his forehead and swung the tip of his finger forward, followed by pointing to his chest: *Wait for me.*

Her face contorted as her tears mingled with the bath water. Then she signed: *When?* And then: *Why?*

Elijah smiled and signed back all the words to the song 'You Are My Sunshine'.

Audrey placed her head into her hands and sobbed until she couldn't weep anymore. Elijah thought the tub was at risk of overflowing.

At last she looked at him through red-rimmed eyes and whispered, 'So this is what death feels like.'

Elijah slid over to her side of the bath and held onto her heaving body as tears rolled down his cheeks, too. They stayed there until their fingers were shrivelled like prunes. Elijah released some of the lukewarm bath water and topped it up with more hot water, then he washed her body with the cake of Lux soap, which promised to soften the skin as it cleanses. He also washed her hair while she lay silent and still. Elijah enjoyed taking care of her; after all, he was her protector and provider. He had already sworn upon it, even though in the eyes of the law she was still Miss Hughes.

Eventually Elijah helped Audrey out of the tub, drying her off and dressing her in a cotton robe that the lodge supplied. He then sat her on the bed and switched on the telly. An episode of *Bewitched* was playing. He wrapped a towel around his waist and left her staring at the TV screen while he ventured to the kettle to make tea. When he returned, he placed the cups and saucers on the bedside table, jumped on the bed, and sat behind her while towel-drying her golden hair.

By now she had put her earpiece back in so they could communicate, and she surprised him by saying, 'I'm sorry.'

'What for, my love?'

'For not being more supportive. I should do these things for you. I'm being selfish and I can *only* imagine how you must be feeling – going off to fight in another country. I wish I could be stronger for you.'

Her words touched Elijah, but he wasn't fazed. He could be strong enough for both of them. Or at least he could act like it. 'Hey,' he said from behind her, stopping his towel-drying actions, 'I would be a little concerned if you didn't react this way.'

'It's too overwhelming. I cannot believe your parents kept this from you to keep us separated. What must they think of me if this is how they treat you to keep us apart?'

'Do you think I give a damn what those nutcases think? And I mean about anything in general? I couldn't care less what they – or Lloyd – think.' Then he chuckled. 'I have half a mind to say I'm a homosexual so they'll die of shock and disappointment.' His mouth tightened as he shook his head. 'I don't wish them dead … it just pisses me off how they've gone about this.'

'Did they ever treat Georgie like this?'

Elijah lowered his head. 'Sweetheart, let's not spend the night talking about them.'

He kissed the back of her head and wrapped his arms around her belly. His legs stretched out either side of her body as she sat on the edge of the bed watching Samantha quarrel with Darrin, who was quarrelling with Endora.

Elijah nestled his chin in the hollow beside her neck. 'Think of this as me going away on a business trip for a short time, but I'll be back before you know it. As soon as I get back, and I mean the *second* I get back, we are going straight to the real estate place and getting us a nice house and ... we're going to start creating our own family, and I mean that same night, too!' He said it with a cheeky smile, although she couldn't see his face.

'Don't forget Corey.' The quiver in her voice told him she'd started crying again.

'Well, we might have to find another dog as I'm certain someone will fall in love with Corey in the meantime. Does it have to be a German shepherd?'

When she nodded emphatically, he chuckled. 'Sounds good to me, beautiful. When I return I'll buy us a new Corey, then head on over to your house and pick you up. Does that sound like a plan?'

Her body constricted before she nodded once.

'Sweetheart,' he whispered, planting another kiss on her head, 'our tea will get cold.'

He manoeuvred around her, rose and grabbed her tea before placing the saucer in her hands. She took it, but still had that thousand-yard stare. He sighed and knelt on the carpet to gaze into her solemn, bloodshot eyes.

'Do you really love me?'
'More than you'll ever know,' she said, holding his gaze.
His fingers tightened around her ankles. 'Then wait for me!'

Chapter 54

THEN – 1965

THEY WATCHED TV for a while afterwards – as a distraction rather than for entertainment. Neither spoke, and Audrey's hot tears bathed his naked chest until she fell asleep.

Elijah remained propped against the headboard, Audrey's head on the pillow beside him and one arm draped around his waist. He inhaled and exhaled, savouring every second of the delicious feeling of Audrey's body next to his. Just holding her, hearing her breathe, were the simple pleasures he wanted to capture and remember on the long nights he would be spending in 'Nam. He stared at the TV as his mind's theatre flashed images before his eyes, imagining what fighting in 'Nam and killing other men would be like. He wondered how he would survive without Audrey's love; how holding their son or daughter would feel and yes, dammit, even Corey featured in the montage. He also thought of Grace, wondering how she would survive in the house of subjugation on her own, without her brother as her ally.

After a while, Elijah rose again to go to the bathroom and when he returned, he made another cup of tea. He dragged a chair beside the bed to watch Audrey sleep, her face bathed in the glow of the blue moon that filtered through the window. Tears escaped and rolled down his cheeks

– she was just the most *beautiful* creature his eyes had ever beheld. After lighting a cigarette, he continued to stare, memorising every feature, every curve on her delicate face before he stubbed his cigarette, drew the curtains closed, and climbed back into bed to hold his saviour.

Minutes converged into hours and before long, darkness surrendered as sunlight permeated the gaps in the curtains.

Elijah kissed Audrey's head. They would need to shake a leg and get a wriggle on. He hadn't even packed his bags. He didn't know how he was getting down to the docks, or if his parents would even accompany him. He loved them because they were his parents and they had brought him into this world, even if it was one of glitz and glamour. But as people, he wouldn't have pissed on them if they were on fire. Let's face it, they wouldn't have done so for Audrey.

Elijah knew the exact moment Audrey woke as her body jerked, then she looked at him once she got her bearings. He smoothed her hair back from her face before she creased her eyebrows and whispered, 'So, it wasn't just a nightmare?'

The corner of his mouth tilted and he shook his head.

Audrey clenched her puffy eyes shut and whimpered as her forehead bumped his chest.

'We need to get going now, angel.'

She shook her head and dug her nails into his torso. 'I'm not ready for this.' Her lips quivered against his flesh.

'I'm not either, my love, but we're only delaying the inevitable. Come on; let's go downstairs for breakfast.'

'I'm not hungry! I'm too sick in the stomach.'

Her tears trickled into his belly button. 'Me too, but I need to have coffee before the drive back.'

Elijah snapped mental images of everything about her that morning as he had done the night before. He had never seen her look worse but still, even with red-rimmed eyes, hair frayed and skin a sickly white, she was more beguiling than any woman he had ever known.

They went downstairs to the dining hall dressed in the attire they had arrived in, and braved the guests who stared open-mouthed at them like they were two greasers high on dope. Elijah grabbed two white circular plates, but Audrey shook her head, looking at the ground while wrapping her arms around her stomach.

'Please eat something – for me?' Elijah whispered.

'I'm sorry I'm not stronger; I just don't know how to be.'

'You just worry about finding us a table, angel.' He winked at her as she turned around to find them a table, choosing one in the back corner next to a floor-to-ceiling window overlooking meandering hills and vineyards. Elijah smiled at her before returning to the buffet, serving himself generous portions of scrambled eggs, fried bacon, mushrooms, oven-baked tomatoes, broiled pork sausages, and white toast. He walked over to Audrey with his hands full, and placed the plates on the white tablecloth just as a little kid ran past him, a Dinky die-cast fire truck in his pudgy hand.

'Am I seeing you off today?'

His eyes locked with hers. 'I wouldn't have it any other way.'

'Are your parents going to be okay with that?'

'I don't give a damn what they're okay with.' He doused his eggs with salt and pepper, knowing that he'd have to scarf if they were to make it back in time. 'I'd rather have you there than any of my other family members or friends, although you'll be the hardest to say goodbye to.' He raised his index finger. 'Hang loose, baby girl, I'll be back.' He returned to the buffet table and grabbed fresh coffee and orange juice for them both, before rejoining his fair lady.

'Golly, I wish I had more time to get accustomed to the idea. I cannot fathom why you need to go to war; it's all too unreal – this isn't even our fight.'

Elijah picked up a fork and raked it through the steaming hot breakfast, and was glad when Audrey spread Vegemite onto her buttered white toast.

'Good girl,' he whispered, then glanced beyond the windowpane as the sun cast a miraculous tangerine glow, its hue illuminating every crevice of the land.

She nibbled at the corner of her toast. 'Do you have any idea when you'll be coming back; can you give me a ballpark answer at least?'

Elijah raised the porcelain coffee cup to his lips and paused. 'A term lasts for twelve months or so – pending circumstances. Plus, I will have a break about midway through, where they'll fly me wherever I wanna go, and I promise you, I'll come back here when they send me. So, it could only be about six months before I see you again – not a year.' He lowered the cup, fear gripping him like a vice. 'But it won't be a problem, right? You are going to wait for me, aren't you?'

Audrey reached over and placed a reassuring hand on his. 'No matter how much time goes by, I'll be waiting.' The coil around Elijah's heart loosened. 'Just promise you'll come home soon and breathe life back into me, for the love of God.'

When they returned to their room, they began making love as if it was to be the last time ever. Elijah kissed her hard while rocking into her, fusing their hands together as if to never let go. Afterwards, Elijah held her tight, but management made it clear their time was up by knocking at nine o'clock on the dot. As Elijah pulled up his pants, he looked at Audrey, who now sat facing the dressing table mirror, brushing her glorious hair by using her fingers. Elijah stared at her, mesmerised, before he hopped off the bed, zipped up his fly and walked towards her. She glanced up through half-closed eyes as he draped a hand on her shoulder.

'Dance with me.'

Audrey's head drooped and his own tears sprung to the surface once more. Her right hand reached up and squeezed the hand that rested upon her shoulder as he struggled hard against the threatening tears. Elijah walked around to her left side and helped her to stand because she seemed unable to move by her own accord. He turned up the ham radio as 'Save the Last Dance for Me' by the Drifters came on, before wrapping her in his embrace. She placed her arms around his neck and squished her face against his chest. Tears cascaded from Elijah's closed eyes as they swayed together, ignoring the employee banging on the door. Elijah reached down behind him, a hand still draped around her waist, and turned the radio volume up higher as they floated about the room like Fred and Ginger.

When the song finished, he pulled away from Audrey's embrace and tilted her wet chin towards his face. He grabbed her hand, placed it over his beating heart while looking into her doleful eyes and said, 'This will *always* belong to you.'

Chapter 55

THEN – 1965

ELIJAH DROVE BACK to Wollongong, his eyes closing then snapping open, despite three cups of strong black coffee. On two occasions, he drifted over to the other lane. He'd dropped Audrey off at Lloyd's because she wanted to get something from inside and to change her clothes. Elijah then drove home to be welcomed by frantic parents and a crying sister as soon as he opened the front door. They shouted at him for leaving the night before, but Elijah noted his folks had been nice enough to have Arthur pack his clothes and items they thought he might need.

'You're just in time to leave,' Arthur said, mouth downturned and head bowed, looking gloomier than Eeyore as though *he* were the one saying goodbye to a son. Elijah walked over to Grace, who sat at the dining room table, sobbing. All he could do was place a hand on her shoulder.

Margaret came in soon after, wearing a yellow silk dress and sparkling diamante shoes. *The ones she uses to walk all over people*, Elijah thought. 'Georgie has just arrived; it's time to go now.'

Elijah's eye twitched and his chest expanded. 'What?!'

'We thought you'd want to say your goodbyes, so she's accompanying us.'

'You're completely daft!' Elijah ran out the front door only to see Georgie all dolled up in a light-pink baby doll dress, standing beside Howard's Bentley. Elijah felt a tad guilty as he stormed past the girl he had known since high school. 'Sorry, I don't have time, Georgie.' He jumped into the EH and sped to Audrey's, pushing the image of Georgie's wounded expression from his thoughts.

When he and Audrey arrived at the bustling docks, they remained in the car. Audrey stared at the HMAS *Sydney*, which was to be accompanied by HMAS *Duchess* on the journey to South Vietnam. Servicemen walked around aimlessly; one guy was throwing up over the side of the docks, and men from the Prince of Wales's Light Horse Regiment were talking to a group of journalists.

Elijah handed his car keys to Audrey and said, 'My gift to you. Lucky we had driving lessons in this thing, huh?'

She argued over the gesture and they quibbled back and forth until she understood she had no choice but to accept them.

'I have a gift for you, too.' She dabbed her tears with a pink handkerchief. Audrey leaned into the back seat of his car and pulled out the bag she had brought along. 'I know it's bulky and not worth carrying, but even if you just *look* at it now. Take joy in knowing what we have to look forward to in the future. The saga of Audrey and EJ has just begun.'

Elijah looked through the pages of the photo album she handed him. She had personalised an inscription on the inside front cover. His heart pumped harder than he thought possible while reading her words.

When he closed the album, he closed his eyes and held it to his chest. That was when his beloved also presented him with a new maroon journal – the same type of journal she had been using to document her life since her arrival in Wollongong and the preceding events. She'd once explained to Elijah her psychologist recommended journal-keeping as therapy after the death of her parents.

He frowned, exhaling. 'Goddammit, I love you so *fucking* much it hurts.'

Audrey wrapped her arms around Elijah and held him until the horn of Howard's Bentley startled them from behind. 'I don't want them to see me.' She shuffled back over to her seat, wiping her face.

'Screw them all. I'd choose you over anyone, any day. I hope you know that? You're worth your weight in gold; don't let anyone make you feel otherwise.'

Audrey blotted her eyes with her hanky once more before he kissed her. They then stepped outside as his parents rushed over.

'Oh, honestly, do *not* embarrass us,' Margaret warned through clenched teeth, maintaining a smile in case of any onlookers. Elijah pushed past her and walked over to Grace with a quivering Audrey in his grasp.

'Take care of Audrey for me, please.'

Grace hugged him tight before he stepped back. 'Love you, doofus.' She wiped away her tears with a palm.

'Me too,' he mumbled, tousling her brown hair before turning away.

Audrey focused on the ground as Georgie held her head high, Margaret's arm around her waist. Sometimes Elijah wondered if his parents shared one brain between the two of them. They both had more money than sense – he knew that for a fact.

Elijah stepped over to Georgie and gave her a brief hug, noting her quivering bottom lip. She kissed his cheek as a hand cupped the back of his head. 'Come back soon.' She then took his face in her hands.

'Take care, Georgie.' He pulled away and turned to face his parents. 'I'm giving ownership of my car to Audrey. Don't fight her about it; you never liked the EH, anyway.' Margaret rolled her eyes. 'When I get back, I will do my best to never see either of you again. I'm going to marry Audrey and we're going to move as far away from you lot as possible. No offence, Grace.' He glanced at his sister, and she smiled knowingly. 'I don't know what I did to displease you so much, so in case I die, then I suppose I'll say I'm sorry here and now for being a disappointment.'

Elijah thought he saw his mother allow one tear to form in her left eye. 'Oh, honestly, stop the theatrics,' Margaret said. Beaming with overt pride, his chest stuck out like a proud peacock, Howard's attention was fixed on the men hurrying around them.

Elijah turned to Audrey, who had stepped away from the semicircle. 'Keep the album with you, baby, and anytime you get lonely or sad, look through it and imagine us going through those stages of our lives together.' He paused, searching her eyes before leaning in close. 'If the unthinkable happens, never forget the love we shared,' he whispered into her ear before tilting her backwards and kissing her silly.

Margaret gasped louder than the surrounding chatter – like Elijah gave a damn. He held Audrey tighter and kissed her, savouring the sensation of demonstrating their love for each other.

The ship's bell clanged back and forth – the brassy sound telling the pale-faced and wide-eyed young men it was time to board the HMAS *Sydney*. Howard pulled him away from Audrey's arms. 'Come on, son, it's time to go.'

'I love you!' she mouthed, clasping the album to her chest, tears flowing freely.

Margaret lit a Tareyton and glanced at her diamond-encrusted wrist-watch. Georgie placed her hands over her mouth, and Grace pressed her lips together as her face scrunched up.

'Wait for me,' were the last words Elijah said to Audrey as he walked backwards, being led to the gangway by his father who repeated: 'It's time to go.'

Soon Elijah Samuels became lost amidst the swarm of men, some of whom were shaking and holding back tears at being pried away from their loved one's arms. Howard dragged Elijah through mothers blotting their eyes, wives wailing and sisters trembling. Daughters clasped onto teddy bears, thumbs stuck in their mouths as they wept, not comprehending where Daddy was going or why.

All Elijah could hear was hysteria and caterwauling, with some boos intermingled from protestors as he kept walking backwards, seeing fleeting glimpses of Audrey, who had her head in her hands, album propped under an armpit. She was by herself, far away from his mother, Georgie, and Grace.

Elijah faced the gangway latched to the HMAS *Sydney* and soon he was shaking his father's hand before taking the kitbag that Arthur had brought along. 'Go nuke those commie bastards, son; make Australia proud. We, as a nation, would rather be *dead* than red.'

Elijah inhaled, chin tilting. 'Goodbye, Dad.' He turned to search the sea of animated people to look for Audrey as they hauled his arse into the carrier. After he settled into his stateroom, he ran to the top deck on the port side, but unfortunately he got there too late as he couldn't get a decent view of the people below. The maritime sound signal blew in one prolonged six-second blast, and soon the ship was pulling out of the harbour. To Elijah, it seemed they were being tagged, dragged, and forced into solitary confinement like cattle being led to the abattoir.

Chapter 56

ELIJAH PEERED OVER the top of his glasses and saw not one pair of dry eyes in the room. Soft sobs came from everyone (except Tida, who was dozing off, a hand on her stomach).

Elijah closed the diary; his hands shaking more than usual. 'I need to go to the little boys' room.' Jamie blubbered as she wiped tears away, so he added: 'Relax; you all know the outcome.'

It broke the tension, and Jamie chuckled while shaking her head. 'We never knew. We never once heard about *any* of this. It's just so strange.'

Elijah raised his eyebrows to show he agreed.

Nurse Mildred, who had snuck in for another session of storytelling (using the excuse of checking the Urimaax drainage bag and to rub Audrey's cracked lips with ointment), helped Elijah hobble to the bathroom, for which he was grateful.

He winced as he limped along. 'You're not here to give me a hand, are you?'

She swotted his arm at the innuendo. 'I'm sorry.'

'For what? It wasn't you who sent me to 'Nam.' He flashed her a reassuring smile, as a male resident walked past, drool hanging from his mottled purple lower lip. Elijah thought he looked like an extra from *Night of the Living Dead*. 'Never let me turn out like *that* guy, please. I give you permission to use a frying pan on my noggin if it'll save me from going to the crapper in my own trousers without realising. Poor guy.'

Nurse Mildred tugged on his arm. 'Eli! I'm sorry that yer life didn't turn out the way ya wanted.' They shuffled further down the corridor towards the communal bathrooms. 'A love like yers is an inspiration 'n' hope ta us all.'

'So that's the silver lining, is it?' He chuckled.

'Nah, somethin' was meant ta happen from this; ya jist don't know it yet. By the by, don't think I ain't been pickin' up on yer coughin'.'

He glanced towards her as he limped with every step. 'It'll get better. It always does.'

When Elijah and Nurse Mildred returned to room 217 a short while later, the room was as silent and still as an empty house. All eyes were fixed on a man who, only a few days ago, had been a complete stranger to them all, and yet it seemed he had been the love of Audrey's life.

As Elijah settled in his chair with immense effort, commotion emanated from the hallway. Nurse Mildred's eyes widened at the sound of metallic clanging and a distressed moaning, and she took off.

Elijah coughed again and used his hanky to catch whatever chunky gunk came up, refusing to look at whatever his sickly body produced, and took a sip of cool apple juice that slid down his throat like liquid silk.

'Sounds like you need a break from reading,' Jamie said.

Chloe raised a hand, lips pressed together. 'Well, would you like to know what Nanna's journal entry said about that day?'

Would I like to? I've only been waiting since 1965! 'Sure thing, kid. I would damn well love to know what happened on that day and, in fact, the day after that, and so on.'

Chloe raised the diary to her eyeline. *30th May 1965. Dear Diary, forgive me for not writing sooner, but I have been living in hell. It has been three torturous days since the love of my life left for Vietnam. Since the day he left, my life has been agony. It's an endless cycle of days blurring into the night, and night giving way to dawn. I sleep on and off, hoping that when I wake, it'll all be a bad dream. After Howard pried EJ and me apart at the docks, I got stuck with his family and Georgie – of all people! EJ was kind enough to leave his car in my possession and he even informed his parents of that, but after he left, Margaret requested the keys back. Who was I to argue with her? They already think I am after his money. I handed them over before his charming mother pulled me aside and let's just say, it wasn't pretty.*

'It has been three days yet I already miss him so much; the pain is excruciating and I don't know how much longer I can mentally go on. After losing Mum and Dad, why would God want to take anything else from me? This is cruel! And what Uncle Lloyd doesn't understand, or even try to, is that it isn't as though EJ has gone away on vacation. This is war! Many wives become widowed; many babies will never get to see their fathers; many pending weddings could be cancelled because at any time a bullet could end it all. I have taken some time off work, but it won't do me any good if I don't have an income. I was thinking this morning of buying Corey with the remaining money I have left from my bowling win. If I buy Corey, it will remind me that EJ and I still have a future to build.

'I know I have to be strong, same as I know EJ will write to me when he can. I suppose Uncle Lloyd doesn't know how to handle my sadness – although he was more than supportive when my parents passed on. But ... it was his brother who passed away, so I guess that was why. He spoke to me the day I got back from the docks, but since then he's hardly said two words. He brings food to my room (which I can barely stomach to look at, let alone eat), then he disappears for hours on end without even checking up on me. He has been going out more, but I don't know where or with whom. All I know is, I cry myself to sleep every night and curse the fact I am not rich enough to marry someone like EJ. If my lack of money doesn't bother him, then why does Margaret care so much? How much longer can I expect to go on feeling like this? Lord, please help me.'

Chapter 57

THEN – 1965

'YOU'VE HAD YOUR fun with my son, now it's time to move on,' Margaret said, eyes cemented on Audrey's face, which was warped with pain. 'I want you to appreciate that his future is at stake, so I refuse to sit by and watch him waste his life because he had too much fun with a girl in the back seat of his car. I have nothing against *you* personally, but my family's reputation is paramount. Plus, I think you should understand he still harbours feelings for Georgie; you are a mere whimsical distraction before he settles down. I think it's astonishing' – Margaret gave an eye flick and a shoulder raise – 'that he brought you along to say goodbye, but this obsession of yours will only cause tension and drama in our tight-knit family. I comprehend that you've fallen for him and I don't blame you. My son is handsome, rich, and intelligent, so I can only imagine being in your second-hand shoes looking at him – to you, he must be a god.'

Audrey's legs felt no wider and no stronger than a blade of grass, and she caught Georgie's smirk as she observed the situation from afar. The belting sun caused Audrey to break out in a sweat, and even though she knew it was ridiculous, she felt everyone's eyes staring at her as Margaret gave her a verbal bashing.

'However, I understand your current financial situation. Considering I am not heartless, I will help you out, dear. I will hand you his car keys right now if you promise to never contact my son again … that is, of course, if he even *chooses* to write to you from overseas – let's not be presumptuous.' She added a quaint laugh for good measure. Margaret then dangled the car keys in Audrey's face, smiling, acting like she was doing *her* a favour – being the good Samaritan she was.

Audrey looked at Grace, who was wiping away tears as she glanced at the ship. Hundreds of men with arms flailing about, faced the crowd of sobbing women on the quay.

Audrey turned back to Margaret as a triphammer pulsed in her chest. 'I'm sorry I am not what you would want in a daughter-in-law. But, Mrs Samuels, I guarantee that no-one will *ever* love your son the way I do. Isn't that enough?' Margaret raised a hand to the side of her mouth, stifling a smirk as her eyes danced with amusement. 'I might not have any money to my name, but I would make a damn good wife to EJ, because of just how much I love him. If he had no money, my love wouldn't waver. Please, take his car; I don't care – I never wanted it *or* his money. I want *him* – and I know he loves me, too.'

Margaret's eyes squinted to mere slits. 'I will offer this to you one last time.' She raised the keys again, higher. They glittered in the sunlight. 'Take the car and … this cheque.' Margaret retrieved a piece of folded paper from her honey-brown suede Margaux handbag. It was a bank cheque for eight thousand pounds. The money plus his car as a bribe to stay away and break all communication. Realisation that this was all pre-meditated was what hurt Audrey the most. Little did Margaret know that ten times that much wasn't enough to keep Audrey away. She could have given Audrey ownership of the sun, the moon, a tropical island in The Bahamas or even the world itself, but nothing would ever be enough to keep Audrey away from him. She wouldn't walk away with anything less than she deserved: Elijah Samuels.

Audrey lowered her head as tears streamed down her cheeks. 'I'm sorry, Mrs Samuels, but I would walk from here all the way back to Wollongong to prove my love to "your son" as you keep referring to him.'

Margaret gave a curt: 'Ha!'

Audrey snatched another quick gulp of air as her jaw quaked. 'Georgie could never love him the way I do, and I will take good care of him until his last breath, I promise you that.' She glanced up with desperate eyes, her hands rising to her chest. 'Please don't keep us apart; he is my family, too.'

Margaret took a final step to close the gap, her lips a paper-thin line. 'I offered, and you refused. Poor, deaf, *and* stupid. Oh, honestly, I have no idea what he sees in you at all.' Audrey clutched at her deflated heart, her lungs screaming for air. 'However, I shan't let you walk home; you may go with Arthur in my son's car, and I'll get my husband to drive *our* family back. Good day.'

Margaret snatched the album from Audrey, spun around with a flourish, and left Audrey standing amongst a crowd of weeping strangers as the maritime sound signal exploded in a trombone-like blast. A symphony of tears and screams erupted as Australian flags and anti-Vietnam placards were unanimously raised higher in the air and the HMAS *Sydney* pulled away from the dock. Audrey searched the throng of rowdy men aboard the top deck, but try as she might, she could not locate Elijah. As optimistic as she tried to be, she could not help the sinking feeling of despair that crept into her bones: that his disappearance was a presage of events to come.

Chapter 58

ELIJAH REMAINED SILENT. A shroud of fabrication and secrecy had covered that particular time and place. He needed a moment to let it sink in. Chloe peered up from the diary.

'She refused to take the EH, huh?' Elijah exhaled through his nostrils and closed his weary eyes. 'I got told she took the car, and that was the last they saw of her.' Chloe looked at her grandmother and then at Elijah. 'I did not know what transpired that day, so I am grateful that after all this time I have some answers.' Elijah glanced at Audrey – ashamed at how they had treated his girl. 'It's surprising even to me how my mother behaved. I can only imagine how Audrey felt.' Elijah then smiled, ruminating. 'She didn't take the car, huh?' he repeated, as if to himself.

'Yoo-hoo,' Nurse Mildred sung from the doorway. 'Anyone fancy some grub?' She wheeled in a silver trolley with trays upon trays of food for the occupants of room 217.

'What do we have here, Winifred?' Timothy said as she wheeled the trolley past his nose, catching the tip of Tida's pointy black shoe.

'Ow!'

Ignoring Tida's cry of pain, Nurse Mildred peered at them over her glasses. 'Cattleman's beef stew with steamed veg 'n' rice.'

'Are you happy with beef, sweetie?' Timothy asked his wife, who rubbed her foot but nodded all the same.

'If she ain't, she can always have some of my homemade gumbo,' Nurse Mildred said, smirking. 'That'll clear yer system right out, oh, Lord! Prob'ly bring out the bubba, too!'

Timothy chuckled half-heartedly.

'How much do you want per tray?' Angela asked, reaching for her Gucci bag.

'Oh, hush now, precious, they happened ta make six meals extra,' Nurse Mildred said with a conspicuous wink.

'Better not let them go to waste, then.' Timothy rubbed his hands together.

Nurse Mildred consulted her fob watch. They all stared at her as she looked up and cupped a hand to her ear, as if listening for something in particular. Elijah scrunched his brow in confusion when, as if right on cue, the banging sound from Montgomery's room began. Elijah smiled when he understood what was about to occur.

'Nurse ... Nurse?!' the frail voice screamed.

Nurse Mildred sighed and shrugged as if to say *What can you do?* She handed each of them a tray on which was the bowl of stew, a dinner roll, a banana muffin, a tub of berry yoghurt, and a cup of white tea with sugar satchels in the saucer. Chloe received her own special vegetarian dish.

'You're most kind,' Elijah said, silently wishing her nothing but happiness as he took a tray.

'Nurse, I'm hungry!' the feeble voice yelled from next door.

Nurse Mildred closed her eyes. 'Doggone it, George; I spoke ta yer 'bout this before!' She looked around the room and feigned a weary smile before she wheeled the squeaky trolley out backwards. 'Enjoy.'

After lunch, Elijah said, 'Believe it or not, I don't enjoy being the centre of attention, folks. I have been talking non-stop about myself and Audrey for the past four days. Perhaps someone else would like to shed some insight into their life?'

Angela swallowed a spoonful of steaming vegetables before clearing her throat. 'Well, see, we already know each other, it's *you* we want to find out about. Besides, I was talking to Nurse Olsson yesterday just before we left. She was wondering why Mildred has been acting so jolly as of late, so I told her what's been going on in this room. Anyway, Nurse Olsson said it might in fact be *your* storytelling that's keeping Mum going.'

An unexpected tidal wave of emotion swirled inside Elijah's stomach, as though *he* had been chosen for the sole responsibility – the safeguard – of Audrey's life; as though it were in the palm of his hands. If that was the case, then he'd read every single day and night to keep her going. He wished he could save her; he wanted her to have many more years here on earth with her loving family, whom he was starting to tolerate. If only it were an option to sacrifice his miserable life for hers. Hot tears burned his eyes, and his stomach muscles tensed while attempting to fulfil his vow of never allowing himself to cry in front of strangers.

He lowered the spoon he'd been clutching and maintained his uneven breathing. 'Very well, if that's the case, then the next entry in my diary started on the first morning I landed in South Vietnam.'

Chapter 59

THEN – 1965 – VIETNAM

ABOARD THE FORMER aircraft carrier HMAS *Sydney* with Rear Admiral Gordon 'Buster' Crabb at the helm, tensions were high. For most on board, this would be their first experience of war. A few men spoke of how they were looking forward to shooting the enemy, but most of them kept quiet. The fear of death was in their eyes. Elijah Samuels only had one thing on his mind.

After an arduous journey at sea, the day he had been dreading arrived on 8th June at 0800. The men, dressed in green fatigues and slouch hats, with their Australian self-loading rifles in place, were ready for anything. The first thing that hit Elijah during the early morning hours as they docked at the port of Vũng Tàu, was the stench. The humidity made the foul odour of decaying bodies all the more pungent. Black body bags that lined the sides of the fields were being pelted by rain in a pitter-patter, while transportation trucks with wire around the back idled nearby, their exhausts spewing diesel into the dense atmosphere. General Westmoreland welcomed the new arrivals, alongside the Australian Ambassador, Mr Anderson, and Colonel Jackson, before one by one soldiers began filing into the trucks, which pulled away until the shoreline became a mere thin slit in the horizon behind them.

In the beginning, Aussies from the First Battalion in the Royal Australian Regiment – 1 RAR – were posted under the operational control of the

US 173rd Airborne Brigade. Their motto was 'Duty first'. The Australian Headquarters was at the Biên Hòa Air Base, about thirty klicks north-east of Saigon. The cruel irony was that Biên Hòa translated to 'land of peaceful frontiers'.

When Elijah first arrived at base camp, he discovered the Yanks had established their base at the north flank of the airfield, which resembled one of those movie-set frontier towns, with honky-tonk bars and Vietnamese staff working as slushies. That night, as four or five soldiers went off to form a night perimeter to secure a defence near a rubber plantation, the camp became alive with throbbing noise from assorted generators, air conditioners, jukeboxes, and radios playing the latest tunes from Tom Jones, the Rolling Stones, and the Beach Boys over the major field radio, AN/PRC-25. 'Eve of Destruction' by Barry McGuire was a favourite amongst the men, while some played their harmonicas to 'Waltzing Matilda', which was the battalions' official marching song. They had a cookout using dehydrated steaks, and tinned fruit cocktails served as dessert.

On Elijah's first night, he holed up in a two-man army tent perched on duckboards and surrounded by sandbags, with a man called Danny Garrison. Garrison hailed from Camden, NSW, and had left behind a wife and newborn son. Under the blue moonlight as rustling palm trees serenaded Elijah, he wrote Audrey a letter telling her he had arrived, that he missed her, and that he would return home as soon as he could.

During the early days in South Vietnam, things were quiet and Elijah had yet to even *see* 'Charlie'. His battalion experienced only sporadic contact with the enemy and suffered no combat fatalities. It was a relief because Elijah's mind travelled to his lady day and night, wondering what she was doing and how she was coping. He hoped she would meet up with his family now and then – but he realised he was fantasising; his folks were likely to slam the door in her pretty face if she popped around for a chat. Elijah also hoped that Grace wasn't having too much of a hard time by herself, but there was no way to know for sure as no correspondence had begun. Communication with loved ones was hard for the blokes because they were on the move, or sometimes mail got lost or even blown up in air combat.

Elijah's service during early to mid-June saw no action. In fact, sometimes he wondered what the haste had been; why he and the other soldiers had rushed to uproot their lives to be five thousand miles away in South Vietnam. As far as he could tell, all seemed peaceful. The Australian Government didn't want 1 RAR involved too much; initially they provided security to the air base and to patrol their tactical area of responsibility. For the first two weeks, Elijah and the other men walked around camp drinking cans of beer or played volleyball – the Aussies versus the Yanks, of course.

It took Elijah a while to get used to the informal showers and urinating in a pissaphone (a corrugated-iron fence blocking off a hole in the ground), not to mention taking a dump in what was called 'the shitter'. Soldiers dubbed the cooks 'ration assassins' who would dish up hearty meals – chicken mostly. Elijah reckoned the worst was 'shit on a shingle', a slice of toast with chopped beef and gravy, but the sight looked like some poor bastard had relieved themselves of last night's curry onto a piece of white toast.

While a few men went off to stand guard at various posts during the nights, the rest listened to camp stories about war, sex and drugs. One African-American described Vietnam to the grunts as 'days of boredom punctuated by the occasional short bursts of paralysing terror'.

While the Yanks and Aussies enjoyed having a yarn and taking the piss out of each other, nothing eventful happened. Until 26th June, when an incident occurred that shook Elijah to his core.

For Elijah, it felt like it was about eighty-two degrees under the midday sun as a truck pulled up to transport men back to base camp. The radio blasted out 'My Girl' by the Temptations over AFVN – American Forces Vietnam Network – and an American flag flapped in the hot wind as they climbed on board; some of them already sparking up cancer sticks. Upon arriving back at camp, an eager NASHO, Trent Smith, was gung-ho as he leaped to the ground – but he didn't quite make it. Unfortunately, an M26 hand grenade attached to his webbing somehow caught on the edge of the truck Elijah was sitting in, causing it to detonate. The blast killed Smithy instantly, as well as one American, three more Aussies, and wounding eleven others. Men on the truck sat like stunned mullets while chunks of bloodied, seared flesh slid down their faces and blood dripped from the roof above.

'Far fucking out ...' someone whispered.

Is that idiot tripping on acid? Smithy was only nineteen, for fuck's sake, Elijah thought as he scooped a piece of Smithy's scalp from his eye.

Less than a month later, Elijah's initial opinions began to change when he witnessed men slit their own wrists in order to escape this hellhole. What made it worse was the men didn't know a Viet Cong from a South Vietnamese, so they were constantly on edge that they'd get a knife in the back as the cunning VC were so well-camouflaged. Elijah began looking at the South Vietnamese with contempt. Not *once* did any of the villagers say 'Don't go down there' or 'The enemy is hiding in this hut'. He wondered what the hell it was all for, if the helpless weren't helping the helpers. When one of his mates was ambushed and shot, he couldn't help but hold the villagers responsible, too, as they had covered up the evil instead of exposing it. Some of the local villagers spat on passing military vehicles, or took it a step further by holding up banners stating 'Go home, foreigners!'

Why the fuck are we even here for, then? Elijah wondered on multiple occasions.

Some days Elijah forgot what a clear blue sky looked like, thanks to napalm, Agent Orange, and the amount of smoke that wafted through the sky from something or even some*one* like a monk burning himself to a crisp.

He was also increasingly concerned that he hadn't received any letters from Audrey, but it was early days and he'd heard from the men already stationed that it could take over a month at both ends for letters to be received. However, Elijah's concerns grew when he started receiving letters from his folks, and Grace and Georgie. He was grateful to receive letters from home, at least. Sometimes they were his saving grace, but the only time they mentioned *her* name was when they replied to his constant questioning of her whereabouts. Their response was always: 'We haven't heard from her'.

Worrying about Audrey proved to be a distraction, which wasn't a good thing when as quick as a flick of lights he could be in full-blown combat. Soldiers had to be switched on at every moment and most of the time it felt like they were functioning on autopilot, waiting for kick-off. Elijah tried to deal with his loneliness by making friends with some of the younger guys, the ink barely dry on their high school certificates.

Two days after the horrific death of Smithy, which had traumatised Elijah and his mates, his battalion was involved in its first major operation – a joint airborne American–Vietnamese sweep of War Zone D involving nine battalions and support units. Over 10,000 troops were engaged, making it the largest troop lift in the war to date. The Australian battalions' task was to secure a fire-support base on the edge of War Zone D, which Elijah thought sounded simple enough.

Torrential rain pelted when operations began. The men ate breakfast at 0700 and then dressed in their fatigues, fitting a 90-pound harness pack onto their backs before walking along a rain-soaked airfield to a row of roaring helicopters. *Whuppa-whuppa-whuppa.* The humidity was in the nineties, even at that early hour. Dozens of helicopters flew men to the edge of War Zone D, which appeared to be a grassy field. But as the first bunch of soldiers jumped out of the Chinooks into the field below, the others stared in horror from above as they watched them sink into the quagmire that the field had become. The men pleaded for help, some even using their emergency flares in a desperate attempt to do *something* to survive, the onlookers apprehensive as they realised their comrades' vulnerability to enemy attack.

Then, the frantic screams were no longer.

While watching their mates disappear into the morass, their last breaths surfacing as air bubbles, a concerto of exploding bombs and aerial napalm attacks on nearby hamlets erupted as choppers sliced through the inky sky.

Fortunately, the Viet Cong had decided against ambushing that landing zone, assuming it was a 'boondoggle' – an 'absurd' choice. It was safe to assume that any professional military operation would have chosen a more suitable, solid landing site. By luck, despite the egregious tactical error the operation proved a success. War Zone D was a purported Viet Cong fortress area, yet the brigade and the South Vietnamese units penetrated it with ease. Victory, however, was an illusion.

One scorching day, a group of Viet Cong waiting in ambush in the thick jungle almost blew an American M113 armoured personnel carrier driver clean in half by throwing a command-detonated mine into the vehicle. Elijah heard men outside screaming: '*Incoming!* Charlie's here! Mortar, *mortar!*' The mine had landed under the American driver's seat, and when it exploded it tipped the APC upside down and tossed the eleven men in the back around like rag dolls into a bloodied and battered heap. As Elijah swallowed his own blood amidst men screaming, he believed his former self was fading like an apparition.

A few months after Elijah's arrival, he and Danny Garrison had moved over to a six-man tent with Corporal Ronald James Kelly – or Ned, as they called him – Taffy, Johnson, and Spider. Most men went by nicknames; half the time Elijah didn't know what their actual names were, but the men got along like brothers. Brothers who had morphed into someone who was like a mutation of their former selves. In hindsight, Elijah knew the nicknames were merely created to de-identify, serve and survive; to do the job required as commanded, while ensuring they could sleep at night. It was a transition from being a human being to a weapon so that moral purgatory wouldn't weigh them down. One night, Elijah wryly recalled a quote he'd learned at school by the English writer Samuel Johnson: 'He who makes a beast of himself gets rid of the pain of being a man.'

Elijah learned Ned had been married for just nineteen days before jumping on a Boeing 707 to fight in South Vietnam. He showed Elijah pictures of his wife, Diane, and often spoke about rekindling their dream of having children and buying a house once he returned to 'real life'.

During their downtime when they weren't on patrol, soldiers constructed a pub called the Ettamogah, which issued one can of beer per day to each bloke. Inside the pub they had memorial plaques for the fallen, along with photos of the deceased. The men had visits from Australian entertainers such as Big Pretzel, Lucky Star, and the Delltones; they even had their own open-air movie theatre. Elijah made audio tapes for Audrey – even though he wasn't sure if she had a tape player – expressing how much he fucking *missed* her. He also sent home postcards, as there was free postage for military personnel. When the conditions were right, men went surfing, and some even went hunting, as it required no licences for either that or fishing.

However, Elijah was reminded they were in the middle of a vicious war on one humid day at the end of September, when an incident occurred which would haunt him for countless years to follow.

Ned, Garrison, Johnson and Elijah were on an operation walking under the searing tropical sun, buckets of sweat pouring off their sticky flesh as they travelled through rice paddy fields and hamlets to reach their objective. The men reached Thunder Road on Highway 1, fighting off insects and dodging the many-banded krait snake – known as the 'two-step' (aptly named because if bitten you'd be dead within two steps … or so the rumour went). The overpowering smell of diesel from the patrol boats roaring up the Đồng Nai River beside them was noxious, and a group of F-100D Super Sabre fighter-bombers carrying napalm, white phosphorus and foo gas impaired their hearing.

As they walked along the dusty road, their tired feet kicking up clouds of fine powder, a Vietnamese woman wearing a long, silky-white áo dài with printed green leaves, walked towards them, her eyes hidden beneath a conical leaf hat. Something in the way she moved and the way she held another conical hat under her left arm made Ned halt. The others stopped, too, and then Ned motioned for them to move aside and wait under a palm tree while he kept his gaze on the woman, who was now walking with her face completely hidden.

'What's up, boss?' Garrison asked, wiping sweat and grit from his creased brow with his damp sleeve.

Ned jerked his chin in her direction, waiting for the noise of a squadron of Skyhawks above to cease, as it made whispered conversation difficult. 'Somethin's not right, fellas.'

The others looked on and Johnson verbalised what the rest were all thinking: 'Whaddaya mean? You sensin' something about that slope, Ned? You think she's a fuckin' Co Cong?'

Ned spat a glob of tobacco on the ground but never took his eyes off her. 'If she reaches into that spare hat she's holding onto like a newborn ... shoot her.'

Elijah studied Ned's profile, watching as he wiped brown spittle from his chin, before his lids narrowed to thin slits. Sweat collected in the creases at the corner of his eye. Elijah turned back to the woman, who was now peering up at them from under her hat.

Elijah caught the shifty look in her eyes – the look that Ned had noticed before any of them – and as quick as lightning, she sure as hell reached inside her spare hat. Like a knee-jerk reaction, the men raised their barrels.

Elijah would never forget the look of pain and fright in her face as her tanned skin split open with every bullet, blood pouring from her scalp down into her horrified eyes as she sank to her knees before sprawling in the dust. Screams from the locals rang out as Elijah stood there, shaking. Alarm sirens in the nearby village went off, dogs barked, front doors slammed shut, and people peddled away on bicycles or rickshaws as quick as their bony legs could manage.

Johnson spat on the ground and used a forearm to wipe his brow. 'Fuckin' dink bitch! That coulda been *fuckin'* hairy.'

The men knew she was dead, but Ned wanted confirmation in case of any apprehension or formal questioning afterwards that could lead to a bad conduct discharge or an AAR – after-action report. The small group walked over while women and children fled the scene. Smoke billowed in twirling tendrils from the woman's fresh wounds. Elijah's stomach dropped like a dumbwaiter; he had to push back the rising mucus in his burning throat. Ned bent to one knee and lifted the hat out of her bloodied grasp, as the dry dirt beneath sucked up her blood like a thirsty sponge. Ten RG-42 grenades fell out of the hat onto the surrounding ground.

Chapter 60

THEN – 1965 – VIETNAM

ON 25th SEPTEMBER, Ned sustained injuries during a patrol in Bến Cát, resulting in him being out of action for a few weeks. Army Headquarters sent an urgent telegram to his wife, Diane, against Ned's request, as he had wanted to write to her himself. During Ned's absence, the men continued their patrols while sorting through the photographs they had sent off for development. Elijah wrote to Audrey every single day, and felt pride in sending off pictures of himself and his buddies (Ned, Garrison, and some others), hoping they'd give her strength and serve as a reminder he was thinking of nothing and no-one but her.

But he had yet to receive word from his dearest.

Soldiers used to call home through an American station system called MARS – Military Affiliate Radio Station. Some soldiers affiliated with the Yanks could use it to call home via Signal Corps and ham radio equipment over shortwave radio. They deployed stations throughout Vietnam and allowed each soldier a five-minute personal radio telephone call. This was not easy; it was more of a science than anything else. There was, of course, a waiting list as every Tom, Dick and Harry wanted to call home, plus there was an endless list of protocols. If you were lucky enough to enter the station (Elijah's was MARS AB8AG) you were given strict instructions: You were *not* to mention a word about where you were or what you were doing in-country, and they enforced the time limit. The only cost was a collect-call charge the family had to accept from the ham's location.

When the day *finally* came for Elijah to enter the station, he was shaking with adrenaline at the thought of hearing Audrey's sweet voice. He sat at the desk with quivering hands and a dry mouth as two men connected him up, but the operator soon came back to him and said the collect-call charges were not accepted.

Fuckin' Lloyd! was Elijah's first thought as his eyes and fists clenched. He then tried to contact Grace, but to no avail either. He wobbled on rickety legs as he left, because of all the palaver in order to make a call, the average amount of times a bloke got to use the MARS system while on tour was twice – for some it was only at Christmastime, if they were lucky. That night he went into town, got wasted on Bière 33 (a Vietnamese beer that tasted like formaldehyde) and played billiards while picturing Lloyd's ugly, fat mug on every ball he smashed with his cue stick.

During the months that had passed since their arrival, Danny Garrison was also changing; Elijah could see it in his sunken, soulless eyes. Every single night without fail, like a priest saying his prayers, Danny held a picture of his wife, Mary, up in the air and stared at it for hours. Danny transported himself to another world; for him, it was vital there was light against the dark. At night, Elijah did the same thing as he lay on a hammock outside the tents, smoking, dreaming open-eyed about Audrey and what the future would provide. Imagination kept him going. On the days when Danny received a letter from Mary, his entire personality changed. Then the vicious cycle would repeat itself until he received another letter. Still, Elijah was envious of the attention and affection Danny received – it was the thing he craved most.

One late-September night, the men were lying shirtless in their own racks. Johnson was flipping through a nudie magazine called *Modern Man*; Spider was smoking a Pall Mall while reading the latest edition of *Stars and Stripes*; Ned – who had been given the all-clear by the nurses – was writing a letter to Diane; and Elijah was resting, head on pillow, hands behind his head. They had the wireless crackling away in the background as Walter Cronkite did a broadcast about the popularity of the Vietnam War … or rather, the lack of it.

Everyone is turning against us, Elijah thought.

'Do you think she has a Jody by now?' Danny said, cutting through Elijah's bitter thoughts.

Elijah turned to Danny, who was looking at Mary's picture through unshed tears. 'Jody' was a term used to describe someone back home stealing your girl while you were away fighting. For some, they feared a 'Jody' more than facing off with the Viet Cong, because you could do fuck all about it from all the way over here.

'Why would you think that?' Elijah said. 'Of course not. At least your girl writes to you. Are you on the waiting list for MARS?'

Danny's mouth twitched. 'Yes, but she sounds different now. At first there were pages upon pages about how much she loves me, but now she'd rather talk about some pop music newspaper, *Go-Set*, and her love for the Bee Gees. And … and I keep remembering how my brother used to ogle her. She mentions in her previous letter that he popped around to see how she was going.'

Elijah inhaled and gazed towards the roof of their tent. It was a hot, balmy night, and it seemed like neither one of them would get any sleep, so naturally their thoughts swam with neuroses. The truth was Elijah had no idea if Danny's lady was having it off with his brother; it was not uncommon. But damned if he'd be the one to say so.

'Mary loves you, buddy. One day she'll be in your arms again and this will all seem like a nightmarish fuckin' dream.'

'If I receive a "Dear John", I honestly don't know how I would handle it. She's the only thing I live for – apart from my son, of course.'

It seemed like the Vietnam War was inspiring more 'Dear John' letters than any other conflict. Back home, the war was so damned unpopular that women felt ashamed at being linked to a man who was fighting in it.

Elijah propped himself up on one elbow, swiped at a mosquito and stared at Danny. 'From what you've told me, nothing could tear you guys apart. She's only distracting herself so the pain of missing you won't seem so overwhelming. I promise she'll be waiting for you when you get back. I *promise*.'

Garrison never took his eyes off Mary's picture. 'I told her about you. I said we're sorta like brothers.'

'But we are, Danny. We really friggin' are.'

Chapter 61

THEN – 1965 – VIETNAM

BY THIS POINT Elijah had seen things he wouldn't have wished upon his worst enemy. Depression had him within its grasp. Elijah was trying to comprehend, amongst other things, why Audrey hadn't had the decency to write even one letter. Yes, he knew it had upset her that he left after everything she'd gone through, but *surely* she knew this wasn't a voluntary suicide mission; their own government had forced him to go. It was as simple as that; did she not know what he was going through?

On patrol missions, after hours of forced marching, the men ate tinned food – or C-Rations – heated by using C-4 explosives. They drank contaminated water out of canteens and added iodine tablets to help purify the water, but dead thingies were still floating around inside like tea leaves from a broken tea bag. The terrain itself was torture, and they woke up with insect bites all over their body after sleeping out in the humid jungle. To ward off malaria, each Monday the soldiers were given CP pills as well as drugs to help with other diseases and ailments. In the mornings the men would be up at sparrow fart, ready to fight another day; sometimes walking for hours on end through the jungle – sometimes soaked to the bone from trekking during a monsoonal storm.

On patrol they saw men hanging by their necks from trees, or the decapitated heads of village elders on spiked bamboo poles as a warning from the VC. At one point it seemed every village they rolled through had houses and buildings burned to the ground and the VC flag swung from almost every post – like a dog pissing on every tree to mark its territory.

All of this made the thought of receiving a simple love letter from Audrey not a luxury, but a necessity for Elijah.

The two abbreviations any soldier wanted to hear about more than any other were R&R and DEROS – date of expected return from overseas. Each man was issued one R&R, which was a three-to-seven-day rest and recuperation vacation to wherever he wanted to go. Bangkok was popular amongst the single lads, whilst Hawaii was most popular for the married fellas, as they could plan to holiday with their spouse.

The Department of Defence tried in vain to suppress soldiers engaging with prostitutes, but the soldiers relied upon it to combat the battlefield trauma they faced. Many Asian women worked in bathhouses, massage parlours and nightclubs around notorious R&R villas in Asia, for the appeasement of soldiers for whom R&R meant I&I: 'intoxication and intercourse', but unfortunately these R&R escapes came a little too late for some who couldn't cope.

Elijah's R&R was issued on 1st October. Few returned to Australia for their R&R, but Elijah couldn't wait to hug Grace, maybe have a quick, flavoursome meal heated on electrical elements for a change, then head straight over to Audrey's for a long-awaited explanation as to why she'd abandoned him when he needed her the most. He had sent two telegrams before his departure – one to Audrey, and one to his folks – informing them when he was touching down. But as luck would have it, the plane he was due to fly out on broke down. Twice.

Chapter 62

THEN – 1965

ARTHUR MOORE GREETED Elijah upon his return at Sydney Kingsford Smith Airport. Not Audrey or even his parents, but the butler. At the house, Arthur pulled into the garage and said, 'Ah, it looks like Mr and Mrs Samuels are home now. Why don't you go inside and rest? I will take care of your bag.'

Elijah jumped out of the car, his mixed emotions swirling around prompting nausea. He would have loved to have gone straight to Audrey's house as he'd already lost so much time, but he didn't look decent enough. He needed to shave and shower, which was partially psychological as he felt tainted by bloodshed – he needed spiritual cleansing as well as physical before he saw his sweetheart.

He also wanted to dress in his best outfit in case he had to persuade her what she still meant to him, and that he was serious about their future.

As Elijah entered the front door his folks walked over. He gave each of them a hug of sorts. Even though Elijah could hold a grudge, they were his parents and he had missed them more than he allowed himself to dare admit.

'Good to have you back, son.' Howard slapped his son's upper arm, then frowned before squeezing it twice. 'Christ, you've lost some beef, haven't you?'

Margaret resembled Greta Garbo in a mauve silk dress. 'It's so nice to see you again, Elijah.' She managed some crocodile tears. *Nice touch,* he thought. 'You'll have to get cleaned up. We have the McMahon's coming to dine with us in an hour.'

As much as Elijah liked Sonia and William McMahon, it was neither the time nor the place, and he hated the fact his parents had used his brief arrival as an excuse to invite those Liberals over to discuss politics over Coffin Bay oysters.

'Where's Audrey?' Elijah said.

His parents looked at each other and chorused a mild laugh.

'Oh, honestly, this is rich,' Margaret said. 'The first thing you ask after months of absence is regarding some girl, not about us or the family?'

Elijah gritted his teeth. 'I know how you are, Mother. Nothing will ever change with you two. So now, where's my girl?'

Margaret's head tilted and her eyes narrowed, while Howard conjured a phoney smile. 'Don't you even want to sit down and have a nice cup of tea, son?'

'No, Dad, I don't! I want to know, as I have asked in *all* my letters, where the hell is my fiancée? What have you guys done, or said to her?'

Margaret raised her hand to her throat and fingered her diamond necklace. 'I keep saying this, Elijah, but you've obviously had too many knocks to the head! We haven't seen her since she sped off in your car. It's not up to your father and me to chase your girlfriends.'

'Be realistic, son, we both have full-time jobs.'

Hearing footsteps behind him, Elijah turned to a teary-eyed Grace near the kitchen door. She held hands with some tall, handsome chap who Elijah guessed must be Benjamin Wilson, the new beau she had been raving about in her letters – the one she'd moved in with during Elijah's absence. Grace shrieked in delight, ran over, and threw her arms around Elijah's neck. He wrapped his arms around her waist and closed his eyes, thanking God that she was well, as were his family, whom he loved somewhere deep down.

Elijah leaned back and faced Grace, before he spoke in a whisper; his energy seemed to have vanished like a grain of sand in a windstorm. 'Grace, enough bullshit. Tell me where Audrey is, *please.*' He grabbed her upper arms.

Grace frowned, her eyes creased. 'You mean, Audrey still hasn't written to you? She still hasn't told you?'

Elijah squeezed her arms tighter than intended. 'Told me *what*, goddammit?!'

Grace glanced at Benjamin with pressed lips, then back to her brother. 'EJ, she moved out of Wollongong months ago.'

Chapter 63

THEN – 1965

ELIJAH STOOD IN front of the crooked path that led to Audrey's house. It appeared to have received a facelift, like someone had put in immense effort – not just into the house, but the lawn as well. He stole a deep, shaky breath as his heart raced.

As soon as he stepped on to the repainted porch, an overpowering smell of curry leaves assaulted his senses. After scrutinising the different furnishings through the side window, he knocked on the panel.

A middle-aged, dark-skinned woman opened the door and stood behind the fly screen, peering at Elijah with such intensity, he thought he was standing in a police line-up. *'Number 5, step forward, please.'*

'Hello, ma'am. My name is Elijah Samuels, and I was wondering if you knew where Audrey or Lloyd Hughes moved to?'

'Huh?' she grunted, eyeing him through thin slits, as if fearing he might bust in and clock her on the head or rape her. Anger flared within him, but *misunderstood* was his middle name. He should have been used to *that look*.

'I'm a friend of the family,' Elijah continued. 'You must have bought this house off Lloyd Hughes – am I right?' The woman shook her head and shrugged, which told Elijah that English wasn't her first language. 'Please, can't you tell me something?'

'I no speak English,' she said in a thick Indian accent, grabbing at her peach-coloured apron.

'Hughes, dammit! H.U.G—'

The lady shook her head and closed the door.

'*Shit*!' He jumped back into his father's Bentley and sped over to Betty-Sue's ice cream parlour. When he arrived, his heart almost collapsed, and he thought he was hallucinating when he saw a *SOLD* sign on the door.

He walked over to the streaky window and cupped his hands to the sides of his face to peer inside. Betty-Sue's was as bare as Bettie Page; nothing at all like the ice cream parlour he had grown to love. He looked over towards the back where his friends used to sit in their usual seafoam-green booth and saw stained outlines on the floor where the seats and tables once rested. They had torn down the 1950s movie star posters, and the spot where Audrey and he first laid eyes on each other was nothing more than a pile of concrete rubble and wooden planks with nails sticking out. Elijah ran around the side of the building and faced the tall fibreglass ice-cream cone he used to park next to. It had been vandalised; smashed and with spray-painted graffiti about the Vietnam War. The peace symbol was daubed over the exterior of his 'second home'.

He took a step back, running his hands through his sweat-slicked hair when another idea knocked on his skull. He hopped back into the Bentley and raced up the mountainside to where Audrey and he hoped to buy their first home. He got lost along the way, but eventually found it due to it being a standout. Another young couple sat on the veranda, each drinking from a bottle of Bulimba Gold Top. Elijah chewed his bottom lip in frustration. When the taste of iron covered his tongue, he drove to the last location his haywire mind could think of. He pulled the Bentley to the kerb and jumped out to run inside Bryce's Pet Store, which had once housed a furry German shepherd pup. An olive-skinned man with a black moustache seated behind the counter with a half-eaten croissant next to the register looked up from his *Everybody* magazine once the door slammed shut. Christos laughed when Elijah had asked him if he remembered selling a cute German shepherd to a young, attractive female.

After Christos laughed his arse off, in a Greek accent, his response was: 'Do you know how many animals we sell here in a year? And you want me to remember who we sold them to?' He placed a hand across his stomach, slapping the counter as he wheeze-laughed. 'Mister, you must be crazy.'

It was a crushing blow for Elijah, despite knowing it was a long shot. He couldn't believe it. He had *no* idea where to begin; how would he even function?

His exact last words to Audrey were 'Wait for me.' *Typical woman, does whatever she wants to do and bugger the rest.*

And just like that, his 'rest and recuperation' time in Australia ended.

Chapter 64

THEN – 1965 – VIETNAM

WHEN ELIJAH ARRIVED back in 'Nam, bitter and even more depressed, he spit-shined a bullet and kept it with him at all times. When his mate Red Rover asked him why he had a single bullet in his webbing, Elijah told him: 'In case I get caught in a crossfire with the VC closing in on me. This baby has my name written all over it.' And he meant it. Elijah wasn't born to be a prisoner, and he wasn't going to live out his life as a POW, knowing he'd never see Audrey again. Fuck that!

That night Elijah bought his first Zippo lighter from the American Post Exchange (a sort of military department store). They were the simple utilitarian tool any soldier could rely on, besides their usual purpose, they could also heat food, illuminate letters, or set fire to the huts of suspected VC – coined as 'Zippo Raids' by many of the G.I.'s.

Zippo in hand, Elijah went to a sidewalk tent in the bustling, luminous streets of Saigon to have a message engraved on the lighter, as many of his fellow soldiers had done before him. Gene 'Shagger' Wilson had *Fighter by day, lover by night, drunkard by choice, soldier by mistake.* A young Aboriginal man known only as Ace of Spades had *Though I walk through the valley of the shadow of death, I fear no evil, for I am the evilest motherfucker in the valley.* It took all but two seconds for Elijah to think of his: *My flame will always burn for Audrey Hughes.*

On 9th October, Elijah was with a group of soldiers walking along a dusty road, enchanted by the Agent Orange sunset with red dust clouds ahead, when twenty-year-old Aussie Jack Evans dropped like a sack of mail. A sniper shot him clean through his left eye, spraying his brains across the ground like someone hurling a tray of lasagna. Jack's best mate Kenny panicked and started letting loose into the dense jungle with his F1 submachine gun.

Kenny ceased fire only to scream out: 'I'll kill every last one of you fuckin' slope bastards!' Spittle flew from his mouth, his face purple with rage. 'Do ya hear me, *Charlie*?!'

When Kenny's magazine was empty, he collapsed to his knees to hold the rest of Jack's head in his lap as he wept, his body heaving, while Elijah and the rest of the soldiers searched through the dense foliage for VC bodies or blood trails. There were none.

When soldiers were out on a mission, heating their tinned food was forbidden, as light was too dangerous. So that night the men sat in a silent circle, their only light source was the moonlight that filtered through the cloud cover in geometric beams, eating from cans of cold lima beans and ham. Kenny said nothing. Kenny ate nothing, and hardly any of them got a wink of sleep that night, as they were close to enemy territory. Every snap of a twig in the impenetrable, silent darkness sent pulses racing and eyelids popping open. The next night, after another banal dinner, Elijah ducked away from the group and moved to a secluded area to sit under a fig tree and listen to a blue-eared barbet twittering. Once again he reached out to Audrey by writing her a letter as best he could in the poor moonlight – heedless of his tears dripping onto his writing pad and making the ink run. This was fruitless, as Audrey no longer had the same address, but it helped him somewhat; even voicing his emotions on a tape recorder felt like a weight being lifted. He signed off with: 'You don't need to die in order to go to hell.'

The next afternoon, back at base camp after another successful oper-ation, the men sat down with anticipation in front of a clerk who had a hessian mailbag. One by one, he called out names as the rest looked on in envy while soldiers hurried to the front to grab an envelope or goody package before scurrying off to read in private. Some letters were laced with a hint of perfume and were passed around camp to share the wondrous, female fragrance – a momentary respite from the terrible smells that they endured (especially when the shit-burning began). Soldiers re-read their letters dozens of times before photos were showcased around the platoon, and good news was extended before the letters were burned, never to be read again. Elijah never vocalised how embarrassing it was to be one of the few lads left sitting there alone – time after time – because they didn't call his name. He began feeling like a fucking charity case when guys kept asking if Elijah wanted their sister or female cousin to make contact. Once the hessian bag was emptied, Elijah was left sitting there like the boy in school no-one picks to be on their sports team, with no choice but to amble back to his tent and wait to hear all about the good news his brothers had to share.

But this time, the clerk had one letter left. The balding, jug-eared man looked at Elijah with a raised eyebrow. 'Jack Evans?'

Elijah's heart rate accelerated on hearing the name of the deceased kid. He glanced around base camp, seeing guys engrossed in their letters, taking note that he was at least fifteen metres away from the nearest bloke.

He swallowed a lump in his throat the size of a fist, and turned back to the clerk with a curt nod.

Baldy handed Elijah the wafer-thin envelope before heading back to the helicopter waiting nearby. Elijah knew it was a major breach of privacy reading a dead man's letter (not to mention morally reprehensible), but he felt compelled to accept it on Jack's behalf. Elijah held it close to his chest as he walked past a few guys, some crying, some laughing.

Spider looked up, a Kent dangling between his curved lips, and said, 'Finally got one, eh?' as Elijah made his way to an isolated patch of grass. Under the dwindling sun, with shaky fingers, he tore the top off and pulled out a folded piece of purple paper. When he opened it, sparkling pink confetti fell over his crossed legs, followed by a square photo tumbling out. On the piece of paper there were two bold words in glittering gold: *Congratulations, Daddy!* Elijah turned the photo over and saw a bundled child with a caption at the bottom: *Welcome to the world, Miss Viola Evans! (She has your eyes, darling.)*

A week later, a group set out along the northern border of Phước Tuy Province in the Courtenay Rubber Plantation, to collect their fallen so they could escort the bodies back in order to prepare them for repatriation. Caribou cargo planes flew overhead as the men patrolled in silence; each of them enduring the private agony of memories from back home, or thoughts of the men they were going to collect. A few moaned and groaned from the pain of their blistered feet and aching muscles; some suffered charley horses. The sweltering sun beat down relentlessly, their fatigues soaked in sweat, and a few guys began dry retching once they arrived at the plantation. The smell of decay was rancid, and the flies on the dead bodies ... Elijah told Grace in one of his letters: 'If you ever left a chicken carcass outside for a week during summer, then you'd know what I mean.'

When the men grabbed onto the arms of the fallen, sometimes they could drag them only a few feet before their limbs tore off, revealing the infestation of maggots crawling around inside the cadavers.

It became clear to Elijah one afternoon, as he watched villages burning and had the smell of gasoline wafting around him, as bombs fell from the skies with absurd elegance, that there were only two ways out of 'Nam: victory or death.

Chapter 65

THEN – 1965 – VIETNAM

ONE NIGHT A Sky Soldier named Fred Duvall killed himself by playing chop suey with razor blades to the wrists after having received a 'Dear John'. To distract himself from this news, Elijah had Danny Garrison tattoo Audrey's name across his chest, over his heart – sort of like a 'good' omen. Visions of Audrey clouded his mind regardless if he wanted them to, and he felt bitter at her sudden disappearance because he suspected foul play by his parents. But he had no proof, and he didn't know what else to do – he couldn't exactly catch a fucking taxi and leave, could he?

While the men went off in search of the nearest brothel or steam bath to ease their minds, Elijah found himself gazing at the sickle moon, hoping Audrey was doing the same thing at the same moment, especially when his wristwatch ticked over to 6:29 pm. Most of the men who frequented the brothels were married with kids (true, some only married hoping it would exclude them from war), but it took the sting off their loneliness; after all, to these guys it was only physical. On the occasion where Elijah began slipping down into the deepest, darkest recesses of his mind, he wandered into the village, contemplating letting out his frustrations and hurt on the cheapest prostitute, too. But no matter how badly Audrey had hurt him, he couldn't do it.

In early November, he stood outside a shoddy timber shack called Monaco Bar – a place the soldiers liked to frequent because it was close by and cheap. The moans and grunts from the men inside rose above the piano music. One man in particular, Teddy Levi, was a married guy of eight years with three young boys. When Teddy stumbled outside the shack and saw Elijah leaning against a palm tree, a bottle of gin dangling in his hand, he stopped. The combination of guilt and sadness in Teddy's eyes was more palpable than Elijah had ever seen. Teddy tucked his rumpled shirt into his pants as he staggered towards Elijah with tears in his eyes; the smell of whiskey on his breath was potent as he leaned in close to Elijah's face: 'Why does God hate us?'

Listening to the throes of lust inside the brothel carved Elijah up as he thought of Audrey being with another man. It tore him in two because he didn't know – he just didn't *know* if by this point she'd found someone else. The constant, repetitive, torturous thinking swamped his mind. It was corrosive and fuelled by alcohol, which was fast replacing his H_2O intake. He had no solid answers and was subjected to the monotonous cruelty going on inside his damaged mind. Where the hell had she gone?!

There was a part of him that wanted to go inside the brothel that night, but it was more so for female companionship, and the bewitching feminine touch. Instead of selling his soul and contracting a disease, he collapsed on the dusty ground after Teddy left and sobbed into his hands until the effects of alcohol and emotional exhaustion consumed him.

When Elijah had first arrived in 'Nam, he didn't understand at all how happily married men with kids could even *think* of paying for sex with cheap, degrading prostitutes. However, as the months rolled on and the turmoil in Elijah's heart and mind climaxed, he sympathised with the phrase: 'Do not judge me until you've walked a mile in my shoes'. The things he saw ... the things he did ... the things he heard ... the things he wished he never knew; it weighed on his mind like a cement blanket, and he felt dragged towards the abyss of earth's molten core.

Late one night in mid-spring, while all the lads were out in the open-air theatre watching *Sex and the Single Girl* starring Tony Curtis and Natalie Wood, Elijah's mate, Jimmy Walker, came into his tent, blitzed as a skunk, and tried to persuade Elijah to go to a steam and cream.

Elijah, who sat over the side of his rack with elbows rested on his thighs and hands dangling between his parted legs, shook his head. His dog tags swung and tinkled as his head lowered.

Jimmy walked over to sit beside him. 'Your girl ain't ever gonna find out, man, just come – one time. She'll never know.'

Elijah opened his eyes as a red mist seeped through every pore on his body. He was angry at Audrey; angry at everything and everyone!

'She might not, Jimmy, but I will.' Then Elijah faced Jimmy, who reacted to his moistened eyes by leaning back, mouth agape. 'How could I ever look at her again if I went with you tonight?'

The sound of Jimmy slapping the bare skin on Elijah's bare back reverberated around the empty tent. 'You've got strength, my man ... you *must* be happy. Bro, all I know is if I don't get me some sweet *poontang* tonight I'm gonna fuckin' explode!' He stood up with a grunt, arching his back. 'Just think about it; it's only a bit of boom-boom, man. Christ, you haven't even fuckin' heard a word from her; how do you know your girl ain't bangin' some bloke right now? Or your best mate who's gone over to "comfort her",' he said with air quotations, before swiping at an insect that flew too close for comfort. Elijah glared at Jimmy while his clenched knuckles pulsed.

Jimmy held up his hands in defence. 'I'm just saying, man, she ain't eeeever gonna know.' He took off his wedding ring and shoved it into his pants pocket before exiting the tent.

Elijah never knew how a woman could affect a man until he went to 'Nam and saw firsthand the power they can hold over blokes, especially if one received a 'Dear John'. Some of those letters were bitter, cold, and straight to the point – 'I slept with someone else'.

Elijah wrote a letter to Grace about the time when Eddie 'Slasher' Jenkins received a 'Dear John', for it was something worth sharing. Eddie had kept quiet about his letter, burning it and adopting an *I-don't-give-a-shit-about-anything* attitude. He moped around camp, his fuse was shorter than a pubic hair, and on occasions he'd take off during the night. When a group of lads saw Eddie by himself in the dense jungle one afternoon during a siesta, they went out after him – fearing he was contemplating stepping on a Claymore mine. Eddie confided in them that his high school sweetheart – the one he presented an engagement ring to the day before he left for war – had written to say she'd cheated on him twice, and no longer supported his role in Vietnam – twisting the blade even further by admitting to participating in anti-war demonstrations with her girlfriends.

Upon getting wind of this, one of the Yanks, Alan 'Brightspark' Clements, suggested they gather all the other lads' photos of their lady, cousin, or sister. Once they'd rounded up about thirty-odd photos of gorgeous women, Alan then dictated a letter, which Eddie handwrote, something to the effect of: 'Dear Janice, I'm so sorry, but I can't seem to remember who the hell you are. Please take your picture from the pile of photos and send the rest back to me. Take care, Eddie.'

Women … Elijah thought, shaking his head, *God, if they think it's tough for them, how the fuck do they think* we *feel?*

On quite a few nights, Elijah heard Danny (a hefty bloke standing at 6'4") sobbing, calling out Mary's name. No doubt calling for her to mollify his broken spirit.

In 'Nam Elijah thought of love as a type of ironic cruelty; the way it crippled his mind, body, and soul. On one occasion he awoke during the middle of the sticky night after having a nightmare about Audrey fornicating with another man. She then left him for dead on the cold Vietnamese soil as he reached out his bloodied hand for her to hold on to, but she and the anonymous man walked away, laughing. It wasn't the first time Elijah jerked awake from having a nightmare along the same lines, and that one was rather mild compared to the others.

Chapter 66

THEN – 1965 – VIETNAM

THEN CAME THE day in 'Nam where Elijah Samuels' life changed indefinitely. On 8th November, during Operation Hump, a battalion of the 173rd stumbled into a VC regiment, ensconced in a camouflaged bunker complex where they became ambushed by 1,200 members of the Viet Cong. From there they had a vicious nose-to-nose firefight lasting four hours. Everything from AK-47s to CAR-15s were being used.

Their machine A-gunner, Joe, was blown sky-high thanks to a rocket-propelled grenade launcher, which showered Danny and Elijah in rubble as they stood close by. The Allies lost forty-nine men that day, one of whom was Danny. They'd shot him through the neck; his severed trachea couldn't have been patched up even if medics had had a tonne of gauze. It was a T&T wound (through and through). Elijah held Danny in his arms, watching his best mate gasping for air, choking on his own blood as it rippled through his exposed oesophagus like bubbling water. Danny's eyes were full of fear as he gasped for oxygen, blood coming out in explosive bursts of crimson phlegm. Elijah was screaming out that they needed medical aid, but no medevac helicopter lands where there is gunfire, so they had to wait for a lull in the firing.

As Elijah held Danny, willing him to stay alive, he didn't know what to do or say, as they both knew it was the end. Elijah didn't want Danny's last few moments here on earth to be filled with bullshit: 'You're gonna be okay, mate!'

Instead, Elijah held on to let Danny know he would not die alone. He would stay with Danny until the end. As Danny's life slipped away in the palms of Elijah's bloodied hands, Lieutenant Colonel A.V. Preece shouted at Elijah to get up and keep fighting. Elijah ignored his CO and held Danny until Garrison's head lolled to the side. The last thing Danny *tried* to tell Elijah was: 'Tell Mary I love her.' The only thing he'd be able to do, however, was move his mouth muscles like a fish out of water.

Laying Danny down, Elijah got up, fighting back tears and blinded by pure rage, realising he was cornered. Soldiers – his brothers – dropped like sandbags around him, while Danny's lifeless, bloodied corpse lay at his feet. They shot Elijah four times, and as his knees gave way, he collapsed next to Danny, staring into his dead friend's frightened, open eyes. Everything around Elijah distorted; the humming from the Hueys and air cavalry above blocked his hearing, and his visual surroundings seemed to move in slow motion. Words and shouts came in gentle oscillations, fading in and out.

As he coughed and choked on his pain, with the belief he was honestly dying, he channelled his thoughts to Audrey and prayed that she would be taken care of. Eventually, he passed out, thankful that the bastards had moved on and presumed him dead like the surrounding others. They'd shot Elijah in the stomach, chest, and thigh. He survived thanks to the aid of his fellow servicemen, but on that day something within him died, along with Danny.

Elijah was taken back to an aid station by the medevac helicopter, but at that point, he didn't give a toss if he pulled through. They transferred him to the hospital, which soldiers dubbed the 'meat factory' where they extracted the metal fragments from his bones and flesh. At first, they took him to the 'expectants' ward (a place where casualties would go if they were expected to die), until Dr Hazlo upgraded Elijah to a 'walking wounded' status. The chaplain came around and asked Elijah for his parents' contact details to inform them of what happened, but he couldn't utter a single word. That night he wondered if he was going to die – if not from the wounds, by his own volition.

A week later, as Elijah lay bandaged up inside his own tent again, he looked over to the empty rack beside him as the little square picture of Mary stuck out from under Danny's pillow. He limped over there and picked it up to see an attractive raven-haired beauty who had enticing Bambi-like brown eyes and seductive ruby lips. Elijah could definitely see the appeal, and the provocative photo was obviously a private one Mary had taken just for her husband, probably to keep in his pocket as a subtle reminder that he was a married man. Elijah flipped over the picture, which had a message on the back:

To my darling husband,
I will be eagerly awaiting (with bated breath) for your return to try
for baby number 2, and to have you in my loving arms once more.
We miss you already, my dearest!
All our love, Mary and baby Brendan xox

Elijah's rage intensified in that moment; not only was he reliving Danny die in his arms but also picturing Mary at the point in time where two black-suited men would notify her that the love of her life, and the father of her child, had died in battle. Elijah wondered if he himself died, would Audrey even care? Audrey and he hadn't had any contact for months; it was driving him insane and to the point of exhaustion. He cursed God for placing him in this situation and for tearing him away from Audrey's arms. He cursed God for taking Danny, and he cursed God for the war, which they had no business being involved in. Elijah thought if there was such a thing as the Second Coming, the Vietnam War would have been pretty fucking apt!

Elijah punched a timber pole of the tent with full force whilst holding Mary's picture in his other shaking hand. Razor-sharp pain rippled through his shoulder with jagged teeth, but he needed to feel *something*. Before long, his stomach started giving him grief, signalling it was time to rest and take it easy. They'd relieved him of duty, pending clearance from the nurses. They gave strict orders to stay on light duties, and to spend the next few weeks lazing about, which was what soldiers called 'spine-bashing'. But far worse irreparable damage had been done to his psyche than to his actual physical form.

Elijah didn't know how he did it, but that night in the tent he took a step back from Satan's claws and chucked a razor blade that'd ended up in his hands during a disorienting miasma, as far as the eye could see. They assigned every battalion with a barber, and in his battalion it was Garrett Bakersfield. Elijah reported to him (or the other lads while on foot patrol) to keep his appearance intact. Elijah Samuels didn't pick up a razor or pair of scissors until over a year later, just as a precaution.

Christmas came around in Biên Hòa. It was a time of rest, yet also laughter thanks to Bob Hope, who arrived from the United States to stage one of his bizarre extravaganzas. Christmas during 'Nam was a time of recreation and presents and packages. Elijah received one.

His parents sent him an expensive designer sweater (even though it was boiling hot and sticky) and a whiskey flask, plus a card with: *From Mum, Dad, and Grace*, written at the bottom; no *Love* was included. It never had been.

An American G.I. next to Elijah held a short-timer stick in one hand, and a picture of his lady (who was naked except for a Santa hat, positioned on a bed in a seductive pose) in the other. The short-timer stick he held meant he was going back home to 'The World'. That stick, which was the equivalent of crossing days off in the calendar, meant you had less than two months left to serve.

The G.I. stared at the picture of his buxom girl with tears rimming his eyelids. 'Man, the sooner I board that fuckin' Freedom Bird, the sooner I can get home to *this*!' He flicked the photo and nudged Elijah's shoulder before kissing the picture. *Mwah!* 'I'm coming home soon, *baby*!' he yelled with a jovial grin. Twelve days later, he was killed in combat. Elijah never even knew his name.

As Elijah chewed on a dry Anzac biscuit, he thought of the contrast between his previous Christmas, which had comprised of making love and mucking around with Audrey at Jenolan Caves, compared to this one: alone in another country fighting in a war that the public condemned. It was so bizarre that he turned his head around to see if Rod Serling was hosting this episode of *The Twilight Zone*; certain he'd be hearing the voice-over anytime now. He also wondered who Audrey would spend the festive season with, and he needed to know if she even thought of him at all. All Elijah knew for sure was, if he arrived back home and found Audrey in the arms of another man, it wouldn't end well for the prick. Elijah had become disgruntled, irascible, and dispirited. Mixed with seeing violence on a constant basis, he was a powder keg of emotions, ready for anything.

Through it all, Elijah had to admit it was nice, however, to see the general spirit of things pick up around camp as the men received care packages, which were like a 'touch from home'. A care package contained letters, photos, homemade food like biscuits (which were usually crumbs, only suitable for a cheesecake base by the time of arrival), and clothing garments. Some big guns brought out their acoustic guitars and they all sang songs that made Christmas Day, which was typically spent with loved ones, somewhat bearable. Lunch consisted of cream of tomato soup for entrée, and seasoned turkey, leg of ham, and roast leg of pork for main. They shovelled down plum pudding before distributing decks of cards on crates, as they made bets on poker and euchre.

There wasn't much time for cavorting, however, because as of 8ᵗʰ January 1966, the US 1ˢᵗ Infantry Division led a mission, Operation Crimp, to search-and-destroy a famed Viet Cong stronghold – the Hồ Bò Woods in Bình Dương Province, where they uncovered the Viet Congs' underground labyrinth headquarters – the Củ Chi Tunnels. They hadn't held operations there for three or four years because of Viet Cong strength, but thanks to the US 173rd Airborne Brigade having the Aussies' backing, it was full speed ahead into the hornet's nest.

Chapter 67

AS CHLOE LISTENED to Elijah's descriptive account of his 'Nam nightmare, she sneak-peeked through Audrey's diary. Her heart plunged as she read what had happened. They never stood a chance.

'... at the end of that month, the First Battalion withdrew to Biên Hòa for an Anzac Day parade and to meet the new Australian Prime Minister, Harold Holt, who had succeeded Sir Robert Menzies. Then it was time to leave South Vietnam.

'We returned to Australia on HMAS *Sydney* on 8th June 1966, just two months shy of the infamous Battle of Long Tan, where the VC outnumbered us Aussies twenty to one.

'Our welcome home march through the streets of Sydney was a triumphant ticker-tape parade. Three-hundred thousand Sydneysiders standing twenty deep applauded as we marched in our greens to the sound of drums. As we neared Town Hall, we saw a female protestor covered in kerosene and red paint. She wasn't protesting the war, nor did she represent any political groups; she was merely a psycho making a personal display. However, some of us felt she was a bad omen, foretelling troubled times to come for us soldiers because not everyone thought of us as heroic warriors. Save Our Sons and others labelled us mindless killing machines, controlled and manufactured by our government. In fact, because of some public outcry, some of our mates returned to Sydney in the dead of night, to remain aloof. But that had unforeseeable consequences because the condition in which a soldier returned affected how he reconditioned himself back into society, see? Those like me, who had returned to a positive response, settled back in with "relative ease", but those who returned in secret, with no accolade, battled the inner turmoil and sometimes dealt with that by sticking a hose through their car window, tickling their brain with a bullet, or kissing the concrete from ninety feet above.

'We were subjected to harsh labels: baby killers, rapists, murderers, and I personally hope that those demonstrators who spat in my face forever feel ashamed. A lot of us felt the public were quick to condemn the soldiers, but not so much the politicians who had conducted the war. But images such as children being burned by napalm, or the footage of a South Vietnamese general blowing the brains out of a member of the Viet Cong in the streets of Saigon, had a profound effect of public opinion and public understanding. I am, however, sinfully proud of having been an enlisted man and offer no apologies to one-sided civilians. Whenever someone asks about my limp, I say it's a token from Vietnam. Usually their look suggests I deserved it and that much more. To this day, not one person has *ever* thanked me for my service during the war, which became a literal war within myself.'

Jamie shook her head, a hand to her breast, while Angela diverted her gaze, closing her eyes.

Elijah licked his dry lips and took a minute to catch his breath. He'd never spoken this much for this long in all his life. Whilst he hated being the centre of attention, it felt good to be in the company of others; for someone to have a keen interest in him beyond the realm of doctors, nurses and pharmaceutical specialists.

He swallowed to lubricate his dry throat. 'Considering we witnessed our friends get blown apart, had to shoot men and sometimes women who aimed a gun at us, and the fact we were never the same again, we were appalled at how having done the job required of us by our government was now being used against us. Even some RSL clubs proved less than welcoming – can you believe it? I know a few men who've harboured lifelong resentment towards these organisations from which we expected so much more.

'Because much of this played on our minds for years to come, myself and some 7,000 others joined the Vietnam Veterans' Association of Australia, which was formed by former veterans like me to help those who suffered the effects of herbicides, suicidal tendencies, PTSD, and defoliants used in Vietnam. Our motto is: *Honour the dead but fight like hell for the living.*'

'There would have been *some* citizens proud of who you were and what you'd done, right?' Timothy said. 'Those at the march applauded you guys.'

Elijah's lips curled. 'Considering the amount of backlash and having words like *murderer* spray-painted on our cars or picket fences, it wouldn't surprise you that the statistics of suicide and failed marriages are higher for Vietnam vets than in any other war the Aussies have fought in.'

'But we're up to the part where you return, right?' Jamie said, smiling. 'I mean, no longer were you in that nightmare; you got your life back, huh?'

Elijah sneered. 'Love, my return to Australia was so painful and lonely, some nights I wished I was with my brothers back in Vietnam.'

Chapter 68

THEN – 1966

THE DAY ELIJAH arrived back in Sydney was bittersweet. He had prayed to God, asking for help to move on with his life, trying to push facts and reality aside to cope with the man he had become. Elijah had informed his parents of his DEROS, and Arthur was scheduled to pick him up. Knowing Audrey would not greet him got to Elijah more than anything.

He hadn't had a smile on his face in as long as he could remember, and today was no exception. As 1 RAR arrived back after their march, soldiers in the streets launched into the arms of their loved ones. Over in 'Nam Elijah hadn't seen many men cry, but when a soldier laid eyes on his wife, or mother, or child, the waterworks flowed like Niagara and it stole Elijah's breath because no woman was waiting with open arms for him – not even his own fucking mother.

Teddy Levi dropped his burlap sack on the ground and fell to his knees when his attractive wife, holding one of their sons, ran to him. Teddy wrapped his arms around them both and bawled, holding onto them for dear life while he remained on his knees. He held them so hard his knuckles turned white.

Diane Kelly sprinted to Ned and they embraced in a tearful hug. As Diane wailed, behind her stood her sisters and Ned's father. Elijah recognised them all by name and face from the pictures Ned had shown so often.

Arthur arrived and the two men shook hands, as anything more than a well-rounded handshake with a Samuels was deemed unprofessional and too familiar.

'Good to see you again, sir,' Arthur said, taking the burlap sack and walking Elijah over to a candy apple red 1966 Dodge Dart convertible, which Margaret had purchased with her loose change. 'I see you've brought a limp back with you.'

Elijah sneered, then focused on a raven-haired woman raining kisses over her man's face. She chanted: 'I love you, I love you, I love you,' in between kisses. The man held her so fiercely her upper arms turned red.

Facing front, Elijah clenched his aching jaw and cleared his congested throat. 'Yeah, it's a souvenir to make sure I never forget the grand time I had.' He glanced at every blonde-haired woman standing amidst the mammoth crowd as pain raked unrelenting, scorching talons over his constricted chest. 'Where are my parents?'

'I'm afraid they couldn't make it, but they should be home by the time we arrive back.'

'Oh goodie.' Elijah placed a pair of black Ray-Bans over his eyes, hoping to shield himself from this bizarre world he had returned to.

Chapter 69

'IT MAKES NO sense,' Jamie said, shaking her head. 'It is evident Mum loved you; why would she abandon you? Something seems fishy here.'

Elijah scoffed. 'You're telling me!'

Angela stood up, shaking her legs. 'I want to hear more, but I am dying for another coffee. Would you ...?'

'Oh, no, go ahead. I need to use the facilities again myself; I have the bladder of a pregnant woman, it appears.' Angela chuckled and helped Elijah out of his chair as he whispered in her ear. 'Don't, ah, wait around.' She shot him a puzzled look. 'I need to drop the kids off at the pool.'

Angela's smirk belied the fact his comment repulsed her. 'What would you like to drink?'

'Oh, um, a strong flat white with two sugars, please.'

As they walked the length of the corridor side by side, Elijah grinned at the thought of how far he had come in a few short days. On his introduction to the family they had barely looked at him; now they were helping him to the bathroom, buying him dinner, and welcoming his stories instead of denouncing them.

Once everyone in the room had settled back down, Chloe had the daunting task of unravelling the mystery by reading from Audrey's diary. Elijah looked on with bated breath, almost crushing the paper cup encircled in his hands.

Chloe inhaled, licked her dry lips, and began: *'9th June 1965. Dear Diary, today Uncle Lloyd informed me we are leaving this house in a few weeks' time.*

I cried and begged him to reconsider! I don't understand what the rush is, and when I asked him where he got the money from, he told me he won it gambling. Isn't it suspicious? But what more can I say or do? Something isn't right – he won't tell me the address so I can pass it on to my friends, or even to Grace so she can tell EJ. I tried calling Grace as soon as Lloyd dropped the A-bomb, but no-one in the Samuels' house answered. I held onto Corey and cried until I physically couldn't. I feel like I don't belong on this planet. I always felt like that until EJ came into my life and made me feel alive and worthy to walk amongst "normal" people. I cannot give up hope for our future; it is my only salvation. Somehow, some way, I'll reunite with him again—'

Angela's phone rang. She tutted as she retrieved it from her bag and apologised while everyone else remained silent. 'Hi ... what? No, Bruce, I told Michelle to send the draft to Gavin before she sends it to Louise.'

No-one said a word. All they could hear was a man yelling into Angela's ear.

Angela stood and raised a hand to her forehead, pacing. 'I am sorry, but I am still with my mother and I thought my instructions were pretty clear. Besides, when do we send a draft to a client without clarification from the board? It's unprofessional. I know Michelle's a temp, but it's not rocket science.'

The mood shifted from sadness to awkwardness, as everyone heard Angela get a thrashing from her boss over a balls-up. Angela threw her free hand in the air, shaking her head. 'I can't come in, Bruce. I am trying to—'

Angela closed her eyes, her jaw clenching as she lowered the phone. She clicked her tongue, then looked around the room, putting on a brave face as she chucked the phone in her bag. 'I might have to duck out for a while; there's been a mix-up at work.'

'Tell him to get effing stuffed,' Elijah said with a straight face, side-gazing Chloe.

Angela rolled her eyes and pinched the bridge of her nose as she turned to Jamie. 'I trust I can leave Chloe in your capable hands?'

'Of course.' Jamie smiled. 'I think I'll walk you out. I need a cigarette.'

'Mmm, I think we'll stretch our legs for a moment, too,' Timothy said, rubbing Tida's back as she sat forward in the chair.

As if realising, they all looked at Elijah, who said, 'I'll hold down the fort.'

'On our way back, do you want us to get you guys something from the café?' Jamie said.

Elijah looked at Chloe, letting her speak first. 'Just a caramel milkshake, please.'

Jamie nodded then looked at Elijah who said: 'Yes, I would like a schnitzel roll with gravy and hell, gimme another hot flat white with two, please.' He lifted his backside so he could retrieve his wallet from a pocket.

'As opposed to a *cold* flat white?' Angela said with a smirk as she grabbed her bag. He gave her the bird in a mocking gesture, accompanied by a wide grin. 'And don't worry about the money, it's on us.'

Twenty minutes later, Jamie, Tida and Timothy returned with provisions, empty bladders, and phones switched back to silent as Nurse Mildred trailed behind.

Chloe opened the diary with one hand, slurping her milkshake through a striped straw with the other.

'Shouldn't we wait for Ange?' Jamie said, munching on a sausage roll covered with runny tomato sauce.

'She'll be hours,' Chloe said while searching for the page where she'd left off.

'Dammit, some of us have work ta do,' Nurse Mildred directed at Jamie before turning to Chloe, grinning. 'Go 'head, angel.'

Elijah chuckled as Nurse Mildred hijacked Angela's vacant chair, then struggled to tear the lid off her wonton noodle soup. *Work my wrinkly arse.*

'I can tell Mother what happens when I see her later on – deal?' Chloe said.

'Wait, I have a question,' Timothy said, not realising chocolate powder from his cappuccino had smeared the corners of his mouth.

Elijah stifled a deep sense of gratitude that they were no longer shunning him. Instead, they had embarked on this adventure into the past with as much enthusiasm as Chloe. 'I'm all ears.'

Timothy cleared his throat and licked his lips as the snaking line of vapour from his cappuccino wafted in front of his face. 'Didn't most soldiers serve two tours in 'Nam?'

Elijah raised his eyebrows before protruding his bottom lip, nodding.

Timothy smirked and shrugged. 'I only remember because we brushed on this during modern history in high school.'

'Very good. Yes, some did, and 1 RAR started back up in '68 – year of the infamous Tet Offensive and Khe Sanh. Not only did I *not* want to go back, but they deemed me FNT, which means fit non-tropical. It meant although enlisted with the Australian Army, I couldn't fight in the tropics or else I would break out in hives, rashes, and swelling – which is what was happening to me in 'Nam.'

'Oh,' Nurse Mildred mouthed, raising a spoon cradling a wonton and popping it into her mouth.

Timothy leaned forward. 'Why didn't they send you home while you were in 'Nam, then?'

'The doctors didn't know what to bloody make of it while I was over there. Doc Norton, head of the Saigon Medical Centre, prescribed me with some Benadryl, and without knowing what to do, or how to treat it, he was pushing for an RTA – Return To Australia, but it never happened. By God, the hives were bloody embarrassing though, the lads nicknamed me "Bubbles" for the remainder of my term—' He sneezed into his hanky one-handed, as the other held his schnitzel roll. 'Excuse me.' He rubbed the base of his nose while sniffling. 'But yes, Tim, they could have sent me to fight in the desert, for example. However, jungle places like Vietnam were out of the question, and because I'd been shot, I wouldn't have passed a physical as it left a permanent limp in my step. I couldn't have outrun my grandmother if she were chasing me. It meant I was at high risk, but rather than get rid of me, they stuck me on light duties for the rest of my term – seeing as I was already there. I knew of men who smashed a foot by slamming it with the butt of a gun to shatter every bone as a way of escaping from going back to that hellhole a second time. Once veterans left Vietnam and returned to the arms of loved ones, it was hard to go back. Some even wore T-shirts stating "I no longer fear hell, for I have served in Vietnam".'

'It must have been,' Timothy said, looking towards the floor, then added: 'And also, what happened to the guitar you left at Lloyd's place? I've been thinking about that for a while now. You never once mentioned joining in with the others in Vietnam when they played the guitar.'

Elijah's cheeks puffed out on an exhale. 'Lloyd destroyed it. Smashed it to smithereens, according to Audrey when I saw her the next day after the police chase. I never picked up another guitar afterwards. I had no motivation to play again after Audrey did the Harold Holt on me.'

'Harold Holt?' Chloe said, frowning. She then waved a hand, shaking her head. 'Wait, it doesn't matter. Can't I continue reading? Pleeeeease.'

'Sorry, kid,' Elijah said, smirking. 'The floor's all yours.'

Chapter 70

'14th July 1965. *Dear Diary, I am writing to you from my new home in Mosman. I hate it. Water surrounds us, but the house is so modern it lacks charm. This morning I took the train to the Samuels' house, but Margaret caught me at the front gate; she was in her fancy golf clothes. I had a letter for her to give to EJ explaining what has happened. It was my only hope; it was the only thing I could think of to do to reach EJ. The letter informed him of my new address so when he comes back to Australia, he can find me. Margaret said she would give it to him. I doubt I can trust her, but I think she saw the desperation in my eyes. I cried all day as perhaps Margaret may not do it — but either way, I have a plan.*

'I am going to become rich. So rich, that the next time I go to the Samuels' house they won't recognise me, because I will be covered from head-to-toe in the finest things money can buy. If money is the only thing standing in the way of them letting EJ and me be together, then groovy. I am thinking long and hard about how I can turn my fortune around so they'll accept me into the family, then there won't be any excuses. As of tomorrow, this Audrey that you and I know so well will change. Peace out.'

Chloe lowered the diary and folded her lips inward as she gauged Elijah's reaction.

'Oh my God,' Jamie said, trance-like, her eyes roaming the ground as though everything was falling into place.

'Yes, oh my God,' Elijah whispered, shaking his head. These were revelations he was hearing decades after the fact. These diary entries were proof that Audrey had loved him as much as he had loved her, and were validation that their brief – yet explosive – encounter was real. Elijah's eyes never wavered off Chloe, hanging onto the edge of his seat as though he were watching a Hitchcock movie, his schnitzel roll left untouched.

'Hurry 'n' read on,' Nurse Mildred urged Chloe, flicking her hand as if shooing a cat.

Chloe placed the milkshake glass on the ground beside the leg of her chair. She straightened and brushed a strand of loose hair behind her ear before lowering her eyes to the open diary that lay across her knees. *'27ᵗʰ October 1965. Dear Diary, I still have not heard from EJ, so forgive me for not writing sooner, but I feel like a zombie. These past five months have been miserable, and apart from when my parents became angels, this is the worst I have felt. The last time I went to the Samuels' house back in September, Georgie answered the door! She informed me that EJ writes to her all the time; she also told me that Grace moved out with her new beau. Call me gullible, but I don't believe that EJ writes to Georgie. I DO NOT BELIEVE HER and I know EJ will return to ME. I need to mention I tried calling the Samuels' phone again in August, but they've disconnected the number.*

'In mid-August, I went to our old place in Wollongong and gave the new owner, Mr Balakrishnan, a letter to give to EJ, should he go looking for me there. No doubt he will, right? This cannot be the end of us! While I was in Wollongong, I went to the post office to see if they had any letters that hadn't been redirected to my new house. A man behind the counter, who introduced himself as Mr Nielsen, looked in the storage room, but came back shaking his head. I almost broke down. Also, I went to see Betty Wallis, but the parlour had closed down. Betty did tell me once that her third husband was ill and they may need to fly to the US for this complicated neurological surgery. I didn't even get to say goodbye, otherwise I would have given her my new address to give to EJ. I enjoyed working there. Especially the memories that came with it. Speaking of work, I have a proper 9-to-5 job at Commonwealth Savings Bank. I am making good dough and I have already saved up a bit.

'Even though I haven't spoken to EJ, I am excited that when he returns, he will have a respectable lady who even his parents would be proud of. Corey and Misty are doing well, and even though I am lonely, I have made a few new friends at work. It's groovy because they're sophisticated people who I am learning so much from. They think I have a lot of money behind me because I live in Mosman, proving that 'social status' can be deceptive. The ladies even invited me out for cocktails next Friday. Although life without EJ is tough, there are things I focus on to ease the pain. To distract myself, I have learned to sew, I am taking French-speaking classes, and I am now in the process of a total makeover. Oh, I have also cut my hair and started wearing make-up, including filing my new acrylic nails in a feminine oval shape like Lorraine at work. I hope EJ will appreciate this. I love him and need him by my side so I can breathe again. Audrey.'

Nurse Mildred twirled her index finger around in the air with closed eyes, as if to say *Don't stop readin', darlin', we don't have all day.*

Chloe flicked through the pages, her eyes widening. 'Wow, the dates of the entries are getting further and further apart.' She grabbed her glass and took another sip of milkshake, while everyone in the room stared at her expectantly, as if they *needed* to know how the story finished. She once more placed the milkshake glass beside her chair as a group of male nurses glanced inside room 217 as they walked by.

'27th June 1966. Dear Diary, it has been one year and one month since I last saw EJ. Only today did I feel ready to face his narcissistic parents once again. I upgraded my aid, plus I also changed my hairstyle. To spruce myself up, I bought a Yves Saint Laurent Le Smoking suit and matching hat. It took a long time to save the money for these items, but I had a goal to better myself and to change my status. The hard work paid off. Operation: successful. Plus, for the first time ever, I have a car – a black 1964 Pontiac GTO – and golly, does it have speed! I thought about taking Corey with me to the Samuels', but then I decided against it. Besides, he was having fun digging his way to China.

'On 8th June, 1 RAR returned to Australia. I saw it mentioned in the papers as I had been keeping an eye out, so when I read an article on EJ's battalion,

I had to go down to the march in Sydney. I took the day off work and waited amongst the thousands upon thousands of spectators. I tried to get a decent spot, but I couldn't see too well from where I was standing. I don't think I blinked the entire time as the soldiers marched by; it was an endless sea of green – like migrating turtles. But I didn't see EJ. I wanted to drive to his house, but by the time the crowd departed and I walked all the way back to my car, hours had already passed. Then a panic attack hit me: What if he did rekindle what he had with Georgie while he was away? Or worse, what if EJ died? Am I ready for that after what happened to my parents? After weeks of chewing it over, I decided I need closure (no matter what it is), so I arrived at the Samuels' around midday (surprised to find their new electric gates with a fancy intercom had been left open). My heart pounded fiercely, so I sat in the car for a moment and reapplied my lipstick before making my way up the steps.

'Arthur opened the door. Then, as I was trying to get more information from Arthur – who I knew had been given strict orders from the Nazis not to talk to me – General Margaret walked past right when Arthur told me that the love of my life had indeed returned home ...'

Chapter 71

THEN – 1966

AUDREY'S HEART KICKED up a notch, not only at the sight of Margaret, but on hearing from Arthur that EJ was back. Elijah Samuels was back in Australia! This was the chance she had been waiting for.

'Hello, Margaret. Good to see you again.'

Margaret waltzed over, squinting while appraising the visitor. 'I'm sorry, do I—?'

Audrey's chin tilted. 'Yes, you do. It's Audrey. Audrey Hughes.'

The look on Margaret's face was one of surprise and bemusement.

Maybe there is a chance after all? Audrey thought with glee, eyes roaming past Margaret, trying to catch a glimpse of Elijah.

Margaret put her hand to her throat in a shocked, melodramatic way. 'My goodness, look at you.'

'I want to see Elijah.'

Margaret stood straighter and dropped her pretentious smile. 'My son's with Georgie at the moment. Can I help you with something?'

That blow impacted Audrey's heart, but if Elijah was going to abandon her, then she needed to hear it from the horse's mouth. 'Yes. I want to know why – if he is in fact back from 'Nam – have I not heard from him? You never gave him the letter stating my new address, *did* you?' Margaret pushed hair away from her forehead using the back of an index finger, eyes trailing skyward as she inhaled. 'What have I ever done to you that could warrant such pure hatred?'

Margaret lowered her eyes and pushed Arthur aside – she could handle this peasant. Margaret stepped close enough for Audrey to smell her Dana perfume. 'Dear, it's a little awkward for me to state the obvious, but he doesn't want you. Who would?'

Audrey scowled. *Do not cry*! *Do not let her win*! 'With all due respect, I don't believe that.'

Margaret's face split into a grin. 'Don't, or won't?'

'Is there a difference?'

Margaret pressed her tongue to the middle of her top lip. 'It's easy to believe what you want to believe, isn't it? For example, you showing up at my door in your new–old car, dressed in the latest suit, bought from a man who wouldn't know haute couture from op shop.'

Audrey dragged oxygen through her flared nostrils. She'd vowed she would *not* break down.

'Exuding importance and wealth can lead you to believe you're something other than what you are. Well, dear, you can put any fancy name like Fabergé on a rotten egg because it's covered by a decorative shell, but the truth will seep out. Soon the cracks appear and people will see you for what you are on the inside – do you see my point?' Margaret raised a plucked eyebrow. 'If you don't, then surely "mutton dressed as lamb" will ring true?' She paused to let the sting sink deep into Audrey's bones. All false hope of victory was lost on Audrey, who felt suffocated by Margaret's toxicity. 'I wish you the best in life, but it is not with my son.' Audrey opened her mouth, but Margaret held up a hand, closing her eyes in a way suggestive of an oncoming migraine. 'Please don't grovel or beg. Have the decency to take it like the woman you so often purport to be, and walk away with your head held high knowing you didn't waste your embarrassment of a life chasing after the wrong man. You might still think of him, but he isn't thinking of you. Please run along and let us get back to our day. I wish you the very best, my dear.'

With that, Margaret Samuels closed the door in Audrey's ashen face.

Chapter 72

'LORDY, CAN I jist say that yo' mama was colder than a witch's tit in a brass bra! I know we're all thinkin' it – am I right, folks? Mm-hmm,' Nurse Mildred said with a hooked brow and a click of her fingers.

Chloe giggled, but Jamie's cheeks burned – anger tattooed on her flushed face over what Margaret had said.

Elijah placed his untouched schnitzel roll on the overbed table and took a moment before responding. It had been one big revelation after the other – like the climax of a suspense novel. 'I didn't know about half the stuff that went on, and that's the truth. It wouldn't surprise you to know that my mother's parents, Julius and Cornelia, were the same with her as she was with me. That's why I was so determined to break the cycle. As far as I am aware, my grandparents never hugged or kissed their daughter when she was a child, and brainwashed her to think that money was the *only* thing that mattered.'

'Typical snowball effect,' Timothy said, squeezing Tida's knee.

'That's exactly what it was, which is why I was so rebellious; I craved to be someone different from the mould my parents had cut out for me as a child.'

'I'm surprised Aud didn't smack her one!' Nurse Mildred said, flicking her hand as if to demonstrate. 'Yo' mama was so stuck-up she'd drown in a rainstorm!'

Elijah laughed, then blew his nose. 'Audrey was a bona fide lady; violence was beneath her. I wouldn't have blamed her, though.' He glanced at Audrey. 'It hurts me to know she tried so hard to get word to me. And I had no idea she was at the march; how could I? Don't forget, ladies and gent, back in those days we didn't have what you people have.' Chloe shuffled in her chair and sat forward. 'There were no mobile phones; no Internet. If we needed answers, for most people it meant hopping on a bicycle and riding to the local library.'

'Ah, yes, I 'member those days,' Nurse Mildred said as a smile crept on her face, her eyes misty with memories.

'If you wanted to locate someone, there was no bloody Facebook – there was the White Pages or word-of-mouth,' Elijah added. 'So it wasn't that we didn't *try* to get back together, it was just that our paths wouldn't cross – or should I say, were *kept* from crossing.' Elijah's shoulders slumped as his head followed.

'Speaking of the Pages; didn't you look up Lloyd?' Timothy said.

Elijah's head snapped back. 'You bet your arse I did! On the day I arrived back in '66, as a matter of fact. I searched the Pages for any Hughes starting with an L or an A. From memory, there was an L. Hughes in Armidale, but ah … that didn't work out too well for me now, did it?'

'No, I guess not. Hey, I'm just curious – going off topic here – but what surprised you the most about being in a war? You had your fair share of drills, guerrilla combat and survival training at being out in the jungle, but did anything take you by surprise?'

'Apart from taking a life for real? I suppose there could never be enough training to combat what I went through *after*wards, but I would have to say the noise. I've seen many war movies in my time and the one thing they collectively screw up is the tremendous noise of *battle*. Bombs exploding, Hueys, men screaming, flamethrowers, bullets cracking through trees … It's a cacophony that's almost deafening. But those sounds became the lullaby to which I fell asleep at night.'

'I could never imagine it,' Timothy said, rubbing his chin and staring at the wall. 'The fellas from work organised a paintball thingy one time, and that was hard enough.'

'I don't understand why it's as glorified as it is. I joined the Australian Army for my own reasons. I felt like I actually belonged somewhere for the first time in my life; as though it was my home, because my fellow soldiers were like family. Fighting for something bigger than yourself – as in, the love for your nation – is a far better and more noble option than fighting on the street.'

'Just another question, if I may?' Timothy said, and Elijah nodded. 'Did you write back to Jack Evans' wife when you saw the letter about his daughter being born and the photo?'

Elijah looked towards the floor. 'No, I, ah, couldn't bear to, and the guilt for opening his mail weighed me down. I knew government officials would inform his wife about his death. There was nothing I *could* write back.'

'What did you do with the photo?' Timothy asked.

'Of Viola?' Timothy nodded. 'I kept it on me – sort of like my guardian angel. I must admit, I prayed for her – growing up without a father and all – he was a top bloke, too. I still have Mary Garrison's photo, as well.'

Jamie placed a hand over her heart. 'That's very sweet and touching.'

Chloe cleared her throat, looking at the wall clock. 'I want to find out more. Do you?' Her eyes wandered the room. 'I'll skip a few entries in between because they're sort of the same – Nan pining over you, is this okay?'

Nurse Mildred grinned, Jamie gave the thumbs up, Timothy nodded, and Tida yawned while glancing at the wall clock herself.

'Yes, go ahead,' Elijah mumbled, sipping on his bland flat white to lubricate his dry throat.

27th May 1967. Dear Diary, it has been exactly two years to the day since I last saw EJ. I realise now that it's time to move on. I cannot keep going back to the Samuels' mansion and begging. The last time I went, Arthur told me through the gate intercom that none of them were there, so I planned to stay outside in my car with Corey for hours, trying to glimpse EJ returning home. But while I waited, Margaret came outside to my car and told me if I didn't leave she would call the fuzz and have me charged for harassment! I demanded to know EJ's whereabouts, but she told me he was now living with Georgie.

'How heartbreaking! I was certain he was as happy as I was in our rela- tionship – or was that what I wanted to believe? There's a part of me that thinks it's all a lie, but either way, I decided to start a new chapter. How could I possibly accept them as my in-laws when they despise me so? I will always hold EJ close to my heart, but I cannot keep living this way. For two years, whenever someone knocks on the door, whenever the phone rings, whenever I get a mysterious letter, I hope to God it will be him. On a few occasions I thought I saw him – walking the streets, running along the beach, sitting in a restaurant. Even the familiar smell of his Camel cigarettes makes my head turn to check. My poor heart can't take anymore. So, with all that to consider, tonight marks the start of something new.

'My friend Dawn has set me up with a man. I kept delaying the blind date, but I can't hold off any longer. If EJ wanted to see me, he could have tracked me down somehow, right? Anyway, it doesn't matter; I am about to meet Russell. All I know is that he is an accountant, he is two years older than me and he's tall. Dawn tells me he and I are to meet in Sydney, at Ruby's Seafood at seven o'clock. Admittedly, I am looking forward to this. It has been such a long time of living with loneliness. Audrey.'

'Oh my Lord, she's movin' on?!' Nurse Mildred yelled, which caused Tida to flinch and glare.

'Oh, *Jesus*! You knew she must have, right?' Elijah said, pointing to Audrey's direct descendants.

Nurse Mildred's shoulders touched her earlobes. 'I know, but ... but I jist—'

He lowered his register. 'Can you blame her? How humiliating for her to be threatened like that by my mother. And to hear I'd shacked up with Georgie again.' He hung his head like a dead man. 'I probably wouldn't have returned, either. Who in their right mind would want to be in a relationship where your in-laws wouldn't save you from drowning in a bathtub?'

Nurse Mildred slapped her meaty thigh, hard. 'Now ya sound like yer stickin' up fo' her actions!'

Elijah chuckled, which brought on another short cough before he swallowed the gunk. 'It would have been selfish of me to expect her to remain single all her life in the hopes of us *maybe* getting back together.'

'Oh, but why didn't ya try *harder*!' Nurse Mildred spoke as though it were the bleeding obvious – as though that was all he'd had to do – try harder.

'She wasn't listed in the White Pages and as I said, things were different back then – you of all people should know, Mildred! We communicated via phones that had cords attached to a wall, for goodness' sake. You had a rotary dial, so it took an age to spin each number separately, and if you stuffed up the seventh number, you had to hang up and dial it all over again. It was a bitch of a thing. If you stuffed it up a second time, the phone set was likely to fly out the window and into the next-door neighbour's yard.'

Chloe laughed. 'Yes, I saw a picture of one of those in a history book the other day.'

Elijah frowned as silence descended on the room. 'What ... you guys don't think I tried?' He paused, waiting for an answer – reassurance they believed him. 'You don't think I searched for her, asked everyone I knew, drove around aimlessly for hours, for God's sake?!'

Nurse Mildred's head lowered. 'I jist ...'

Elijah admired the fire in her belly with quiet regard. 'I know; me too.'

Timothy looked into Elijah's eyes and then prompted Chloe. 'How's about the next chapter, sweetheart?'

Chapter 73

'28th May 1967. *Dear Diary, I had a good time last night. First, Russell presented me with roses when I approached his table, and he looked so debonair in a pink-and-black suit. Even though the air was nippy, I wore the latest dress by Versace, and fire-engine-red high heels. We dined on oysters and lobster at Ruby's, accompanied by Barossa Valley chardonnay. Then we walked to the Globe Newsreel Theatre on George Street to watch* Bonnie and Clyde *– starring* Faye Dunaway and Warren Beatty. *It was nothing like I have ever seen before (in a groovy way), and afterwards we drove around in his Ford Cortina GT, getting to know each other, before we took a stroll along Balmoral Beach.*

'I did enjoy myself, I confess, but I couldn't stop thinking of EJ, especially when we walked along the beach. I want him, *not Russell, nor anybody, but I have to be realistic in saying that what we had is gone. It's time to stop living in la-la land and cut my losses. In my heart of hearts I know EJ and I loved each other more than two people could, but for whatever reason, it hasn't worked out.*

'Russell is a pleasant choice; he would make a fine husband. But not my *husband. Not unless he can live up to the standard that EJ set, and somehow I don't think that's possible. No-one I've ever met holds a candle to EJ. So, I have decided not to pursue Russell or accept his advances. It wouldn't be right. Am I still waiting around for something that will never happen? No, I just need more time before I can give my heart to someone else. Audrey.'*

''Course it didn't work with Russell; she were still in love with Eli!' Nurse Mildred's voice boomed like a hectoring coach on the sideline, as clusters of crumbs from an Arnott's biscuit fell from her mouth and onto Tida's shoes.

'Nurse, please,' Jamie said, chuckling. 'We all know the outcome.'

Nurse Mildred shrugged. 'Still, someone needed ta smack her silly, 'n' let her know her true love was right 'round the corner! This is too intense; I should git back ta work 'fore I git all worked up ah-gain.'

Nurse Mildred stepped outside, mumbling to herself. Tida then made use of the toilet in Audrey's room, Jamie turned her phone back on, and Elijah downed the lukewarm cup of flat white that had a glug of half-melted sugar at the bottom.

'Hey, the entry before this one mentioned you living with Georgie,' Timothy said, as if remembering.

'Yeah, what's up with that?' Jamie added, looking up from her phone. 'It is a lie concocted by Margaret, right?'

'Of course, although, I saw Georgie a few times upon my return.' Jamie's eyes widened and Timothy cocked his head to the left, inquisitive eyebrows on alert. 'Hey, now, our families were close, so it was natural for us to bump into each other and for her to rock up to the house on an occasion.'

'Bump into each other, eh?' Timothy said.

'Did, ah, anything happen between you two?' Jamie said, colour spilling over her cheeks like an ink stain.

'Sexually?'

She nodded as Tida emerged from the en suite and shuffled over.

'Hell no; those days were over. Any time Georgie saw me I was talking about Audrey in some way, asking for advice on where to search, et cetera.'

A minute later, Nurse Mildred re-entered the room, scoffing the last of her biscuits. 'Ohh-kay, I jist checked 'n' everyone seems ta be as happy as a possum eatin' a sweet tater. Continue, angel,' she said to Chloe, with a scrunch of her nose.

Chapter 74

'31ˢᵗ MARCH 1971. *Dear Diary, at work I act like I have no demons in my closet. I laugh. I make jokes. I pretend nothing bothers me. But at night, even after all this time, I dream of EJ holding me. Kissing me. Making passionate love to me. I dream about his cheeky smile and the way his green eyes light up when he gets excited. But I cannot remain a prisoner to my love for a man who may as well be dead. I have already lost some of the best years of my life pining over him; now I need to live again before I wake up on my fiftieth birthday, wondering where my life went and why I held on to something that was no longer there. It's like grasping at fog.*

'I want children. I want a husband. I want to buy a house. And I don't think it's selfish to say, because wanting and needing those things is a part of nature. So on that note, I accepted to go on a date with Donald (Buck) Arlington, an investment banker on Crown Street. Yes, there have been suitors before this, but I met Buck at a party my friend was hosting and we spoke for hours on end, resulting in me giving him my number. I thought about him after I left. It has been such a long time since anyone's held me. I am used to wiping my own tears away; I just want to be taken care of again.

'My love for EJ has turned into feelings of bitterness and resentment, and I don't want it to be like that. I want to be a jolly person and they say the best way to get over a man is in the arms of another. I accepted to go with Buck to the Sydney Royal Easter Show, followed by dinner at Lucky Jade's Chinese. I cannot wait to see what the future holds. Anything has to be better than this. Audrey.'

Chloe peered at Elijah, hesitant to see his reaction. As expected, his eyes were as sombre as an innocent prisoner behind bars.

'I have a question,' Nurse Mildred said to Elijah, as a young man holding a bunch of pink roses walked past the room, looking at the door numbers.

Elijah lifted his glasses, pinched the bridge of his nose, and groaned. 'I'm all ears.'

'Were ya *really* not home at all durin' those times Aud came ta the house? It seems suspicious that each time she went, ya were never there.'

Elijah glanced up with weary eyes. 'Do you *honestly* think I would have ignored the love of my life if I knew she was at my doorstep?'

'Well, I don't know what's goin' on,' she said, crossing her eyes, which made everyone laugh. 'I'm as confused as a fart in a fan factory!'

Timothy laughed and Chloe giggled before Elijah continued. 'I didn't know that Audrey had come to my house, no. The only reason I stayed with my parents when I got back was because I knew if Audrey looked for me, then she would have come there. My mother never told me that Audrey had come to the house, so I don't know whether I was in the house at the time or not. In retrospect, there's a good chance I may have been when some of this occurred, yes.'

'Don't that jist put a burr in yer saddle?' Nurse Mildred shivered as though someone had walked on her grave.

Elijah paused on hearing the unmistakable sound of heels clacking through the corridor before Angela strode in, panting, cheeks as red as winter apples. Nurse Mildred sprang from her chair like a jack-in-the-box, and observed Audrey's chart, bobbing her head at what she saw, finger to her chin.

'Sorry, everyone.' Angela flicked loose strands of hair from her forehead.

'Hello,' Chloe said as Angela placed her Gucci bag on the ground and sighed.

Timothy leaned forward, a hand on his knee. 'Are you all right?'

Angela nodded, resumed her position in the chair, and sipped from a takeaway Starbucks cup. 'So, where are we in the Audrey and Elijah saga?'

'Dad's just arrived,' Timothy said.

Chloe raised the diary. 'And I'm about to read another entry.'

Angela glanced at her Guess wristwatch. 'Go ahead, then we'll have to get going—'

Jamie then let out an anguished sob, which diverted everyone's attention.

'What's wrong?' Timothy asked, frowning. 'What just happened?'

Jamie used her wrist to wipe away the tears. 'I'm so sorry; I ... I miss Dad. I miss him so *damn* much!'

Timothy got up and wrapped his arms around Jamie as she wept. It had been a long couple of years without Buck, and the only man in her life right now was a lying, cheating mongrel – even Timothy was no source of stability. Things with Boyd were going from bad to worse, with 'office work' exceeding his limits. Sometimes, all a girl needed was a hug from her daddy, no matter how old she may be. Yes, there was a part of her that felt guilty over letting Elijah talk about romantic stories involving her mother, but she understood everyone has a past, and it could also be said that in some ways, Elijah was like a substitute. But days like today, knowing her last parent would soon cross the threshold, was a crushing, immobilising thought. This mini-meltdown had been imminent. She remembered all too well, waking up after losing her father and just ... well, existing. She slept all day, doing nothing but breathing and blinking in between. Breathing and blinking, as though in a vegetative state. She had to be nursed back to health by Boyd (he wasn't 'working nights' at this stage). She wasn't ready to face that depressing stage again with the loss of her mother. It was way too soon. Her heart had not yet mended from Buck. Nor did she think it ever would. Even referring to him in the past tense felt surreal.

'You all good now?' Timothy said, stepping back and bending down to inspect her face.

Nurse Mildred handed Jamie a box of Kleenex that she'd grabbed from the overbed table.

'Here's a tissue fo' yer issue, sugah.'

'Thanks.' Jamie took a tissue from the box and blew her nose. 'I'm sorry, everyone. But God, life can be *so* unfair.'

'Don't apologise,' Angela whispered, rubbing Jamie's back with soothing strokes. 'We'll get through this together. As a family.'

'I'm all good now, guys.' Jamie dabbed her eyes with a second tissue. 'You can read on.'

Chloe nodded before picking up the diary. *'27ᵗʰ June 1971. Dear Diary, I know it has only been a few months, but here goes: I'm engaged! Buck proposed to me last night and I couldn't be happier. To top off the proposal, he bought me a new car! As you know, this relationship has nothing to do with money, but it means I will be secure and so will my children. I feel like I am living in a dream world on a constant basis, and I thank God that Buck has pulled me out of limbo.*

'It's funny how life changes. I'm sure by now EJ has kids and is as equally satisfied with his life. No doubt his parents are jubilant, and it will be one big, pretty picture. I hope he is happy with Georgie; I barely thought of him last night, anyway. It's obvious this "peasant" wasn't worth fighting for. It doesn't matter anymore, anyway, because I'm in love with Buck. Today we looked at houses in Woolwich, which is steeped in history, with reserves, harbourside restaurants and parklands; perfect for entertaining people and raising children. We both liked this six-bedroom house that has a pool, large white pillars around the courtyard, en suites in the two master bedrooms, an alfresco dining area, and a large shed, which is convenient to store Buck's boat—'

'Yeah-yeah-yeah,' Nurse Mildred said, turning to face Elijah. 'Did ya marry that tramp, Georgie?'

Everyone turned to face Nurse Mildred, who had propped herself against the doorframe.

Elijah removed his glasses and looked her straight in the eyes, despite his vision being a little blurred. 'What do *you* think?'

She shrugged and brushed a bit of white fluff off her uniform. 'I'm jist curious as ta why her name keeps gittin' brought up time after time, 'n' she *was* at the house when Aud popped over that one time. Li'l suspicious, innit?'

He stared at her as though he'd just had a frontal lobotomy. 'If you don't know me by now, then you'll never know. If my love wasn't obvious, then I must be the world's worst lover.' He paused to hack into a napkin. 'Excuse me.' He crumpled the napkin and cleared his burning throat before placing his glasses over his eyes again. 'Look, as far as I can tell, Georgie played it cool around me, but I think she kept the light on, even though she was with Brad. My mother loved her, of course. It didn't matter to my mother that she couldn't carry a conversation, or cook, or even wash dishes lest she chip her painted nails. Georgie just fitted the bill. My mother and Georgie remained close friends for a while, but of course, I didn't go back to Georgie after I returned. Not even after years had gone by.'

'Whatever happened to her?' Timothy said, shifting in his seat.

'Georgie married a German stockbroker and they had four children, one of whom passed on from a motorbike accident a week after his twenty-first birthday – Kevin, I believe his name was. That's pretty much all I know.'

'Don't git me wrong, I know ya didn't love her; I jist wondered if ya ever got lonely 'n' wandered over yonder. Some folk I know cain't go without a companion fo' long, 'n' I jist wondered if ya did, is all.'

Elijah coughed into a fist and shook his head. *God, I'm feeling worse,* he thought as a thunderbolt of pain shot through his left arm like Poseidon's trident, causing his face to contort.

'Are you okay?' Timothy said, his forehead marred by worry lines. 'You seem to do that a lot now.'

'I'll be right as rain,' Elijah said with a smile. Timothy and Jamie swapped troubled glances as Elijah cleared his throat. 'And no, Mildred, I feel sorry for those who go from relationship to relationship, because they'll never be happy. How can they give their whole heart from one to the next? It's impossible. Because I was truly, deeply in love with Audrey, I didn't venture down an old, worn-out, well-travelled path. I held on for as long as I could before I had to come to terms with the crossroad that was right in front of me.'

'Excuse me,' Timothy whispered as he got up and shook his legs. 'I'll just go to the bathroom.'

'Why don't anyone ever use the john in here?' Nurse Mildred pointed to the en suite.

'I don't think anyone wants to hear *me* on the crapper,' Elijah mumbled, removing his glasses again to clean them with a tissue from the Kleenex box.

Jamie laughed, and Angela shook her head.

'I'd like to stretch my legs for a bit, anyway,' Timothy said, walking past Nurse Mildred, who shuffled aside before she turned to everyone, clutching a fist to her breast.

'A woman's heart is as deep as any gator swamp in Mississippi. I've been marred fo' thirty-four years ta a great fella: Joseph. But truth be told, when I was a young'un – poorer than a church mouse – I gave my heart ta another fella, Torrance Jackson.' Her head flew back as she gushed, eyes beaming brighter than any lighthouse. 'Oh, Lordy, I was head over heels in love with that fetchin' rebel 'n' used ta git all gussied up fo' our dates 'n' the like. We were goin' strong fo' oh, 'bout eight months, but when he asked my papa fo' my hand in marriage, Daddy objected 'cause Torrance believed in a different faith. My daddy said we had ta go our separate ways, so … Torrance skedaddled.' She inhaled through flared nostrils. 'Back in those days, kids listened ta their folks, so that was the end of us 'n' I never saw him ah-gain. I have ta admit, I still think 'bout Torrance even after all these moons. I haven't mentioned a word 'bout him ta Joseph. There are some things a hubby don't need ta know – am I right, sisters?'

At that moment, the PA system bellowed out over a speaker just outside the room and a woman with a thick British accent said: 'Paging Nurse Mildred. Nurse Mildred, please return to your station.'

A 'click' signalled the end of the call-out.

'Ah *shit!*' Nurse Mildred threw her hands in the air and skedaddled out the door.

'She's a funny one,' Elijah said, smiling from ear-to-ear once the room settled.

When Timothy returned, he looked at Chloe and smiled. 'Okay, sweet pea, you may continue if everyone else is good to go?'

Chloe didn't need to be asked twice, so she opened the diary to where the ribbon was at.

'Hold up now!' Nurse Mildred said as she skidded back into the room. 'I've been thinkin'…'

'Shouldn't you be working, love?' Elijah asked, smirking.

'Didn't Aud ever call ya? Or send a letter under an alias or – or *somethin*'?' She looked around the room as all eyes were on Elijah.

'Mum mentioned in a previous entry that Margaret had the number disconnected,' Jamie said.

Elijah snapped his fingers and pointed at Jamie. 'Correct, Mum *did* have the phone number changed. We were never listed in the Pages to begin with, and I assume my parents and Arthur kept a close eye on the mail Grace and I received.'

Nurse Mildred raised a finger. 'There's a sayin' in the south that goes: "cain't never could." Now ya jist think 'bout that fo' a jiffy.'

Elijah tutted. 'Jesus, I'm not speaking just so I can mimic my arsehole! I tried with every fibre of my being to get her back. God, I even parked my arse out the front of my house for days on end in case she happened by. I slept at the beach under our boardwalk at nights. Christ, I asked around as though I were a private investigator! You think I did sweet Fanny Adams, do you?'

'Calm down, sugah, or yer'll bust ya poofer valve.'

Elijah's chest heaved, but he cracked a smile and even chuckled at her lame attempt to calm him down. He coughed into his hanky and caught Angela eyeing him, so he shook his head and waved a free hand as if to say he was okay. 'Mildred, I thought you were supposed to be working?'

Nurse Mildred's mouth dropped open. 'I *am* workin'! I'm checkin' up on Aud if ya don't mind!' She walked over to the bed, humming, and started fidgeting with the corners of the bed and fluffing the pillows beneath Audrey's head, which flopped from side to side. Everyone stared, slack-jawed, until Nurse Mildred turned around. 'Well, don't mind me – continue!'

Angela exhaled and leaned forward, hands on her knees. 'Look, everybody, I think we should call it a night—'

'Wait!' Chloe held up a hand, her eyes fixed on the page.

'Wh-What is it?' Jamie said, looking from Chloe's face to the diary.

Chloe glanced around, her lips parted. 'There's only one more entry left, and it's written years later.' She flipped through the rest of the pages – as blank as a starless sky.

Everyone stared at Angela (the matriarch), who sat back and gave her attention to Chloe.

Elijah's heart thwacked, he *needed* to know what that last entry said; needed it perhaps more than his next breath.

Everyone shuffled their chairs closer to Chloe, as tiny beads of sweat appeared on her temples. Then, as it became quiet enough to hear the clouds move, Chloe took a deep breath and … Angela's phone rang.

'Oh, fo' the love of *God*, woman!'

'If you don't throw it away, I will!' Elijah cautioned as Angela checked her bleating phone.

'Calm down, people; it's only Seth – probably wondering if he needs to make his own dinner.'

'He's a big boy; he can figure out Pizza Hut's number,' Elijah mumbled.

'*Soh-ree*, grumblebum, I'll put it on silent.' Angela rejected the call from her husband before chucking the phone into her bag.

'Good,' Elijah muttered, and a sharp pain shot up his left side. 'Hurry!'

Angela winked at Chloe. 'Go ahead.'

Elijah clutched the steel arms of the chair as though he were a punter with high stakes watching the Melbourne Cup.

Chapter 75

'31ˢᵗ OCTOBER 1980. Dear Diary, I used to feel that you were something to look over as I got older; to reflect upon and remember certain things, regarding EJ – my intended husband – and to laugh at the things he and I used to get up to. But the truth is, I don't want to remember my past. I want and need to look to the future, for my family's sake.

'Golly, you have helped me through hard times – but now that I have everything I've ever wanted, I no longer need you. I don't think it's fair to write about the two main men of my life within the same journal. Perhaps I shall start another with Buck as the headliner this time.

'To catch you up, Buck and I are living in Woolwich inside our flawless homestead. We have a daughter named Angela (named after his grandmother), and we are expecting our second child any day now. We don't know whether it's a boy or girl – that's the beauty about this miracle. Buck and I have our own business, Arlington Inc., which buys rundown and dilapidated buildings from owners who can no longer afford to keep them, then renovates and sells them off at a higher price. After we flew back from our Hawaiian honeymoon, I became the CEO of Buck's company, and we have offices opening up in Auckland, Tokyo and San Francisco. Our empire is booming, ensuring my children's future. I'd now have more money than the Samuels family had. Ironic, isn't it? I hope my parents are looking down with pride.

'Corey has long since passed, taking with him everything I hoped for with EJ, signalling my past officially buried. Buck and I have a beagle, Sally, who is better looked after than most people I know. Right now she's lying beside me

in the hammock as the sun shines bright … I read the Mosman Daily *one morning a while back, and saw a picture of a handsome little boy. His last name was Samuels, and he featured because he came 1st in a mathematics competition across the country, which won him a sponsorship deal. His father, Elijah Samuels, commented: "This is one of the happiest days of our lives".*

'I always knew EJ would make a wonderful father. I think meeting him and his parents gave me the ambition I needed to change and become a better person. If it wasn't for him, I wouldn't be where I am today, and where I am is priceless. But that doesn't mean from time to time I don't still think about Elijah Samuels. The sting of his betrayal and abandonment has long since gone, especially when I look around and see what I have. I don't curse his name anymore; rather, I thank God that I was fortunate enough to have someone like him in my life, even if for a brief period.

'Elijah gave me a new lease on life; he made me feel like I could do anything I put my mind to. Him "loving" me (or whatever that was) was his way of saving me. In 35 years, I have not met a single soul like EJ, so I take it as a blessing our paths crossed. Even though I am a strong, independent woman, it still hurts when I open up this diary on occasion and read how happy I once was with someone else. I look back in here at the movie stubs, the love notes EJ left, part of the wrapping paper from the gift he bought me for Christmas in the blissful bubble we created at Jenolan Caves back in '64.

'Thank you, dear Diary, for being there for me when I needed you – only you will ever know my deepest, darkest secrets and desires. Not even someone who's flesh and blood, and with whom I share the same last name, knows half the things you do.

'Maybe one day I will tell someone else about EJ and how he stole – and broke – my heart. Then again, maybe it's best to leave the Band-Aid on. I've often wondered in the future if EJ ever tracked me down (because he's bored with Georgie or the like), whether I would take him back. The answer would be no. You and I both know deep down there's a part of me that can't let go. But I would not trade what I have with my husband and children for anybody. Angela is the most important thing in my life, followed by Buck, who saved me

from the brink of extinction. In saying that, if years from now Angela brought home two men on either arm – one like EJ, the other like Buck – I know which one I'd secretly hope she goes for. The sensible mother in me would verbally say Buck, but the helpless, incurable romantic who could live vicariously through her would long for the one like EJ.

'God help me, I can still remember the time he possessed me on the staircase before we could even make it to my bedroom. If I am honest, images like these still make me restless late at night, but when I turn around into Buck's loving arms, it feels like I've reached home base. My life may not be as passionate and wild with Buck as it was with EJ, but I am where I am meant to be (but if need be, in my darkest hours of longing, I will always possess these memories of then). Whatever happens in the future I am not worried about, because I have my husband and my children (not to mention Sally) by my side.

'So, dear Diary, I suppose I shall say thank you and goodbye to you and the life I once knew. Yours truly (a now all-grown-up), Audrey.'

Chloe refused to look up, the book shaking in her hands, as sniffles and harsh exhaling erupted around the room like verbal applause.

'Oh, so many misunderstandings,' Elijah whispered in a strained voice, looking at Audrey.

'I think ya need ta do some explainin', boy,' Nurse Mildred said from the doorway, unwrapping a protein bar.

Elijah exhaled. 'First, you want to know what I think after hearing about all the shit that went down?' He glanced about the room. 'I reckon my darling mother and father contacted not only Lloyd, but the postman, too.'

Seeking agreement, he looked at Nurse Mildred. She stopped chewing and frowned, cocking her head to the side.

'I'm saying, I think my parents offered Lloyd a hard-to-resist sum to move out of Wollongong.' Nurse Mildred eyed the ceiling as if giving his assumption the once-over. 'No doubt about it, my parents went to extreme lengths to keep us apart: changing our phone number, upgrading our driveway gates, and scrapping the EH that I'd intended for Audrey.

I also believe they paid Mr Nielsen, the local postmaster, to destroy all letters addressed to me and to keep my letters for Audrey away from her.'

'Well, butter my butt 'n' call me a biscuit!' Nurse Mildred slapped her thigh. 'Ain't that jist the darndest way ta keep ya lovebirds 'part?'

Timothy winced. 'I don't know, Elijah, it's a big stretch. Would they risk it, knowing you could have found Mum and then the beans would have been spilled?'

'Because *that's* how much keeping up appearances meant to them. They would risk losing their own son to save face. They didn't give a shit about me, let's be frank here. They thought I was scraping the bottom of the barrel with Audrey. She wasn't rich, she had an impediment, and she worked at an ice cream parlour.'

'It's unfair to judge someone like that,' Jamie said, shaking her head.

'Hey, it wasn't me, love. Don't mix us up, please, otherwise you'll insult me.' He turned to admire the sunset outside, which was losing its fiery glow. 'It's ironic that Audrey is where she is today because of me – well, through meeting me at least.'

'I have question,' Tida said, raising a hand. Everyone in the room stared at her agape (including Timothy). Even Nurse Mildred double-blinked, her open mouth full of food.

Elijah recovered first and smiled. 'Go ahead, love.'

'Why you not go in the Whit Pages so she find you?'

'Yeah … yeah good question, Tinder,' Nurse Mildred said with a serious expression, causing Jamie to smirk. 'Why didn't ya make it easier fo' her ta find ya?'

'Because I wasn't sure how long I wanted to stay at my folks' place, and I honestly did not expect that it would have been as hard as it was to track her down. It ended up being about as hard as climbing Mount Everest in thongs, if you need an analogy to comprehend it.'

'Thongs?' Tida's head reeled back, glancing towards his crotch.

He tried to stifle a burgeoning grin. 'The ones on your feet, love. Your *feet.*'

Tida turned to Timothy, but he smiled and waved a dismissive hand, and told her he'd explain later.

Nurse Mildred shook her head. 'I think ya could've made it easier fo' Aud ta find ya in the Pages, though … yessiree, I do!'

Elijah stuck his index finger inside his ear and wiggled it. 'I received death threats in the mail from the people in Wollongong about my service in Vietnam. I didn't want to deal with any more of that shit, so I never became listed in the Pages once I moved out. In the end, when it seemed clear I wasn't going to find Audrey, all I wanted to do was just friggin' disappear into nothingness.'

It took a while for the next person to speak – clearly they were all mulling their own interpretations and theories on the events.

Jamie raised a hand. 'I also have a question.'

'Yes, love.'

'How did Grace know Mum had left Wollongong? When you arrived home during your R&R, it was Grace who informed you Mum had left town – but she was living with Benjamin Wilson at this point, correct?' Elijah nodded. 'Do you think your sister was an accomplice to your parents, perhaps?'

He shook his head. 'No way in hell; she's been pretty much the only woman I *can* trust. When I hadn't heard from Audrey during those first few months of my term, one of my letters to Grace asked if she could go to Lloyd's and see what was up. I gave Lloyd's address to Grace and she drove over to find a *SOLD* sign erected in the front yard. I arrived home on my R&R before her letter telling me this had arrived. I received it weeks later, after I arrived back in 'Nam.'

Jamie nodded, satisfied. 'I just wondered is all.'

'No, it's okay; Grace would have lied to my parents over me any day of the week, and I would have done the same for her. Siblings have a special bond that cannot be substituted.'

Jamie looked at Angela with a smile before facing Timothy, who had a downcast gaze.

'Well, you mentioned you found out about Mum being in here because of Grace, didn't you?' Angela said. 'I don't think I ever asked: how did Grace find out Mum is here, in a coma?'

Elijah rubbed at his bottom lip with a pinkie. 'Grace is always on the bloody computer. It's mentioned on there somewhere, I believe.'

Timothy nodded. 'It is. On the plane as we were coming over we saw it mentioned on *9News*. People could leave comments to give well wishes to the "entrepreneur and visionary in business, who paved the way for women to stand tall within the commercial industry". Even had a photo of her and Dad back in the late eighties.'

'How the hell did the news team find out about it in the first place?' Elijah said.

'There are lots of "famous" folk in here; didn't ya know?' Nurse Mildred said.

Elijah cocked his head. 'Like who?'

'Like writers, artists, models, socialites …' Nurse Mildred trailed off. 'Word spreads faster than diarrhoea in these halls.'

Angela's brows shot north. 'So, there's a news correspondent roaming around—'

'Mot*her*, can we carry on now, please?' Chloe's knees bobbed up and down.

Elijah shoved the soiled napkin in his pocket and opened his diary. Each page felt like he was uncovering another long-hidden scar, so he paused and looked up.

Jamie smiled and whispered: 'Go on.'

'Yeah, don't tug my short 'n' curlies any longer; I'm wantin' ta find out 'bout this son of yers! Is it true? Do ya have a son?!'

Breathing in deeply through his nostrils, Elijah bobbed his head once. 'Yes.'

Chapter 76

NURSE MILDRED WHEEZE-gasped as the others cast curious glances as if to say: *Why hasn't he mentioned his son before?*

'How could ya do that ta her, ya egg-suckin' *dog*?!'

Elijah rolled a thumb over his tongue to pick up where he'd left off, unaffected by Nurse Mildred's lashing. 'Everyone okay to hear some more?'

'Well—' Angela began, looking out the window at the diminishing sunlight.

'Stick a cork in it 'n' let the man speak!'

'When I returned to Australia in '66, things seemed abnormal in every bloody aspect. Even the damned currency had changed. Shortly after I arrived, I visited the local post office and demanded they check the back rooms, under counters, under the carpet, just to find one goddamned letter from Audrey explaining *why*. But the postmaster, Mr Nielsen, came back from the storage room empty-handed. No matter who I talked to, whether it was Georgie, Alison, Jonathan, Grace, Lawrence, Mum, Dad, Arthur … no-one could or would tell me anything. The last night Audrey and I shared together when we held each other in the motel room was as real as you could get. I did not buy for a single damned second that she'd just decided it was over the minute I left the soil.

'One evening when I arrived home after another gruelling day of searching for what seemed like a missing person – interviewing people and making phone calls – I saw my parents sitting at the dinner table, mouths down-turned.' Elijah struggled to turn the page with his shaking fingers, so he tutted and twisted his lips. 'Damn thing. There we go – you see, after I got back from the war, my mother – being her usual melodramatic, hypochondriac-self – tried to force me to go to the doctor for a check-up as she knew I'd been shot. I refused to go, but being the stubborn woman she was, she brought a doctor to the house where he performed oral, physical, and psychological exams on me in the private environment of my bedroom. The reason my folks looked glum was because my results had come back, and my mother couldn't help herself – once again she sneaked a look at the letter before I had a chance. In short, without getting technical, it said I would never sire an heir.'

Angela and Jamie glanced at each other, frowning, and looked back at Elijah.

'The sixties turned into the seventies, and soon the year 1972 was upon me. Gone were the days of "power to the people"; now it was all about the Village People. Chest hair replaced long hair; we said goodbye to rock 'n' roll and hello to disco. The only three things I remember about that year are Jane Fonda posing on an anti-aircraft gun with North Vietnamese troops in Hanoi, the Watergate scandal, and Grace informing me that Audrey was about to get married.

'By the beginning of '72, I was living in Windsor – a quaint town near Richmond at the foothills of the Blue Mountains – seeking peace and solitude, as there were still members of the public who didn't want me to forget that I had served in 'Nam. If I couldn't walk down the street without having members of Save Our Sons spitting in my face for defending this country, then something was *very* wrong.

'The doctor back in Wollongong diagnosed me with PTSD and severe anxiety. I sometimes woke up in the dead of night with sweat pouring down my face after having vivid dreams of being in 'Nam, and living with my parents without Grace in the house was just too much in the end.

'I'd barely got used to accepting the fact I would never see Audrey again, when one rainy night at a local Irish pub in Windsor called O'Donoghue's, a buxom woman carrying a glass of red wine bumped into me, staining my paisley shirt ...'

Chapter 77

THEN – 1972

ELIJAH SAT ALONE on a stool behind the oakwood bar of O'Dono-ghue's, nursing another whiskey, reminiscing about the road not travelled. Why was he always taking those same old, well-worn paths that led him to the same place?

On some of his bigger self-loathing whiskey binges he had given in to a more intrinsic reflection of his superb flaws and detractors, which would lead him time and again to this same stool, at the same bar, drinking the same Kentucky bourbon that warmed the body but left the heart cold. He also had to accept the one fact that he never spoke about: he suffered survivor's guilt. It was something that gnawed away at him, no matter how much he tried to numb himself. As he rose to take a much-needed piss in the men's room, cold liquid ran down one side of his arm.

In Elijah's drunken stupor, he glanced down at his right arm to see that a red liquid smelling like port had stained the fabric. He looked up with blurred vision as a brown-haired woman stared back.

A hand flew to her cheek. 'Goodness, I am *so* sorry!'

Elijah gave a lopsided smile. 'Not the worst thing that's happened to me in this place, darlin'.'

She smiled and her eyes softened. As he moved his stool away with the back of his leg, she placed her free hand on his chest, stopping him.

He swayed on his feet, looking at her with inquisitive eyes as 'Long Cool Woman (in a Black Dress)' by the Hollies came over the jukebox.

'My name's Harriet. Baker.'

His eyelids struggled to stay open and his bladder, which felt like the size of a balloon, pressed against other organs. 'Have a good night, Mrs Baker, don't worry about the shirt.'

He went to move, but she once again blocked him, this time with her body. A shamrock-green floral jumpsuit with long, flared sleeves hugged her curves. He glared at her. Thunder clapped like cupped hands, and she moistened her dark-red lips with a quick, nervous flick of her tongue. Elijah's eyes darted from one person to the next behind her. Who was she here with? A husband? A group of girlfriends? Or a mere buxom vixen out on the town by herself, looking for hot action?

'I've seen you here before,' Harriet said, running a hand through her feathered brown hair. 'You drink a lot.'

He snorted and used his left hand to steady himself on the bar stool as her hand went to his wrist to keep him upright.

'Why?'

Elijah glared into her eyes that were rimmed with black eyeliner and had little 'flicks' outwards from her eyelids. In his drunken state he couldn't tell (nor did he even fucking care) if her lashes were that fake crap women glued on, or if they were the real deal. But they were long eyelashes. *Very* long.

'Why *what?*'

'A handsome man like you frequently in this dirty dive, alone. Why?'

Elijah's nostrils flared. Who the fuck was she to ask such a personal question of a complete stranger – one whom she was calling a drunkard? He felt hot, he was pissed, and he needed *to* piss more than anything, but her invasiveness deserved an attack.

'You really wanna know?' he said, looking deep into her hazel eyes. She nodded, her eyes searching his. He leaned in close. 'It's as if the alcohol injects my soul. I can laugh, smile, feel the sun on my face. For a fleeting moment I am alive again, but then the alcohol wears off and the sun goes away. The doors close and the cold seeps through again and I remember, as if I had never forgotten, that this is who and what I am. And *that* will never change. I am a lost man who has been given back to those who hate themselves enough to love me, broken. I know that the happiness others feel isn't allowed for me, so I live just to spite the universe.' A tear escaped and ran down his face as he grabbed her arms. 'Let me tell you, Harriet *Baker*, for a man there ain't no bigger kick in the gut to realise what he thought of as his biggest accomplishment, is now his biggest failure.' He released her arms. 'Satisfied?'

Harriet stared at him with parted lips. The rain belted on the tin roof harder, drowning out whatever song was now playing over the jukebox. Her eyes seemed to mist over as though she understood *exactly* what he felt. Then she turned and left. It had been enough to scare her away. *Good*, Elijah thought, remembering he needed to pee. *It's for the best.* A man who had done and would continue to do the things he did could not be entertaining worldly desires.

This was the price to pay.

As he staggered off to the men's, Harriet interrupted his booze-fuelled hatred of existence by walking over to him carrying her umbrella and a brown suede fringe shoulder bag.

Many would say this woman was 'ordinary' but to him, she was the kind of beautiful, dangerous ordinary that you just can't leave alone. He was now looking at this hard-luck woman as though she were his weakness. His drinking wasn't about the tale of a man who was keeping love at arm's length through emotional distance and refusal to love himself. It was about the tale of a man and his wasted minutes, knowing he was going to die alone, just not knowing when to expect it.

As it continued to rain, the two of them stayed talking inside O'Donoghue's until the early morning sun shone through the windows. Elijah discovered Harriet worked at Ethel's Hair Salon in Glossodia – a place not far from Windsor. Harriet was older than him by a few years, plus she had a little boy, Lance, who was barely walking. Her husband, Richard, had taken off with some young barmaid and had left Harriet to raise Lance by herself.

From there on, Elijah and Harriet began seeing each other on a casual basis, and would meet for midnight romps in a motel room or in the back of his or her car, until eventually he allowed her to come back to his place. After a while, as things burgeoned into something more, she hinted she wanted to move in with him. Elijah was happy but not thrilled, although he tried hard to be, and taking on the father-figure role for Lance proved challenging.

Elijah had just arrived home from work one Thursday evening in September (he now worked for the local council doing menial jobs) when the phone rang. Harriet was in the kitchen making a pot roast for dinner, so he grabbed a bottle of Resch's Pilsener from the fridge and limped into the lounge room to answer the phone. It was Grace …

Chapter 78

THEN – 1972

'HOW ARE YOU?' Grace said. Call it instinct, call it what you will, he *knew* something was wrong, and so did the tiny hairs on his arms and neck.

'What's up; what's happened?' Elijah wondered if it was something to do with their parents. By this stage Howard's dementia had kicked in and Margaret was popping pills like John Belushi.

'I'm not going to bullshit,' Grace said. She drew on her cigarette as Elijah's German shepherd, Butch, bounded through the back door to greet him.

He held the chilled bottleneck to his lips and took a huge gulp, wincing as the effervescent mouthful burned his throat. 'Good. Don't. What is it?' He wiped his wet lips with the back of his hand.

'Audrey is getting married.'

Elijah's knees gave way as he dropped into his chair in stunned silence. It was like God Himself had smashed a giant boulder into Elijah's gut. Trying to find oxygen was like searching for Wally. It seemed an age before his mind kicked into gear.

Then, in a faint whisper he said, 'Wait, what? Audrey, a-as in *my* Audrey?'

Grace inhaled as though something was blocking her windpipe. 'Yes, I'm so sorry, but I thought you should know. I saw it mentioned in the business section of a magazine.' She tested his patience by dragging on the cigarette again. 'EJ, I know you're hurting and your pride is wounded, but I'm telling you it's a sign that you should go to her.'

He sat there for a second and fantasised what it would feel like to be young and carefree with Audrey again, running around on the beach under the moonlight, chasing her through the sand as she squealed and laughed, then landing on top of her, kissing her silly under the boardwalk and making love.

The forgotten feeling washed over him as though someone had dunked him underwater in the Fountain of Youth, but that joy soon morphed into anger. A fierce type of anger that was borne of the direct result of hurt so unimaginable, it may as well have been a medical condition. His nostrils flared as the anger seeped deep into his bones, twisting his heart. She was getting hitched to another guy.

He looked to the metal TV tray table beside him and placed his beer on top of the September issue of *TV Week*, covering Mary Jane Boyd's pretty face with a perfect ring of condensation, and stared ahead at the yellow floral wallpaper. 'You read that Audrey's getting married, and you think it's a sign for us to be together?' He faked a laugh as best he could through his tight throat. 'Only *you* could make that connection!'

'I was walking by a magazine stand and something drew me to look inside *POL*. I never buy it, but something *drew* me to it. Besides, I'm a woman, aren't I? I'm telling you, EJ: she still loves you.'

Elijah wasn't even aware that he was grinding his teeth until his jaw ached. 'If she brags about her wedding in a magazine, then I'm pretty sure she's happy!'

Grace sighed and Elijah stared at Butch lying at his feet on the orange shag pile carpet. The dog's ears pulled back and he gazed into his master's eyes, as though sensing his angst.

'I'm sure she is where she wants to be, but thanks for the phone call,' he added.

'Christ Almighty! Stop being so stubborn, you *bastard*.' Grace paused to huff and bang something – to Elijah it sounded like she palm-slapped a table. 'Trust me; listen to just one person in your goddamn life when I tell you: if you walked back into her life tomorrow and declared your love for her, she would drop *everything* for you!' She paused long enough to fill her lungs with toxins once more, and her son, Ryan, began crying in the background. 'EJ, I know deep down you still love her. We all know. You're my baby brother and it upsets me you're only settling with your life; you're not happy at all like, well ... at least not like you pretend to be, anyway.'

A touch of guilt pricked him as Harriet continued humming away to Rod Stewart's 'You Wear It Well', which was playing over their new Astor transistor radio in the kitchen.

'You've already lost seven years of your life over this, and I am so sure about my hunch, I would wager money on it.' Grace expected him to laugh. 'I will bet you my portion of the inheritance that Audrey would take you back in a second. A love like yours could never die, so what else do you have to lose apart from the rest of your life?'

Elijah glanced at a framed photo on the cane-woven coffee table of Harriet, Lance, and himself, taken at Taronga Zoo. Harriet had surprised him with tickets. They looked like a genuinely happy family, so a sting of contrition pricked his heart as Harriet hummed while mashing spuds and cracking pepper.

'What about Harriet and Lance?' he wheezed out; the pressure on his chest felt like someone had dropped an engine block on him.

Grace took a moment, as if she hadn't thought much of Harriet or her son at all, or how Elijah's absence would affect them. 'Harriet is a pleasant woman; I have nothing personal against her whatsoever.'

'*But?*'

'But you've never once looked at her the way you did at Audrey.' She took another drag of her cigarette as his eyes stung like third-degree sunburn. 'Remember the night you brought Audrey home to meet Mum and Dad?'

He gritted his teeth, his fingernails digging into the fabric of his chair. A question so preposterous he almost laughed. 'Do I remember? Grace, I remember *everything*. It was one of the most painful, awkward moments of my life – and I've had a colonoscopy!'

Grace expelled the smoke as Elijah closed his eyes, reminiscing. 'When I saw you two together, I knew she was "the one". You seemed so carefree, like a little boy again, and the smile on her face, oh my God, it must have hurt her cheeks!' She chuckled as tears rimmed Elijah's eyelids. He moved the mouthpiece away from his trembling lips as he gasped for air. 'I just *knew*. She awakened something in you, and you did in her. That is pure love; *that* is the epitome of the word *soulmate*.'

Elijah lowered his voice, cupping the mouthpiece. 'So, you're suggesting I walk back into her life and tell her I ... you know?'

'Mm-hmm.'

'And then everything will be hunky-dory?'

'Yep! Try it.'

Elijah slammed the phone in its cradle and stared at Butch as his chest rose and fell. He had often imagined what he and Audrey's reunion would be like if they were ever to have one. He imagined all the things he would say to her; all the things he would do to her, buy her, show her, explain to her.

But the more he sat there and pondered, the more he worked himself up. He couldn't believe she was marrying someone else. If she loved Elijah, she would have held off; she would have refused and waited for him like she'd *promised*.

As he swiped away a tear, Harriet emerged from the kitchen in her corduroy pinafore and white sweater, her brown feathered hair bouncing as brass tassel earrings swayed with each step.

'Honey, why are you sitting in here alone?' She glanced at the blank Philips TV.

He tried to fake a smile, but he guessed, even in the fading light, she could see through him like he was a sheet of cellophane, because frown lines marred her smooth forehead.

'Who was that on the phone?'

He cleared his throat and clenched his stomach in the hope of holding back tears. 'Grace.'

'Is everything okay?' She reached for the light switch.

He shielded his eyes by raising a horizontal arm. There was no denying Harriet loved him, and he felt bad because he could never give her something he had lost a long time ago. He wanted Harriet and needed her, but he could never *love* her. She was a top woman – it wasn't her fault he was broken. If he were being truthful, he couldn't fault her. She was a great lover; a wonderful, doting mother, and a shoulder for Elijah to cry on if he ever needed to. In theory, she was perfect – as if designed by God Himself. But even after all of that considered, his heart yearned for someone else.

He couldn't concentrate on the future when he lived in the past. He told Harriet he needed to leave for a few days, as tsunami waves of guilt slammed into his queasy stomach.

Lines of concern stretched across her forehead. 'Why; what's happened?'

'I, um, I need to sort out some family affairs.'

'Oh,' she mouthed, clutching the pepper grinder to her bosom.

He hated being the one who caused her pain, but he just needed to see for himself. Maybe Grace was on to something. Maybe—

Harriet lowered her head and spoke to the carpet. 'Is it because of *her?*'

Elijah swallowed past the rusty nails lodged in his throat and flared his nostrils, trying to maintain control. He wasn't a liar – he never had been, but he didn't want to confess his private turmoil, either. 'Who?'

Her lips parted as her bottom lip tremored. 'The woman whose name you have tattooed on your chest. The woman who you see whenever you look at me.'

His jaw hardened as his pulse raced. He wanted to implode – to hell with this awful circumstance, he didn't want anyone to get hurt. 'I need to sort things out, is all. I'll be back in a few days.'

She licked her lips as her stormy eyes met his. 'Then that's a yes, otherwise you would have said "no".' Harriet's lips sucked inwards as she closed her eyes. 'Are you going to come back home to us, or is this going to be something else I have to survive?'

Elijah looked away as a nervous tic played havoc on his knee. The word 'us' was not lost on him. Harriet let out an anguished sob and leaned back against the kitchen doorway. No doubt the memories of Richard's betrayal had come flooding back to her. Then, serendipitously, Lance bawled his eyes out, so Elijah used that as a cue to leave. He felt like the scummiest man in the world, but he didn't want to wake up one morning years later thinking *what if*? How often did people get a second chance at true love?

After he tended to Lance, he went to the master bedroom and started packing – his hands shaking at the mere thought of seeing Audrey again after all this time. He walked back outside as Harriet sat on the lounge with a thousand-yard stare, and it reminded him of Audrey when he told her he was leaving for 'Nam. *That* look alone made him rethink this whole situation. He wasn't in love with Harriet, nor would he ever be. But causing someone heartache how it'd been done to him ... that was something else. He was comfortable and content – why screw that up?

'I will come back; this is just something I need to do. Trust me, sweetheart, I won't abandon you, too.'

Chapter 79

THEN – 1972

AUDREY SCHEDULED HER wedding for Saturday, 16th September. Elijah was in his latest beige Cadillac DeVille driving down to Ulladulla, where Audrey and this fella, Buck, were getting married. He didn't have a game plan. But it was a second chance, so he was going to reach out and grab it, come hell or high water.

He did, however, feel terrible about Harriet with how he'd left things. He'd packed his bag and kissed her forehead before jumping into his car and driving to his sister's place. Elijah wasn't open with Grace; he never had been – especially about his feelings – that just wasn't his thing. However, last night he'd gone over there and Grace's husband, Quinton, greeted him at the front door, flanked by their son, Ryan (who'd just started walking), and their pit bull, Tortoise (so-called because he was fat and barely moved unless being called for dinner).

Grace had greeted her younger brother with a kiss on the cheek and took him inside her spacious two-storey fibro house. 'I've got homemade Pavlova,' she said. 'Tea?'

Elijah nodded and Grace disappeared into the kitchen to prepare Pavlova with extra whipped cream and passionfruit pulp. Just the way he liked it.

Sitting at the dinner table cradling a cup of tea, Elijah stared at the spinning ceiling fan as images of Hueys flashed across his damaged mind.

Grace returned and gasped. 'Oh, shit, *sorry*! I didn't even think—' She put the Pavlova down and reached for the fan's switch. She then turned down the knob of the Drake ham radio that was tuned into 2GB. Quinton had given them privacy by going out into the garage to work on his Simca Vedette, which had been leaking oil on the driveway. Ryan went along to be Daddy's little helper.

Grace pushed her paperback copy of *The Exorcist* aside and placed a plate of Pavlova in front of her brother, wiping the cream on her thumb onto her dark-blue flared jeans.

When she tried small talk, he looked at her, almost pleading with her not to bother.

'Grace, what do I do?'

She took a sip from her mug of tea before saying, 'I only have one thing to say to you.' Reaching under the table to the chair next to her, she pulled out an album that Elijah had not seen in years. 'Is this what you want to leave behind?'

Elijah stared wide-eyed as Grace handed him the photo album Audrey had given him the day he'd left for 'Nam. He broke out in goosebumps and grabbed it as 'Nights in White Satin' played over the crackling radio. 'How did you—?'

'I rescued it from the trash, courtesy of Mother – the day after you left for Vietnam.'

The thought of his mother discarding it in the bin like it was nothing more than a soiled tissue infuriated Elijah. He pulled out his pack of Camels and offered his sister a lung-buster as the haunting sound of the Mellotron used by the Moody Blues banished the silence.

He drew on the end of his butt, pushing his untouched plate of Pavlova aside. 'Mum said Audrey drove off in my EH and you guys never saw her again.'

Grace took a drag. 'It is true that I never saw her again after you left for 'Nam – her or your car.'

Smoke jetted from his nostrils. 'Then how did Mum get this album? Why the *hell* didn't you give me this before?'

She faltered, twisting her beaded bangles. 'It sounded like Audrey wanted to be left alone, and when she moved out of the Gong without even telling me, it was pretty obvious she was hurting and wanted nothing to do with us. Of course I asked Mum how she came to have the album, and she told me Audrey left it behind at the docks. As I've told you a thousand times before, Mum said Arthur went with her to make sure she knew how to handle the transmission. After that, he *did* arrive back at our place in a taxi – I saw it with my own two eyes. When you came back from 'Nam and I saw your mental state, I *truly* didn't see how giving you this album would have helped. It was not a map to Audrey's new place. I thought at the time it would have done more harm than good.' She placed a hand over his wrist. 'Apart from this, that's the *only* thing I've kept from you. I swear on Ryan's life.'

'There's no way Audrey would have left this album behind.'

'Hey, I believe that Audrey loved you beyond words, and it does seem off. But how did Mum get the album? Why did Audrey keep your car? Why did I never hear from her again?'

They sat in silence, their thoughts clanging around like billiard balls until the sound of Quinton revving the engine, followed by Ryan squealing in delight, interrupted them. For seven years, Elijah had nursed the hope that one day, somewhere, somehow, Audrey would return to him – had his parents had something more to do with it than he initially thought?

'Forgive me, but I had to look through it,' she said, eyeing the album. 'Don't let pride come between something so beautiful.' Elijah detected tears in her eyes, something that was a rarity as their folks had conditioned it out of them both at a young age. Even Quinton said Grace had the emotional range of a thumbnail.

'But what about Harriet?' he whispered, opening the album, which opened old wounds, like stitches being ripped out. Seeing Audrey's dainty inscription on the inside front cover was almost too much to bear. His teeth ground together like a pestle and mortar as his stomach muscles tightened.

Grace sparked another cigarette, shrouding them both in plume. 'But what about *you*?'

After Elijah got the details of the wedding, which were listed in *POL* magazine along with a dazzling picture of the young entrepreneurs, he slept as best he could in a spare bedroom before waking up early the next morning, determined to stop the wedding.

'A Horse with No Name' by America played over TUNE!FM as he sped down the highway.

Elijah's love for Audrey would never fade. It tainted him. It was too powerful, and no matter how hard he tried, he could never love Harriet – or any other woman – the way he loved Audrey.

At one point he decided to barge into the chapel and yell: 'I object!' Then the next minute, he decided against it. As he argued with himself back and forth, a miracle – or perhaps an omen – happened: the song 'Everything I Own' by Bread came on.

After listening to the relatable lyrics, Elijah conceded, as wind whistled through his open window, that he would not be one of those fools who sung about lost love. He put the pedal to the metal and floored it right to where all the signs were pointing. It was difficult using a map while driving sixty miles per hour, but somehow he made it in time to see what could only be described as a Disney castle as he crept along the estate's driveway.

Thunderbirds, Monaros and Fairlanes lined the driveway littered with pink-and-white petals, which fell from cherry blossom trees that seemed to stretch from one side to the other, as though reaching out to intertwine their branches. Elijah had to double-check he was at the right venue. He hadn't a clue how much money Audrey had come into; the last he saw of her, she was living at Lloyd's wearing no-name clothing. He parked next to a lime-green metallic Torana under a willow tree, and focused on calming his erratic breathing as he stepped outside. It was more like a scene from one of his parents' parties than Audrey's wedding. People wearing white silk suits and ties wandered around the immaculate grounds, talking in idle banter while sipping on the finest champagne offered by waiters with white tea cloths draped over their forearms. He realised he would stand out like dogs' balls wearing bootcut jeans and a black flannel T-shirt – but he found this whole scenario ironic. Once it was *his* family who snubbed Audrey, now the roles were reversed.

He managed a small smile for the benefit of guests, who eyed him with suspicion. Fear proliferated inside him once he thought of the bigger picture. If he had changed, then how much had Audrey? Had the money gone to her head like it had to his parents'? Elijah overheard people referring to his girl as 'Aud' – a real upper-class version of Audrey – and he didn't like it. Was this 'Aud' a reinvention after the tumultuous time in her previous life?

He needed another smoke beforehand, but as he limped away to find seclusion, people gasped. Elijah turned around as a Rolls-Royce Silver Shadow cruised along the gravel driveway as cherry blossom petals floated from above like confetti. A lump formed in his throat the size of a bowling ball. Inside that car was the love of his life. He had waited for this day for seven long years.

The driver of the Silver Shadow, clad in braces and a comical pair of spectacles, stepped out and then opened a rear door. Three bridesmaids, none of whom Elijah recognised (although why would he?), hopped out first. Their coral-coloured poly chiffon dresses rippled in the gentle springtime breeze as guests started piling into the church with fevered pitch to the accompaniment of music. Then the driver reached in as a dainty, white-lace glove-covered hand – her hand – clasped onto his, followed by her sparkling silver high heels. She emerged like a vision; Elijah's knees buckled at the sight of her. *Translucent* didn't cover it. It were as if Audrey was an angel who had benignly graced them all with her presence. How trivial he felt in that instant.

Elijah's heart jump-started and he wanted to run to her. But he couldn't. She'd transfixed him by her smile and the sound of her laughter with her bridesmaids, so he leaned against a tree for support. She looked so different – so mature and proper.

Her transcendent gown would have cost a mint. Her sophisticated, done-up hair shimmered; her teeth looked professionally whitened, and she had a golden tan and long, manicured nails – heck, even her mannerisms had changed. Elijah knew deep down, after looking at the way she moved and acted, that she was not the spirited girl he fell in love with, merely a shell of who she used to be. A cloud of disappointment washed over him.

'Look at me, baby, *please*,' he whispered through a dry mouth as his heart wreaked havoc. He held out a shaky hand as if to touch the mirage in front of him. After working up the courage, Elijah's lips parted and his lungs sucked in air to speak, just as the middle-aged photographer moved and blocked his view of her. Before long, she had glided through the sandstone entrance and up to a water fountain in front of the steps that led to the church where Lloyd waited for her. Elijah took three goes to light his Camel before leaning against his car to get a better view of the commotion.

A free hand clutched his nauseous stomach. If she wasn't the same girl he fell in love with, then how would it work between them, if what they had was no longer the same?

It was like they were from another time and place altogether; it seemed they didn't stand a hope in hell of rekindling what they had experienced in a different galaxy.

Elijah wished he had a crystal ball to peer into the future, to see if ruining her wedding day would be worth it. Then the song by Bread came into his mind and he agreed he couldn't let her go without a fight. Whatever problems lay before them, they could overcome them with the love they had. It was now or never: to rescue her once more and live out their lives together as they were destined to do. Elijah ground the cigarette butt under his heel and set off through the sandstone gates, determined to be hated by every single person in that church.

However, all notions flew out the window as soon as he peered inside. Looking at her, any thought of being her saviour evaporated like smoke sucked up an air vent. Audrey held hands with her new beau, and the jubilance on her face was something Elijah would never forget. He admitted to himself then that he was too late. The dam he had constructed to hold back the heartache, loss and hurt gave way, as if it had waited for this moment of weakness, and all the while his heart was laughing at his head for being so futile and childish.

A typhoon of submerged feelings cascaded over him and he was washed away. He was no longer at the church entrance watching his love marry another man; it was that first moment he saw her walk through the door of Betty-Sue's. Captured then by her elegant walk and air of grace; a seductress weaving her magic with nothing more than a timid smile and the sway of her hips. Never had the world seemed so colourful. In that moment when their eyes had locked while she was behind the counter, he was a god made mortal. In the next instant he was mesmerised by her sleeping in his arms after they first made love. His graceful tigress looking as carefree as a kitten, her dreams finally untroubled by anything. He had her, and she had him.

He tumbled through forgotten memories of their arms around each other as they walked through the drizzling, foggy streets of Sydney one night to Rowe Street Records to buy Bob Dylan's latest album; of singing along to the latest rock 'n' roll song in his EH; and of her unbridled passion when they made love.

She was one of a kind.

She was his dream.

But he was not hers.

With this immobilising thought, it broke his reverie like a ship crashing against rocks in a violent storm. His heart sank and it felt like it would never hit the bottom.

She was looking at Buck, and he at her. Elijah couldn't grasp the ravelled ends of his thoughts to gain composure, to grasp on to reality.

When the priest said: 'Speak now or forever hold your peace,' Elijah was on the edge of the precipice, about to scream out.

But the priest continued, so Elijah closed his mouth as a tear trickled down his face. His teeth clenched – to call his pain excruciating would be an understatement. They'd shot him four times in 'Nam, but here at the church, witnessing *his* Audrey marry another man, hurt far worse than bullet wounds. He could never give her what she truly wanted; they could never be as happy as they had imagined. Elijah Samuels was not the rich boy she once knew; he was a middle-class, infertile man, and no matter how much he loved her, he could never give her children, which would forever be the missing jigsaw piece – rendering their dream incomplete.

'Soulmates' and 'commitment' and then 'till death do us part' floated through the thick air. 'You may now kiss the bride,' the priest said at last, and the handsome chap lifted Audrey's veil. They kissed as the hundreds of guests clapped and wiped away tears of joy. Elijah dug his fingernails into the wooden doorframe and closed his eyes, face contorted in the cruelty of it all. He had to get out of there before anyone saw him, so in a zombie-like state he limped back to his car, not knowing if he had just made the biggest mistake of his miserable life.

Elijah punched the willow tree, splitting the skin on his knuckles and causing blood to smear his hand, before lighting another cigarette. Once back in the driver's seat, he screamed at the top of his lungs as though it could expel every ache and pain he'd experienced and suppressed over seven years in a drawn-out howl.

Panting harshly, lungs hooking in oxygen, he looked up through thick tears to witness the jovial guests throwing rice and confetti over the happy couple as they walked hand-in-hand down the steps and into a waiting Chrysler, which had a sign on the back that read 'Just Married'.

Sitting in his idling car, holding a lit Camel out the window, Elijah glanced up after a long while and, through blurred vision, he saw Lloyd's disbelieving eyes boring directly into his. Elijah swore there was the briefest glimmer of guilt – as well as shock – in Lloyd's wide eyes. He took a cautionary step towards the car before stopping. They continued to stare at each other before Lloyd's eyes roamed the ground, as though looking for answers amongst the fallen leaves.

Does he know that my heart is fucking shattered?

Lloyd gave Elijah one final, almost apologetic look before turning away. Elijah sat there motionless, watching the guests leave one by one as tears slid down his face. Once the sun dipped behind the church and his was the only car left, he took off home to Harriet and Lance, a soldier returning from a war that he wasn't sure what he had been fighting for. And that day was the last time he saw Audrey's smile.

Chapter 80

'*WHAT?*' NURSE MILDRED screeched. 'Ya mean that was it? Why didn't ya fight fo' her? She loved ya, ya *idiot*!'

Elijah squared his shoulders and faced Nurse Mildred. 'It was the hardest damn thing I ever did. Remember, though, I've only heard these stories from Audrey's diary for the first time – decades after the fact. I did not know about her trying to contact me; I wasn't aware she felt the way she did years after I left for 'Nam. Nor did I know my parents ruined what we could have had by keeping us apart, thanks to them buying everyone off.' He shrugged. 'I didn't know any of it.'

No-one spoke. His story consumed them, each reserving their own opinions about what Elijah should have done on the day of the wedding. As no-one said a word, he continued.

'Have you ever had it in your head all the things you will say and how you will say it when you're planning a discussion or argument with someone? Then comes crunch time, it goes nothing like you envisioned.' Everyone except Tida nodded, especially Jamie. 'When I peered inside the church, Audrey looked *happy* and what's more, so did the guy she was marrying. Audrey was not the same woman I fell in love with, and I didn't want her settling for me when I couldn't make her feel complete.'

'But how do ya know that? Her love fo' ya has shaken us all like a fish in the jaws of a gator.' Timothy, Angela and Jamie remained silent. After all, the man Elijah was referring to was their father.

'I may not have got the life I wanted, but at least she got the life she deserved. I can't ask for much more than that.' Nurse Mildred cocked her head to the side and gazed down. 'For years I felt resentment, guilt, anger – you name it – towards the whole situation. So, when Grace told me Audrey was in here, I *had* to come and see her again, no matter how painful. And you know what?' His eyes lingered on Chloe's tear-stained face. 'I am glad I did. Not only did I get to see Audrey again' – he glanced towards her on the bed – 'but I got to meet all of you, and now the pieces of the puzzle fit into place.' Smiles appeared on the faces around the room. 'If I had swooped in and stopped the wedding, this here, now, would never have happened. I could never have given her what your father did. As much as I hated him for many years for hijacking the life meant for me … I thank him.'

Angela placed her arm around Jamie's slumped shoulders. Timothy squeezed Tida's knee and she beamed, and Nurse Mildred pulled Chloe's face into her bosom in a fierce embrace.

'I suppose on some level I knew as I drove to her wedding that I wasn't capable of stopping it. I think it was more to make sure she would be taken care of. I still felt like her protector, and as soon as I saw her beaming smile, it was time for me to move on – for good. As for closure, seeing Audrey marry another fella was as good as any, I guess. The finale to our story.' He paused while Angela handed out tissues to Chloe and Jamie. Nurse Mildred had her own supply.

'Sorry ta seem too big fo' me britches, but couldn't ya have adopted, sugah? What ya had was as rare as lips on a chicken; I feel like ya sorta … gave up.'

Elijah scoffed a little too hard, which stirred his coughing. 'Gave up? I still haven't given up, and I am almost six feet under.' Laughter replaced the sniffling around the room. 'Besides, a woman wants to feel a baby grow inside her, to have a child of her own, you know?' He assumed their silence was in agreement. 'What's done is done, and after meeting you all, I'm glad I did what I did.'

'What did you do after you left the wedding?' Chloe said as a trio of nurses strolled past in the corridor.

'I arrived home just after midnight. As I stood in our bedroom doorway, I saw Harriet tangled in the bedsheets, naked, wiping tears away. She hadn't heard me arrive. I crawled into bed and hugged her from behind. She clung onto my arm with what felt like steel talons.

'"You came back," she whispered. "Of course I did," I said, holding my tears at bay, thankful she couldn't see my face. A fantasy played out that night; it was all I could do to keep from falling apart. I knew what it was like to love someone with everything you have, then they disappear from your life in an instant. I had a type of loyalty to Harriet, and I didn't want to destroy her just because someone had shattered me like a dropped glass plate. I knew what the pain felt like, and Harriet had never done anything to me that could justify me hurting her. Don't get me wrong; it was the hardest thing I had ever done, but I left Audrey where she wanted to be. It was clear she didn't need me anymore.

'Harriet turned around and kissed me hard, pinning me beneath her as her tears dripped over my face. We made intense love as if I had been gone for years. It was the reunion Audrey and I should have had, and during a relapse – God help me, I looked up and envisioned Audrey's face.' He eyed everyone over his spectacles to gauge their reaction. Angela swallowed, looking away. Timothy shifted in his seat and cleared his throat. 'Harriet and I never got married. I couldn't give her any children, but Lance called me Dad, and I called him son. We also legally changed his surname to Samuels early on. Harriet and I stayed together until her premature death in '89, when she passed away from cancer – she was also an avid smoker. I remained faithful to her over the years of hardship and certainly wept over her death.'

'Do you still speak to Lance?' Timothy said.

The corner of his mouth pulled back. 'He calls me sometimes, but it's not how it used to be when the three of us were under the one roof. When Harriet became an angel, Lance and I moved out of Windsor and he ended up going to university. He has his own family now – I don't think his wife is too fond of me. I have been on my own since Lance moved out, and that's when Audrey popped into my head even more. I have to admit, the strength of her memory surprised even me. I never thought love was as fierce and corrosive as this and, like a fool, I assumed time would heal all wounds.' He glanced out the window to take in the fading sunlight; darkness gobbling up the remaining blue. 'When people say it's better to have loved and lost than never to have loved at all, I concur. As my life is drawing to an end, it's easy for me to point fingers and to blame. Not Audrey or Buck. But I could blame my parents. I could blame the dirty Vietnamese who shot me. I could even blame the government for sending me to 'Nam. Whatever the case, I have spent too much time pondering the past when I should have spent more time focusing on the future; I just always assumed Audrey *was* my future.'

Jamie sniffled, rose, and walked to the bed, wiping her wet cheeks. She stroked the side of Audrey's weathered face (being careful of the tubes) and whispered, 'Come back to us, Mum. There are people here to see you; to tell you they love you.' She sniffled again and waited for something, *anything*. She sucked her bottom lip inside her mouth as she stared at her mother, her tears hitting the blanket.

After a hopeless wait, Jamie heaved a sigh, turned, and resumed her position next to Angela.

'At least I got to meet you lovely, albeit slightly weird, bunch of people.'

Everyone laughed, including Tida, who gave off an exaggerated laugh as if desperate to join in with the others.

Elijah dipped his head. 'Thank you for allowing me to come into your lives, and for listening to this old fart's tales of the past.'

Angela rolled her eyes, but her unshed tears glimmered. He placed a hand over his beating heart, the place where Audrey's faded name would forever remain, in this life and surely the next.

'You have a special family, so please take this geezer's advice: don't fight, don't argue, and don't waste petty time ignoring one another if some miniscule thing happens.' Timothy diverted his gaze. 'Life is way too short. The things you're all worrying about today like work, money, social life, social media,' he said, holding his brittle fingers up to rattle them off, 'will not matter in the slightest when you are writing your will.'

He turned to Chloe, who was as wide-eyed as a young doe. She was the one who had believed in him from the start; the one who had fought for him every step of the way. She would be the one he missed the most. 'Chloe, even though your mother can be a pain in the arse,' he said, ignoring Angela, who shook her head, 'listen to her because she's a damn good one at that. Also, remember, if you have a dream, don't worry about failures; worry about the chances you'll miss when you don't even try.'

Chloe ran to him and threw her arms around his brittle neck. His spine stiffened, and the two sisters swapped smiles before he relented and wrapped his arms around her petite frame. She offered him a tiny kiss on his cheek before she retreated and stepped back to Nurse Mildred's arms.

Elijah turned to Jamie, who dabbed the corners of her eyes with a crumpled tissue. 'Jamie, ditch the bitch. You know what I mean.' She let out a laugh but Chloe and Timothy both frowned. 'You can't start the next chapter of your life if you keep re-reading the last one.' Angela nodded her agreement. She stood up to shake her legs, while Jamie nodded her appreciation.

'Tim, take care of your family and don't be a stranger to them. Yes, you have moved away, but your responsibility of being the only male sibling doesn't fade, and a good old heart-to-heart with your sisters won't go astray.'

Timothy nodded in appreciation of the pep talk.

Elijah drew air into his nostrils. 'Tida ... good luck with the baby, love, and may God help you push a human out of that body of yours.'

Jamie cracked up as Elijah turned to the lady whom he admired almost as much as Audrey. 'Winifred Mildred.'

Her entire face widened as she pointed towards her chest as if to say *Who, me?*

'May the world shine as bright as your smile. Your husband is a very lucky man. You're an inspiration, and I hope you never change. I'm glad I met you and, here …' He reached into his inside breast pocket. 'I have a present for you.'

Nurse Mildred's eyes filled at the sight of a Snickers bar. From behind her horn-rimmed glasses the tears looked amplified. She ran over to hug him, almost knocking his chair backwards. It was a tender moment that Elijah would remember, even if she was only hugging him over a chocolate bar.

'Angela,' he said, noting her bottom lip tremor as she braced herself against the window ledge. 'Loosen the stick a little and you might enjoy life a bit more.' She shook her head, but a wide grin accompanied it. 'When you're on your deathbed, you'll flick through your mental photo album of memories – that's what life is about, and now you can pass down more memories to people you meet after having met me – the crazy kook.' He smiled through the sharp pain stabbing his sternum. 'Thank you, Angela, for taking care of the family. I know it sounds strange coming from me, but as I said, no matter how old Audrey gets, she'll always be my girl.'

A timid knock at the door stole their focus; an elderly nurse gave Nurse Mildred a quizzical look before turning to the rest of the occupants. 'Sorry to disturb you all. Winifred, Harry's asking for you again. He's pulled his catheter out, and you're the only one he'll allow to touch his …'

She sprang to her feet. 'Hold on, Harry, I'mma comin'!'

Once Nurse Mildred left the room, Elijah slapped his knees and cleared his phlegmy throat. 'Ladies and gent, with all due respect, I would like to have a minute alone with Audrey, please.'

Chapter 81

ONCE EVERYONE LEFT, Elijah studied Audrey. Her face had yielded to age, yet her ethereal beauty remained; it had outlasted time itself. He'd had the opportunity to be alone with her a few nights back, when Nurse Mildred suggested he eat dinner in Audrey's room. But he'd passed up the opportunity to speak to her then. His emotions had been too erratic, as he still harboured anger towards her that he'd carried for decades, for what he perceived to be her abandonment. He'd declined Nurse Mildred's offer and went home to Sheba instead. But now that he knew the director's cut version (the *actual* story), there was nothing that would stop him from acknowledging and admitting the flame still burned for her as bright as it ever did.

Hot torrents of grief coursed down his wrinkled cheeks, the pain still raw, as he moved his trembling hand to hers and held on like it was the last time. Her bony, paper-dry hand felt cool. He was gripping a tentative last thread between the world of the living and whatever lay after.

Elijah struggled for words, so instead, using his free hand, he stroked the sides of her face, brushing a thumb over cheeks that used to display such happiness.

He bent down to her ear, forced his dry lips apart, and whispered: 'Did you save the last dance for me?'

The room spun, teleporting him back to the day he was leaving for 'Nam. They were inside the motel room at Picton, dancing in each other's arms, only this time he wasn't saying goodbye. Instead, he welcomed the start of his new life.

He imagined never leaving her behind, knowing that jail would have been preferable over the years of suffering he'd endured at losing her; at how he was technically a prisoner of war, anyway. He contorted his face and gave his emotions free rein, desperately gasping for air as he visualised them gliding around *this* room, telling each other all the things they had wanted to say since 1965. He pictured holding her, kissing her, proving to her that the only accomplishment that ever mattered to him was to love her unconditionally; this was the only thing he wanted engraved on his epitaph.

As the sound of a helicopter outside sliced into the vivid image, he opened his eyes to stare at his soulmate. With bated breath, he sniffed and let out an *ahhh*, expelling pent-up pressure like gas escaping a soft drink bottle. His lips quivered, his head pounded and, for the briefest moment, he pictured her opening her eyes.

When the cold reality set in, he again leaned close to her ear. His eyes felt as though they were bleeding with pain. He grabbed her lifeless hand and his lips quivered. 'I love you, Audrey. I always have, and I always will.'

Audrey's fingers tightened around his. He gasped and looked at their entwined hands. His gaze returned to her face, but she hadn't opened her eyes. Elijah's heart thwacked inside his sternum as he moved his trembling hands to cup the sides of her face.

'*Audrey!* Please wake up, sweetheart. *Please!* I'm so sorry I left you. I should have known better – there *was* n-no life without you – *please* open your eyes!' He fought for breath as he moved closer to her ear. 'I need to know you can forgive me.'

When silence greeted him with no further reaction, he let out a tormented wail, which prompted Nurse Mildred to rush in on a heartbeat.

'What on ear—?'

'Sh-Sh-She squeezed my hand!' He stood back, struggling for oxygen, wiping the tears from his face.

Nurse Mildred frowned and moved over to the bed to study the machine before glancing at Audrey.

'I don't think so, Eli,' she whispered, creasing her eyes.

He shook his head. 'No, I'm *telling* you! I held onto her hand and she squeezed it back; I know what I felt. She *can* hear and understand everything that is going on around her. I knew it! She's still fighting for something; there's a reason she's hanging on.'

Nurse Mildred patted Elijah's back. 'Darlin', sometimes their eyes can twitch; their hands will flicker 'n' folk'll think—'

'No, this was different. It was *her*.'

She offered a gentle smile before looking towards Audrey, then heading out the door.

Elijah wiped his face with the back of a hand and sat on the edge of the bed, breathing in and out as he stared at his hand on hers. He closed his eyes and savoured the moment. When he opened his stinging eyes, Audrey had not moved. The machines were not behaving erratically, her brainwaves had not spiked, but as sure as he knew that he loved her, he knew something remarkable had passed between them.

After an age, he rose and shuffled to the door. Turning and looking at Audrey one last time, he smiled as realisation hit him: *Terminal lucidity.*

Chapter 82

ELIJAH SAID HIS goodbyes to the family (omitting to tell them of the hand squeeze) and went to sit at the taxi shelter. Once he was seated on the cold bench, Angela called his name. He looked over, expecting to hear Audrey was awake, that he could go back and speak to her.

Angela was panting by the time she reached him.

'What is it?'

'I–I wanted to say that even without hearing Mum's side, I always knew she had something buried deep inside of her. Maybe it's a woman's intuition?' Elijah's frown demanded further explanation. 'I, ah, I never paid too much attention to it when I was younger because I was unaware and ignorant – never having been in love. But I thought you should know that she thought of you all the time.'

After a beat, he tapped the space on the aluminium bench beside him. It wasn't quite the conversation he'd hoped for, but he was grateful all the same. She sat and crossed her legs, the fluorescent lighting above them attracting a gazillion bugs.

'As I got older, I used to study my mother's behaviour. On numerous occasions I caught Mum out in the backyard, sitting on a swing, iced tea in hand, gazing into the sky. I always used to wonder what she was thinking about.' This time Angela was the one who coughed. Placing a hand at the base of her throat, she said, 'I also want to confess that I lied about something.'

'Oh?'

She turned to face him. 'I wasn't entirely truthful before when I said that not once had we heard your name.'

Elijah manoeuvred to hear better, as the crickets and distant sound of ambulance sirens were playing havoc with his hearing capabilities.

'I remember a time when I was about eleven or twelve. I was reading a book in bed when I heard my mother yell out, and I didn't know it then, but she was calling your name in her sleep. I forgot until recently that my parents got into a terrible row because she'd called out another man's name. My father demanded to know who the man was, but she swore she wasn't having an affair and said he was overreacting to a dream.'

Elijah turned away and inhaled as a cool breeze blew over them, all sounds in the background suddenly fading into silence.

'It's clear you weren't the only one missing a lost loved one.' She nodded with certainty. 'I sometimes used to think Mum was depressed.' Her mouth twisted. 'My mother tried to act strong and she was a fearless businesswoman, but even now I can remember certain times at the dinner table, when she would be there, but she wasn't – if that makes sense?' She turned to Elijah, who remained silent, monopolised by his own thoughts. 'In retrospect, I realise she was thinking of you; picturing her life with you at that given moment. I guarantee she would have wondered if it would have mirrored what was in front of her.'

A car horn blasted in the distance, startling them, and for a moment Elijah thought of telling Angela to stop talking because his poor heart couldn't take anymore.

'This is hard and sort of weird – me talking to you about this considering Buck is my father – but I thought you deserved the truth and, well ... closure. It is a shame, but who knows? Maybe you two would have ended up hating each other like many long-term married couples I know. Maybe it was a *good* thing fate preserved your love like a time capsule. Does that make sense?' Elijah lowered his head, shielding his face in the darkness. 'Your love was pure; maybe it should remain like that. And it can satisfy you knowing you shared a love most people only ever *dream* about. We can't have it all, as they say.'

'Your mother did,' Elijah whispered.

'Hmm, maybe if you asked her, she would have a different answer. That she brought her journal here to the nursing home, and not even her own wedding album, speaks for itself.'

Elijah shot her a doubtful glance. *No, you're lying.*

'It's true.' She nodded as if reading his mind. 'I found the wedding album at home when I was doing a spring clean-out, along with other stuff I thought was odd she didn't bring with her.'

'Do you think she was *happy*?'

She stared off into the distance. 'From my perspective, before I knew about you, yes.' She chuckled. 'My parents loved each other very much. It would please you to know that my father took exceptional care of her, and gave us kids the most magical childhood.' She glanced at her entwined hands wrapped around a knee and smiled, teary-eyed. 'I remember many trips we took together as a family when we were younger.' She swatted a fly, and a lone tear fell. 'They did argue – I mean, what married couples don't? But my mother brought out the best in Dad and he doted on her, worshipped her. As far as I am aware, neither of them had an affair, but after meeting you, nothing would shock me about my parents' past life.'

'I ... I just would have given anything to experience what being married to her would have been like. I dreamed about it for so damn long it hurts to know I never had a chance because it wasn't in the cards we were dealt.' Angela placed a hand on his knee as he used his hands to emphasise communication. 'I pictured in my mind so many countless times what it would feel like coming home to her cooking us dinner; sharing a laugh around the dinner table with our kids, before holding each other in bed late at night. Going away on family vacations, seeing our children in school plays, watching them graduate from university.' He shook his head. 'God, there were *so* many things I wanted to experience with her.' Elijah looked skyward. 'Harriet, please forgive me.'

'I'm so sorry, EJ. But I believe now my mother must have spent a good portion of her time wondering the same thing about you.'

He clenched his eyes in an attempt to restrain another onslaught of tears. If the dam burst he might end up on the ground in a dishevelled heap, sobbing like a child. 'The most precious thing about the past, in my humble opinion, is that it's so beautiful because it's untouchable, ya know? All the memories, all the feelings, smells, sights and sounds, the times you laughed, cried, played with neighbourhood kids – no-one can ever erase your memories. The past is a fact, whether it is a lesson, a blessing or a disappointment – it's stuck with you for life.'

'All we need is a time machine.'

Elijah waited for a group of rambunctious teens to run by before he said, 'If you don't mind my asking, how did your father pass away?'

'Prostate cancer. He dropped the bombshell on us and six months later he passed on.'

He patted her knee. 'I'm sorry to hear that. Honest to God, I am.'

She offered an appreciative smile while looking at the ground. 'Thank you. It was hard on us all – especially Jamie. Tim went off the rails because of it. Dad was a terrific man and, as weird as this is going to sound, I believe you two would have got on like a house on fire.'

Elijah gave an honest, hearty laugh. 'Why, because we have the same taste in women?'

She nudged his shoulder with hers. 'No, because he was down-to-earth and generous to a fault. Whatever my mother desired, he made sure she got.'

He contorted his face, attempting to stop his tear ducts from leaking again. 'Then, I can't ask for much more than that, can I? She had a wonderful life, so I am happy.'

'Are you?'

Elijah gave a mirthless smile and patted her hand that remained on his knee as a car with blazing high beams and Meat Loaf's 'Bat Out of Hell' blaring, pulled up to the taxi shelter.

'Jesus H. Christ, I think this is my driver,' Elijah said in a tone that made Angela throw her head back and laugh. Elijah noted how attractive she was without her scowl, and now that he observed her in a different light (literally, beneath the electric streetlamps) and under different circumstances, there were similarities to Audrey's features, including high, rounded cheekbones.

'That's the first time I've ever heard you laugh. It's quite infectious.'

Angela's smile faded and she turned away. 'Yours, too, grumblebum.'

He coughed and patted his chest before he stared at the ground. 'You know, I used to smile and mean it. Now, I just smile.'

'EJ?'

'Mmm?'

'The woman in Vietnam – the one you shot – Tida reminds you of her, doesn't she?'

Elijah licked his lips and inhaled. 'Maybe it was my punishment.' His eyes were still on the ground. 'I took a woman's life, so one got taken away from me.'

She shook her head. 'You can't think like that!'

His nostrils flared as he closed his eyes. 'Regret has been my constant companion for as long as I can remember. It's never failed me.'

'You did what you had to do. It was her or you, remember?'

He opened his eyes. 'Yeah … as if that's what helps me sleep at night.'

Angela paused, deliberating. 'And here I thought you were just a racist arsehole.' She grinned.

He chortled. 'I don't have a racist bone in my body; what happened, happened. I don't hold it against them, same as they shouldn't hold it against me.' He turned to her. 'Maybe you're more astute and switched on to situations than I thought.' He paused upon reflection. 'I should take it a bit easier on Tinder.'

'Tida!'

'Huh? Well, who's Tinder?'

'No-one; it's a dating app!'

'*App*alling by the sounds of it.' She shook her head, grinning. 'Thank you for everything, Angela.'

'Are you *sure* you don't want a lift home?'

'You live in the opposite direction. Besides, I like to live life on the edge.' His chin jutted towards the taxi driver, who was now playing the air guitar.

'Shall I see you tomorrow, then?' she asked, glancing at Ozzy Osbourne's doppelgänger behind the wheel as he flicked a cigarette butt into a nearby bush and belched.

'Well, that all depends on this nitwit.' Elijah jerked a thumb in the vibrating car's direction.

Angela leaned over and kissed his wet cheek. She leaned back and smiled. 'Why, Mr Samuels, I believe you are blushing.'

'Shut up and help me up!'

'Jeez, Louise, all right …' Angela obeyed his order and offered him her arm as they walked over to the idling taxi, grinning all the way.

Chapter 83

WINIFRED MILDRED HAD been at home on a well-deserved day off when she got the early morning call. She ditched her efforts at planting Swiss chard seedlings to drive to the nursing home, in the belief Elijah shouldn't have to deal with this on his own, or be delivered the news by strangers. She had walked into the empty room and waited by the window, glancing out to the horizon as Sydney stirred and the morning sun bathed every square inch of the city with its warm rays.

Winifred was recalling a funny incident last Valentine's Day between Audrey and another resident, which had involved a hot glue gun, when she heard Elijah's footsteps shuffling towards room 217; she thought she heard him humming 'I Want to Hold Your Hand'.

A strange sensation washed over Elijah like a pall as he shuffled along the unoccupied corridor, lilacs in hand. Nearing the entrance to Audrey's room, he spotted the empty bed first, and noticed that the oddly reassuring sound of the respirator was absent.

Nurse Mildred stood by the window looking out over the garden, dressed casually in denim jeans and a brown cardigan. She turned around slowly. 'I'm so sorry, Eli.'

'No!' He shook his head, clutching his tight chest with his free hand.

'I thought there might have been a chance that—' She whimpered as fresh tears erupted.

Elijah dropped the bunch of lilacs and grabbed the doorframe for support, his face warping. *'When?'*

'This mornin' at six twenty-nine the machine recorded her last breath. I think she let go of what she needed—'

'Six twenty-nine?' Bile rose in his throat and he doubled over, still clutching his chest. 'Why ... didn't anyone call me?'

Nurse Mildred approached him. 'It's the home's policy, darlin'. Yer not next of kin or her proxy. They notified her children 'course; it devastated them, 'n' that sweet li'l child—' She cupped her mouth and clenched her eyes as tears oozed out.

Elijah stared at the wall in front of him as he thought back to when Audrey squeezed his hand just hours ago. He damn well knew it was Audrey responding, and not a trick of his hopeful imagination. If he had known that in a few scant hours after their emotional encounter she would pass, he would have held onto her before striking a bargain with God. *Two birds, one stone.*

'Please believe that this is God's will—'

Elijah staggered off, treading over the fallen lilacs as Nurse Mildred's voice faded out like the end of a song. Opening the front door of the home, he staggered out into a blazing sun and cloud-free, blue sky, and limped off the grounds in a hallucinatory haze.

The weight of hot tears soaked his lashes before rolling down his face in an endless stream, as the indifferent sun, which promised a glorious day, shone brightly as if to taunt him.

A group of young kids rode in his direction on bicycles, but they skidded to a stop and stared at him with slack jaws. How often did you see an elderly gentleman crying on the street?

The world around him seemed different; as though the earth was off-kilter now that she was truly *gone*.

Even this morning, he'd felt something was askew by the way he'd jerked awake; it was as though someone had shaken him. Because he hadn't heard otherwise from the nursing home, he'd brushed the odd feeling aside. Then he remembered looking at the digital clock beside his bed: *6:29 am.*

Chapter 84

A FEW MONTHS after Audrey's passing, Elijah received an early morning phone call. As usual, he cursed the world and all its interruptions.

He jammed his false teeth in and picked up the receiver of the phone next to his bed. 'Who is it and whaddaya want?'

'Eli, it's me!' a squeaky voice replied.

He frowned before realisation dawned and excitement raced through him, his forehead smoothing out. 'Chloe?'

'Uh-huh. Who else would it be?'

Still in bed, Elijah sat upright and rubbed the sleep from his puffy eyes, as Sheba lay asleep on the floor, twitching through an apparent nightmare.

He yawned before clearing his throat. 'Sorry, sweetheart. How have you been?'

'Mother wants to talk to you.'

'Oh, God, what have I done now?'

She giggled. 'Nothing, I think she was just nervous to call you herself,' Chloe whispered into the phone. 'Okay, here she is.' Elijah guessed from the muffled sounds and various noises that they were grappling back and forth with the phone.

'Ah, EJ, it's Angela. How are you?'

He clutched his aching side, wincing. 'Oh I'm hanging in there like an old pair.'

Angela tutted. 'Are you for real?'

Elijah chuckled. 'Would you have me any other way?'

Her silence signalled she was contemplating it. 'No. I wouldn't.'

'Good, well, I'm not too bad for a young fella on a Sunday morning; how's about yourself? It's been a long time.'

'Mmm, yes it has, and I'm … doing about as well as can be expected, thank you.' Her audible swallow gave the truth away, but he didn't push. He understood all too well now that she *had* to be the brave one – it was all she'd ever known. 'Listen, um, sorry to bother you. I wanted to, ah, call and see what your plans were for Christmas.'

Elijah's mind hit fast-forward to the usual turkey roast they served at the local RSL club. 'I haven't thought that far ahead yet. At my age it's best not to, so I can't disappoint.'

Angela chuckled. 'Well, I don't want to intrude, but I – we – hoped if you weren't too busy you might like to come to our place for lunch?'

His ears perked up, and it took a moment for him to respond. Angela was inviting *him* over for Christmas? 'Hmm, are you going to be the chef?'

She clicked her tongue. 'Does it matter if I am?'

'Are you as good a cook as your mum was?' He closed his eyes, still hating the fact he now had to refer to his beloved in the past tense. It didn't sound right. He leaned over the side of his bed to ease Sheba out of the nasty dream she was having. It had always felt good to take care of others – dogs were no exception. Sheba opened her eyes with a startle and wagged her tail upon seeing his face looming over hers. Elijah greeted her with a big smile as his fingers kneaded into her neck and shoulders before he sat upright on the bed again, although it was a struggle. The pain came back with a vengeance and his leg jerked.

'I believe so, yes.'

His throat constricted. He felt wanted; *needed*; perhaps even – missed? 'Do I have to buy presents for everyone – what's the deal?'

'Mmm, seeing as it's Christmas and all, it's sort of tradition. But we understand that this isn't a normal situation, so don't feel obliged to bring any.'

'Okay, suits me. When and what time?'

Angela laughed. 'Goof! Twenty-fifth December – at eleven in the morning. I will send you an invitation if you like?'

An invitation. Hmm, it's funny how you miss the small things in life. 'Thank you for the invite. I appreciate it and if I remember, then I will come.'

'You'd better remember because everyone will be here and you'll get to meet Tim and Tida's baby girl. They're flying down for the festive season, which will be a wonderful change.'

Despite the pain shooting through his body like a scorching prod, he smiled. Elijah heard her *Proud Aunt* voice, and he revelled in the fact the Arlingtons were catching on to what mattered the most, even if it had stemmed from Audrey's passing. 'Yes, that'll be lovely. What's bubba's name?'

'Her name is Ligaya.'

Elijah's face scrunched up, reminding him of the time when his nephew Ryan had given him a sour gumdrop as a gag. His silence prompted Angela to say, 'Don't start!'

His brittle shoulders lifted. 'I didn't say one word.'

'You didn't have to; I know you too well!'

There was another pregnant pause as Elijah fingered the phone cord, but damned if he could help himself. 'Whatever happened to classic names like Gaylord or Bethel; Franklin or Ruth?'

Angela exhaled. 'Jesus, do you want her to be ridiculed in the playground by both students *and* teachers?' Elijah laughed. 'By the way, not that you would know, but Ligaya is a Philippine name meaning happiness.'

Elijah paused again, scrunching his brow even harder. 'But Tinder is Malaysian—?'

'*Tida!* Gosh, you're as bad as Mildred. Look, don't start, I said!' Angela sighed. 'Anyway, apart from all of that, how are things with you, stranger?'

Their last encounter was at Audrey's funeral. Angela had been more than accommodating and even let him sit in the front pews alongside the immediate family, and at his suggestion, they had played 'Wild Horses' by the Rolling Stones during the slideshow memorandum. She even included the picture of the two lovebirds taken at Jenolan Caves in the exhibition. He felt honoured, but had never extended his gratitude to Angela, as he didn't know how.

Elijah did not go to the wake; instead, he did a tour in a taxi (this time with a more respectable driver) of all the places in Wollongong that held nostalgia for him. It started off at Lloyd's house, then Betty-Sue's ice cream parlour, followed by the bowling alley, and finished with a stroll along the beach. It proved to be a struggle with his deteriorating bones, but it was worth it when he crouched down low and ran a shaky hand over the faded love heart encasing their initials that he'd engraved under the boardwalk using his army-issued pocketknife all those decades ago. He listened to sounds of children laughing and adults playing volleyball and for the briefest moment (in his reverie), he saw his sky-blue EH parked on the sand. Through the passenger-side window, Audrey's head tilted back as her dainty hand touched the base of her throat. Her round cheeks were red from laughter, and she wiped a tear away, as she had the night they'd escaped from the police.

But the image disappeared when someone yelled: 'Hey, bro! Can we help you?!'

Elijah blinked and turned as a shirtless Pacific Islander-looking man loomed over him. When Elijah glanced back to where he had visualised his EH, he realised he'd been staring at what he assumed was this guy's family.

'Sorry,' Elijah mumbled as the middle-aged guy stepped back a few inches while watching Elijah struggle to his feet.

'Move along, bro!' the beefy guy ordered, and his family laughed. 'Fuckin' weirdo!'

Elijah offered an apologetic smile towards a tattooed teenager dressed in a low-cut black bikini, but she scoffed and flipped him the bird. 'Perv!'

Elijah conceded this was not his beach. This was not his time anymore.

Despite that incident, the day offered minor pleasures. Of course, the parlour, Lloyd's house and the bowling alley had all changed – relinquished to the gods of commerce to make way for espresso bars and upmarket fashion stores – but his vivid memories endured of chasing Audrey on the beach, driving down the mountain to get away from the police, and arguing with her in Betty-Sue's. It was all thanks to Angela that he'd got to tell Audrey he loved her one last time.

'EJ?' Angela said. 'Are you still there?'

He cleared his throat. 'Sorry – yes, ah, I've been well.'

Angela hesitated. He knew she knew he was lying, as did he, with her diplomatic response. But what else was there to say? 'Listen, I'd better get Chloe ready for ballet, but it's been so nice chatting to you.'

Holy fuck, she sounds sincere! 'You too. Take care, Angela. Bye for now.' Elijah hung up the phone as a smile crept onto his craggy face.

Chapter 85

ANGELA LIFTED HER fur collar higher about her neck as they approached Pinegrove Memorial Park. She'd hopped out of her warm Mercedes into an icy breeze before purchasing a bunch of lilacs from Aunty Poppy's Flower Shop.

'My b-br-braces are hurting now,' Chloe said, her teeth chattering like a novelty wind-up toy.

Angela sniffed and blew out condensation. 'We'll pay our respects then we'll head home, o-okay?' She placed black leather gloves over her trembling hands after she'd put her purse back in her bag.

Chloe wiped away the tears collecting at the base of her nose, which was as red as Anzac Day poppies, and they tramped across the silvery sheen of grass, its wintry whiteness illuminated by the sun's nascent rays.

As they trudged along, shielding their faces from the biting wind, Angela's numb hands dropped the bunch of lilacs onto the dew-laden grass. After picking them up with stiff fingers, she turned back and caught the imprints of her shoes, recording the direction of her journey towards an electronic sign at the Guardian Funerals chapel that read: ELIJAH SAMUELS 1940–2021.

They spotted Winifred Mildred and her husband standing by themselves in a huddle, as background music harmonised with the endless chatter.

As Angela and Chloe approached the small crowd, which included several Vietnam veterans wearing uniforms, a tall man in a black suit and navy-blue tie handed them an order of service. 'I'm Elijah's son, Lance. I don't believe we've met?'

Angela stared at the middle-aged man with sandy-coloured hair and a dimpled chin. He had a light-coloured moustache, and his grey eyes peered at her through round-framed eyewear.

Twin girls clung to either side of his long legs, and a blonde-haired woman with plumped-up lips and cheeks, who exuded no warmth or sympathy, stood behind him in a tight-fitting black dress.

'No, we recently came into contact with Elijah through a ... mutual friend,' Angela said, giving Chloe a wink. Chloe clutched the order of service, which they had yet to look at.

'Well, thank you for coming despite the crazy weather. I'm sure Dad would have appreciated it.' Lance turned to his stoic wife before making his way over to other guests who braved the freezing weather.

'Aunt Grace!' Lance called out. Angela looked towards a round, colourful flowerbed as an elderly woman stood beside a frail man, both smoking. Grace's dull green eyes showed a considerable amount of tribulation, and a small group of people consoled her, including someone who Angela presumed must be her middle-aged son, Ryan. A teary-eyed German shepherd resting its head on outstretched paws lay behind Grace, its pink leash attached to a pole.

If Angela had known Grace (which she partly felt like she did), she would have gone up and offered her condolences. Instead, she squeezed Chloe's stiff hand and walked through the small crowd to get out of the harsh breeze.

As the guests upturned their collars to shield their necks from the bitter wind, Angela glanced at the latest arrival – an elderly lady dressed in a purple-and-black suit, being pushed in a wheelchair by a man of similar age, whom Angela presumed was her husband.

'Georgie!' another elderly woman called out, and with a walking cane in hand, she hobbled her way over to the wheelchair-bound lady.

So, that's the woman my mother thought was a threat to her, Angela thought as she scrutinised Georgie. She had a sadness about her that her dazzling designer accessories could not mask. Her withered face drooped with obvious pain (it was hard to know whether physical or emotional) and, judging by the inflammation of her purple ankles that were exposed beneath her black pants, it appeared she hadn't walked in years. Her frail husband propped himself against the wheelchair. He adjusted his thick tortoiseshell spectacles and seemed worn-out; perhaps he felt a little uncomfortable being at the funeral of his wife's ex-flame. It was depressing seeing Georgie in her current state when Elijah had spoken so fondly about her glamour in her younger years, and the adventures they had embarked upon.

Time had not been kind to Miss Georgie Brown. Angela surmised that there comes a point where life stops giving and starts taking away.

A framed picture of Elijah's youthful, handsome face sat on a wooden easel near the church's double doors. Angela peered at the photo, then turned to the silver registry book, black pen in stiff hand, and wondered why the name Mary Garrison rang a bell.

Chapter 86

OBSERVING FROM AFAR, whilst standing in the frigid air – the last breath of winter's reign – Winifred Mildred prayed no-one could see the truth in her eyes, for she felt consumed by guilt. When she had received a call from Elijah eight days earlier asking her to pay him a visit, she had no idea she would leave his house with such a heavy heart.

She had opened the unlocked front door and ambled up the stairs as the ticking of the grandfather clock added suspense with each step – as though she were in a Kubrick film. After knocking on the bedroom door, she entered and saw Elijah lying on the bed with Sheba by his side.

'What's goin' on?' Winifred whispered, noticing tears spilling from the corners of his eyes and a photo album propped on a nearby chair. Bloodied tissues, vomit bags and prescription pill bottles lay beside a mountainous ashtray that decorated his bedside table.

He inhaled and turned his head. 'I'm tired, love.' He wheeze-coughed.

'Well, rest up. I can leave 'n'—'

He shook his head. 'No. I am … *tired.*'

She looked on as he hacked and, with a shaky hand, he reached over and grabbed a small white box that lay next to an old cassette player, which was also on his bedside table. Winifred treaded across the carpet to the other side of the bed closest to the window and gasped when he opened the box.

'I think … I'm ready now,' he choked, his chest rattling like a cat's toy.

Winifred cupped her mouth as an anguished cry escaped. She shook her head, tears collecting in the rims of her glasses, before slipping down her cheeks. 'I cain't! Please don't ask me. I'll lose my job; my—' The sight of him reaching for a lit cigarette in the ashtray cut her short. He put the butt to his mouth with a wobbly hand, sucking on the filter as though it were an oxygen mask.

Elijah closed his eyes, struggling to stay awake, and lay his head back on the pillow, patting Sheba's stomach while stubbing out the cigarette in the mound of extinguished butts, each of them so small yet so powerful in their devastating effect. He breathed in through his nostrils and expelled the smoke. 'It's time for me to go now.' He opened his drooping eyelids.

'Please don't ask me ta kill ya.'

'Don't give me any of that suicide/murder crap. This is a simple *coup de grâce*. Audrey's gone; my decrepit body's dying; this isn't living, this is torture. I've d-done all I can do in this world, and I've already told you: I ain't going to no damn hospital.'

Winifred doubled over on a cry, as he extended the needle. 'How'd ya git hold of this?'

He gave a humourless smile. 'Does it matter?'

She shook her head, her glasses now askew. 'I *save* folk, not kill 'em! How could I live with myself?' She adjusted her wet glasses.

'If you don't do it, I will, but I can't see my damn veins.' He wheezed before coughing. 'I could … be here for hours.' He smirked as a tear escaped while he tried to hand her the needle.

Her head flew from side to side, tears spurting. But when she saw the look in his eyes, all judicious intentions flew out the window. It was like looking into a torch with flat batteries as the light fades, so she capitulated and took the needle.

'You're a nurse helping a patient, that's all this is.' He coughed, gasping for breath. 'Please, let me find some peace.'

'I cain't do it!'

'Do you know what euthanasia means?'

Winifred wept. She knew. Of course she knew.

'It's Greek, meaning "good death".'

Her head flailed about. 'I *cain't*! This is the coward's way out.'

Elijah looked at her through laboured breathing. '*Coward?* I've been f-fighting my whole life. It takes … courage to say goodbye to everything I know and love; to cross a threshold with no idea where it … where it leads. I fought throughout my w-whole life. Who was there to … to fight for me?'

They maintained a prolonged battle of wills, Winifred travelling through the labyrinth of moral dilemmas in her mind, sobbing as Elijah struggled to breathe.

'I *c-cain't*,' she choked on a whisper.

Elijah's lips trembled, his chin quivering. 'Can you hear the Hueys outside?'

She sniffled and frowned. 'No?'

'I can.'

Winifred's body crumpled; her resolve was slipping. 'Please, stop.'

'For once,' Elijah began, reaching for her hand. 'For once in my goddamned rotten life, let me be in control. Just this one time. *Please.*'

Winifred looked deep into his pleading, desperate, bloodshot eyes, and knelt down beside his bed. She wouldn't want to see a dog in this kind of agony, let alone a human being.

'Wait,' he slurred, grabbing a wad of necklaces from the top drawer of his bedside table. Each gold chain had a religious symbol attached. Elijah's slight moving about prompted an onslaught of phlegmy coughing.

'What are those fo'? Ya ain't religious.' Winifred eyed the Star of David on one of the chains as she rose.

He forced a smile and swallowed. 'I know, but just in case … I don't want to miss out on upstairs because of a technicality.'

She smiled and managed a weak laugh before grabbing her pocket-sized Bible from her black handbag, sniffling. 'I'll make sure ya git in.' She placed his right hand, which was shaking like a leaf in a hurricane, on the Bible's leather cover, as she did the same while whispering with closed eyes.

'Oh, before I forget,' Elijah said, wheezing, 'give Sheba to Grace, and make sure you inform Angela. I have something for her and Chloe.'

Winifred reluctantly knelt by the bed, weighed down by her heavy heart. Elijah turned up the volume on his cassette player and extended his bare, bony arm, which Winifred held in her hand.

She exhaled in a prolonged sigh, as 'My Way' by Frank Sinatra filled the room.

The cold metal pinprick touched his loose skin before it entered the blue vein.

Elijah looked at Sheba, who was looking at him with raised ears and a cocked head. 'I love you, my sweetheart,' he whispered to her. 'I promise to come find you at Rainbow Bridge when y-your time is done. But for now, I want you to raise as much hell for Grace as you … can.' He turned to Winifred, tears raining down her face. 'B-By the way … Sheba … likes chicken necks. T-Tell Grace for me, please.' He paused for breath, gasping, stealing as much oxygen as his useless lungs could manage. 'Oh … and Sheba likes rubs behind the n-n-neck.' He finished by hacking, a smear of blood trickling down the side of his chin.

Winifred nodded, lips inward. 'I surely will.' She snivelled, wiping her wet chin on her forearm. 'Goodbye, my friend.'

She muttered to herself while pushing the syringe as his other hand caressed Sheba's fur. Strange sensations ran through his body; he stopped feeling so much pressure in his sternum and his heart rate seemed to steady. An ice-cold sensation ran through his veins. He smiled and gazed at the ceiling as images played through his mind of Audrey and him dancing beneath the silver moonlight on the boardwalk at Wollongong Beach.

'Lord, please forgive me,' Winifred choked out, pushing down on the syringe – the liquid emptying into his arm as pearl-shaped tears raced down her cheeks and heavy sobs tore from her throat.

With blurred vision, he looked into Winifred's solemn eyes just as Sheba whimpered. 'Take care, old girl. Until we meet again.' Then he turned once more to look into Sheba's distressed eyes. His fingers no longer feeling the comfort of her fur, or the warmth of her paw. His ray of sunshine was the last image he saw until Frank Sinatra's voice finally helped him to drift off into eternal slumber.

Chapter 87

JAMIE WAS OVERSEAS on a much-needed, soul-searching vacation after receiving the news that she had PCOS – polycystic ovarian syndrome – and could never conceive. Angela had decided not to inform her of Elijah's passing in her already fragile state, and Timothy couldn't afford to take any more time off work to fly back and attend the funeral.

Angela felt a wave of disappointment when she walked through the church and discovered only a handful of pews were occupied. The empty benches were not a testament to Elijah's character, at least not in Angela's opinion. She thought back to their time together last Christmas, and it conjured a smile. Elijah had seemed relaxed, and he'd even held baby Ligaya (wearing a Batgirl onesie he'd bought her under the advice of Grace) while they posed for family photos.

Elijah bought everyone gifts, ranging from hundred-dollar gift vouchers to make-up kits, perfume, jewellery and DVDs. Elijah even bought the box set of *The Twilight Zone* and gave it to Chloe, telling her, 'This will be the best damn TV series you'll ever watch!'

Elijah had also provided Chloe with a clothing store voucher (according to the gothic-dressed shop assistant, 'all the cool babes shop here!') and a new, top-of-the-line artist kit, which included oil pastel crayons, coloured pencils, acrylic paint in glass jars and six different-sized paintbrushes.

They had all shared stories about Audrey, whose photo Angela had enlarged, printed and framed, and it had pride of place in the lounge room overlooking the festivities.

Angela had gone to immense effort to please everyone; she even made a homemade batch of eggnog, which was Elijah's favourite guilty pleasure, especially with brandy added. Lunch had consisted of turkey, maple-glazed leg of ham, honey-glazed carrots, string beans, roasted pumpkin with rosemary, Paris-style mashed potato and gravy. Seth poured generous servings from a seemingly endless bottle of Brown Brothers moscato to accompany the meal, and he kept Elijah entertained with his political views and knowledge of sports like cricket and tennis. Boyd Patterson had not been present, and Jamie gave no reason why, but it was just as well because Elijah told Angela he had a hankering to give Boyd a clip around the ear for his ill-treatment of her sister.

Afterwards, the family sat in the lounge room once more and watched *National Lampoon's Christmas Vacation* and ate Angela's homemade custard trifle.

On Boxing Day, Elijah called Angela to thank her for her hospitality and for giving him 'the best Christmas since 1964'. Those words would remain etched in Angela's memory for as long as she breathed.

As Chloe and Angela took their seats on the cold pew, Angela glanced down at the program Chloe held, and her eyes widened: 'A celebration of the life of Elijah Timothy Samuels.'

'Mum, look!' Chloe pointed to the exact word Angela eyed: *Timothy.*

'My mother never ceases to amaze me,' Angela whispered as the tears that she'd kept at bay spilled in a graceful stream.

After 'Auld Lang Syne' ended, an elderly man dressed in green fatigues with a poppy pinned on his shirt lapel walked towards the chancel. Elijah's cherry-veneer coffin had an Australian flag draped over it, and on top amid a wreath of poppies was a framed picture of him as a soldier wearing his slouch hat and greens.

'Ladies and gentlemen, my name is Ronald Kelly – Ned – as my brother here used to call me. On behalf of the Vietnam Veterans' Association, St Marys Outpost, I convey our deepest sympathies to the family and friends who have assembled here to honour one of our own, Elijah Timothy Samuels, a comrade-in-arms.'

Chapter 88

SIX MONTHS LATER, Angela sat inside her office in her comfy black swivel chair overlooking the harbour and its inhabitants. She stared, pondering whether to go down to the nearest newsagency and buy a diary to carry on Audrey and Elijah's tradition. *What is there to write about, though?* She envisioned what an entry in her diary would look like:

Dear Diary,

Had a slice of rye toast and avocado for breakfast.
Kissed Seth goodbye and dropped Chloe off at school.
Collected the usual coffee orders before arriving at work.
Worked on this account and that.
Lunch was a quinoa tuna salad and a Diet Coke.
Went to the dry cleaners to pick up my suits and went back to the office.
After a few Zoom meetings, phone calls, printing a few thousand papers and adding the finishing touches to my Stapleton Ltd. account, I drove home.
Made dinner: garlic chicken and mash with veg and gravy.
Showered, then set the alarm before bed.

Angela.

Angela's buzzing intercom startled her from her reverie, causing her to bang her left knee on the side of a filing cabinet. *Dammit!*

'Ange, I have a man on line one who says he needs to talk to you about a private family matter; he says he's not selling anything.'

Angela rubbed her knee and mumbled, 'Thanks, Tanya, I'll take it.' She picked up the phone and pressed the flashing blue Line 1 button.

A man's accented voice blasted into her ear. 'Hello, am I speaking with Angela Tawny?'

'Yes, speaking.'

'Mrs Tawny, my name is Sunny Solomon. I was Mr Elijah Samuels' solicitor. First, I am sorry to hear about your loss.' Angela noted the lack of sincerity in his tone, picturing him patting down his oily hair while gazing into his mirrored reflection with a wink. 'Second, this call is to advise you that before his passing, Mr Samuels placed your daughter in his last will and testament. Are you able to come in for a chat this week?'

Angela's body and face froze. At first she didn't comprehend what he'd said. Maybe it was his thick accent, or maybe she didn't appreciate how much of a bond her daughter and Elijah Samuels had forged. She blinked herself back to alertness. 'Wow, this is quite a surprise. Ah, yes, I can.' Angela moved the mouthpiece away from her trembling lips, waiting to be hit with an ambush of tears.

Damn that charming, unpredictable man; I need to concentrate on the McLaren project, not blubber like a Kardashian over EJ's overwhelming gestures!

'How is this Thursday, ma'am?'

Angela's chest rose and fell while she checked her appointment diary that lay on her spotless desk, seeing pencil scribbled everywhere. She couldn't afford to spare a single second, but she hadn't stopped thinking about Elijah since he'd passed. It surprised her, and she understood perhaps why her mother had always kept the light on for Mr Samuels. He sure was hard to forget.

Her eyes roamed the pages below as a lone tear smudged her pencil scribble. 'Where are you located, Mr Solomon?' She wiped her cheek with the back of her free hand.

'My office is in Bondi. How about eleven o'clock this Thursday morning?'

'Sounds good to me.' Angela looked at the list of people she was going to piss off by rescheduling, but smiling all the while.

'Great, I shall see you then and in the meantime, I'll send your secretary an email with the confirmation. Good day.'

Angela sat back, staring at the wall in front. *Elijah included Chloe in his will?* It was the ultimate honour. Angela would keep this a secret from the rest of the family until she found out what the will actually stipulated; no use ruffling feathers without good reason.

Besides, now wasn't the time to bring it up with Jamie, seeing as she was living alone. Angela remembered hearing Elijah give Jamie advice during their Christmas together, something to the effect of: 'Sometimes hanging on can be more harmful than letting go.'

Angela always sensed something was off about Boyd, so she was only too happy that Elijah had had the guts to tell it how it was. Jamie had eventually kicked Pretty Boy Boyd out, even with no hard proof of infidelity, because Elijah also told her: 'Love is not just about how you feel towards the other person, but how they make you feel about yourself.'

Auspiciously, just when Jamie thought she'd thrown in the towel too early, the truth of Boyd's multiple affairs spanning over the last few months unfolded like lotus leaves, due to scorned women (one of them married) contacting Jamie through Facebook (some apologising, others hurling abuse at her for dumping him because he was no longer the same tender lover). Thus, Jamie confided to Angela that if it hadn't been for Elijah, she would still be stuck in a rut. If Angela was honest, they *all* missed having Elijah around, like a homeless cat you take in and grow to love. Elijah had come into their lives like a whirlwind, tossing everything into chaos, before retreating in much the same fashion, but with the effect of everything being not only restored, but reinvigorated.

****

When Angela arrived home that evening, she flopped backwards onto her king-sized bed and stared at the ceiling. Not long after, Chloe walked in, catching the back end of a sniffle.

'Are you okay?' Chloe whispered, sitting on the edge of the bed.

Angela wiped her face dry and braved a smile. 'Of course.' She cringed, knowing her poor attempt at acting 'fine' could win her a Golden Raspberry.

'I painted a picture; would you like to see it?'

Angela sat upright, smoothing over her skirt.

Chloe shuffled over on the bed and revealed her painting that she said she'd spent the past few months perfecting. It was a picture showing one large hand, withered like a flower devoid of water, held by a much smaller, youthful hand.

Granddaughter and grandmother. The beginning of life; the beginning of death.

Chapter 89

SUNNY SOLOMON SHOOK hands with Angela as he introduced himself, before inviting her to sit in a brown leather chair facing his desk. He sat in front of shelves containing legal books and a wall decorated with accolades. Wearing a bespoke navy-blue suit, he seemed like the sort of solicitor who charged five hundred dollars a phone call and two hundred per email. He stared at her through chestnut eyes, adjusting a red-and-blue striped silk tie.

'Thank you for coming today, Mrs Tawny. Would you like a tea or coffee?'

Angela adjusted the collar on her white silk blouse as rivulets of perspiration gathered at her temples. 'A black tea with a slice of lemon will do just fine.'

Sunny pressed the intercom buzzer on his desk and ordered their beverages before capturing her eyes once more. 'I am going to keep this brief, Mrs Tawny,' he began, fusing his palms together on the desk. 'A short while before Mr Samuels passed, he changed his will. When someone changes a will on short notice before they pass, it has to be investigated for legal reasons. For example: was this person of sound mind? Is this a case of fraud? Is this identity theft? And that's why it took a while for me to contact you; we had to wait for the all-clear. I am aware you arrived in Elijah's life not long before he passed; you'd never met him before that, right?'

'That's correct.'

His bushy eyebrows rose as he blinked. 'You must have made quite an impression because he has left a considerable sum to you – or, more specifically – to your daughter.'

A middle-aged woman with a Mrs Brown hairdo appeared at the doorway, carrying a laden tray of piping hot tea for Angela and a flat white for Sunny.

'Thank you,' Angela said, taking her fragrant citrus tea from the silver tray. The woman bowed and left without a peep, closing the door upon exiting. Angela turned back to Sunny. 'Well, Mr Solomon, this is a pleasant surprise.'

He swirled a sugar cube through his porcelain cup and smiled behind his thick, black moustache, before tapping the teaspoon on the gold rim three times. 'I'm sure it is, but I have to warn you that this comes with some conditions.'

Of course there are. Angela frowned while peering over the slender-lipped rim of her steaming Chinoiserie teacup.

'The money will remain in a trust fund until the day Chloe turns eighteen. The money is also meant to be spent specifically as per Elijah's wishes.'

Angela blotted her lips, staining the white tissue she'd grabbed from a box on his desk a light shade of brown.

'Mr Samuels left a note for you, plus a box of his treasured items.'

It was only then that Angela noticed a mahogany box, wide enough for a diary, resting at the edge of the rosewood desk.

Sunny nestled his cup in the saucer, and removed a white envelope from the top drawer, which he placed atop the box before pushing it across the desk towards her. 'I suggest you read this at home.' She raised an inquisitive eyebrow. 'It'll be better to cope with the content, but of course, you may do as you wish.'

***

When Angela arrived home later that night, after a gruelling afternoon of endless meetings and abusive phone calls from demanding clients who weren't short of a quid, Seth greeted her with an obligatory kiss, mobile phone pressed to his ear, before she dragged her carcass upstairs and, for the first time in a long time, she drew a steaming hot bath with a few drops of lavender oil.

She also poured a glass of Wolf Blass chardonnay, before stripping and reclining in the bubble-filled bathtub, closing her heavy eyes. She conjured up images from her happy childhood; of the friendly little girl she had once been. Her hands gripped the sides of the tub as tears plummeted. Hidden beneath everything was one simple truth that she daren't tell anyone: losing Elijah had been like losing a father-figure all over again. Her eyes flew open once the sharp pain became unbearable, and they zeroed in on tiny water droplets slipping from the faucet; one by one the tear-shaped blobs hit the bath water, their sound as regular as a metronome, and she stared, hypnotised. When the droplets slowed, she dried her hands with a towel from the floor, and opened Elijah's letter, which had been calling out to her all day from her desk's bottom drawer:

Dearest Angela,

If you are reading this, it means I have croaked it.

Finally, Audrey and I will reunite, even if it is in a spiritual form.

Thank you for providing me with happiness and joy in the last few months of my life. Your family (especially Chloe) stoked the cold embers, and for that I am eternally grateful.

I would like to prove my gratitude by giving Chloe a share in my inheritance.

I want to stipulate though: I don't want her to have access to the money until she turns 18.

The reason being, I want her to enjoy life as a child, without being corrupted by the image money represents.

I know you well enough to know you will have a stronghold on her finances, anyway (don't roll your eyes at me) – and I don't blame you. But still – 18 and not a day younger! I've left more than enough money for Chloe to buy a ticket to France and study at the Paris College of Art. Of course, I cannot force her. But this is my wish.

On a side note:

As I reflect on my life, I realise I spent too much time 'dying'.

I was dying to join the army.

After that I was dying to get a new car;

I was dying to marry Audrey, and dying to have children.

And now, as I write this, I realise as I am actually dying, that I half-lived my life.

My advice from the grave is: Don't let life get in the way of living.

If things aren't meant to be, then don't turn out like me – bitter and cranky; trust that everything has its place.

Also, I left a box for you to do with as you please;

I assumed you would like this, rather than it being tossed in the trash.

Now get out and start living, and just remember: you managed to do something that no-one else had in a long time: You made me feel that my life was worthwhile.

Through this experience, it reminded me of the man I used to be.

Bugging you for the last time,

EJ xx

P.S. I will always remember our Christmas together, even though the turkey was a bit dry.

I'm just kidding. It was absolutely <u>perfect</u>.

Angela wrapped a towel around her shivering body and walked, dripping wet, to her bedroom to sit on the springy mattress before taking the box in her hands. She sat there, breathing hard as water droplets fell from her hair. Upon opening the lid, she saw Elijah's diary, four wartime medals, his engraved Zippo lighter and Vietnam lapel pins. There was an order of service from Audrey's funeral, noteworthy newspaper clippings – including some on Audrey and Buck regarding their contributions to societies and foundations. There were also old pictures of Elijah from when he was a strapping young lad, including some black-and-white shots of him and his buddies in South Vietnam. And finally, a picture that Chloe had drawn inside the nursing home while they all sat together: Elijah had his head buried in his diary, glasses perched at the tip of his nose, as the rest of the family (plus Winifred) gazed on with intrigue. This picture, which Chloe had given him for Christmas, was striking as it captured the very essence of an unspoken truth: he was part of their family, whether they'd verbalised it or not.

Chapter 90

ONE WEEK LATER, Angela waited for her triple-shot caramel espresso at the Starbucks' drive-thru, fingers strumming the leather steering wheel, knees bouncing from the thought of the presentation she was giving on the new McLaren Financial Advisers' account. They were not easy to impress; in fact, Angela had been up all night worrying – finding it hard to focus when her mind was all around Elijah and Audrey. Seth (on more than one occasion), whilst yawning and rubbing his eyes, had told Angela to come back to bed, but she wanted to make sure the advertising pitch was nothing short of the *Maxwell Standard*.

Angela was already running late because Chloe had had trouble locating her Featherdale Wildlife Park excursion permission slip, but she feared without coffee she'd look and act like a woman having a midlife crisis who'd been out on an all-night bender.

After they sped off from Starbucks, Angela resumed mumbling her rehearsed pitch that she would deliver in front of her boss and two hedge fund managers from McLaren, who both came with more demands than Mariah Carey.

As she gazed out the window at an unravelling medley of colours and blurred shapes that sped by, Chloe said, 'Can I have Denise over on Friday night for a sleepover?'

Angela's mind at that point comprised only numbers, codes, and acquisitions – until her bleating phone startled her.

Speaking via the Bluetooth piece in her ear, Angela said, 'Good morning, Bruce! I'll be in soon; I'm dropping Chloe off to school—'

To which Bruce went off like Gordon Ramsay until he *had* to pause for breath.

'Seth had already left for work—'

Bruce hung up on Angela for the millionth time in the past six months alone. With a grunt, Angela put her foot down, whizzing past cars so fast they looked stationary.

'Mother, have you forgotten my presentation tomorrow?'

'What?' Angela mumbled, checking her side-mirror before merging lanes.

'I have my drawing presentation tomorrow morning, remember?'

Angela took a second to register what she was talking about. 'I don't think I can, but I'll try and make sure Dad will be there, okay?'

'Oh, I see.'

'Please don't guilt trip me. I don't have time for this! One day you will become an adult, too, and that means having responsibilities like paying bills, which can only come from having a *job*.'

'I know – work first, us second.'

Angela pressed the brakes, merging back into the other lane again. 'Excuse me, young lady, that attitude is uncalled for.'

They spent the rest of the drive to McClifford's Private School in silence.

Angela pulled up into the school drop-off bay, clipping the gutter in her haste.

'Have a good day at sch—' She received another phone call mid-sentence and let out a harsh exhale before answering.

Chloe got out of the car and slammed the door before walking through the school archway, her head down.

While Angela was on the phone, emotions churned inside of her like a raging maelstrom. Just as Bruce started dropping the f-bombs, a school bus spewing grey fumes pulled up in front of her view. The back of the bus had a Nikon digital camera advertisement that read: **Sometimes you will never know the true value of a moment until it becomes a memory.**

It's a sign from above. An augury from Elijah; no doubt about it.

As she glanced around the busy street, it dawned on Angela that she felt as though she were inside a metal coffin on an assembly line headed straight for the incendiary pit as she watched the blur of other cars around her, observing the robotic drivers who, like her, looked like they were 'over it'. *We are nothing but mass-produced carbon copies, but no matter which way we turn, run, drive, walk or gallop, we are all headed for the one destination.*

Through tears, Angela turned to see Chloe walking away as the driver inside a white Nissan Pulsar behind her started honking.

Angela looked from her rear-view mirror back to the bus ahead. She lowered the passenger-side window with a button on her driver's side door and yelled, 'Chloe, come back!'

Chloe turned around, frowning.

'Hurry!' Angela yelled as the driver behind leaned on the horn. Chloe returned and as she reached the door Angela shouted, 'Quick, hop in!'

'Huh?'

'Hurry, we have to go; come on!'

Chloe frowned, but she took off her schoolbag and opened the door, got inside and buckled up, as Speedy Gonzales screeched off, flipping the bird to the honky-tonk driver behind.

'Mother, what's going on?'

Angela throttled the steering wheel, eyes on the road. 'Chloe, from here on out, things are going to be *very* different.'

'What do you mean? You're being cryptic.'

Through a cracking voice, Angela said, 'I'm so sorry for not being around, but things are going to change. I promise.' She leaned over and patted Chloe's knee before returning her hand to the wheel.

'Where are we going; what about your job?' As if on cue, Angela's mobile rang.

Bruce's name flashed across the screen like a warning signal. 'Meh, screw ya.' She threw her mobile out the car window as she continued driving.

Chloe gasped as though choking for air, which prompted Angela to say, 'Let's just say, there's a bit of Elijah's rebellion in me, too!'

Chloe looked at Angela dead-on. 'Mother, there's no such word as "ya"; it's "you".'

Chapter 91

OVER AN HOUR later, after Angela had called in to pick up Jamie from her loft and then stopped in at home to retrieve something – which she shielded and placed in the car's boot – they were on the road again.

'What do you think about going away for a holiday, ladies?' Angela said, eyes focused on the traffic ahead, elbow propped against her window ledge.

Jamie remained silent.

'What's got into you?' Chloe said after an awkward spell. 'We *never* have holidays.'

Angela licked her dry lips. 'I know; that's all going to change, though. I want to *live* before I die. To start off with, I'm thinking maybe Batemans Bay – although, Dubbo has a zoo.'

'You're acting weird,' Chloe muttered, looking back at her aunt, who shrugged as if to say *Don't look at me, she's your mum.*

'No, baby girl, for once' – Angela raised an index finger – 'I am acting *normal.* For once I am acting how a mother should. You just don't recognise it and ... that hurts – but it's not your fault.' She cleared her throat. 'You're no longer going to come second to anything. I can always get another job, but I'll only ever have one family. So, starting from today, I will no longer take that for granted.'

As they reached the lookout, Chloe stared at the miraculous view in front, her jaw dropping. Jamie unbuckled her seatbelt and leaned forward between the two front seats.

'Wow,' Chloe whispered, inhaling the aromatic, salty sea air through the passenger window. 'This would be amazing to draw. So, this is—'

'Yes,' Angela said, smiling. 'Ladies, welcome to Wollongong.'

All three occupants hopped out of the Mercedes, and Angela collected the mysterious item from the boot. 'Come on, girls, we're going to give Mama one last ride.'

Chloe pointed to the urn. 'Is that Nan?'

Angela nodded, glancing at the golden urn that held her mother's ashes.

Unbeknownst to them, a car had rocked up in the parking lot behind them as Jamie trailed off, capturing snaps of the magnificent view with her smartphone.

'Oh. My. God,' Angela said, as Lance Samuels hopped out of the grey Mazda with his twin girls, who were holding hands and wearing matching white frilly dresses. Lance held a green urn and Angela thought for a moment she was hallucinating; this was too bizarre to be true.

'What's wrong?' Chloe said as Angela stood in stunned silence, the wind ruffling her blouse collar.

Lance smiled at Angela before he trailed off in a different direction, breaking her trance.

'I'm sorry; excuse me!' Angela raced over to Lance, who spun around. 'Yes?'

'Um, I am so sorry, I don't know how to put this, but you're Lance, aren't you?'

Lance nodded, his eyes roaming her face, trying to place her.

Angela noted his wife wasn't present, and a faint white strip of flesh on his finger marked where a wedding ring used to reside. 'And forgive me, but you're holding onto Elijah Samuels, aren't you?'

Lance looked at Angela's urn, then back to her face, squinting. 'I'm sorry, do I—?'

'We met at your father's funeral. I'm Angela, and this is my daughter, Chloe.'

Lance glanced towards Chloe with a tender smile, then back to Angela. 'Ah, I apologise. I can't remember much about that day.' Lance gave a slight shake of the head as a gentle wind whistled around them. 'It all seems like a blur.'

'I understand; I lost my father, too. There's no pain on earth like it, is there?' Angela stepped aside and turned around. 'By the way, this is my sister, Jamie.'

Lance's lips parted when Jamie stepped forward, the sun illuminating her eyes. She offered a smile and held out her hand, which Lance took without looking at it; his eyes as wide as flying saucers. 'It's a pleasure to meet you.'

Angela interrupted their prolonged handshake by clearing her throat. 'Look, this is going to sound even weirder and ... I can't quite believe that you're *actually* here,' she said with a short, disbelieving laugh, 'but I am holding my mother, Audrey, and—'

Lance's concentration broke, and he turned to her. 'Wait, you mean *the* Audrey? As in, Audrey Hughes?'

'You know about my mother?' Angela said, noticing Chloe's own mystified expression. 'We were under the assumption that EJ didn't mention Audrey to you or—'

'Or my mother, Harriet? No, not while he was alive. When Dad passed away, he left me a sixteen-page letter that outlined some unspoken issues, including the reasons he never married my mother and, of course, Audrey's name popped up on nearly every single page. She sure left quite an impression on him.'

Angela looked at Jamie, who hadn't taken her eyes off Lance, then back to him. 'Their brief romance was a well-kept secret. I, too, had no idea.'

'You know, it's weird,' Lance began, gazing out towards the vast horizon, 'I had this overwhelming feeling today; it's as though Dad was pushing me to come here.' His eyes settled on Jamie before returning to Angela. 'He mentions this spot in his letter.'

Angela's mouth twitched and her eyes widened. 'I had the *exact* same feeling as I was dropping Chloe off to school. Now here we all are, and I do *not* think this is a coincidence.'

'No; I don't believe in them,' Lance said, side-gazing Jamie. She grinned as she swept her flyaway hair behind an ear.

Lance looked back and forth between the two women and then to Chloe, who was focusing on his daughters. 'Gosh, where are my manners? These are my two girls, Chelsea and Ashley.' He gazed down at them with overt pride. 'Come on out now and say hello, girls.'

The twins peered out from behind his long legs with curious glances. Chloe walked over and said, 'Hi, I'm Chloe; it's nice to meet you.' The girls glanced at each other before stepping out, holding hands, walking over to Chloe, who hugged them both as if they were long-lost friends.

Lance chuckled and tore his gaze away. 'So, if I'm holding Dad, and you're holding your mother, and we both came here to …'

Angela nodded, her chest expanding, emotions swirling like the waves below. 'Yes, if you're okay with it. Shall we?'

He looked out over the glistening ocean as seagulls soared, and the brilliant sun hugged the land with its golden arms. 'I say we give them what they both deserve. I can't imagine anything that would make my old man happier.'

'Is this all right with you, sweetheart?' Angela said to Chloe, who had rejoined the circle.

She nodded, wiping her red-rimmed eyes with the sleeve of her school uniform.

Lance then focused his attention on Jamie. 'Is this okay with you, Mrs …?'

'Miss,' she corrected with a smile, presenting her left hand, which was bare except for a sterling silver ring on her index finger.

He grinned sheepishly and looked down before turning away, inhaling. 'Okay, on the count of three …' Lance paused as they all stood on the edge of the cliff. 'You can count down, angel,' Lance whispered to Chloe, who was clinging onto her mum, as his kids were to him.

'Three... t-two... one,' Chloe choked out through tears, to which Angela and Lance lifted the lid off their respective urns to let the wind embrace the ashes. Salty tears ran down Angela's face as she witnessed the particles rise and combine, and then drift and glide through the air in a seductive dance, down the mountainside towards the rippling ocean. Lance wiped a tear away from under his glasses using a knuckle and looked at Chloe, who now had an arm around both Chelsea and Ashley.

As they watched the ashes return to nature, Lance looked out over the turbulent waves and smiled. 'Now they shall be together always.'

While the ashes faded into the distance, the onlookers turned around towards the sound of a crackling PA speaker behind them, connected to the exterior of the former Rickard's Tackle and Bait shop, now a café, and a song began to play.

Lance and Jamie swapped comforting smiles as Angela gazed into the cloudless, blue sky. She visualised her mother and Elijah together again, side by side, smiling from above as Jamie, Lance and she linked arms and listened as 'Never Tear Us Apart' by INXS floated past them and out from the clifftop, over the land of Wollongong.

**PHOTOGRAPH OF
CORPORAL RONALD JAMES KELLY – 'NED' –
AND HIS 'DARLING DIANE', CIRCA 2004**

They have been together since 1963 and are the proud parents of
two children, who grew up and rewarded them
with seven grandchildren.

They never gave up hope.

For the Fallen – An extract from the poem by Robert Laurence Binyon
(1869–1943)

They shall grow not old, as we that are left grow old.
Age shall not weary them, nor the years condemn.
At the going down of the sun and in the morning,
We will remember them.

Lest we forget.

Acknowledgements

It was always my intention to present this book factually as well as respect-fully, for the Vietnam War is one of modern history's most controversial events. To do this, I immersed myself in researching history books, documentaries, newspaper clippings, music and movies. I also had the pleasure of being invited into the home of Corporal Ronald James Kelly – 'Ned' – and his 'darling Diane', where he retold personal, touching and sometimes harrowing tales from his time as a corporal in 1 RAR. I thank them both for allowing me to pick their brains, which must have felt like the equivalent of a lobotomy (maybe more painful) and for allowing me access to personal items such as photos and private love letters.

I also extend my appreciation to William (Bill) Roberts and Frank Cole at the Vietnam Veterans' Federation of Australia in Granville. Your generosity and insight during your time in the war has not been forgotten.

My research was thorough, but I would like to express my sincere apologies if my account of the war in this novel offends anyone (especially Vietnam veterans here or abroad); it was not my intention and some derogatory comments made by characters are not my personal beliefs. But never let it be said I did a disservice to or created injustice amongst my characters. Art is to be interpreted, so thank you for taking the time to interpret mine; I hope you have enjoyed reading this book as much as I enjoyed writing it. I had to take liberties with stretching some minor truths. For example: Jenolan Caves didn't open its secluded cabins until the

'80s, and they don't have a waxed dance floor inside Chisolm's Restaurant. Forgive my poetic licence!

Second, I would like to thank Sally Asnicar from Full Proofreading Services for extending her professional services to me. I am indebted to you, Sally, for your time and help. I would recommend her services to anyone seeking to have a book edited, and I also want to give my heartfelt thanks to my beta reader, Catherine O'Farrell!

Third, I must thank my loving parents, Kathleen and Edward. As always, your strength and support provide me with the courage I need to pursue my dreams, no matter how difficult it all seems. I love you both very much and cannot ever repay what you have done for me, although I will certainly try.

Besides family, I give special thanks to my wonderful friends, who have seen me through thick and thin; you are honestly more like brothers and sisters. Blood makes you related, loyalty makes you family. Together, you guys are my backbone.

Now I must do a special shout-out to my supporters! I thank you all for helping me move forward and giving me the potential to create stories through your encouragement. I hope I can continue to inspire, uplift, and urge you to follow your dreams, no matter how big or small.

Last, although certainly not least, I want to praise my fur baby, Corey, who now resides over the Rainbow Bridge. Corey, you were with me during the start of this book, and it breaks my heart you aren't around for its release. I dedicate this book to you, my baby boy; I hope you're proud. You'll never know how much I miss my little buddy being by my side as I write books and look to you for inspiration on speaking about love – and now the pain of loss. I wrote it at the beginning and I'll write it again now: you will always be my sunshine.

Much love,
Stephanie Louise May

Stephanie Louise May is an award-winning international actress-turned-author. After spending years in the acting business, she has turned some of her focus and energy to entertaining people through writing. Stephanie has written novels in genres ranging from romance to horror, and is currently working on a cookbook.

Her pastimes include exploring rural Australia, reading Stephen King novels, and cooking Italian or Mexican cuisine while crooning to hits from the '60s and '70s.

To keep up to date with her journey, please visit www.stephaniemayofficial.com

@stephaniemay14

stephaniemay_90

stephanielouisemay